DESTINY

KALIYA SAHNI BOOK SIX

K.N. BANET

FOREWORD

Hey everyone. This is Kristen. K.N. Banet. I don't do forewords very often, but before you begin the last book of Kaliya Sahni's story, I wanted to talk about something.

I would like to give my deepest love and respect to Hinduism and those who ascribe to it. I hope that love has bled through the pages. I researched for endless hours, finding legends, folklore, and real beliefs to blend with my characters in an attempt to show my deep respect for it as I wrote about a world I wasn't raised in.

To those who don't know, the legends and folklore I reference are from Hinduism, a religion practiced by over fifteen percent of the world's population. Kaliya running from the island of Ramanaka to escape Garuda, only to face Krishna at the Yamuna River. His venom poisoning the river and leaving a lone Kadamba tree. These powerful tales have been written down for thousands of years. You can find the story in the *Bhagavata Purana* or the *Mahābhārata*.

I chose to write about this religion and it's stories for a

few reasons. I was utterly fascinated by the complexity of it, along with the depth and feeling of it. From Kadru and her sister, Vinata, to Garuda and the nagas... The deep undercurrents of rivalry and family. Those are the sorts of stories that reach out to me and touch my heart.

Beyond that, I want my world on the pages to be as big as the world we live in. I want characters from all over the world with different experiences, different beliefs, and so much more.

I took that fascination and my belief in a big world then dove into stories I had little experience with. It became an overwhelming love as I tried to hunt down references between legends, recurring names, interesting tales, everything else I could sink my teeth into surrounding the nagas.

I can't begin to explain how writing with these stories as a backbone has moved and changed me.

I can only hope you see the love and enjoy this final story about Kaliya Sahni.

And even more, I hope you've fallen in love like I have.

1

CHAPTER ONE

MAY 4, 2020

I sat on a large rock in the sun, my favorite place to be. I needed the heat from the sun bearing down on me, so oppressive I wouldn't want to move. It was over a hundred degrees out and would only climb higher. The nights would be warm, only dropping into the eighties. It was my time of year. The blissfully hot summer of Arizona, only an hour outside of Phoenix. It was still early. This was only a short heatwave before real summer hit.

Staring at the desert, I thought of an endless number of things even though my body didn't move an inch. I was far enough from home that no one came looking for me while I spent my lonely hours thinking. If I turned around, I wouldn't be able to see the three-story mansion that was now my home or the isolated neighborhood spread out around it.

They'll expect me back soon.

Leaning back, I let the sun wash over my face. I didn't

make a move to go back to the home I now occupied or ruled, depending on the day and what the problem was.

I was out here to think. As I had been the day before, and the ones before it.

I came out here to stare at my desert every day since I had returned from India over two weeks ago. Staring at the harsh landscape, with its brutal and stark beauty, I hoped to find some measure of inner peace while I planned for the future. A future no one spoke to me about, a future no one could truly understand, weighed heavy on my shoulders. No one except my mate, who had spent his own time staring into the oblivion that was his people's future.

I never found the inner peace, but the plans were coming together, taking shape in my mind as I went through possibilities and put together ideas. I tossed out ideas, endlessly going back and forth about how to do what I knew must be done.

I have to find him.

I have to kill him.

For all the people expecting me to return home soon for the evening, I had to go back to India and end this fight with Garuda once and for all.

Today was the first day I was feeling remotely confident in my plans. That confidence told me it was time for me to do something. Even though the entire plan was half-baked and mad, I had to make my move, or I would lose precious time.

Yeah, today is the day, isn't it? I have to get moving again, or we're all going to stay trapped in this loop of survival and running.

It felt right.

Reaching up, I touched the bundle on my chest, protected in the sling I wore, also enjoying the brutal heat with me like she did every day.

Roshni stirred when I started rubbing her back. I smiled down at her, trying to hide my sadness. Looking at her, I saw her mother every time, and my heart broke a little more. She shifted into her snake form and moved up my chest. I laid back for her, and she shifted back into her human form, a chubby baby, and giggled as she tried to crawl on my chest.

"You know you're not supposed to escape the sling, Roshni," I reminded her, smiling as she reached out and grabbed my nose. "What am I going to do with you, huh?"

She gave me a big baby smile. This was a good day with her. There had been bad ones, too, that came to my mind as I stared at her big smile. Getting her back into her human form had only been step one. For two weeks, we all watched to see how that traumatic time had affected her. Some nights, even sleeping between Raphael and me, she cried and cried. Some days, she didn't let anyone hold her, preferring to stay in her snake form, forcing me to put her in the terrarium for sunbathing until she was ready to be the baby we had to take care of. We kept her human most of the time, but sometimes, we had to wait for her to be ready to be with us. It wasn't so life-threatening anymore as it had been when I had first found her, those agonizing early days, trying to get her to come back. Normally, she only stayed in her snake form for a few hours, and it was after those nights when she couldn't stop crying.

"You miss your mom, don't you?" I asked, touching her dark hair. She tried to pat my cheek and touched my lip ring. I let her have free rein to explore except for my eyes and teeth. The only time I stopped her from touching anything else was when she pulled on the lip ring, which forced me to pull her hand away today.

"Roshni, you know better," I said, sighing. She reached for it again, and I couldn't stop a laugh as she nearly grabbed it, moving faster than a baby her age should have. "Excuse me, little girl, but you definitely know better. Why do we keep having this conversation? You can't pull on the lip ring."

She laughed, and I knew she found my frustration funny, or at least it felt that way. As she went for it again, I sat up and flipped her onto her back into my lap, tickling her as she giggled, and her arms flailed around.

"You little snake, you," I teased. "You're not faster than me."

Stopping before I overwhelmed her, I let her relax on my lap in the sun. She stared at the sky with wide, curious eyes. I wondered if she knew the danger of it. The sun gave us warmth and light, but it also was the home of our greatest predator.

The thoughts turned me down a dark road as I pushed her hair from her forehead.

The sky held the one who had taken her beautiful mother from us and killed her father.

The sky held the one who had killed my parents or

more accurately, had ordered their murders. My mother, my father, my brothers, and Adhar, the crutch I had leaned on for decades, a grandfather to me in his own way. One I argued with endlessly, but who had also tried his best in a situation, he wasn't prepared to handle. A man who had changed as he watched me grow and change as well.

I closed my eyes and tried to banish the thoughts—the rage and sadness—for just a moment. When I was with her, I tried to remain calm.

Today, it was harder.

My plans are nearly done. I just need to handle a few things.

"It's time to head home, little snake."

She just made that happy baby noise I was getting all too used to. I tried to get her back into the sling, but she fought, not wanting to go back into it under any circumstance. Giving up, I slid off the rock with her tight against my chest and landed with a small thud.

"You normally don't wake up while we're out here," I said, knowing she probably barely understood me, if she understood at all. There was just something in her eyes when she looked at me, that knowledge that I had recognized when we met. With her snake form already natural for her, I knew she processed information better than children her age, but there was a lot I didn't know about naga children... a lot no one knew. We couldn't do extensive studies with our very limited population, so most parents just played things by ear.

That was really all I could do, so I kept talking to her

because it felt like the right thing to do. None of this was helped by the simple fact that I wasn't exactly the best person to take care of her. I hadn't had a single moment to read a parenting book. I used what I was given and told how to use, then got on with my long list of duties. There was too much on my plate to dedicate time to educating myself. The only reason I had her was she didn't like being with anyone else for too long. She thought I was safe, which meant I kept her with me.

It can't stay like this, though. I have too much on my shoulders.

I walked back to the compound with her, watching it come into view. Two weeks back from India, my whole world was turned on its head. Nothing looked as it had when Raphael and I left. Nothing was the same—not the world I lived in nor my role in it.

The mansion stood out as the largest thing in the little world I helped rule. Three stories tall, it was a proper mansion with windows on all sides. From any floor, you could view the community springing up around it. There was a fifty-yard radius around it that acted as a yard, something for privacy, but it was often used as a park by everyone who lived in the compound. Small homes were spread out around it, each with their own yard, and the gym stood out on its own, farther from the living areas. A guardhouse was now on the dirt road leaving the compound with a gate. It looked lonely. The stone wall around the compound wasn't done yet, but we had a real gate. More homes had been rushed into construction, but only one was finished so far. I could see the cooking area where Raphael liked to host barbeques, with its pavilion and rows of picnic tables.

It was home. It wasn't the home I had built for myself, where I had spent a long time, living alone and distanced from the world, but it was my home now.

"It's your home, too," I said to my silent companion.

We walked through the small homes, heading for the mansion. I went in through the backdoor. The ground level was by far my least favorite, with offices, meeting rooms, a giant dining room, a couple of sitting areas, and a large kitchen that could fit five people, if not more. It was meant for the community, but that part wasn't the problem. It was just how official it all was. I wasn't used to it and was certain I never really would be.

With the idea of putting Roshni down for a little while, I headed up the stairs, passing by the second floor, which was all guest bedrooms, and right now, we had guests. Until the homes were finished, many of my people lived in the guest suites. Sorcha and Cassius were also over for the night.

The third floor was my piece of the mansion. The entire floor was designed for Raphael and me as a five-bedroom home with a kitchen, three bathrooms, and everything else we needed. We never had to go downstairs if we didn't want to. The extra four bedrooms had been a concession when we had originally designed the home. I wasn't planning on having children yet, didn't even know if we could, but we had put in three suites for children just in case. They all shared a bathroom. Those had been Raphael's decision. The last room was for special guests, someone we would want in our home, like a relative. That had been my decision.

Right now, one of those bedrooms was Roshni's. We hadn't tried to furnish them, so it had been a mad scramble to furnish one as a nursery for her, which was barely used. Normally, she was being carried. Raphael loved hanging out with her in the mornings, and I had her for our afternoons in the desert. Eshika took her whenever neither of us could, though that was only a few hours at a time.

"All right, you little snake. You're going to have a little time with Eshika while I see what's happening downstairs." Putting her in the crib, she yawned and didn't fight me. I smiled as I turned on the baby monitor. "Raphael, I'm coming down," I said, knowing where the other monitor was. He kept it on him all day just for situations like this.

"We're in the large conference room. I'll send Eshika up," he replied.

I sighed heavily at how tired and annoyed he sounded. I needed to figure out what was wrong. Kissing Roshni on the forehead, I left her to play with her toys. Or shift into her snake form and explore the room. That also had required renovations we hadn't expected ever needing.

As I closed the door, I knew she would be safe. She never bit Eshika. She wasn't cuddly with her, but Roshni respected she couldn't bite anyone. Eshika held her more than anyone else, and I leaned on that. I caught the human on the stairs and smiled at her.

"Good day or bad?" Eshika asked, stopping on the

second-floor landing. She looked as tired as I felt most days—tired and haunted with nightmares waking us up every night.

Today, I wasn't tired. Today, I had come to some sort of conclusion, which gave me energy and purpose. Now that I didn't have Roshni, I could act on it.

"Good," I answered, leaning on the railing. I always stopped when I talked to anyone who survived India with me. "Thanks for doing this every day. I know you have your family to be there for right now."

"Helping you, Raphael, and Roshni is one of the most important things I can do, and my family understands that. I would do it more if she was comfortable with it."

"She'll have to get comfortable. Hopefully, you watching her like this every day has prepared her."

I saw the shock in her eyes.

"Prepared her for what, Kaliya?"

"For me to leave." Pushing off the rail, I turned and headed for the last staircase to the ground floor. "I'll tell everyone more tomorrow. There are things I need to do first."

"You don't need to explain," Eshika said as I reached the first step.

Looking over my shoulder, I saw the brave face of a woman who knew what I had on my mind.

If she could do it herself, she would.

I believed that to my very core. If Eshika could go on the hunt I was planning, she would pick up a sword and join me.

Or she would have already left.

"No one else has breathed a word of it, but we all

know, Kaliya. We've just been waiting for you to say something. You've been planning, haven't you?"

"I finally picked my path, yes. I'll announce it tomorrow," I said softly, the words formal, even stiff.

"Of course. I will wait for the declaration of the *Nagaraja*."

Nodding, I jogged down the stairs with that word chasing my heels.

2

CHAPTER TWO

I went into the conference room without knocking. An argument was raging, but I hadn't heard it on the monitor, which surprised me. Raphael sat at the head of the conference table, rubbing his temples, with Mateo behind him. Silent, dangerous Mateo. Sammy couldn't deal with meetings, but Mateo was shaping up to be a good right-hand for Raphael. Raphael didn't need protection, but Mateo was a watcher, the kind of person who observed every little detail of the space he was in, the people in it, what was said, and what wasn't. Watchers were useful to keep around.

Across from each other, Mahavir and Cassius were glaring at each other. Dalar was seated, looking as if he couldn't deal with this anymore. The man never slept. If the twins were terrors in India, they were downright nightmares in Arizona. The massive change in their schedule and environment was the source, and there was nothing anyone could do except ride it out until they adjusted.

Except me. I can do something, and I will.

Vikrant was leaning on the wall behind Mahavir. He didn't look all that happy, but he wasn't screaming like Mahavir.

Looking at the other end of the room, Cassius had a classically frustrated expression I knew all too well. Leith was beside him, arms crossed and fuming, unusual for Leith. Sorcha yawned behind her husband, rolling her eyes.

I looked at Raphael again because no one had realized I was in the room except him. He shook his head a little, telling me a couple of things. He was frustrated with the meeting and didn't care what came out of it, as long as the two parties finally made some sort of decision before he wanted to throw them out. He didn't want to do whatever this was a second time.

"What's going on?" I asked, announcing my presence as I stepped to the opposite end of the table from my mate. Putting my hands on the table, I smiled as silence took over the room, and they all looked in my direction.

"Prince Cassius of the *Fae* won't turn over the rightful archives of the nagas," Mahavir explained. I caught the bite over what Cassius was. "Archives he has no right to keep."

"They're in a secure location where they can be maintained and handled with care. You don't have the proper facilities to keep them here," Cassius retorted.

"We deserve access to them at the least," Mahavir hissed. "Something you haven't given us."

"You can't come to my home right now, and I can't bring the archives here. How many times do I have to explain this?" Cassius snapped. "That was Kaliya's decision, not mine."

"But you can bring pieces of the archives here for short periods of time. You just won't."

"That's a fair point, but then how would you feel if I took them home with me at night? You wouldn't let me, and I'm not in the mood to fight over it."

I slowly raised an eyebrow as Raphael rubbed his temples. He dropped his hand and gave me a very clear look.

This is your problem. Please deal with it.

I drummed my fingers on the table, shrugging a shoulder. I had an easy solution that he'd probably thought of himself, but he hadn't brought up. There were some unofficial rules between him and me now, a balancing act for ruling two different supernatural species without stepping on each other's toes. It had been easy enough for us to figure out, but what was comical about this situation was his refusal to call me back early from my desert time to deal with this before he lost his mind.

My mate doesn't want me bothered by the bullshit. He knows what I've been thinking about.

I listened to the arguing, my presence already forgotten. They were going in circles, and I realized this was a money problem. Neither of these parties would ask Raphael because he wasn't the one who could decide.

They had needed me here.

And I really didn't have time for this bullshit.

"Raphael, find a place here in the mansion, a

conference room or something, to turn into an archive. We have a library, right?"

"We do," he agreed.

"Talk to Cassius and get his experts. Have them renovate the room into a proper space for these sorts of manuscripts and artifacts. I'll pay for it from the naga coffers. This is my house, too, right?"

"Yes, it is," he agreed, smiling. "But the cambions would then lose their library. They need it to continue their education about the world."

"That's right." I had forgotten that. We had a witch homeschooling some cambions there. I looked out the window. From this room, I could see the homes still under construction. "Then we'll build a school and library, two stories. The bottom floor will have room for childcare, like a daycare, and school rooms for any age. The second floor will be a full library for both people. One half will be properly outfitted for the precious archives of my nagas, and the other will be a public library for anyone who needs school books, casual reading, and what have you."

"That's a long project," Cassius pointed out. "What do we do until then? I don't want to come to the compound and get yelled at by Mahavir every time."

"Until then, you'll hold on to the archives—"

"We need them to properly teach our children," Mahavir pointed out. He didn't sound angry, more frustrated. He wasn't a bad guy, just a passionate one. Recent tragedy had made him protective of our people, something I had no problem with. "Devesh is at the age where he needs access to them to further educate himself on our people."

"Raphael, can two cambions be spared if a naga needs to leave the compound to look at the archives at Cassius's residence?" I asked my mate.

"We'll have to work out a schedule, but I'm certain it can be done," he agreed, with a small smile. We worked together well, him and me. My people had thought this was a problem between them and my fae friends and certainly didn't want to ask the cambions for anything. Not because they didn't like my demon mate and his wild people, but the nagas already owed them so much. The cambions had opened their homes to my people in our darkest time.

Asking for more probably felt like taking advantage of the cambions' generosity.

To them. Not to me. I've had to deal with these assholes longer than my nagas have.

By the look on Mahavir's face, my estimation of the problem was correct.

"My Queen, the cambions have done so much..." Mahavir sounded so tentative, his pride clearly about to be wounded by needing more help.

"Mahavir, it's fine. I promise."

"We cambions know how it feels to be alone, but we've always had one ally, helping us every step of the way. She's standing right here." Raphael pointed at me. "We'll do whatever is necessary to make sure your son has access to his heritage... that all of you do. We'll begin the plans for the new building tomorrow, and until it's finished, we will establish something for you to be able to use the archives at Cassius's estate. Mateo, work with Sammy for a schedule to escort the nagas if he's willing to let them visit him."

"Of course, I'm willing," Cassius said, sagging in relief. He looked at me, as exhausted with the meeting as Raphael was. "I've been waiting for you to get here. I was going to offer that as a solution but didn't want to spend your money or Raphael's money without both of you in the room."

"And we certainly weren't going to spend ours," Sorcha mumbled, looking at her nails, but I knew an act when I saw one. She looked up and smiled at me, dropping the bored act. "I'm kidding. We could have offered to pay for it and could afford it, but then we're giving away everything. Your nagas have little experience with other supernaturals, and not everyone is as giving as we are. I told Cassius we could make this into a small lesson about making demands and how to bargain."

"Warn me next time, so I can be here," I said, shaking my head. "Fae."

"I am a fae, yes." Sorcha's smile grew wider. "At least one of them will have to learn to bargain in your place, and none of them are ready. Who else is going to teach them but me?"

"Kaliya, is she serious?" Vikrant asked me, breaking his silence. Dalar only groaned.

"She is," I confirmed. I focused on my fae friends again. "Was this why you came over today, or is there something else?"

"We came to have dinner," Sorcha explained as she

walked to my side. "Cassius also has some news he wanted to pass along."

"Oh?" I raised my eyebrow at him. "Don't make me wait until dinner. I'm probably going to miss it."

"New Tribunal Executioner arrived two days ago. I figured you would want to know a bit about your replacement. Like you, he's planning to make Phoenix his base of operations, considering the prison is just south of here."

"What are we dealing with?" Interested, I crossed my arms. I never planned on dealing with him, but it was good to stay up to date with this sort of thing. I would have to get his phone number and email. It was a priority as a ruler to know how to contact someone locally who worked for the Tribunal. I had Cassius, still a Tribunal Investigator, but knowing both was good.

"Just a fae, but I haven't had the chance to look into it more. Haven't even bothered to read the profile to check for his name. Probably a distant cousin of mine."

"Cassius, they're all distant cousins of yours," I pointed out, smirking as he narrowed his eyes. "Well, that's good to know. Are we done here? I'm going to run some errands tonight."

"Really?" Raphael sat up.

"Yeah."

He was bursting to ask, but I offered no information, and he never lost control and demanded to know where I was going. I hadn't left the compound or let any of the nagas leave since we came back from India. I would be the first to step foot outside our protection.

That was on purpose.

"May I join you?" he finally asked.

"No." I shook my head slowly. "It's for me to do alone."

"Anything else you want to say?" He stood slowly, and I could taste the subtle change in him in the air as his eyes turned black and red. A few slow black veins grew around his eyes as he stared me down.

"Not yet. Not here." I turned to walk out, knowing he was following. We walked out of the house in silence and looked at the world we were building. I led him to the edge, and he turned to study me.

"You've decided."

"I have. I just want to... do a couple of things first," I said, swallowing.

"Kaliya..."

His concern touched me and drove me to explain further, allowing me to be open with him here when I wasn't able to be in front of the others.

"I'm going to see Paden tonight. I haven't spoken to him in months, since before we mated. There are things I think need to be said." I let out a long, slow breath, thinking of everything here. "Tomorrow, I'm going to announce it, and we'll begin preparations. We're going to move fast once I tell my people. Today, I decided it was time to get moving. It's been over two weeks. Roshni will be cared for by Eshika. She tolerates Eshika and will adjust because there will be no other options. Eshika knows how to raise a naga and doesn't have infants to deal with. Elanor hasn't had children with Vikrant, Basanti has twins even younger than Roshni, Sorcha is a fae, and none of the cambions can do it. It has to be Eshika."

"Which is why you've had Eshika watch her when we've needed a break," Raphael said, crossing his arms.

"Yeah." It was one of the first things I'd decided. I couldn't move too fast with it, but after two weeks, I had to hope for the best. I needed to move forward. There would be no peace for me, or for anyone, if I didn't, especially not little Roshni. The future would be hard for her and Eshika, but it was necessary. Better to do this now than later.

"Have you considered if you're ready? You're still underweight, Kaliya. You've been working out every morning, training with everyone through the first half of the day, but you were nearly killed. I'm still amazed you survived the rakshasa attack and that fucker's venom. Are you sure you're ready for this?"

I knew he said the words out of love, but there was only one answer I could give him. It wouldn't make him happy, it wouldn't give him confidence, but it was the only answer I had.

"It doesn't matter if I am or not. It just doesn't matter. The longer I wait, the longer he has to plan. My people have lost their homeland. They lost a man they had all known since they were children. A ruler who they loved and respected. I lost him. It's not just him, though. Roshni lost her parents. Mahavir lost his brother, sister-in-law, and nephew. I lost my parents. Vikrant lost a sister. We've taken losses for centuries and keep taking those losses because we keep waiting. I can't keep waiting, Raphael. I have to be proactive, whether or not I am ready."

He did something that caught me off guard and had my mouth opening slightly. Dropping to one knee, he took my right hand, then my left, held them both to his lips, then looked up at me. His eyes were back to the chocolate brown I loved so much. Normally warm, inviting, and friendly, right now, they were passionate, burning with fire I knew came from his heart.

"I won't tell you not to go or to do this."

"Really?" I pretended to be surprised, but I had known. If he had planned on arguing with me, he would have started over a week ago.

"No, I'm not. I know why you're doing this, and I would never stand in your way. It's what you have to do as queen of your people. I'm going to back you up every step of the way," he promised.

"I know," I whispered. I tried to smile, but I couldn't get it to fully form. "Why are you down there?"

"I'm pledging myself to you, I guess." He chuckled. "It felt like the right thing to do."

"Get up. You're making this weird."

He laughed and let my hands go to stand. We made eye contact, and he pulled me close. I grabbed his shirt at the same time, and our kiss was something for the books. When it was over, the moment felt bittersweet.

"I'll see you when I come home tonight," I promised. "And I will come home. This is just a drive to Paden's. If anyone gives me trouble, I'm the Queen of the Nagas, and they're idiots with suicidal tendencies."

"I know." He let me go. "I'm going to stay out here for a while. Drive safely."

"I will. I need to get ready to leave in a couple of hours."

"Drive safely," he repeated.

I kissed his cheek, then walked away, leaving him to his thoughts. When I looked back, he had his back to me, his hands in his pockets. He was going to need my time away to think about what I had told him.

We were going hunting. It would probably be the most dangerous thing we ever did, and if either of us died, it would probably be me.

I could only hope there was enough time for him to come to terms with it.

3

CHAPTER THREE

Parking at The Jackalope, Paden's bar, I stared at it for twenty minutes before I even cut the engine. My heart was unusually heavy.

There was one thing neither Raphael nor I had said.

I was coming to tell Paden goodbye. There was no guarantee I was coming back. Raphael could come on his own to tell Paden the same thing, but I had to do this by myself.

Getting out of my car, my resolve gave me the strength I needed as I walked toward the bar. I went inside with no fanfare, acting as if this were any other night and ignoring the casual visitors. Supernaturals just there for a drink would never go into the basement bar where I was a patron.

Every person in the bar looked my way, from the bartender on shift to the patrons. The news of my retirement from the Tribunal's employment had spread quickly. Only one thing spread faster, and that was my new title. Few supernaturals saw a queen in their lifetime, even the immortal ones.

I went to the entry into the downstairs basement. Deacon stood there as a bouncer as he did on most nights, his expression completely unreadable. Normally, I would talk to him, but tonight, he only moved and gave me access to the downstairs. As I started walking down, he softly told Paden I was headed down.

As I went into the basement, one thing stood out to me. The Jackalope was exactly as I remembered it. Once, I had come for drinks, kicking up my feet after business. Whether that business was an execution or a bounty, I came here to shoot the shit with Paden.

It was here my life had changed in ways I couldn't fight. I got a drink and picked up my car, unwilling to leave it parked at the airport when the Tribunal needed me for something. It wasn't often the Tribunal needed me onsite, but that occasion had been one of them. Getting home had been wonderful, back to normalcy, or so I had believed.

Until a mysterious bounty on a seemingly human man caught Paden's interest, and he'd asked me to look into it both in an official and unofficial capacity.

Through everything, The Jackalope never changed.

But I had.

It no longer felt like a second home.

Paden was behind the bar, filling a drink before giving it to his patron. He put the bottle down as I slowly walked into the room. Whispers broke out at the tables and booths as people moved away from the bar, clearly making way for me to get a drink. When Paden finally looked up, there was sadness in his eyes.

"Everyone, rise for Kaliya Sahni, The Demon Serpent and Queen of the Nagas," he announced.

There was a sudden hush.

Really Paden? You didn't do this for Cassius. Does Queen of the Nagas rank higher than Prince of your own people?

I nodded my head as a bow of sorts, then continued walking. The key to these moments was to grin and bear it. Accepting the position offered to me by my people and declaring myself the Queen before the Tribunal, I couldn't go back on it just because it made me stand out even more.

"I'm here for a drink," I told them as I looked around the room, taking in the faces of petty criminals, bounty hunters, and so many others I had run into over the years. I ended with Paden. "And to talk to an old friend, if he'll have me."

"Always," Paden said, giving me a sad smile. I leaned on the bar as he prepared a drink for me. "Do you want to talk in my office or here?"

"There's nothing sensitive to worry about." There was a pregnant pause as I decided how to tell him. I went with the most direct option. "I'm leaving soon."

He stopped pouring and gave me a confused expression.

"You only just got back from India. Where are you going?"

"Back to India," I answered, smiling.

His eyes went wide as he looked over me, clearly putting the pieces together. Something bad had happened. Everyone knew that part, but Paden saw more. I looked as though I had been starved, and the nagas were suddenly living in Arizona.

"I never found out what happened in India, but I know it wasn't good," he admitted, finishing with the glass and putting it in front of me. "I only have intel about what you told the Tribunal. No one really understands on this side of the planet."

"I brokered peace with the rakshasa, then was betrayed by them." Sighing, I picked up the glass and took a sip. "They had gotten a better offer, one that let them declare war against the nagas instead of being backed into a political corner by us. I thought I had handled it. Few want to get into a fight with my mate. They didn't know our numbers." I took another drink, this one longer. "However, someone did, told them, and cut a deal. We were attacked during a community gathering... every living naga in one place, our mates, our children. They came and tried to kill us all."

"Kaliya, I'm so sorry," Paden said softly, leaning closer.

"I am too," I admitted, putting the glass down. "I saved who I could and brought them to live with the cambions. A bunch of demon spawn protecting the nagas..." I chuckled darkly. "Let's see anyone try to get through them. Raphael killed two or three dozen rakshasa by himself. Not a single person, who wants my kind dead, can get past the cambions."

"I've heard of his abilities from the fight in the Market. I..." Paden trailed off, putting his hands on the counter behind the bar. "I'm not sorry for talking to Cassius, but I was sorry to hear what happened. I'm sorry

I never tried to call afterward... your abduction, the Market fight. I should have. We've been friends for a long time. It was unkind of me, and you've been right to avoid me."

"I wasn't avoiding you. I was busy... newly mated, planning trips. It's fine, Paden." I meant every word. "I didn't have time to go out and drink. Life and all of its responsibilities caught up with me."

"So, you're going back to India and wanted to stop by for a drink? Finally taking the time to treat yourself nice?" Paden smiled, and this time, it was less sad.

"I'm going back to India and wanted to say goodbye in case I don't come back," I corrected.

His eyes went wide, and his shoulders sagged as that sank in. The bar, which had been silent as it listened in on the conversation, echoed with gasps from the peanut gallery.

"I'm a snake, Paden. I have predators, and the most dangerous of those are always birds of prey. I'm going on a hunt for the most dangerous and powerful. Garuda was the one who convinced the rakshasa to betray our peace treaty. He revealed himself during the battle, thinking they would win. I won't give him another chance to come after my people. They're safe here in Arizona, for now, but he'll come, eventually. He'll pick them off one by one as they grow more secure and comfortable. I can't keep them locked up on the compound forever. I won't do that to them. I'm going to him before any of that can happen. The sooner I act, the better. I'm the *Nagaraja*. It's my duty to protect my people, and if it's the only thing I ever achieve as a queen, I will die knowing I was the best *Nagaraja* I could be."

Paden leaned back, speechless.

"Have a drink, old friend," I said, smiling as I picked up the one he poured for me and sipped the amber liquid. Whiskey. It was my weakness. "We have all night to talk."

He poured himself a large glass of wine and took a long drink.

"Garuda," he finally said. "Isn't he dead?"

"Yeah, my people killed him long after the legends stopped being written down. He was reincarnated, a specialty of supernaturals from India, though probably not limited to us. Normally, we don't get back our memories of past lives, but he's not the only one running around with those, so I can't give him a hard time for it." I took another sip. "Hell, they named me for the naga I was reincarnated from. Have all of his memories as well, thanks to my mother."

"I feel I've missed quite a bit since we've last spoken."

"Oh, you have no idea," I mumbled before finishing my drink. "Another? You can put it on my tab. You know I'm good for it. Or bill it to Cassius if I die. You know he'll cover it without causing a stir."

"Tonight, you drink on the house," he said, waving a hand. The glass refilled without him doing anything.

"Really?"

"If you die, I don't want to be the person who calls the cambion compound about an open tab... or Cassius and Sorcha. I'm not sure which of those options scares me more."

I couldn't stop the laughter as it bubbled out of me. Tossing my head back, it rang out, my first real laugh since I had come back to my favorite place on earth. I was wiping my eyes as I leaned on the bar and sipped my topped-off drink.

"Yeah, good point," I said, falling into a fit of giggles. I let them pass before getting back to the important conversation. "I am going to try my damnedest, you know... to come home alive. I'm going to try."

"I know you will. You're too stubborn to die," Paden said with a snort. "But... you've never taken death so seriously. You've always been honest about it, but you've never... made arrangements."

"He's..." I sighed. "My last life ended because of my fear of him. I ran from him and ended up in a place I shouldn't have been. Pissed off the wrong power and was killed. Gained a name I carry today... The Demon Serpent." I sipped my drink. "I've never met someone I was certain could kill me at my best. He could... and I'm not at my best, Paden."

"I wasn't going to point that out. You look like you were dragged through hell."

"I was bitten by another naga, an assassination attempt that had nothing to do with Garuda and the rakshasa. Venom tried to destroy my body, and it was hell to survive. It happened... maybe a couple of days before the attack. Garuda had been spying on us in his eagle form. I'm certain he saw how weak I was and decided it was the best time to come for us. As a warrior, he would pay attention to those weaknesses."

"Yet you made it out. You might be as good as people say you are."

It wasn't Paden who said that. I turned to see someone leaning on the bar further down. I licked my lips and caught the man's scent as I read his body temperature.

Fae. Sidhe.

"You must be the new Executioner sent by the Tribunal." I didn't recognize him, and I recognized nearly everyone in this city. He had spiked black hair, brilliant blue eyes like Caribbean waters, and several piercings in his human ears and more in his face. Tattoos covered his neck, with more on his hands. A long-sleeve V-neck covered the rest, only offering the smallest peek of a chest tattoo.

"I am." His Sidhe ears became visible, growing longer than I figured they should have. Those ears said a lot about the potential power of a Sidhe. The longer they were, the less human blood was in them. He wasn't like Sorcha and Cassius. Sorcha was unique among the fae, so I couldn't use her to judge, but Cassius was a pureblooded royal with long pointed ears. This guy was pretty damn close to Cassius. He probably had a bit of human in him, but not enough to really matter.

He moved closer.

"Heard you fuck Sidhe," he said, his smile all too suggestive.

"I have before, but I'm off the market. Sorry."

"Too bad," he murmured. "How did you make it out of India? That's what I wanted to ask. You don't look like you're all that much. I mean, I've been an Executioner for a year, and so many people talk about how good you are, but you look like someone chewed on you. Seeing you right now, I don't know how you survived this job, much less being a ruler." He paused, then snapped his fingers. "Oh yeah, you were only a ruler because there weren't any other options."

"Are you trying to be an ass, or is it just something you do naturally?" I asked, tilting my head to the side as I tried to figure out his game.

"A bit of both. Really, I'm just feeling antsy. I heard you used to come around here, and I've never put my skills against another Executioner before. It's not allowed, you know?"

"Yeah, I know." It was highly discouraging. A lot of half-mad people worked the job. I was one of the saner people in the Tribunal's employment, and that was saying something.

"But you're not an Executioner anymore." He smiled, showing sharp, inhuman teeth. "Let's play."

"Let's not," I said softly.

I could *feel* the magic in the air.

As a spell crackled in the air and water started spraying from the faucets behind the bar, the room went dark. I shifted, hissing furiously.

Water and darkness. Fun.

I didn't give him a chance to do anything more. Flying around him, I coiled my tail once I had hold of him. I wasn't a constrictor, but the principle was there.

"What the fuck?" I heard a groan, then he screamed. "Holy shit! Let me out."

"Turn the lights back on, fool," I hissed above him.

With thirty feet of snake body, I could be a very tall creature.

They came on, and people screamed when they saw me. Paden even jumped back with wide eyes. I leaned over the new guy, my fangs visible for him to see and comprehend.

"Do not play games with me," I thundered. Leaning farther down, I met his clear blue eyes.

"Yes, ma'am," he croaked.

I shifted back to my fully human form.

"You wouldn't be fighting another Executioner. You would be fighting the Demon Serpent, and you wouldn't win." I put my hands together in front of me as he gasped for air, his hand on his chest.

"I see," he agreed. "Well, I'll leave you to your evening."

"Probably for the best." I knew how to talk to other Executioners. I rarely had to, but it was a good skill. "We might have to work together one day. I'm close to the Tribunal as a former employee. I'm also the ruler of a Tribunal loyal species. Don't break any of the Laws you enforce or try to attack me again. I'll forgive you this once but not a second time."

"Thanks," he said, stepping back. "Paden, you should have warned me."

"I didn't think you would be that stupid. Have you found your cousin yet? He could have told you what you wanted to know."

I raised an eyebrow between them.

"Cassius? Fuck no. Can't believe they put me in the same city as that fucking asshole." The Sidhe shook his head and walked away. Once he was gone, I turned to Paden.

"It's never boring in this city, is it?" I asked, sighing.

"We used to have boring. We ruined that." Paden gave me a knowing look. He had been the one to send me after Raphael, and things had never been the same since. "Since he never introduced himself, that was Prince Maxen, although not much of a prince. He's only about thirty in human years."

I raised my eyebrows in surprise. Few of the fae had a countable age. It was such a problem, no one tried to age them. That Paden knew how old Maxen was? That was *young*.

"He's the youngest son of the youngest daughter of the royal family, Oberon and Titania's last child. She had an affair with a human. He was the result. He's a prince... because people were feeling nice, and his blood leaned more to fae than not. I mean, Cassius could abdicate the throne and keep his title. Why not give Maxen one? Those titles are handed out like candy now, it seems."

"Cassius doesn't know it's him. Said he figured it was a distant cousin." I shook my head, not surprised by the complex mess that was the fae royal family. "Though, maybe to Cassius, he is one."

"Probably, but this might be a little closer to Cassius than he'd prefer." Paden chuckled. "They'll be fine together, don't worry. Neither of them really care about the royal family they're part of, so..." Paden shrugged. "Maybe they'll bond over it."

"I'm not worried." Cassius could stomp the kid into dust. "Maxen isn't a problem. Young, new to the job, and all the Executioners are some level of insane and stupid. He's a little foolish, but he'll figure it out. In fact..." I chuckled as I realized it was kind of nice. "It's good to see they sent a fucking mess to replace me." I grinned at him. "With me being a respectable ruler and everything, you'll need a new hot mess to work with. It's not like I can take bounties anymore and help you figure out the interesting ones. It's not a good look. It never was, really, but circumstances have made it so much less acceptable."

His silence made me lose my smile. The longer it stretched, the more I worried.

"Paden?"

"We might not be able to work together anymore, but come home, anyway," he said softly. "Come *here.* You're always welcome."

"I'll do my best," I whispered. "But don't ruin my goodbye. It's hard to do, but I need to. I won't lie to either of us by saying this is going to be okay, Paden. I won't do it."

"And I respect the hell out of you for it even though it hurts more than anything I've ever experienced."

We shared another drink, then another. Clinking our glasses, a toast to our friendship, we talked about that friendship long into the night, telling old stories and sharing laughter. The bar remained respectfully quiet. No one bothered us, and a second bartender came downstairs to take orders, so Paden could stay with me. We went through a couple bottles of wine and whiskey, laughing, but with an undercurrent of sadness always there.

Then it was closing time, the bar completely empty,

and I knew Paden had to go home to his wife and me to my mate. We were surrounded by empty bottles, a testament to how much history we had. I didn't feel a buzz, though. The mood was too somber, and my body was processing it faster than it ever had.

"Goodbye, Paden," I said as I put my empty glass down.

"Goodbye, Kaliya."

I left, not knowing if I would ever see him and this place ever again.

4

CHAPTER FOUR

The next day, Raphael and I were up before the sun rose over the horizon. He had waited up for me, keeping Roshni company well into the night. She adored him and went to sleep quickly while he stayed up for me. We were both used to losing sleep, so the early morning didn't bother us. Another day, another list of things to do.

Sitting up in bed, with a laptop on my lap and little Roshni lying beside me, I was looking at flights. I wanted us out of the country in less than twenty-four hours, and he had no complaints.

"Where are we going first?" he asked as he got dressed.

"The Yamuna River," I answered absent-mindedly, not really considering how that was going to land with my mate. I looked up when I didn't get a reply. His deafening silence and frozen body were all I needed to know about how he was taking it. I closed my laptop and sighed.

"I died there. Well, he died there, my previous incarnation. It seems like a good place to start." I watched black veins slowly spread over Raphael's face, knowing my words weren't helping. He needed more information. "I just want to see it. I have no plans of staying or going into the water or anything like that. I don't plan on poisoning the water with my venom like I did in my previous life. I just want to see it. I keep thinking about it. I have for months. It's not about the plan or hunting Garuda. I want to put my past life to rest, or… maybe it's picking up where he left off. He died there, but he had options he didn't use. Krishna told him to go back to the island of Ramanaka. I want to start there and walk away from the river." I needed to make sure he understood I wasn't trying to get myself killed. I *wanted* to come back.

"You want to rewrite history," Raphael said, the veins finally retreating. "Instead of dying in the river, you'll leave and go on the journey *he* should have taken… not you. You're smarter than he was, different. Don't take his mistakes on your shoulders. You didn't commit them."

"That's my hope," I confirmed, putting the laptop aside. "As for not taking his mistakes for myself, I don't think I have an option, Raphael. Garuda certainly won't give me one. He doesn't see me as a new person. He sees me as the naga who ran from him thousands of years ago." I got out of bed, stretching. Today was the day. I'd waited and planned, and now it was time to send it all into action.

My plan and my allies are all I have. Garuda could kill me at my best, and I'm nowhere near my best.

Looking down at my naked body, I was still bony. There wasn't enough food or exercise in the world to bring back in only two short weeks what I had lost to

Pavan's venom. I'd gained ten pounds, my muscles still worked, and the small run-in with Maxen had been a good reminder my full naga form was still powerful enough to do what my human form couldn't.

"This is only a man's wishful thinking, but I had hoped you would take more time," Raphael admitted as he came around the bed and wrapped his arms around me. I leaned back into him. He was so observant, my mate. He knew what I had been doing—judging myself as I did every morning.

"We don't have time," I reminded him.

"I know. Besides, if we held this off any longer, you would drop from exhaustion. You don't sleep well." One of his hands reached up and cupped my cheek, turning my head as he leaned down to kiss my lips, a soft, fluttering touch. We stayed there for a moment, his chocolate brown eyes full of the same concern that had been there for days and days. "When this is over, you're going to lie down and sleep for me. One entire night. That's all I'm asking for."

"I welcome it," I whispered. Freeing myself, I went to shower, then went to find something to wear in our walk-in closet. By the time I was dressed, Raphael was ready with Roshni, her diaper freshly changed and her outfit ready for the day. Taking a moment, I watched him tickle and play with her in the middle of the bed as she giggled and kicked her legs.

The scene broke my heart as much as it tried to heal it.

Saranya should be here. She should be...

I had to turn away and wipe my eyes.

"Kaliya?"

"Sorry," I mumbled as I looked at him and her there. "Do you think she'll be okay with Eshika while we're gone?"

"I think they'll have a few bad days, then she'll settle," Raphael said, sighing heavily. Rolling off the bed, he swooped her up, letting her fly before catching her. I smiled like a fool at her excited baby babble.

Healing and pain, hand in hand. For every moment I felt guilty Roshni had lost her parents, I felt immense love and joy, knowing she was alive and seeing Raphael with her.

He didn't give her to me, and I didn't reach for her either. Right now, she was clearly happy with her warm cambion man, and I wouldn't get in the way of that. Not when there wasn't much time left.

"What time was the flight you found?"

"We can fly out tonight at midnight if you're okay with leaving that quickly."

"I'm okay with it. Who do you want to leave to plan the library? I was thinking of Mateo, Cassius, and Vikrant."

"Yeah, let's keep Sorcha and Mahavir out of it. She'll try to play games to teach them. Mahavir definitely needs to learn, but this needs to go smoothly while we're gone. It's too important." I met him at the door, and we walked out together. "Vikrant is calmer, more leveled-headed, but lacks seniority. Mahavir is also pretty smart. This isn't a good one for him to deal with. He loses his temper when it's a family thing. Clearly, he thinks it's important Devesh's education continues, and I agree. He's old enough to see the archives and should have them available."

"It's something more, though, isn't it?" Raphael readjusted how he was holding Roshni, who was still laughing about whatever she found so funny. "You didn't lose your temper. You were so calm the entire thing. Not that it's a bad thing, but normally, you come into arguments with a boom, not a whisper."

"We just lost our homeland, Raph. They lost their homes, the places where they were raised and planned to raise their children. Homes that had been in their family for years." I stopped at the top of the stairs, looking at him as the pain cut deep. "They're afraid they're going to lose their heritage, too. I know Cassius wouldn't withhold our archives without good reason or indefinitely, but they don't know him. He's looking out for us, but they don't know him. He knows I agree with him, but they—"

He leaned down and kissed my cheek. "I know you wouldn't let that happen to them," he murmured.

"I've only been their Queen two weeks," I reminded him, and he nodded in reply. "They're trusting me to solve all their problems, but they don't know me. And… I haven't exactly been kind to our heritage. So, Mahavir yelled at Cassius. It's not the worst problem we have in front of us. It's very small, considering." Reaching up, I poked Roshni's nose. "Let's get someone breakfast and find the only person I can trust to keep her while we're gone."

We walked down the stairs to the ground floor. I was expecting the woman I found in the ground floor kitchen.

Eshika was already prepping to cook breakfast for us and looked up with a smile.

"Mahavir said you came into the meeting yesterday and handled it," she said as I went to help her.

"Oh yeah. Cassius and Sorcha are nice, but the cambions were easier to train than the nagas," I explained, chuckling. Taking the bowl and wooden spoon from her, I stirred so she could knead the bread. "Less ego when it came to politics, age, heritage, and all that."

"He was grateful for you to come in and decide what would happen. He had considered asking Raphael for similar, but..." Eshika sighed and rolled her eyes.

"It's better he waited for me. I am the *Nagaraja* and all that."

"He could have asked me," Raphael pointed out, finally interrupting lady-time as he put Roshni on the counter in front of him. I didn't always help Eshika, but this morning, I felt the need to keep my hands active. Other mornings, helping her let me pretend I was younger, helping an older woman in the kitchen as I had sometimes helped my mother. It took the weight off my shoulders and comfort I hadn't had for so long.

"He would have never," Eshika said, laughing. "He considered it, which is a big step for him. You're the ruler of the cambions, though. We already owe you so much."

Yup, I was right.

"It's really not—"

"Then pay us back," I said, cutting off my mate. Eshika raised her eyebrows. She knew I didn't mean money. I knew the wealth of every single naga now, and as a ruler, since I was a child, I was by far the wealthiest. "I asked you yesterday to wait for an announcement. You need to know earlier, though, to prepare. You know what's happening, but it's... We're leaving tonight. Raphael and I, we're leaving. I need you to care for Roshni full-time."

Eshika's surprise shifted from concern and worry to pain and more. I saw the emotions of a lifetime flash by as she absorbed what I said.

"For how long?" she finally asked.

"Until I come back... *if* I come back." I swallowed the pain I felt saying those words to her. We nagas and our humans, we had lost so many, and I was asking Eshika to take Roshni into her home and keep her, perhaps for the rest of her life. A baby, one who had already lost parents and was traumatized from it. One who thought only I was safe, and Raphael was a decent second to me.

"I know how to raise a naga." Eshika nodded and went back to kneading bread as her eyes went to Roshni. "I will do this for you... for both of you. I know why you're leaving, and it's the *right* thing to do, but I would like you to promise me something."

"Tell me, then we'll see."

"Adopt her," Eshika whispered. She gave me a fiery look that probably struck terror into the hearts of her husband and son. "When, not if, but *when* you come back, adopt her into your household. Raise her as your own, daughter of the *Nagaraja*. Not a lost child in the community, but a cherished member of your family. Give her privilege and love and safety. Adopt Roshni."

I opened my mouth then closed it. Looking at my

mate, searching his eyes, I wondered what he was thinking. He offered me nothing but looked down and focused on Roshni. Roshni didn't catch the emotional currents between the adults around her. She flailed her arms and tried to touch Raphael's face, babbling about whatever was happening in her head.

My heart broke and healed a little as Raphael leaned down and gave her what she wanted.

He didn't offer his opinion, and I didn't know how to feel about that. He just politely ignored the conversation, keeping the little girl busy as she ran her chubby hands through his hair and laughed.

As I watched, I knew I wouldn't be able to find an answer yet.

"I'll consider it," I answered as I looked at Eshika again. It was all I could say.

I'm not the motherly type. I wouldn't know what to do full-time. The only reason we've made it this far is with her, Raphael's, and everyone else's help. Even Sorcha knows more about babies than I do. I just... never had that in my life plan.

I didn't think I would live to see it.

Eshika shook her head, clearly disappointed.

"Why?" she asked after a silent, drawn-out moment.

Because I'm the reason her mother is dead. Because I didn't recognize the threat soon enough. Because I would have to raise her with the expectations of being in my shoes one day.

"There's too many to say," I whispered, looking away from her.

"Kaliya, you're the closest thing she has to a mother right now."

And what a fucking tragedy that is.

"She trusts me because she knows we're the same, not because she knows or loves me," I reminded her. "You're the same as her mother. She's nice to Basanti, too, and for the same reason. She's getting used to the other cambions, thanks to Raphael. She has bad days, but they're not outwardly aggressive. She just cries less for me, but that's all."

Eshika only stared at me, and I saw my pain echoed in her eyes.

"Give me one, just one of your reasons," she pleaded.

"No." I couldn't properly put them into words and express the depth of my feelings on the matter. "I'm sorry it's not the answer you wanted, Eshika, but I said I would consider."

"Is this a problem with her becoming your heir?" Eshika asked, still prying. "Because she wouldn't be. We've all sat down and already had this discussion. From here on, the *Nagaraja* will be the naga or nagini capable of doing the job. Mahavir and Vikrant are working to learn to be your advisors... and your heirs if necessary. They were your choices, so they know they can make themselves capable if it becomes necessary. We would never put that burden on her shoulders—"

"Eshika. Stop," I ordered. "This is not up for discussion anymore. Let's have breakfast, then we need to get everyone from the compound." I looked at my mate before she had the chance to respond. "Raphael, did Cassius and Sorcha stay last night? I knew they stayed the night before."

"Yeah. After you left, I asked them to stay for another day," he confirmed.

"Thank you."

Sitting, I stared at the table until food was put in front of me. I ate, but not enough. Most days, I ate like something twice my size with an endless stomach, trying to put weight back on, but today, I picked at it. The moment I lost interest and my stomach wasn't growling, I stopped and left Raphael to give Roshni breakfast and eat with Eshika.

Raphael could call his cambions to him without a problem, but I wanted to get every naga for the meeting myself. As I walked to the first house, someone caught up to me.

"Good morning, Cassius. Thank you for staying another night. There's a meeting—"

"Don't do this," he whispered, stepping in front of me.

"Not even a good morning?" I stopped, trying not to run into him. "Cassius, you know—"

"I know a lot of things, yes, and one of those is I don't want you to die. Just listen to me."

"I can't." I wasn't upset he kept cutting me off, just sad. "There's nothing you can say, Cassius. Listening... only makes this harder."

"Your people are safe here. You have the wealth and resources to keep them under some of the strongest protections this world offers. Garuda can't get to them here," Cassius ranted, even though I had just told him it wouldn't make a difference. "I know the legends and stories about you and your previous life. I know the twisted history you and your people have with him. I know you lost India, and the nagas have lost their home, but... you can't go get revenge. It will kill you."

I had known Cassius for so long, it felt as though I had grown up with him. In all of those years, he and I had strong emotions about each other. We made for a toxic, bad romantic relationship, but we were powerful friends.

It seemed to always come back to this. Cassius pleaded with me not to do something else dangerous, pleading for me not to take the next step, to go further, or to push myself too hard. I hadn't told him a single one of my plans, but he knew. Most days, he knew me so well, it was hard for me to surprise him anymore.

He's wrong this time.

"It's not revenge," I corrected, but I wasn't given a chance to explain. Revenge was part of it, but not all of it. It wasn't the most important piece.

"If it's not revenge, then it's the same obsessive need you've had since before we met. This time, it will be the death of you, and you know it."

"It's not obsession either," I promised. "Cassius, let me explain."

"No! Kaliya, we've been through hell together, which is the only reason I think I have the right to tell you this. Ruler to ruler. Royal to royal. Don't walk away from your people to chase this. It will do more harm than good."

"I won't have a people if I *don't*," I countered, keeping my eyes locked on his. "Royal to royal? You know the job of a ruler when a threat is out there, waiting to hunt down and destroy those who rely on you. Neutralize the threat before it gains power, solidifies its plan, and attacks. We're at *war*, Cassius. I don't have a *choice*. I *have* to fight Garuda one day, so I'm doing it on my terms, not his. I won't run or hide from him. To do so would be a disservice to my people, leaving them vulnerable and looking at the sky for the rest of their lives, wondering if one day, the great eagle will swoop down and come for them." I sighed.

"I'm not doing this purely out of revenge or obsession. I'm doing this because my people deserve better than lifetimes of fear and eternities of secrecy. They deserve better than wondering if their loved ones will come home from a trip to the grocery store. They deserve the land they grew up in, their homes, their history, and so much more. They deserve more than raising *orphans*." I stared him down, the strong fear for me leaving them.

"I am the *Nagaraja*. Revenge is a personal goal, and obsession is part of who I am, but the thing driving my feet is *duty*. It's up to *me* to give them what I believe they deserve as my people—all the glory and goodness of a good life and their children safe and *free*. That is the job of a ruler, and I accepted the role this time. It wasn't thrown on my shoulders because I was an option. They asked, and I said yes. I told them I would be the *Nagaraja,* and I mean to be everything they need me to be. I will fight to my last breath to give them everything they should have had all these centuries. So, there is nothing you, Sorcha, Raphael, or anyone else can say to stop me." I waited impatiently for his argument, but his face was blank, then he smiled. Of all the expressions he could have had at the end of my speech, a smile wasn't what I expected.

"You're a better person than I was," he said, holding out an arm. I took the invitation and let him hold me to his side, his arm over my shoulder. After a moment, he wrapped his other arm around me, and I wrapped mine around his waist and held on tight.

It took me a moment to figure out what he meant, but it clicked.

"No, I'm not," I mumbled into his chest.

"We'll argue about it when you get home." He let me go and backed away. "I need to wake up Sorcha. I've been out here for hours, walking around, trying to find the right thing to say to keep you from doing this. Hearing you, though… I'll be at the meeting, and I'll be here, helping everyone, so you know they're safe."

"Thank you." I kept walking as he turned back toward the mansion.

5

CHAPTER FIVE

Mahavir and Devesh were ready for the day when I went to their home with Eshika. She got up early to help me, and I firmly believed they got up in solidarity.

"I need you both in the large conference room, the one that fits everyone," I told them as I stood in the entryway, able to taste human, cambion, and naga on the air as I nervously licked my lips. The human and cambion scents were fainter because they weren't sharing with a cambion like Vikrant and Eleanor were. The cambion who had claimed the home when it was built had moved in with another to give the family more space and keep them together.

"We will go right now," Mahavir promised. Devesh looked between his father and me but didn't have the confused expression I expected. In fact, there was concern and surprise as though something bad was going to happen, and it was going to happen soon.

His parents must have talked to him, letting him know what they believed would happen.

"Thank you. I'm going to get the others." I turned to head back out, able to escape before anyone thought to ask me a question. I wasted no time in heading for the home of Vikrant and Eleanor. They were still getting dressed when I knocked, evidenced by Vikrant buttoning his shirt as he opened the front door.

"Kaliya, come in." He opened the door wider, but I shook my head. There was no reason for me to go in.

"Kaliya?" Eleanor's head came out of the kitchen. "Are you here for breakfast? David and I can make a plate. Right, Vikrant?"

One of the cambions looked out, and I recognized David, whose eyes went wide.

He knows. Raphael probably told Mateo last night and let the word quietly spread.

"Of course, we can, but I think our queen is here for something other than breakfast," Vikrant replied as he kept the door open with his foot and finished buttoning his shirt. "What do you need?"

"I need all of my people in the large conference room. Mahavir and Devesh are already on their way. Eshika is at the mansion, and I'm going to Dalar and Basanti now." I looked around him, seeing David hadn't moved. "Raphael—"

"He told us to come when you called for the nagas. Whoever sees it first will alert the others," he answered, telling me my mate was one step ahead of me. "I'll leave with them and send out a text. We'll all be there."

"Enjoy breakfast." Backing away, I turned to walk

down the path to the dirt roads we were wearing into the desert around the compound. I knew Vikrant watched me the whole way, his mind probably mulling over the orders I'd just given him and David's acknowledgment the cambions knew it was coming.

As I walked down the road, I thought of Raphael's plans that would be put on hold. He wanted to pave the drive into the compound and these roads. He wanted this place to seem like a real town or neighborhood. He'd started writing down his plans before we left for India the first time. Coming back, he hadn't wanted to start anything. He just reached out, and with my help, we launched the construction of the new homes needed.

I'd left Dalar and Basanti's home for last because I didn't want to interrupt any possible sleep they could get or breakfast with the twins. Dalar, with bags under his eyes, opened the door, let me in, and went back toward the kitchen.

"How are Devaj and Ishir?" I asked gently, patting his shoulder as I saw Basanti cleaning the kitchen.

"Down for a nap after breakfast," he answered.

"Oh, then I need to offer an apology," I said, sighing. "I need everyone in the large conference room at the mansion. All the other nagas and cambions will be attending."

Dropping the plate she was holding into the sink, Basanti turned and started shaking her head.

"No," she whispered, a small plea.

"It's not a discussion, and this is not a democracy. Basanti, just come to the meeting."

"You can't do this. You just can't. We need you here and alive, and you aren't healed and—"

"The Queen will do what she believes is in the best interest of our people," Dalar said, his head down.

"I'll do what's in the best interest of your children, not just their safety but for the long lives ahead of them. Come to the conference room as quickly as you can and listen," I said, leaving them there.

I didn't head straight back to the mansion. My heart pounding, I went to the gym, knowing I could find solace there, not in being alone, but in being with a tough-as-nails friend, who I knew would agree with me.

"Sammy?" I called as I went inside.

"Here!" she called from the other side, next to the equipment. She put the weights down and grabbed a towel as I walked in her direction. Throwing it over her shoulder, she used one end to wipe her forehead.

"Normally, we're not here this early, so I didn't know if I would find you here," I said, reaching out to shake her hand as we met in the center of the gym.

"Heard some things, so I wanted to get a good workout in to think." She gave me a one-shoulder shrug. "You know, things about people going on suicide missions with no idea what direction they should take."

"Just because I haven't told anyone doesn't mean I don't know the direction," I countered. "What do you think I've been doing for the last two weeks?"

"Grieving like a normal person." She smirked, bringing a sense of youth and levity to her expression as a strand of her long blonde hair fell into her face. "But we're not normal, are we?"

"No, we're not."

"We're tough bitches who don't take shit from anyone."

"Sure." Maybe I had once felt that way, but I didn't anymore. In fact, I was at my most powerful when it came to my magic and my abilities, but there wasn't a moment in my life when I'd felt more fragile. Maybe as a child, but not as an adult.

Sammy must have caught my mood. Pushing the strand out of her face, she looked around, checking over her shoulder as if she wanted us to be alone. When she looked at me again, I continued my silent patience. I was getting used to this. Everyone reacted a little differently.

"I get it," she finally said. "Some shit just hits you harder some days. Knocks you down, and it's harder to get back up."

"Yeah," I agreed softly. "When those days hit, they put shit into perspective. No matter how powerful, experienced, or well-trained you are, there's a way for life to hit back and make it hurt. There's always something that can kill you, a weakness you can't do anything about."

"Oh yeah." Sammy nodded, then sighed. "We're rooting for you. We'll be here when you get back, and *no one* is getting to your nagas. Mateo and I are going to make fucking sure of that. You had our back, Kaliya. We didn't even know you, you didn't know us, but you came to the labs, and you got us out. Sure, you lied to me about the thing between you and Raphael, and I held on to that longer than I should have. Considering everything you did for us..." Sammy turned away and wiped her eyes.

"Damn, now you've got me crying like a fucking little girl. This is why I came to work out. I was a bitch to you after we got out of that hellhole, then I was a bitch because you weren't ready to talk about mating, so you lied. Fuck, I ruined the time I had to get the one woman who fucking gets it to be my friend."

"Sorcha gets it, too," I said, trying not to bleed out from an emotional wound I never realized I had. "There are a lot of other women who do, too. Mateo isn't a girl, but he's a warrior."

"Life's fucking hard for us, though," Sammy said, finally looking at me again. "The dangers are different."

"Sometimes," I agreed. "By statistics, definitely. Sammy—"

"Don't bullshit me with trying to walk around it. You *know*. You've been through some of the same shit I have. You *have* to come back. You're the only person I know who might *understand,* and I need someone who *understands*. I've never been able to... talk about any of it and was hoping we would get to that one day. Now, you're leaving on a fucking suicide mission without a map."

My heart shattered, and I had to fight the tears. Oh yeah, I understood the haunted pain in her eyes, the shaky plea, the desperation. The timing couldn't be worse. Sammy was damaged but was admitting she was ready to reach out and let someone help her. She had probably been thinking about this for weeks and was now realizing the person she had picked was leaving.

Everyone in the compound was damaged, but I knew her damage. It resonated all too well. I saw it in my face for decades, heard it in my voice and in my head. Women like us had the tendency to find each other and recognize it. It wasn't as though I didn't know what Sammy and the other cambions had been through. I had general explanations and assumptions I could build with those.

"You've got to come back," Sammy repeated.

"I'll do my best." It was the only thing I could give any of them.

"Yeah, I know you will, and even if you screw up, Raphael will be there to save you," Sammy said, rubbing her eyes. "There's not a lot that can kill him out there, I bet. Use him as cover."

"You're not wrong, and I will."

We stood in silence until I reached out and hugged her. I was certain I surprised her by the frozen way she held herself for the first thirty seconds, but I didn't let go until she hugged me back. It was tentative at first, then grew more confident and comfortable.

"I'm heading back to the mansion," I told her as I finally let her go. "Do you want to walk with me? No one is going to care that you haven't showered yet."

"Yeah, I'll walk with you."

We left the gym together. I saw other cambions jogging for the mansion, and more than half saw us, slowing to let us catch up and pass them. One even stopped and waited for us to pass before joining the small pack growing behind Sammy and me.

It wasn't normal, but I didn't question it. The cambions were a somewhat weird bunch, and I still hadn't figured out their wiring. Every supernatural species had some stereotypes and generalizations. Werecats liked to be alone; werewolves didn't. Nagas liked the heat. It was more obvious in some supernaturals, the worst in ones that were once human, but there was always something.

And cambions are just strange.

Cole ran around Sammy and me to get the door. Sammy stopped and let me go through first. Me and five cambions went to the large conference room, where Sammy got the door this time.

Everyone was there, waiting on me and the stragglers. All of my nagas sat close together at a few tables close to the front. Dalar and Basanti were rocking one of the twins, pacing in circles, and the only two not seated. The cambions were more spread out. Sammy and the ones following me broke off to see their friends and get seats. Cassius and Sorcha were at the front, leaning on the wall behind Raphael. Gabi was flitting about, checking on people until Sammy snapped her fingers and pointed at a chair, which prompted the Nephilim to sit down.

I stopped beside my mate and sighed when I saw he was still holding Roshni.

"You have to give her to someone else, eventually," I said gently.

"Yes, but not yet," he countered. "After the meeting."

"Okay." I could accept that. I looked over the room again, and every eye was on me. "No one is wondering why we're here right now. Raphael and I leave for India tonight." I saw mouths open, and some stood in surprise at that timeline. "This is *not* a discussion. You will follow the lead of Cassius, Prince of the Fae, and his wife, Lady

Sorcha. Mahavir and Vikrant, you'll be in charge of the nagas as a *team*."

"Mateo, you'll be in charge in my stead," Raphael said. "You'll work on the library with Prince Cassius, making sure it fits the needs of the nagas and the cambions. You will do so impartially." Mateo gave a sharp nod and crossed his arms.

"Mahavir, you'll let Vikrant help Mateo while you make sure the families of our people have what they need. He will handle situations with other species while you handle our people," I said, shifting my weight. "I need all of you to promise that you will work together while we're gone and that you'll do everything to keep each other safe until we both come back."

I saw heads nodding, every one of them. This was too serious for anyone to mess around.

"Good. Now, Roshni will be in Eshika's care and *only* in Eshika's care. If she needs any of you for anything, you will drop what you're doing and help unless it would hurt or kill someone. You will follow her orders regarding Roshni. If I come back and hear otherwise, I'll find an appropriately cruel punishment to hand out." A couple of faces paled, and I was certain I had gotten the point across. "I expect the same level of assistance extended to Basanti and Dalar with their twins, am I clear?" They all nodded. "Good. I think that covers everything."

"Eshika," Raphael called softly.

Jogging forward, she took Roshni but didn't back away with her. She leaned the baby toward me, and I kissed the girl's forehead.

"Be good," I murmured as tears filled my eyes. Eshika

took her away, and I looked over the group but didn't have much else to say.

"Good luck," Mahavir said.

That started a chorus of everyone repeating it.

I nodded as I blinked away the tears.

"Thanks."

6

CHAPTER SIX

Used to moving quickly, Raphael and I were packed by lunch. We packed light, knowing it was next to impossible to know how long we'd be gone, so there was no way to plan for everything. No one bothered us as we silently filled two bags each—his with clothing and survival gear, mine with clothing and weapons. We staged them in the garage next to the SUV Sorcha would drive us to the airport. My dear friend had been quiet for the meeting, but I knew I would hear it when we were on the way to the airport.

As Raphael and I surveyed and went over what we packed, I heard a door and turned to see Mahavir and Vikrant walking in. Mahavir carried a little wooden box that intrigued me.

"We hoped you were here," Mahavir said, sighing. "We're not here to tell you not to do this. We wanted to ask about your plans, though. We won't tell anyone, not even our mates, but we're hoping we might be able to give you information or advice."

I leaned on the SUV and sighed.

"I have told no one because most of it doesn't... make any sense," I admitted. "But okay. My plan is to go to the banks of the Yamuna River in Vrindavan to see the kadamba tree."

"That seems very dang—"

"Yeah. Raphael and I went over this already. I won't get in the water or try to cause any trouble. I mean, really. There will be humans there, and if I keep my head down, they'll never know I was the naga who poisoned the river with my venom."

"I mean, you're not," Raphael pointed out.

"Yeah, there is that, but I want to see it, and starting elsewhere makes little sense."

"What's your logic?" Vikrant asked, leaning against the truck next to our SUV.

"Simple. Krishna told Kaliya to leave Vrindavan and go back to Ramanaka. He didn't. Krishna killed him. I will leave the river and go to Ramanaka, which is where this gets complicated."

"Oh, definitely complicated and probably impossible." Mahavir crossed his arms, frowning. "Kaliya, the naga haven't seen Ramanaka for thousands of years. Adhar didn't even know how to go back. How do you expect to find it, and do you really think Garuda would know how when we don't?"

What Mahavir was asking was reasonable and were the questions I had spent two weeks answering over and over in my head. Long, quiet walks and sitting in the desert with Roshni, trying to understand, trying to put the pieces together, so I could make my plan.

"I think..." I looked down at my hands, curling them tight into fists. "Garuda hid from us for centuries. He reincarnated as himself somehow and restarted his war against us. He's behind most of it. I believe he's been running a secret campaign to have our people poached like animals and that he's gathered allies in the shadows to do the murders for him, so he never had to reveal himself. He learned from his first life. He was bolder in his first life and was willing to meet us on a battlefield when we had more numbers. His overconfidence was how we killed him the first time before anyone here was even born." There were no nagas left alive from that time.

Adhar had been the only one close, and we lost him. *I* lost him. For a moment, my heart was fragile as I remembered him and wished I had him back to tell me more, give me the information I needed, or tell me how to find it. *Anything.*

"He was reincarnated and learned, just like I am. Maybe he did it the same way I did, or a better way to say it would be how it was done to me. My mother and Devika developed a spell, and it unlocked the memories of my past life. They were only trying to find out who I was reincarnated from. They learned, but... so did I. Then they locked away the memories." I ran a hand through my hair. I hadn't sat down and explained this to the other nagas yet. "I unlocked them when I mated with Raphael. That's its own story. Adhar knew, and we told Nakul when Raphael and I arrived in India. You see... the original Kaliya? He had a cambion as a mate, too. Not that anyone knew until I got his memories."

"That's close to... blasphemy," Mahavir said carefully.

"Yeah, I'm surprised Adhar and Nakul never pointed that out or used that word," I replied, nodding. "That's not the point. Kaliya probably knew how to find Ramanaka. I can't find the memory for it. I've thought about it for days and days, but I can't summon that memory. I wonder if something else is at play there, *but* no one knew about Rama. If they knew about her, it was believed she was a human, possibly a witch." I gave Mahavir a wobbly smile. I couldn't look at Raphael. I couldn't do it.

"Rama being?" Mahavir was confused.

"Kaliya's first cambion mate," Raphael answered. "We're going to find her?" I heard the undercurrent of excitement and hope. I knew he wanted to. He and Adhar had both been very much for that idea.

It made me uncomfortable, as so much did these days. These were powers and people I was scared to face. Especially her, a woman I could remember touching, kissing, and making love to. A woman who had told me her deepest secrets.

Not me. Him. She told her mate, and I'm not her mate.

"Yeah," I finally confirmed for *my* mate. "If none of the nagas know how to return, she might. They lived there together before they ran from Garuda. Cambions are immortal once their powers are activated. She had her powers because they altered Kaliya. Like yours altered me."

"Which is why you have been so powerful in both lives." Mahavir's mental light bulb blinked on, and I nodded as his eyes grew. "The Demon Serpent."

"It's a bit on the nose, isn't it?" I chuckled darkly as

Mahavir nodded. “Yeah, that’s where the name comes from. I feel stupid for missing it all these years. Back on topic. I can use demon or cambion magic.” I shrugged. “None of us really know how or what it does, though. Everything I’ve done so far has been a ‘hope and pray it works’ situation like surviving Paven’s venom. It was the benefits of being a cambion’s mate that allowed me to heal, even as his venom was destroying my body. It kept the venom from reaching vital areas of my body. I had to keep focused, though. If I lost concentration or passed out, I was going to die.”

“How did Kaliya poison the river?” Vikrant asked, his thoughtful and intense eyes meeting mine when I looked his way.

“He...” I trailed off and thought about it, letting the memory play in my head like a movie. I could feel the tangible thickness of his fear as he devised his defenses to protect his mate and her mother. I had no idea where Rama’s father was, but Kaliya was protecting them both. I felt a pang of ache in my fangs as he milked them in his memory, and I caught the red glow of cambion magic. Then he poured it into the river, never telling his mate what he did until he’d done it.

“He milked his own venom, did something with the magic granted by his mating with Rama, then poured it into the river,” I finally answered. “Clearly, I will never do that. We all know not to put our venom in water sources, even without amplifying it with magic.”

“Let’s go back to your plan. You’re going to Vrindavan, which is poetic, and a quest should begin in a poetic way.” Mahavir paced. “Make no mistake, Kaliya, you are on a quest. This is a story that matches tales of old. Then you will hunt down someone from your previous life, and hopefully, she will have the answers you need to continue. Once you reach Ramanaka, you hope to find Garuda, face him, and defeat him."

"And hopefully not die in the process," I finished. "It's not even easy on paper. Adhar was going to help put my memories to real locations and hopefully find where Rama once lived in today's geography... but we don't have Adhar anymore, and it probably wouldn't have worked. She's probably moved around in the last *four to five thousand years*. I'm going in blind, but I won't sit here and wait for the answers to come to me." I felt the need to explain that.

"See, I have contacts all over the world, except in India now. In fact, very little leaves our homeland about our people and other species there. It's one of the few places in the world that can be very insular. That Garuda has kept his name out of the mouths of everyone for so long only proves we're dealing with something I won't be able to research from home. At the time, Rama also had a father and mother. Her father was also a cambion, and her mother was his human mate. Clearly, Raphael would like to know what they have to say about the cambions. All of this rides on if they're even alive. All of it. If I can't find them, but I find another way to Ramanaka, then I'll go deal with Garuda, and we'll keep hunting for the ancient cambions when it's over."

"Allow us to do research from here," Vikrant said, pushing off the truck. "We can look for details about

Ramanaka, perhaps clues that may help. We will email what we find."

"I considered that, but if Adhar had looked through those archives for hundreds of years and found nothing to take our people back..."

"Then it's unlikely we will, but we can try again," Vikrant countered. "If not information about Ramanaka, then about Rama and her family."

"All the material I have read through about my previous incarnation and his mate is sparse and inaccurate. Adhar told me much, if not all, of male-Kaliya's actual writings are missing and have been for centuries," I said, shaking my head. "Keep your focus here on our mates, our people, our future. I need you to do that while I'm gone. I don't know if this will take a month or if it'll take a year. If we've gotten nowhere in a year, we'll come back, but..." I sighed. "Just promise me you'll keep safe. Listen to the cambions, Cassius, and Sorcha. They're all wonderful people. They'll protect and help you. Mahavir, you're going to have a baby in your household. Vikrant, Dalar and Basanti need help from you and Eleanor. Work together because if I fail, all you'll have is each other."

"I don't like this." Mahavir stopped his pacing. "You want to go hunt down people and places no one has seen in millennia with no help? It's madness."

"I have help. I'm taking Raphael. I have memories of my past life, so in a way, my mother and Devika gave me a head start. Plus, there are potentially millions of supernaturals in India... and none of them will be ready for the Queen of the Nagas. I don't plan on hiding. I'm certain some of my enemies and those who want to stop me will come straight for me. I just don't think there's anything you can do from home. Feel free to try. I will welcome email updates on everyone while I'm gone. All I want is for your focus to be on our people. That's what I'm trusting you with."

The two capable men looked at each other, then back at me, and bowed in sync.

"We'll do as the *Nagaraja* wishes," Mahavir said as they straightened.

"And we'll do it with pride, to the fullest of our capabilities," Vikrant added.

Mahavir followed Vikrant out, then turned back to us and held out the box.

"You might need this," he said, his hand shaking.

I took it and peeked inside, my eyes going wide for only a second.

"I picked up as many as I could before we left and put them in there. It took up space when we had to hurry, but it felt important at the time. I've been holding on to them since, not sure..." Mahavir shook his head as he turned to follow Vikrant again.

Closing the box, I put it in one of our bags without thinking more about it.

As they left, they were talking about a division of tasks, and I turned to my mate.

"They'll be fine," I said, hoping I believed it enough for him to believe me.

"They will," he agreed. "So... why didn't you tell me we were going to try finding Rama on this... mission?"

"Oh, you don't like calling it a quest, either?" I

chuckled. "It makes me uncomfortable to be compared to the legends of old. I am one... but not. I don't want to be one."

"Not the conversation. Why didn't you tell me?"

"Because..." I leaned on the SUV. "I knew your answer, and my hesitancy has nothing to do with you. *I* needed to convince myself. Over and over, I considered the story of my previous life and how I would go about hunting down Garuda. Over and over and over, I thought about the history of my people to now and how it's unfolded, leaving us a decimated culture. I thought about how Garuda has remained hidden for long... and Ramanaka continued to be the *only* answer. All roads point to Ramanaka. After that, I had to figure out how to get there, and the easiest answer, the simplest answer, is to find someone who has been there before and left. Someone who knows how to do it, and there's only one person I can be certain has." I shrugged. "That's Rama... if she's still alive.

"I didn't need your arguments in favor of it. I already knew them, and they don't wipe away how uncomfortable this makes me. I needed time to really think about it without pressure from you. Let's admit when you first had this idea, you played every guilt trip card in the book. Helping the cambions and everything else."

"I..." Raphael groaned. "Yeah, I was excited."

"Everything you said was valid, but I didn't need to hear it again. I even agree we need them. All of us in this compound would benefit from finding them. I just..."

"I understand. There are no words to explain what you're dealing with, what you feel, but I understand."

I could only nod. We stood in silence for a long time, staring at each other. As minutes ticked by, I finally voiced one doubt for him and only him. I couldn't let any of my people know I had *any* doubts.

"I don't know if I'm strong enough for any of this. To be their Queen, to face Rama, to defeat Garuda... I'll do it, but I don't know if I'm strong enough."

"Even if you aren't, *we* are," he whispered, pulling me into his chest. "We are."

7

CHAPTER SEVEN

Leaving the garage, we headed for our last meal with the people we loved and ruled. We all came together, which wasn't common. With the mood in the air, I knew it was for solidarity. Raphael and I didn't talk about our plans, and no one asked. They talked about their plans for the compound, what they wanted to get done, training schedules, trips to Cassius's mansion, and more. It was nice listening to them.

Raphael leaned in and gestured for my phone, so I handed it over. I watched as he looked at our flight information. We were once again flying into Delhi. The tickets were pricy, and we were going commercial, not private. There wasn't a reason to sneak around this time. If Garuda tried to take our plane out of the air with dozens of humans aboard, he was going to have bigger problems than me, the nagas, or the cambions. The Tribunal would hunt him down on their own.

There was a line supernaturals couldn't cross. That was one of them.

Lunch ended, and everyone moved on with their days. Sorcha was the only one left, even Cassius leaving to talk more with Vikrant and Mateo about the new library we were building.

"When do you need to leave for the airport?" she asked.

"Any time before six. Flight leaves at nine," I answered. "I already called my contact at the airport. We won't have a problem with my weapons."

"Good, good..." Sorcha sat down with us, and the time ticked by. I kept waiting for her to join the chorus of people telling me not to do this. Waited for her to demand to know why I felt the need since my people were finally safe with the cambions. I waited for anything.

She said nothing. We sat in silence unless one of the cambions or nagas wanted to run something by us. Raphael confirmed ideas that would be okay during our time away and others that would have to wait. The compound ran efficiently without us, something Raphael had worked hard to make certain of before we had gone to visit my people.

The addition of the nagas had thrown a small wrench into everything, but not so much that we couldn't trust them now. The questions were fairly simple. Could the cambions take the nagas to the grocery store? Only if there were two or three escorts available. Could they include the nagas in their training? Only if Gabi was around because nagas were fragile like humans, and none of them were trained like I was. Could their human mates? I reminded them that Mahavir and Mateo were in charge of that now, so humans wouldn't be going to the larger training sessions.

"It never ends," Raphael said softly.

"Yeah, but at least they're asking now and not later." I understood the sentiment, though. I knew there would be something we missed, but I trusted the people we had here. They wouldn't do anything that couldn't be fixed.

At five-thirty, my closest friend stood, pulling her keys from her pocket as she left. I followed her out, knowing Raphael was behind us.

"Sorcha..." I couldn't stand the silence anymore. "Why won't you say anything?"

"There's nothing to say," she replied once we reached the garage. "You're going to do this, no matter what anyone says."

She and Cassius tell each other everything. He probably already explained the entire conversation from this morning.

"Yeah, but—"

She turned to me, her moon-grey eyes hard like iron, her bone-straight silver hair whipping around her head.

"There's nothing to say," she repeated. "I have no intention of trying to stop you, regardless of what you told Cassius, your people, or the cambions. Why would I try to stand in the way of what I see as the right decision? It will be dangerous, yes. I want you to come home, yes. Neither of those things makes this anything but the right decision. *Twice*, we have all been caught off-guard by the enemies of the nagas. *Twice*, I got a phone call or saw you and wondered if the next time you wouldn't be able to get back up. You must be proactive and destroy them now, and I won't stand in your way." She looked me over. "You could be in better shape, there's no denying that, but time isn't on your side."

"Then you understand." I was overwhelmed by how much that meant to me.

"This? All too well. I didn't survive my days as an arms dealer by not being proactive," she said, a soft expression passing over her face, completely at odds with what she'd said. "Do I wish you and I could have normal lives? Absolutely, but I realize it's never going to happen if we're not willing to shed blood for it. I thought I understood that before, but now, I feel the lesson has sunk in. We are who we are and do what we must do." She waved at the SUV. "Get in. Let's get out of here. We'll talk more on the drive."

We loaded in, and I tried not to think about how I knew someone had touched my bags when I hadn't been in the garage with them. I knew who it was, and it scared me. Four bags, three people. I sat in the front with Sorcha and Raphael stretched across the backseat. Only one person would come back to the compound when all was said and done. We waited until we were off the compound to talk again.

"It's more than just the right decision, though," Sorcha said, sighing. "It's honorable, bold, brave. Pick a good adjective for a hero, and it would probably fit this scenario. It's what I wish my own rulers would do for our people."

"Ah…" That made more sense to me than I wanted to admit. "Oisin is a pretty shitty king."

"Yes, and Alvina is a quiet queen, good but not a force to be reckoned with, but it's more than that. Oberon and

Titania left us to rot. Brion left us to rot... even Cassius. I know all his reasons, understand them, and agree with his choice, but even he couldn't step up for the fae when they needed someone *good* to rule.

"But you? You step up. No matter how great the challenge, no matter who stood at your side, you stood up and fought for them, whether or not they knew it, and you continue to do so. So, no, I can't tell you not to do this. Every day, I wish the rulers of the fae would be so good to their people." Sorcha gave me a smile. "It brings me joy and immense pride to know you're my friend, Kaliya Sahni."

"I'm sorry we have had little time over the last of few weeks," I whispered. I wished we had spent weekends drinking.

"Defeat Garuda, and we'll have all the time in the world... until the next time." She grinned, and I laughed.

"When I get back, we'll go for drinks."

"Maybe we can take the other ladies," she said, chuckling. "Sammy unleashed on Phoenix without Raphael hovering over her shoulder."

My mate made a noise of disapproval.

"Maybe not, but Basanti and Eshika need time away from their families and the *babies*. So many babies. Poor women never get a break from the screaming. For the last few weeks, you've barely had any time away from it."

"I know. We'll take them with us. Eleanor will have to come as well, though we might have to do some convincing. Vikrant is as possessive and protective as that one." I pointed to the backseat with my thumb, then yanked it back before Raphael could grab my hand to do who knew what with it.

"Are you sure? His queen would want to take his mate out on the town. What sort of loyal man denies the woman he loves that honor?"

I wanted to gag.

"Don't say things like that."

"You're the queen, not me. *You* said okay to it." Sorcha snorted as she shook her head.

"Yeah, but..."

"No buts. You said okay."

Her teasing made me smile. We continued to plan out this epic night on the town with the women of the compound—four different species brought together by friendship, family, and circumstance. Raphael relented halfway through the drive to let Sammy and the other female cambions go out without watchful eyes. Even Gabi, which brought the species total up to five.

It was a fun distraction that continued as we parked, and Sorcha walked us into the airport. We were led behind the scenes and around security. The humans of the airport didn't control the persuasive and cunning supernaturals who had to work around them.

At a certain point, Sorcha couldn't continue with us. The fae leading us stopped at the door that would lead us into the terminals, where we would find the right place to sit and wait for boarding.

"This is goodbye," she said, smiling at me. "Hopefully, it's more of a see you soon."

"I hope for that, too. Can I ask a favor?"

"Anything, with no charge," Sorcha said, bringing her

hands together and waiting for whatever I wanted to lay on her.

"Talk to Sammy while I'm gone, try to connect with her." Sorcha nodded, but I wasn't done. "Get my humans together and teach them more about modern makeups and that sort of thing." I took a deep breath, realizing that wasn't enough. "Care for the women. Make sure they get time for themselves, and the nagas help clean up. Don't let them cook for everyone all the time. They'll be run over unintentionally if no one is looking out for them."

"Adhar used to look out for them," Raphael explained softly. "When they visited him, he made sure everyone worked to give the women more time to themselves."

"You worried they'll fall into old habits while you're gone?"

"I just want them happy," I said, shrugging with one shoulder.

"I'll ask Leith to stay with us at the compound. He's a force of nature, our butler. If he thinks anyone is doing too much or not doing their part, he'll correct it." Sorcha made a face. "And I'll see what I can do with Sammy. Girl time with Eshika, Eleanor, and Basanti is easy and enjoyable. I've done it a handful of times while you've been staring at your desert. Sammy..."

"Is harder. I know."

"I'll make an effort, though," Sorcha promised. She turned to the fae with us. "See that their time here is enjoyable and uneventful," she ordered, her regal power turning on. Sorcha was not a noble by birth, but she had taken the role easily from everything I had ever seen from her. This was Lady Sorcha, not the retired criminal I knew as a friend. The fae paled, his back going straight. "Do not embarrass the Sidhe."

The fae's head bobbed up and down as if he were on the dashboard of an eighteen-wheeler.

"Good." Sorcha turned back to me with a bright smile. "Good luck, Kaliya. Keep her alive, Raphael."

"I'll do my best," Raphael promised.

Accepting a fluttering goodbye kiss on my cheek, I watched as Sorcha gave Raphael the same, him having to bend a little for her to reach. Then she marched away, her head held high. I could feel her confidence in us, her faith in the belief we were doing this for the right reasons, no matter the outcome.

The fae let us head to our terminal. When our tickets were called, we boarded and claimed two first-class seats. Raphael put our bags up and finally asked the question I knew had been bugging him much of the day.

"What's in the box?"

"Feathers."

8

CHAPTER EIGHT

We slept for the entire first flight, even getting in a nap at the airport during our layover, which had been ungodly long, thanks to flight delays and malfunctions. I was awake when the second plane entered the skies over India. I woke up Raphael as we drew closer to our destination, once again landing in Delhi.

"We land in an hour. From here on out, things are dangerous," I whispered to him as he opened his eyes as if he hadn't been softly snoring moments before.

"Once we touch down, there's no telling who is our friend or enemy. I know. I'm of the opinion to treat everyone as hostile combatants until proven otherwise."

"Then we're on the same page." These were things he and I could have talked about for days on end before this trip. We had before visiting Adhar's home. This time, I trusted him not to just follow my lead but understand the calls we had to make and make the right ones on his own if I needed him to. Being on the same page was something I had never expected of my mate and me, but then, I had never expected to actually see through the mate bond.

"How are you so perfect?" I asked softly.

"I'm not, and you know it," he said, shaking his head with a chuckle.

"I mean, you kind of are." I raised an eyebrow. "Who else would put up with me and smile about it?"

"Anyone who spends ten minutes learning who you really are." He gave me a sideways look as the plane bounced thanks to turbulence.

I didn't have a response, and he didn't say anymore. It left me with a mix of emotions I couldn't properly untangle.

As we descended, I couldn't try to puzzle out the knot Raphael had created in my chest any longer. My thoughts shifted to what was ahead of us.

The moment we land, we have to assume every supernatural we see is a potential threat. I don't even know what sort of supernaturals we might run into anymore. There's no telling which are still around and which are gone entirely, much less knowing if they're a threat or not.

"What's on your mind?" he asked as the landing drew closer and closer.

"The nairrata," I answered, then paused as my mind quickly shuffled through all the possibilities. "The yaksha and yakshini, the gandharva, the vetala, any of the gana—"

"Supernatural possibilities of the country. Got it." Raphael sighed heavily as the plane turned just enough to create that awful sensation of my stomach lifting. "I've been talking to Mahavir about a lot, but my education in the depth of lore surrounding this part of the world isn't finished."

"I know. There's no way it could be in the decade. I'll let you know if I see anything and tell you what I can, but I think some nagas haven't seen many for centuries. There's just no way of knowing what's left from the ancient times."

"Are any of them possible allies?"

"Um, probably not," I said, giving him an apologetic look.

He only shrugged one shoulder as we had wheels down in India for the second time.

We were good passengers, waiting without trying to stand as the plane rolled to the correct terminal. Being in first class meant we would get off the place quickly, and money had already greased palms to make that even easier. A flight attendant asked everyone to sit back down, then came to us and gestured for us to stand.

We got off the plane quickly. It felt too much like the last time we arrived, but there couldn't be more differences. Last time, we had a plan, every step of the journey carefully laid out to protect us and those more vulnerable. This time, we were going in blind. There was no one waiting for us on the other side. He'd been a wonderful man, that friendly cab driver, and for a second, walking down the passenger bridge, I wondered if he was still alive. He'd been innocent, in my opinion. Those humans who offer services and keep our secrets were just doing their job.

What made the thought harder was the surety I

would never know his fate unless I was lucky enough to see him on the road. The likelihood I was going to flag him down was slim.

"We're renting a car," I told Raphael as we headed for a staff door, where a werewolf was waiting. There weren't many in India, but werewolves were the supernatural equivalent of rabbits. A fast-breeding invasive species that could thrive anywhere, they were finding their foothold in India. I knew the game they played. They traveled into untouched areas and slowly grew a base with wealth and influence by bringing locals into the pack. They always stayed near city centers for the power. There weren't many cities in the world that didn't have a local werewolf pack. They slowly spread out and would buy land near the city for full moons, a secondary base.

Their invasion of India was still a new thing. I didn't believe they would ever become a strong political force, though, no matter how hard they worked. The situation around Eleanor and Vikrant had been a stark reminder that even supernaturals from this beautiful land had problems with the idea of colonists, and when it came to supernatural colonists, I was glad the werewolves would never find the foothold they wanted.

"This way," the female werewolf said politely, her accent thick. She opened the door and let us in before following. I waited for her to direct me to the right place. I knew little about this airport. Late in the evenings after Raphael was asleep, I had looked up its layout, trying to memorize everything, but most airports didn't provide blueprints of their secured areas.

"Thank you," I said as she started walking again. "For

helping us get through the airport without incident." I felt a little bad for her. It was still the afternoon, but that night would be a full moon, and she was working.

"We do this for all supernaturals," she said softly. "So long as we're made aware before arrival. You gave us notice. Short notice but enough." I heard the soft frustration.

"Twenty-four hours' notice is the standard minimum. I gave you nearly thirty-six if you consider the delays we faced," I countered, but it wasn't heated.

Going into a baggage zone, some humans looked our way, but Raphael and I were pretty good at pretending we belonged somewhere, even when we didn't. Remain casual, unconcerned. I was certain one of them would report her, but someone would calmly brush it under the rug. Some of my money given to the airport would grease hands, and today would have never happened. We got our bags without needing to go to baggage claim, a bonus of being wealthy and supernatural.

"We need to rent a car for an undetermined amount of time," I reminded her as she led us out of the staff area and into some VIP zone.

"We've been considering that," she said, continuing her brisk pace. "We will sell you a vehicle at market price, which is what you would have to pay if you lost or destroyed the vehicle you would rent."

"*We* being you and your bosses, I assume." I needed to know. "I gave you enough money to cover that if necessary, so consider it done."

"Yes, we being my bosses and me."

"Other members of the pack?"

She stumbled but recovered fast enough, I was certain a human would have missed it.

"No, the supernaturals who run our... area of the airport," she explained.

"And they are?"

"No one you need to be concerned with."

I looked at Raphael and raised an eyebrow. He was glaring at the back of the werewolf's head.

"We never got your name," I said, smiling as she took us into an elevator. She looked me over and stood as far from Raphael as she could get.

"It's not important. I'm only here to make sure you get what you need to leave the airport without incident."

"Sure."

"Don't cause trouble," she said softly, and her deep brown eyes shifted to amber—wolf eyes. "Delhi is outside of the view of the Tribunal."

"No, it's not. There's a Delhi werewolf pack, isn't there? Someone in the pack probably Changed you."

"Yes, I'm a member of the pack, and my Alpha supports my work here at the airport." There was no missing her warning. Her Alpha would fight for her.

"He reports to Callahan by way of an Alpha Council. The Tribunal has a foothold in your city. You work for it." My smile widened. "I don't need the Tribunal. I'm a naga. This is my homeland."

"The nagas were chased out of India," she said, and I wondered if there was satisfaction in her words. That she even knew was proof it was interesting news to be passed along, worthwhile to know.

"Yeah, we were. I'm here to fix that."

The elevator reached the floor we wanted. As it opened, Raphael stepped in front of me and went out first. Neither of us trusted this werewolf.

We were right not to. As we entered the parking garage, I could taste other supernaturals in the air—werewolves and rakshasa.

"Cats and dogs don't play well together," I murmured, looking over my shoulder at her.

"Money makes everyone play well together." She pulled out a set of keys and threw them on the ground. "This is what we owed you. Now, you're someone else's problem." Then she started running.

Next to me, Raphael was practically vibrating with energy. Reaching down, I picked up the keys. At least they were modern enough to have remote lock and unlock. I hit the buttons but didn't get so much as a honk in return.

"Well, that's rude," I muttered in annoyance. "Keep your eyes open. Werewolves and rakshasa have been down here recently. Clearly, I'm not wanted back in the country."

"I got that vibe as well. Want to bet the only reason they haven't tried to kill us yet is for reputation?"

"I don't take bets I'll lose." I positioned myself next to him, looking over the rows and rows of vehicles. "That's exactly why no one is shooting yet. If something happens in the airport, no one will use it. Humans will come back quickly, but supernaturals? No one will come near it if they believe the system in place isn't safe." I spun the keys on my finger. "I bet you the car is bugged in multiple ways, some I won't be able to deal with here."

"Do you think they were hired by him?"

"Hired, bought, or longtime allies," I said softly as I started walking. I needed to figure out which of these cars was ours. "He was here, flying overhead the last time we landed. He knew our arrival time. I remember his call."

"The leak," Raphael reminded me as he stayed glued to my side. I could only nod. "Someone at the airport heard the information in the leak and reported it to him."

I kept hitting the lock button, knowing it was the one that made cars honk. After twenty feet, we finally heard something.

"Thank the gods, we were just out of range." I released a tired groan. "At least I don't need to try the key in every fucking door." I led the way to a brand-new Mahindra Thar. I had requested something new with off-road capabilities. They had done their job, regardless of how rude the werewolf was at the end.

"Maybe I just made her upset," I said to myself as I gave Raphael the keys. "Hold those and stay here."

"Why?"

"Checking for bombs."

"Kaliya!"

"It's reasonable to check, and you don't know how."

Approaching the car, I got down to look under the vehicle, then opened the driver's side door and checked under the seat. I assessed the dashboard for tampering, then went to the passenger's side. The inspection, which led me to open the hood and check, took twenty minutes, but I had to be thorough while we had the chance to be. In the end, I found two small bugs and dropped them on the ground, crushing them with my heel.

"Clear," I said, waving for him to come closer. He put our bags in the backseat while I got behind the wheel.

"You mean, you think it's clear," Raphael said as he got in and put on his seatbelt.

"Yeah."

I drove out of the parking garage while Raphael played with the GPS. I chuckled as it wasn't in a language he could read. At a stop, I punched in our destination, then checked the time. It was ten in the morning, which meant we would get there before nightfall.

That was when reality sank in.

In less than three hours, we would arrive at Vrindavan.

The last time a naga named Kaliya was there, he died. It was a moment I remembered in perfect clarity.

9

CHAPTER NINE

"Will you tell me more about Vrindavan?" Raphael asked with only an hour and a half left in the trip. "I read up on it, but you probably know more than most."

"Vrindavan is rich in history. A hotbed for the supernaturals and divine beings that call this region of the world home. It's surrounded by other famous places, all culturally and historically important. Every year, millions visit the city and the surrounding area to see the temples and take part in the countless festivals. There are over one-thousand temples dedicated to Radha and Krishna. Radha was Krishna's consort and lover, though there are numerous ways people have described the relationship. Whether they were married or unmarried depends on the person you ask and the texts they subscribe to. I believe everyone agrees they were soulmates, though, two parts of a whole." I repeated an introductory lesson I had once received as a child.

"How did this area become so important?"

"Krishna is said to have been born only nine miles from Vrindavan in the city of Mathura. We don't need to explore it in depth. What you need to know is it will be crowded, so please stay close to me."

"I will," he promised. "It's not like I could talk to anyone else."

I chuckled. He had taken lessons in Arizona, but two weeks probably only taught him how to say hello, goodbye, and ask where the closest bathroom was.

"I would tell you all I know, but I don't see it as... necessary," I admitted. "Not today. I'm sorry."

"You have eternity to tell me all about India's rich culture," he said as I felt his fingers drift over my cheekbone as he tucked my hair behind my ear. "I'm almost jealous. I'm an American boy, Catholic born and raised. There's very little the world doesn't know about Catholicism, thanks to the sheer volume of Catholics."

"Hmmm, yeah, it's hard to avoid in the western world. Think you'll take up practicing again?"

"No."

"Really?" He behaved as though I said something funny, so I ribbed him a little. "You held it pretty close when we met. You stopped going to Mass but carried the guilt, all 'woe is me, I'm a monster now.'"

"I am a monster," he countered without missing a beat. "Learning about the supernatural helped me when I didn't have all of my memories. Seeing you, confident, fully accepting of what you are without guilt? That helped. Cassius and Sorcha, werewolves, vampires, none of them carry guilt all the time, do they?"

"Maybe some of them." I shrugged a shoulder.

"Getting my memories back just reminded me I didn't need to beg for forgiveness. Just because I'm a demon hybrid doesn't mean I'm evil. The awakening of my powers isn't my sin. Why should I carry the guilt and beg forgiveness for an act I didn't orchestrate? And if I've never done anything evil with this power, why is the power evil?" Raphael shook his head. "Someone out there will probably say I'm wrong, that I should repent, but I won't keep something in my life that only shames me. I have more important things to worry about than my immortal soul. The other cambions need me, and I won't look at them and—"

"You want them to be happy and free. Shaming yourself for being a cambion would tell them they should be ashamed, too. Those are incompatible."

"They are." He sighed.

The conversation died off as I drove into Vrindavan. Finding a place to park was possible but a nightmare.

"We'll be walking a lot to get where I want to go," I explained as I looked around the car for potential threats. "Can you grab my weapons bag?"

"I'll bring the survival gear bag as well, in case we end up running." A moment later, I tried to take my bag from him, but he kept it out of my reach. "You lead the way. I'll hold on to these. No one is going to take them from me, and they're not heavy."

"They're probably weightless to you," I said, patting his chest. He leaned down and kissed me, a smile on his lips.

"Yes," he confirmed. "Now lead the way."

"Not yet. Shoes. Take them off. Might as well go

barefoot from here. We can't wear them inside the ghat." I caught myself. "Ghat means… steps down to a river. This temple is actually Kaliya Ghat." I saw him nod, absorbing the new information. "We'll shove them into one of the bags. People can walk barefoot in the city if they choose. We're going to follow their lead, so we don't have to worry about it later. We'll put them back on when we leave the city. I just don't want to get there and fuss with the shoe thing."

Without a word, we pulled off our boots. There was something freeing about going barefoot. Shoving my boots away, I flexed my toes for the first time in hours, then turned away to take in the city. People were everywhere, but I knew that was common for the city.

It was then I realized I did not know where I was going, like a tourist passing through without a plan. With a little shame, I had to pull out my phone and look at the map. Once I was decided on a path, I started walking.

"I've never been here," I said sheepishly as my mate walked by my side.

"I've never been to Rome," he replied. "You think I would know how to show you around the Vatican if we went?"

I couldn't stop a smile. It didn't last long, but he'd gotten one out of me.

The walk through the city was long, but eventually, I found the red stone temple I was looking for. Heart pounding, I stared at it.

"Is this it?" he asked.

"This is it. Kaliya Ghat. The place where Krishna triumphed over the demon serpent," I said softly. It was simple as far as temples went. A stone arch marked its entrance, and there was a pile of shoes waiting for their owners, mostly sandals people could slip on and off with ease.

"Do you want me to go in with you?"

"You can follow me, but... I might ask you to leave."

"Let me know when you want to be alone," he said in a hushed tone.

Walking in, my pulse rang in my ears. Like many temples, things seemed to quiet as you went deeper. Reverence filled people as they journeyed into such places of power.

As I went deeper, it wasn't reverence that filled me. It was a place, and it was deeply important, but because of who and what I was, reverence wasn't it.

It wasn't terror, either. Stairs led down to what was once the riverbank, with an open sky above me—this place wasn't dark and terrifying. It was a beautiful day, and I was doing nothing wrong. I was here to see, to bear witness, to my past, and there was no crime in that.

The kadamba tree came into view, the sun dappling the stone around it, and I recognized it, though not for its outward appearance. Many humans didn't believe it was over five thousand years old, but I could feel it. It had been soaked in power ages ago and still was. The feeling in my chest was a deep well of regret and respect for the tree.

I didn't draw closer yet, looking around and taking in the space. Raphael had wandered off toward a statue, a depiction of an ancient naga, and stopped in front of it.

"Raph?" I called softly.

His head snapped in my direction, his skin paler than was natural. I went to his side and looked down at the statue that made it seem as though he had seen a ghost. I couldn't fault him for the reaction.

"I never told you because I..." I didn't really know why. "I just didn't. I didn't think about it."

"A black snake," Raphael said, going down to one knee in front of it. "He was a black—"

"I know. Why don't you step out and let me,"—I touched his shoulder—"let me think for a minute. Go get some air."

He was up faster than I was ready for and walked quickly out. I stared at the statue of my previous life, wondering if my form was black because I was his reincarnation or my mother's spell awakening that before I took my snake form for the first time.

Moving on, I headed for another statue, which depicted Krishna dancing on his head. I walked the red stone temple until the last thing to see was the resilient ancient kadamba tree. I wasn't sure if I was avoiding it, but I saved it for last. By the time I headed toward the kadamba tree, there was no one in the space with me. Everything was eerily quiet, and I was left staring at a past I wasn't supposed to remember.

It reached skyward, as it always had. Its knotted trunk was thicker than my arms could reach around, though it hadn't been so when my previous incarnation had been here. It provided shade and represented the power and resilience of life. It alone withstood the noxious venom that turned the river into poison. It alone withstood the test of time. It was so powerful and old, it had grown through the stone bed that was placed around it.

Where do I go from here? Ramanaka? No one knows how to go back. Does it still exist?

"Are you here on a pilgrimage?" a man asked in Hindi, startling me. I tasted the air as the breeze moved his scent through it, grateful to discover he was a human. I didn't turn, letting him walk up beside me.

"Something of the sort."

"It's a beautiful thing," he said as his head tilted back and took in the mighty kadamba tree.

"It is," I agreed.

There was a pregnant silence, one that lasted for too long but didn't seem unnatural. This was a place of power, and I wanted to keep soaking it in.

"You shouldn't be here."

It was a remarkably out-of-place comment, said in a benign way that set my heart racing again. I tasted the air again, but he was still only human.

"The temple is open to the public, isn't it?" I asked, my pulse hammering.

"Yes, it is," he agreed as though there was a joke I was missing. "*You* shouldn't be here."

"I'm sorry, I don't know what you mean," I said, in denial a human would say that.

"You shouldn't lie in this place," he chastised. Something about the man reminded me of Adhar, thanks to that line. "You stand here, thinking of what you should do next. A good first step would be to leave. You will not find yourself welcome in this city, not knowing what you know and being who you are. Maybe before you mated, but not now."

As terror filled me, I opened my mouth, trying to find something to say. Power filled my lungs and silenced me.

"I knew who you were the moment you came into the city. I knew long before that," he said, his words still casual. "Tell me you aren't so foolish as one might believe, thanks to your presence."

The power left my lungs, and I could speak again. My mind was scrambled from sheer fear, but the words of my truth were easy to find.

"No. I just wanted to see this place before moving on with my… almost pilgrimage," I explained.

"Ah."

"It felt right to see it." I felt a desperate need to say to him what my goal was. "To…" It clicked why I felt a burning desire to see this place before I continued. "To apologize. I am in a new life, with new experiences and a new fate. I have no intention of repeating the past mistakes of my predecessor, whether or not I have his memories. I came to apologize for those mistakes before forging a new fate because I have the memories of my previous. I know them and committed them in detail. I can't move forward until I reconcile the past."

"Then be on with it."

With his approval, I felt more at ease. My eyes on the tree, I gently touched it and felt power there. I leaned in and closed my eyes, my forehead on the tree as I let that power flow through me.

The kadamba tree was a lesson life had already taught me, one my predecessor never learned.

Real strength was standing tall in the face of adversity, not accolades or victory on the battlefield. It wasn't magical powers or standing on top as a ruler.

Real strength was much simpler, and *anyone* was capable of it.

It's standing against those who would do you harm when no one expects you to. When the odds are so against you, no one dared ask for it. It's standing against an adversary because it was the right thing to do, even if defeat was inevitable.

"I'm sorry for being the battle you fought," I whispered to the kadamba tree. "For being the adversary you had to stand against when the odds weren't in your favor, when you did nothing to deserve the treatment you received. You were innocent. Those you shared the banks of this river with were innocent. I am sorry for giving you pain and tragedy to remember me by. I will do better than I have before."

Leaning back, I looked at the branches, forever reaching for the open sky above us all. I knew I was talking to a tree, but it felt as if it brought a little peace I had spent weeks searching for.

"Thank you. I'll be on my way now," I said, pulling my hand away from the trunk and giving a deep bow to the man with me. "I will not trouble you nor the kadamba tree further." He said nothing as I came up from my bow and walked away. I was nearly halfway to the door when he spoke up.

"I've never known a *Nagaraja* to bow so low," he said, seeming curious. "Wait."

My feet stopped, and I turned to see the still human

man standing in front of me, the kadamba tree framing him.

"The quest you go on is the same, but not," he said, bringing his hands together in front of him. "It would have been easy for him but will be much harder for you. I tried to give him peace by telling him he would not be threatened if he returned to Ramanaka. He rejected it. He did not believe in the possibility of peace. You will now have to earn that peace, for the circumstances have changed. And you will have to believe in it."

"I will do what is necessary to ensure the survival of my people," I said, leaning on my conviction to give me the courage to say the words.

"If only he had considered his people," the man said softly, turning back to the tree. "Maybe he would have been strong enough if they had relied on him the way they now rely on you."

I considered that, then shook my head.

"No, he wouldn't have been," I said, my heart finally slowing as my confidence grew.

"Why do you think that?"

"He let his fear chase him from the battlefield."

"And you have never run from the battlefield?" He sounded humored by me. "Didn't you run from home?"

I wasn't surprised by his knowledge, but it made me stop and think. How was I any different from my predecessor?

"As a child, I ran from Mehar, King of the Rakshasa, because my parents told me to. I had little chance to survive that night. As a young woman, I ran away from home, yes, but not out of fear of the enemy. I couldn't find my enemies at home." I remembered both days with clarity but wished I didn't. "As a grown woman and a warrior, I have spent my life searching for this battlefield and preparing for the day I met my greatest enemy in open war. Running from him has never been my objective... and never will be."

He turned toward me again, his expression thoughtful.

Then he was gone.

Suddenly alone in the temple again, I turned on my heel and walked away, my hands curled into fists tight enough to cut my palms. When I left the red stone structure, Raphael was waiting with our bags, looking several shades less pale.

"You were in there for a while."

"Walk. We can't stay," I said, not missing a step as I passed him. He struggled to keep up as Vrindavan came alive once more, and people entered the temple behind us.

"Kaliya, what's wrong?"

"Krishna wanted to speak for a moment. It's fine, but we need to leave the city before I overstay my welcome."

10

CHAPTER TEN

Wasting no time getting us out of Vrindavan, I drove us back to New Delhi and parked at the hotel, opting not to use the valet. Raphael had booked us a week there, though I wasn't sure we were going to use the whole week. We just needed to pick up our keys and could discuss it once we were settled.

"You're not going to say any more about what happened, are you?" my mate asked, clearly annoyed with the silence I'd held for the entire drive.

"I don't know what to say," I said, shaking my head. How did someone go about explaining a conversation with a literal god? Krishna was both a god and an avatar of Vishnu. "I... never asked for his name, and he never actually offered it, but... well, there are some things only he could say."

"Like what? Kaliya, you met the god who killed you in your last life. Our trip to Vrindavan wasn't supposed to be dangerous, but on the scale of threats, that one is at the top and is in the range where I don't think I would be to help you."

"He..." I sighed. "He let me do what I wanted in the temple. Let me say what I needed to say." I stared at my steering wheel, the boring, mundane thing contrasting the magic of reliving those moments in the temple. "He told me our quest will be harder than the one my previous incarnation would have gone on. Krishna had offered him peace for free, and all he had to do was go home, but I will have to work for peace, and let's be honest, I have to find home. I have to find a way to an island I'm not even sure is real or exists anymore. For all I know, it could be a different realm entirely, and that's how we lost our way back."

"But he never... threatened you?" Raphael asked, clearly looking for confirmation.

"Oh, no, not threats." I shook my head slowly, and Raphael's sag of relief would have been almost comical if it wasn't a real possibility Krishna would have killed me right then and there. In truth, I felt the same relief. Just being out of Vrindavan was a blessing at this point. "Not overtly, at least. He let me know I shouldn't be there, and I'm certain he would have... taken issue if I intended to stay." I leaned back and exhaled a long, drawn-out breath, letting go of the moment and my memories of it. "Let's head inside and get settled for the night. With that done, we can move forward."

"Did you get what you needed out, even with the run-in with a god?" Raphael climbed out as he asked that question. I got out right after him, lost in thought again, thanks to the question. As we grabbed our bags, I pondered it, letting Raphael get the doors for me.

I had apologized for being the adversary of someone innocent. It hadn't been me. I didn't go to that river and decide to poison it. The one who did had been a different person—literally. All I had was his memories and his name.

I apologized because *I have memories and his name. I'm the only person who ever could apologize, and it made me feel better, so...*

"Yes," I finally answered my mate as we stopped in front of our door. I barely remembered checking in. He unlocked and held it open, so I could go in first. Once the door was closed behind us, I put my two bags down on the bed and sat beside them. "I got what I needed out of the stop. Now we need to decide where we're going next and how."

"You..." I saw the light of excitement and apprehension in his gaze as he dropped his bags on the floor. "You wanted to search for Rama and her family because they might be the only people who could be our allies and would remember how to get to Ramanaka."

"You know what's funny about that plan? I don't know if Garuda is there." I snorted, then fell into a fit of hysterics. My laughter bounced off the walls as he touched my shoulder. Being back in India, having a conversation with Krishna, seeing the place I had died once before... it all left me more fragile than I had believed. Insecurities bubbled up as I laughed.

"I have no idea! I'm just... going on a wild hunch that it's where I need to be. If he had lived away from the island all these years, we would have known sooner, but I have *no* idea if he actually is. For all I know, he could live in Sri Lanka." I wiped my eyes. "For all I know, Rama could live in Boston or Atlanta. I don't *know*, Raphael."

"Krishna said it was the same quest," Raphael said, giving me such a look of concern, I wondered if I seemed like I was losing my mind. "But he only told *that* Kaliya to go back to Ramanaka, so it has to be the right hunch. It has to be."

"I don't know the solution, Raphael. I just have a plan, and I'm hoping it's the right one, even if… it doesn't make a lot of sense." There were so many unknowns, so many questions constantly bouncing around my head I didn't dare let whisper into the air. I didn't want to give them the thought they deserved because they were questions about how this could end. So many possible outcomes.

I'm going to see this plan through, regardless of the outcome, so what's the point in wondering?

"We need to think about how to find Rama," he said decisively, nodding as he grabbed the survival bag and searched through it on the closest table, pulling out a stack of maps, then a laptop. He hadn't known why I had asked him to bring it all but had figured it out easily enough.

It's potentially finding the other cambions. Of course, he figured it out. It's his greatest wish to meet older cambions and to learn from them.

"While you get started with that, I'm going to find us something to eat," I said as I stood up and checked for my wallet.

"But—"

"When was the last time we ate?" I interrupted as I walked to the door, ready to leave. "I know the answer, actually. Neither of us has eaten since we were on the plane. I'll get us something before everything closes. That way, we can focus on our plans all night instead of starving."

"Okay, but be safe. Do you want me to go with you? For safety."

"You can, but I'm not planning on leaving the hotel," I explained. "There are a few places I'm sure I can bribe to let me get us something to go."

"We could just call room service," he offered, nodding toward the phone. "You would never have to leave the room, and we could get started while we wait for it."

"You're right. We could do that." I continued to inch my way closer to the door.

"I'm not comfortable with you being out there by yourself right now," he said, his tone growing more serious. He talked like that with the cambions, and it annoyed me he was taking the tone with me. "Kaliya."

"Oh, a warning name. Guess I have to listen." I nearly rolled my eyes. "I want to walk. I want to see the halls. I want to look over the lobby a bit more. I'm also the *Nagaraja*. I will not hide in my room and use room service when all the nice restaurants are open."

"And if someone sees you and picks a fight?"

"It's a good thing I'm probably the most powerful supernatural in the city... aside from you," I countered, grabbing the door handle. "You can always come with me."

Still holding a stack of my maps of the subcontinent, he looked at them, then shook his head.

"Stay out of trouble."

"Planning on it." I left him to ponder the maps. He wouldn't be able to do anything with them, but I considered it a good thing if he tried to familiarize himself with the country a bit more. If he wanted to stew over them, he was more than welcome to.

Going to the elevator, I was on high alert, looking around corners, tasting the air, and hoping, desperately hoping, I didn't catch another supernatural on the air. I was lucky to have an elevator to myself.

The hotel we were staying at was fancy enough to house a handful of upscale restaurants. It was a proper resort with more to offer than a standard room and a continental breakfast. I had to pay extra, but I convinced the Korean restaurant to let me get food to-go, all the while looking over my shoulder. I was heading back to the elevator when I caught the taste of magic in the air. Looking around casually, I didn't see anyone, but when I stopped in front of the elevator, a man walked over and stood too close to me. When the doors opened, I got in first and punched an incorrect number for my floor as he watched intently. He didn't hit anything.

"What floor?" I asked politely.

"I wanted to speak to you privately."

"Sorry, you're not coming back to my room," I snapped. "Pick a floor."

"You're not in a position to make—"

"I'm the *Nagaraja,* and unless you want a diplomatic incident, where I go to Johann and Matilda with your *head*, you'll tell me what you want, and you'll do it on my terms," I snarled as the doors closed, locking me in the elevator with the witch. "Not in the position to make demands? Don't be stupid. I'm a retired Tribunal Executioner, a real queen, and getting more pissed off by the second."

He turned several shades paler.

"Or did you not know who you were speaking to?" I asked with a sweetness that was completely false.

"I knew," he said softly.

"Then you're an idiot who clearly misunderstands the power balance of this situation." I smiled. "What do you want?"

"Someone wishes to speak to you," he said simply. "I was hired to relay the message."

"Really?" *A messenger? Must be an expensive messenger boy.* "Who wants to see me?"

"I can't tell you that. I can give you a location and a time when you can meet them."

"That's too bad. You can tell whoever sent you, I'm not interested if I don't know who they are." The elevator dinged as it stopped on my false floor. I stepped out, blocking the witch's exit. "Go back to whoever hired you and tell them no deal. If they're too cowardly to give me a name, I see no reason to walk into a painfully obvious trap."

"Please." He threw his hand out and stopped the door from closing between us. "My employer would like to see you."

"Tell your employer if he has the courage to give me a name, I'll consider it," I said, looking at his hand. "Until then, there's not a single thing you can do to convince me, so please don't try."

"Maybe you should consider the fact I could find you, which means every supernatural in the city can probably find you. It would be safer if you came with me to speak to my employer."

"I already assumed they could," I said, shrugging a shoulder. It was unsurprising. I figured everyone in the country would know I was here from the moment I left the plane. If the airport didn't leak it—I was certain they had—someone would have seen me on the road. Or someone would have heard in the States and potentially passed it along. There was no way I was going to secretly get into India this time, so I didn't bother trying.

"You're not concerned for your safety?"

"I'm always concerned for my safety. Whether I let that force me to live in fear is another issue altogether. Maybe I'm overconfident, but I'm nearly certain I can handle whatever this city tries to throw at me." I grinned as an idea came to mind. Pulling out my wallet with my free hand, I pulled out all the bills and held them out. "There, you have a new job. Go tell everyone the Queen of the Nagas is here, and she doesn't give a fuck about how they feel about it."

It was bold and stupid, but I was done caring about the small-time bullshit. I had bigger fish to fry, and if someone wanted to pick a fight with me while I was in the country, I was more than okay to destroy them with extreme prejudice.

"I..." He leaned on the doorway of the elevator, which kept trying to close. "You want people to know you're here?" His confusion was so deep, it finally clicked for me.

They're used to nagas being secretive. Most supernaturals on the subcontinent have never seen one of my kind. He probably assumed I wouldn't want anyone to know I was here. His employer probably believed the same thing. It's a reasonable assumption.

A wrong one.

"The time of nagas slithering in the shadows is over," I explained, waving the money around. "If someone wants a pair of snake eyes, they can come and try to take them from me. If they don't leave the encounter with all their limbs or with their lives, for that matter, that's on them."

He stepped back, clearly fearful of me and my offering of cash. It was written all over his face as the doors finally shut and left me alone. I headed toward the closest staircase, trotting down the stairs.

When one needs to go to the wrong floor, it's smart to aim higher than the intended floor.

Going down several flights of stairs was easier than climbing up.

The trip gave me time to think. I was back for less than twenty-four hours, and someone was already trying to reach out. The options of who that person could be were limited, but I wasn't versed in the political powerhouses of the country. Anyone with an interest in the region's political situation would want to speak to the newly crowned *Nagaraja*. I had strong ties to the Tribunal and individuals of power. For all I knew, it could have been the Alpha of the Delhi werewolf pack or the head of a local coven, considering the use of a witch. It could be the rakshasa trying to set up a trap to get revenge for another dead king. I knew, for a fact, not all of their kind had been a part of the attack on Adhar's home. A sizable portion, for sure, but not all of them.

Whoever it was didn't realize just how dangerous I was right now. They hadn't been smart enough to warn their witch messenger that I wasn't someone to strongarm or threaten. Or the person feared for their own life and didn't want me using the messenger to get back to them without proper plans in place for their safety.

So many options, but I tried to stop going down the many rabbit holes. I was in India for one reason—the preservation of the nagas. I was here to find a handful of cambions lost to time, defeat my ancient rival, and if all went well, go home.

One impossible task right after another. I don't care about local politics. Got enough to deal with.

As I got back to the room, I took a deep breath, readying myself to tell Raphael this frustrating turn of events. He wouldn't like it, not that I could blame him.

Day one in India, I had a run-in with a god, and other supernaturals were already trying to drag me into covert meetings.

I didn't open the door. He did, frowning at me as he let me in.

"What happened?"

"Because whenever I'm out of your sight, something must go wrong?"

"Yes."

11

CHAPTER ELEVEN

I didn't have an argument, so I put our food down on the small dining table near the window. Pulling out the to-go containers, I split the food between us.

"Something happened. I felt you go up a few floors, then come back down. Just tell me what's going on."

"A witch tracked me in the lobby and grabbed the same elevator as me." Grabbing a plastic fork, I sat down and started eating as he glowered at me. With clear intent, he locked the deadbolt on our door, then walked to the table. He looked at the food, and I saw the internal debate. He had to be starving. The excitement of the day and moving around might have distracted him from his necessary caloric intake, but there was fresh food in front of him, and my bottomless pit of a mate was going to eat.

He grabbed a plastic fork and sat across from me but stared at me as he started eating as well.

When I thought there could be nothing awkward between him and me, he proved me wrong. There was something immensely weird about him holding eye contact with an expressionless face while he shoved food into his mouth, and I was fairly certain he knew exactly what he was doing.

"He was a messenger boy," I finally continued, unable to deal with the dead-eyed look my mate was giving me. "Well, he was a grown man and was probably powerful enough to give me trouble if I hadn't scared the shit out of him in the elevator. He wanted to tell me his employer wanted a meeting."

"Who?"

I'm lucky he's on my side, and that tone isn't directed at me. If he questioned someone else in that tone, they would probably cry.

"See, that's why I turned down the meeting and scared the witch. He wouldn't give me a name. In fact, he tried to threaten me. The whole 'if I could find you, imagine who else can' sort of deal. We're not going to meetings with people who won't give me their names. Don't worry."

"We've been here less than twenty-four hours, and they've found us. Damn it." Raphael's growl made the table and everything on it shake.

"It's not surprising," I reminded him. "We came in on a commercial flight, I used the publicly available resources to get us a vehicle, and we used my normal credit card to book this hotel room. So long as no one comes here to pick a fight, I don't care if they know I'm here." I took another bite as he glared at the food. "And if someone attacks us... we kill them. If we have to leave a trail of bodies across this country, we will."

"Let's hope it doesn't come to that," he said before he started eating again.

"Agreed."

After we finished our meal, I cleaned up while Raphael covered the table in maps. He sat back down, and once I was seated, he waved a hand over the maps.

"When you left, I realized I didn't even know where to start," he said, sighing heavily.

"Yeah..." I groaned. "Tell me about it. There are a lot of options. They could live remotely, hiding in the jungles and keeping out of the human eye, just like we did as nagas. They could also live in populated areas, moving around." I frowned, then shook my head, something rubbing me wrong about that option. "That doesn't fit the... people we're talking about." As memories flashed through my mind, part of me felt as though I knew these cambions. "They would try to live in one area. They liked having a *home*. It might have changed over the years but not often." Some memories were clearer than others. Anything with Rama was crystal clear, in vivid detail, down to the tears on her eyelashes when she cried or the sparkle in her dark eyes when she laughed. The texture of her hair in my hands...

I got up and paced, not wanting *those* memories.

This happens every time. Every time I think of them, it's her, always her. Everything he *would want to remember, but nothing fucking useful.*

Memory was fickle and frustrating. As I had explained to Adhar, I remembered things as my predecessor would have. He and I had different goals, different ideas of what was important. He wanted to remember Rama as the woman he loved to the point of obsession, to remember the little moments because, to him, they were the most important. It was touching and useless to think about the time he bit her and took her on the banks of a river. Or behind a waterfall. In a deep pool, her legs around his waist...

I covered my face, groaning.

"I'm going to assume you're remembering things you would rather not," Raphael said softly.

"It's hard to think about them and not think of the intimate moments Rama shared with him. It's a chain reaction every time. Think of cambions, think of Rama, think of sleeping with Rama, kissing her... one after the other." I dropped my hands and stared at my mate, who didn't move from his spot while I paced around the room. "Remembering her parents is hard because he only viewed them in relation to her. Trying to think of her parents reminds me of the time he snuck out with Rama to fuck her under the stars, and her father accidentally walked up to them."

"Sohan and Lalika. Maybe if you use their names, it might... make them distinct to her," he said.

"I told you their names once, and you remember them?"

"Of course. There aren't that many cambion names to remember."

"Sohan and Lalika," I repeated, nodding. "Sohan was secretive, protective, definitely a warrior. Lalika was loving and kind, treating her son-in-law as one of her own." Using their names was helpful, more helpful than I would have thought. "Warrior... warrior-caste, I mean. He was definitely like Sammy and Mateo. The longer I think about it, the clearer it is."

"If he's secretive and protective, he would keep everyone out of sight. He would want to defend them in a place he understood and knew well."

"Which is why it feels wrong to think they might move around or live near populated areas. No, the only reason they would move is the fear someone might discover them, either humans moving in too close or someone following Sohan home from one of his... trips." I looked at the maps again. "There aren't many places out there that could host ancient beings living full time in secret, without a considerable amount of magic to throw others off the trail."

"With what we understand about cambion magic, there's a possibility they have that," he suggested as I sat back down. "So, we're talking the jungles."

"Or deep in the mountains," I said, pointing farther north than where he'd indicated. "Highly unlikely they would have left the country unless it was accidentally. Shut-ins like them wouldn't be too bothered to learn new languages. They would want familiar."

"How does someone *accidentally* leave a country?"

"Borders are redrawn," I reminded him. "Or they didn't bother looking at the borders and just moved a little to get away from people. There are many possibilities. The subcontinent is more than just India. Off the top of my head, India, Pakistan, Nepal, Bhutan, Sri Lanka, Bangladesh, and... The Maldives." I almost forgot that last one. "I don't think they're in Sri Lanka, an island that doesn't have enough space. They would have never moved there initially and certainly wouldn't stay there. Pakistan is probably also out and everything near its border with India. Sohan wouldn't want his family living close to human conflict." Grabbing a notepad from the hotel and a pen with the same branding, I started writing my notes, needing to record these thoughts. "Nepal, Bhutan, and Bangladesh are options."

"That leaves thousands of square miles to look over," Raphael pointed out.

"Yeah, it does," I confirmed. Looking up from my scribbles, I saw the sheer disappointment in his eyes and felt it to my core. I put the pen down slowly, straightening my spine under the weight of his gaze.

"Are we going to do it on foot?"

"If we have to."

The stare continued, the disappointment growing. I saw him, *felt* him shutting down.

"Just say it," I whispered, needing the words he was leaving unspoken to be addressed now. I wouldn't leave them to fester between us.

"I thought you had more of a plan than this," he said softly as I held the eye contact. "We could do this at *home*. You know, the place where you could be safe, and your body could keep recovering. This is still..."

"I told you it was barely a plan," I reminded him.

"Why are we here if we're not ready to do anything?"

"Because I wanted to be here. I need to be here."

His expression said he didn't agree.

He got up, but I said nothing as he walked out of the room. In a matter of moments, the comradery of trying to piece together the puzzle was shattered. I wasn't sure what had happened. I had told him I didn't know where the cambions were and that this was all a shot in the dark. I wasn't sure where his sudden shift had come from. All I knew was he'd decided he would rather pace in the hallway than sit here with me.

Unless he had hoped for more than I actually had to give...

I looked at the maps again, fingers dancing over them. It was like going into the archives at Adhar's, hoping for so much when I'd gone in, but in the end, there had been nothing there, just as I had been told. Adhar had read his way through the archive's documents multiple times and would have been able to point to the letter or journal to give me answers.

The answers hadn't been there... had never been there.

Raphael expected me to have answers, and I had none, or I would have already given them to him. If there was something to remember, I would have by now.

Or maybe the answers are *in my memories, and I just don't know how to get to them.*

I got up and paced, thinking as I did laps around the room.

Memories have triggers. A person forgets things until something jogs their memory, and they come back as if they were never forgotten. That's why we have the saying 'jog your memory.' Maybe that's what I need to get around. I need something to jog my memory. I need to go somewhere or do something to bring those memories to the forefront.

I stopped pacing and crossed my arms as I looked around the modern room.

Just like in Vrindavan. I looked at the kadamba tree and

remembered how he saw it centuries ago, how it felt. I didn't remember it having power, but now, it seems like a simple thing I could never forget. How does someone forget a powerful tree, right?

So, where would I go to awaken memories about where Rama and her family could live? Or a way to find her? Most of the time, I can barely tell where I am in the memories.

I clung to the prospect of being able to remember, something I could work with, and I needed that. After several minutes, I was tired of thinking in circles, so I went to the door, opening it to see Raphael starting another lap in the hall.

"I have an idea." He looked up from his feet, acknowledging my presence, but said nothing, so I continued. "I'm sorry I started this without enough concrete planning, but I couldn't just sit in Arizona and do nothing. It felt like it was time to get started, and I could only start here. I had something to handle before I could... focus properly on this."

"Whatever you needed at Vrindavan."

"Yes."

He came back into the room and leaned on the wall as I locked the door.

"I think we need to jog my memories of his life. I'm certain there's relevant information floating just out of my reach. I'm missing something, something he knew instinctually, but I'm clearly out of my depth. It's already happened once since we've been here. I'm certain we can do it again."

"Okay, I can get behind that," he agreed. "Any idea where to start?"

"There are places..." I went back to the window and looked at the view. I was in a modern room, with modern things, but he and Rama would have had none of this. They lived in old structures.

Well, they would be old today if they were still standing.

"I need more than that, Kaliya. We need to narrow down the search a little."

I tapped my foot, thinking about the history of my people, specifically that first generation and their direct children.

"There are temples where nagas of the first generation had great stories, like the one we went to in Vrindavan. It was dedicated to Krishna's defeat of my predecessor, but we could go to others. He would have seen those places or heard about them in letters from his brothers. They would have exchanged stories. Or maybe he was an unnamed member of those stories. I think we should start with Kukke Subramanya Temple. We'll have to take a plane if we want to get there quickly. It's a day's drive out of Bengaluru or a forty-one-hour drive from here."

"Why that temple?"

"It's where Vasuki and several other nagas once took refuge from Garuda. Vrindavan and where nagas live now are much farther north than they used to be. It's just an idea, Raphael. It's a long trip across the country that could yield very little, but it's worth a shot."

I hope.

My mate groaned.

"All that, hoping you remember something... anything that might lead us to Rama—if she's alive—so she can lead us to Ramanaka, a mythical island no naga has been to in thousands of years. And after all that, we can only hope Garuda is using said mythical island to hide and where he's been orchestrating the extinction of the nagas."

"Yeah."

"This is insanity, Kaliya. I can't believe you brought me here with literally no real plan. I really believed you had more than this to go on."

"I know." Oh, I knew all too well. I had come into this knowing it would be a struggle with very little to go on. It hurt that Raphael was already frustrated with me. I had assumed he knew what was happening, which was starting with nothing, and my assumption left us both in a bad place—me looking like an asshole and him frustrated and defeated before we even started.

"Mahavir gave you Garuda's feathers. Could we use them?"

I went to my bag and pulled out the box.

"Potentially..." I sat beside him and opened the box to show him the feathers. "There's nobody I would trust to ask who would be powerful enough to make it worth our while. Devika might have been able to. I don't know how fae magic would play with the legends of my people or Garuda. Besides, unless the spell can open a portal to where we need to be, there's very little it would tell us. A dot on a map in the open ocean? It's not that simple, Raphael. We can't take a boat to this island. I have no memories of how Kaliya left the island. There's nothing there as if it's been purposefully forgotten or removed. I only know that he did."

"Then why are we here?"

"I need to be here if I want to succeed," I answered softly, knowing it was my truth. This was where I needed to be. "Why don't we sleep on everything, then come at this tomorrow with a clear head and start again?"

"Good idea," he said with a groan and stripped, his shirt going first.

I tucked the box of feathers away once again, and we prepared for bed in silence. Once we were in bed, Raphael slept with his back turned to me, and I wondered what he was thinking.

It took longer than I wanted for sleep to claim me.

12

CHAPTER TWELVE

I woke up to a noise. I didn't move, keeping my eyes closed because my instincts screamed at me that the noise wasn't natural. Raphael was still next to me, his breathing even, his chest rising and falling against my back. At some point in the night, he had rolled over and wrapped his arm around my waist.

But that wasn't important.

There was a noise. What was it?

I heard it again, and this time, I recognized it—soft footstep on carpet, a pat of soft material on soft material. Listening more closely, I caught the sound of fabric sliding against itself as it grew louder.

Not louder...

Closer.

I kept my breathing steady, keeping up the appearance of sleep. There were natural noises in the night—creaks of buildings, the movement of someone in bed—but these were noises I knew all too well. I had produced it myself on a number of occasions.

Soft shoes on carpet. Probably flexible for mobility.

Smooth clothing, minimal rustle.

No breathing.

There was someone stalking the room, trying to remain silent, a thief or an assassin. I didn't dare try to taste the air to discover what sort of supernatural I was dealing with, not wanting to give myself away. I knew the moment I moved, whoever it was would recognize I was awake, and so would Raphael.

Instead, I paid attention to the thermal energy of the room. With Raphael pressed against my back, the warm body only a foot from the bed was the intruder. With a masculine form, I decided it had to be a man. All too close to me to be a thief.

Plus, a thief wouldn't keep a sword raised over his head.

It happened quickly. Shifting into snake form as the sword came down, I launched out of the sheets and sank my fangs into the assassin's thigh. He screamed, and something crashed to the ground nearby as I pumped venom into his bloodstream. When I released, I shifted back into human form in a crouch, watching the assassin as he stumbled away. Our door flew open, and two others ran into the room, weapons drawn. I straightened and tasted the air, discovering who my attackers were.

"Fucking rakshasa," I hissed.

"Our first night here, and people are trying to kill us," Raphael snarled as he stepped up beside me. Beside us, the gurgles of a dying man punctuated the situation all too well. "Consider me unsurprised. What did you say over dinner, love? If we have to leave a trail of bodies..."

"We will," I said, glaring at the two in my door. This was their chance to run. A high-end resort hotel was *not* the place I wanted to have a supernatural brawl, especially one in a country where I had no resources to clean up the mess. One body would be frustrating enough to get rid of.

One looked down at their dying comrade, then at me. He lifted his sword, ready to continue the fight. His partner whistled, and I heard more feet running down the hall.

"There's more coming," I said. "Cover me. I need a weapon."

"I've got you," Raphael promised, stepping forward and growing.

"No demon form," I ordered in a rush as the horns erupted from his forehead.

There was no chance for him to reply. The two rakshasa who had breached the room rushed forward, experienced warriors there to take him down. Diving for my bag, I unzipped it while cursing myself for not putting weapons on ready before lying down for the night. I pulled out a chakram first and went to throw it, but Raphael's massive form filled the doorway. He grabbed one of the rakshasa and shoved him into a wall, and the body was immobile. The other brought his blade down, and I could taste black blood in the air as Raphael roared and shifted to the side in reaction to the blow.

Seeing the opening, I took my chance and sent the chakram sailing past my mate, deep into the chest of the rakshasa who had injured him. So long as my mate kept his head, it would be okay. That was logical, but fury ran through me at the scent of his blood. Before another could run into the room, I pulled another chakram from the bag and threw it, watching it hit the neck of another rakshasa. Including the three now dead, there were seven I could see. I grabbed a third chakram in one hand and my katana in the other as they started through the door. Raphael knocked one back as I rushed into the fight, deflecting a blade and throwing my last chakram at the same time. I killed a third with that throw while blood splattered the walls as Raphael tore a body part off another.

Once, I had thought to train my mate with weapons.

There was a reason I didn't waste time on that sort of thing anymore.

That was when I lost my ability to see.

I wasn't standing in the hotel anymore, but a dark cavern, pitch black except for a foot around me as if I glowed.

"Raphael? We're under an illusion!" I called out, hoping he could hear me. Depending on the power of the illusion, there was a chance he couldn't. It took me a moment to realize it was that powerful. I heard nothing but the eerie whisper of wind through the imaginary cavern.

Something hit me from the darkness, and I hit the stone wall of the dark cavern, pain radiating from my back as warm blood poured down my side. Considering exposure was inevitable, a problem I would have to deal with another day, I shifted, not to my snake form but to my powerful naga form. Coiling, I hit things in the darkness, knocking them around.

Using that to tell me where my potential enemies were, I launched at the last one I hit, pinning it to the ground as I sank my fangs in while I coiled around it. There was something primal about the kill, an energy running through me close to rage but deeper. Bones crushed as I flexed. I couldn't hear the screams of the dying, but I could imagine they were there. Something cut into my snake body, and I lashed out in that direction, throwing myself into another attacker. That one I couldn't grab, so I assumed I had knocked him out of my reach.

When I lashed out again, I hit the one I needed to, and the illusion broke. I was coiling around the hotel hallway, hissing furiously at the rakshasa on the ground around me. A number of them were dead, but more than half were still alive, circling and trying to find another opening I tried to find the one who posed the biggest threat, tasting the magic still in the air. I needed to kill the one who could do the illusions, but a roar took me away from that task.

Turning, I looked back into the room to see Raphael fighting against the darkness. While I had broken the illusion around me, I hadn't done it for him. Worse, the rakshasa was taking advantage of separating us, and Raphael was taking hits, his blood staining his body, the walls, and the carpet. I couldn't see where they had hit him. I dove into the room, coiling around my mate as I knocked a rakshasa away.

"I've got you." I touched his shoulders as I was followed into the room by the remaining rakshasa. "Don't shift. The rooms and halls are too small." I could only pray he heard me. The damage he would do was the least of my worries. He would crush me and hurt himself.

"You shouldn't have come back," one of the rakshasa snarled. "Your time killing our people is over!"

"I've never killed a rakshasa who didn't try to kill me first," I hissed, quickly counting the remaining rakshasa. Five left. I could do this. "I will not argue with you tonight. This ends now."

I dove for the one talking, darting to the side at the last moment to avoid his blade. In the same movement, I flung out my tail and sent three into the wall, then got behind the one I wanted and grabbed his head. A quick twist and his body crumpled. I grabbed his sword and blocked a swing of a blade as I shifted back to two feet, wanting the mobility of being smaller. I disarmed the next rakshasa, then reached down for the chakram in the chest of the first one I'd killed and threw it as I came up, killing another in the same way.

Making my way through them, my body was on autopilot, moving faster than it should have. As I killed the fourth of the remaining six, I realized I had tapped into the thing Nakul had pulled out of me. This wasn't just my training. This was how he had once fought. I didn't do it on purpose, but there was something strange about how I deftly cleaned up the group of rakshasa.

Standing over the body of the last one, I turned to my mate, knowing he was out of the illusion now, but he hadn't moved.

"Are you okay?" I asked, dropping the weapons in my hands and letting them hit the floor. Neither of them was mine.

"I don't like the magic," he said, breathing heavily. "They didn't do it when they attacked Adhar's home."

"They had been riding to war. In the chaos, they didn't have a chance to," I explained, searching my mate's expression. "This was a kill squad. The assassin was supposed to kill us, hopefully in silence. Two dead bodies for someone to find later. They were the backup in case things didn't go as planned. Divide and conquer—two powerful illusionists and several warriors to take advantage of our confusion."

"You shifted. I... felt it. It looked like thick vines, but I knew those weren't real." He touched his chest and winced. "They cut me up fairly well."

"How are you healing?" I demanded, finally closing the distance between us. He pulled off the shift, but all I saw was black blood smearing his chest.

"It's healing. Don't worry about it. I need to find a finger, though."

I let my jaw drop open. He lifted his left hand and showed me where a pinky was supposed to go.

"I stupidly lifted my hand and tried to catch a sword. Realized it in time to keep the hand but lost the finger. It's in this mess somewhere. Let me find it while you grab our stuff. I take it we're leaving."

"Damn right, we're leaving." Kissing his cheek, I collected my weapons as quickly as I could, having to pull them out of corpses. It was two in the morning, and I was amazed no one had woken up to see what the commotion was, but we were lucky. No one came running into the hall or our room to investigate. By the time I had the bags collected, Raphael was holding his pinky to his hand, grimacing as he watched it heal, while I stared in fascination. I knew he could but had never seen it, not in real-time. I had chopped off Sammy's hand that once, but Gabi had sped that up. Gabi was a Nephilim, a literal angel-human hybrid, who could heal anything.

It took a few minutes, but Raphael let the pinky go, and it stayed attached to his hand, but when he closed his fist, the pinky didn't fully react.

"It'll take some time for it to feel natural," he said, shaking his head. Then he looked around the room and saw the devastation I had to get through. "Shit. Three supernatural species are going to be exposed because of this."

"Probably, but we don't have time to worry about it. We need to leave before the human authorities get here." Grabbing my weapon bag, I threw it over my shoulder while Raphael grabbed our two bags of clothes. We left the hotel room and tried to casually walk away, but there was a certain haste to our steps.

"We can't use the elevator," I told him as I pointed to the door for the stairs.

Entering the stairwell, we picked up speed. Running down the stairs, we made record time and were in a full sprint when we went to our car, ignoring any humans who might be nearby. With little care, we threw the bags into the car, and I jumped behind the wheel. The tires screeched on the road as I slammed on the gas to get us away from the vicious crime scene we had been forced to leave behind.

"When this is over, we're *never* coming back to India," Raphael said, looking over his shoulder.

"Agreed."

13

CHAPTER THIRTEEN

"Where do we go now?" he asked me as I drove out of the city once again. "Are you going to put us on a forty-hour drive to the temple you were talking about?"

"I don't know since I figured we would have a couple of days to get our feet on the ground. I knew someone would eventually try to kill us, but the first night?" I shook my head. "Now the situation is more complicated, exposing the nagas, rakshasa, and cambions to humanity. I mean…" I couldn't believe rakshasa would take that risk just to get to me. One of the best ways to hide in the supernatural world was to make exposure inevitable if someone attacked. Clearly, they weren't playing by those rules anymore, and there was no way I could go back to the resort and clean up the mess.

Beyond that, I had a fair amount of guilt. I had been more than a little arrogant with that witch, practically daring the world to come for me, hoping a little arrogance and confidence would keep people guessing about me, make them cautious. It had been a tactical maneuver.

It hadn't worked, and the world hit back.

"Why don't we bunker down somewhere, check in with home, and see how this plays out?" Raphael asked. "Is there somewhere close we could hide, even if it's just for the night? So we can get our bearings and actually decide where to go next. We were going to sleep on things and talk more in the morning. We never decided about anything."

He was right. If we were going to be attacked at every turn, we needed somewhere secret to go, so we could talk and sleep without interruption. Racking my brain, I could only come up with one possible option for our new problem.

The only option.

I turned, taking us out farther than I planned. I didn't know the roads or the signs.

But I knew this landscape intimately.

"I have a place," I whispered as I drove in the dark. Eventually, my mental map of the landscape told me it was time to go off-road. "It's been abandoned for a long time."

"Wherever you think we'll be safe for the night, I'll take it," he said, holding the bar over his seat as I road over rocks and through a stream. Deeper and deeper.

An hour out of the city, then two, I finally saw it through the trees. Once, I had made the trip on foot, and it had been farther from civilization at the time. Back then, Delhi wasn't the modern metropolis it was today. It had still been rural, but it would have been abandoned sooner rather than later by the nagas who had lived there.

I parked at the front gate, still locked tight as it always had been when I was a child.

"What is this place?"

"Where I was born. It's the closest naga home I know. This is where I lived my entire life before my family was murdered. Mehar was the only rakshasa who knew about it, and no one knew what he was up to. We've confirmed that much. The others shouldn't know it's here. As for anyone else? I bet you Mehar killed off everyone who knew his secrets because his people were in the dark." I licked my lips and could still taste the powerful magic that defended the home. If I remembered correctly, Devika had done the spells herself.

Which was how the murderers were able to get around them into the estate to kill my family when they were aiming to kill me.

"Stay here," I ordered as I undid my seatbelt. "I'm going to open the gate wide enough to get through, then we'll lock it behind us. I don't know how it'll react to you trying to pry it open, so it's just better if you stay here."

Not giving him time to protest, I got out, went to the gate, and looked up. It wasn't as tall as I remembered. When I was a child, there were times I would come out to stare at the gate, wondering how someone could build the thing. It had touched the sky in my child's brain, and it had blocked me from the entire world, the end of my space, and the beginning of everything else.

Now, it was just a tall gate, twelve feet high with the walls to match. Locked by physical means and magic ones, but I only needed to worry about the magic ones. The locks were old and would be easy to pick. The magic could kill me.

I looked over the gate, tasting the air. The protective magics were concentrated here and threatening, an aura of danger—a warning. My hair stood on end, a classic emotional manipulation for anyone foolish enough to wander too close. Creating the sensation of fear and foreboding kept the curious away and warned the enemy that death was on the other side of this gate.

Daringly, I reached out and touched the metal bars, wondering if the magic would recognize me. When it did, the fear subsided, and my body relaxed. Instead of needing to pick the lock, the chains on the gate slid off and fell to the ground. I stepped back as the gate creaked and rattled, slowly swinging open as if the old home was welcoming me back, beckoning me inside, where I belonged.

My parents would never leave me locked out.

I went back to the vehicle and drove in. Once parked, I went back to the gate, closed it manually, and put the chains back. I couldn't replicate the buildup of vines that had crawled over it, so someone would know it was recently used. Although the likelihood anyone would come here for Raphael and me was slim. They would have to bring someone back from the dead to discover this place even existed.

When I turned back to the car, Raphael was out and grabbing our bags. Nothing crazy happened, and the taste of magic on the air was gone. Once inside, there wasn't any spell that could kill him.

But there are...

"Wait! Don't move!" I called out, jogging toward him. He froze at my first word. As I reached him, I saw the first of what I knew would be dozens of snakes.

"Don't even think about it," I hissed at it as it went toward my mate. Stepping in front of it, the snake coiled into a defensive ball, staring back at me. My parents had surrounded the compound with snakes that ate well by keeping the rodents at bay. Clearly, that hadn't changed.

"Kaliya?" Raphael sounded more than a little afraid. I turned, and another was wrapping its way around its leg. Luckily, it was over his pants.

"Fuck. I forgot about these when I got out. I'm sorry. Don't move. Stay calm, and I'll handle them."

I went down to one knee, and reaching out, I sang, my voice rusty but capable. The magic of a naga charming a snake was a private one, and there wasn't much use for it in my day-to-day life. Helping a friend a couple of years ago with a cobra was the last time I had needed to sing, and I had done so only when necessary.

As I sang to these snakes, I remembered how my mother and father would frequently charm these snakes to stay and defend the home. The closest things to pets I would ever have.

By the end of my song, I had six on me and knew there were another eight in the dark, all focused on me.

"He's my mate. He's mine," I whispered to the closest one in the Hindi of my parents. "No threat here. Be at peace and go find your next meal." I released them from the grip of the charm, and they retreated into the darkness, off to do as I asked.

"They'll ignore you now." I stood up and kissed his cheek. "Promise."

"It's always beautiful to hear you do that," he said softly, looking over his shoulder at me. "Did you ever think to try with Roshni?"

"It wouldn't work on her. A simple lullaby is all that's needed with her, no matter the form," I said, smiling as I grabbed my bags and started for the front door. Thinking of Roshni brought back the heartbreak that had sent me on this damn journey. Standing on the estate of my birthing, I was thinking about another orphan.

An endless cycle of pain, one I needed to break. That was why I was here at the beginning of it all.

I led him into the home of my childhood, covered in dust and overgrown with vegetation. Once, it all had been carefully managed. My family had enjoyed the rich vegetation in their home and the gardens creeping through the windows. Now, the home had been claimed by the gardens, dust and dirt coating each surface, and the furniture was falling apart.

It was a skeleton of the home I had lost. I heard the echoes of my family in every creak and groan and saw the visage of them in every object strewn about.

I relived the night they all died, knowing that night was the reason the table was upside down and broken. That night was the reason the windows were shattered.

Raphael walked around and inspected the house, leaving me to my silent grieving. I heard furniture move, and when he came back into view, he cleaned off surfaces, sweeping dust away from tables and chairs that could be salvaged.

"You never came back here, did you?" he finally asked as he moved two chairs into the open space at the center of the home.

"No, I didn't."

"I'm sorry."

"Don't be," I whispered. "It's exactly what I always figured it would be."

"Oh?"

"A ruin and a graveyard," I elaborated, then walked in deeper. "Let me do a sweep before you keep exploring. Everything is probably safe with me in the building with you, but I don't want any nasty surprises later."

"I'll stay in the main areas. I didn't go into any of the bedrooms."

I nodded, appreciating his forethought. I had to check those myself. As if running on autopilot, I went to my room first, opening the door without thinking.

It was the room of a girl I didn't recognize—toys on the floor, wooden things my father had carved for me. I tried to remember the games I played with them but couldn't. There were some memories, some periods of life, I was okay with forgetting. At nearly one hundred and twenty years old, I was okay not remembering the tea parties I'd had with the wooden carvings.

Continuing my hunt, I left my room. I didn't want to get lost in this. We were only here to hide out while we planned our next move, not for me to go down memory lane.

I cleared each room of potential traps and spells... and snakes. I couldn't forget about the snakes.

Then I reached a locked door. Frowning, I tried it

several times, eventually slamming my shoulder into it. Doing that reminded me of the cut on my side, and I hissed in pain and frustration. Forgetting the door for a moment, I yanked my shirt up to see the shallow but long cut the rakshasa had given me. Adrenaline only lasted so long, and my exertion brought the pain of the injury to the forefront of my mind, making it impossible to ignore any longer. I would have tended it sooner if I had thought it was fatal. It was already half-closed, anyway. I healed faster than other nagas, thanks to my mating with the cambion.

Not going to my mate for stitches. I focused on the cut and pulled on the power I knew had I had, like getting a bucket from a well or turning on a faucet. Red magic flowed around me, and the wound sealed completely, closing into a scar.

My bill to get that removed is going to be steep.

Sighing, I focused again on the locked door. My parents had been keen to keep this room secure, and not even their murderers had breached it.

"What was this room?" I asked out loud, tilting my head to the side. Raphael wasn't screaming or anything, so I had time to ponder it. The memories of my childhood were fuzzy. Like my predecessor, I remembered the good parts, but there was a lot of data dumping, things that were important now but hadn't been when I was a child. Like whatever this room was.

I couldn't bring myself to walk away from it, so I pushed, pulled, and jiggled the handle. I even looked for any obvious locks but couldn't find anything to pick open. Desperate, I licked the damn handle and tasted the magic through the dust and dirt. Spitting out the shit in disgust, I had my answer to the room.

Magic locks, huh? Well, the gate responded to me because it remembered me. Daughter of the estate. This door must have been told to recognize only my parents or brothers.

"Kaliya, what are you doing?" Raphael asked. I looked down the hall to see him frowning at me.

"This door is locked, and I want to find out why and how," I explained as if it was obvious. "I don't remember what's behind it. I've already checked the bedrooms, offices, storage closets. Somehow, after all these years, this room has remained unbreached. I need to know why."

My mate, picked for me by the gods, sighed heavily and smiled.

"Okay. I'm nearly done setting us up in the main... courtyard thing. It's a lot like Adhar's. The kitchen seems usable, too. I'll just need to remember Eshika's lessons about how to use some of the wooden burning stuff."

"Thank you. See if you can get an internet connection from here. Phones, laptops, anything. Did we bring a satellite phone? If we did, try it out. If any of those work, we can check on home. If I need help with this, I'll come get you."

"I'll see what I can do with the electronics." He wandered off and left me to my puzzle.

Weirdly, the drama of the day before and the wakeup we'd had was forgotten. The conversation felt perfectly normal, and it brightened my mood.

Going back to the door, I inspected it further. It was a

normal door, made of wood but felt unbreakable. I walked away from it, heading outside to the wall where it should have a window.

No window.

"Keeping secrets," I whispered as I realized this was more than a small mystery. "My parents kept a lot of secrets." I knew that all too well. "I wonder if Adhar had puzzled over this door when he came here and found their bodies. He probably just forgot to mention it over the years, figuring it was something for me to deal with, wondering if I would one day open it and reveal its secrets."

It was my shame to carry that Adhar wasn't around for me to ask. It was my shame I had never attempted to return to my childhood home to discover this puzzle decades beforehand.

"Kaliya?"

Raphael's call made me snap out of my thoughts. I went back inside to find him where I just had been standing. He looked up at me, then at the door, practically jumping out of his skin for no reason.

"What?"

"The door..." He pointed at it. "It... wasn't here, just a second ago."

I tried to process that.

"Excuse me?"

"It wasn't there. I came over to tell you I was able to get a wifi hotspot set up and that everything was working, but you weren't here, and *neither was the door*."

14

CHAPTER FOURTEEN

"Oh…" I didn't know how to react. I knew he was telling the truth. He wouldn't miss an entire door. "What was there when I was gone?"

"A wall. The same wall." He gestured to the hallway. "It was as if it was never there."

"Holy shit," I mumbled, walking to the door again. "So, it's here when I am, which explains why it's never been opened. No wonder Adhar never mentioned it. He probably didn't know it was here." I nodded, accepting that. "Powerful magic then. If it's here for me, then why is it locked?"

"I don't know, but this house gives me the creeps. A disappearing, magic door?" Raphael shook his head and walked away.

On a hunch, I grabbed him and made it clear I wanted him to stay.

"Try to open it with me."

"Why? I don't know if I want to touch the magically

haunted door, Kaliya." My mate, my fearless, cambion warlord mate, was genuinely freaked out by this door.

I couldn't blame him. I was as well, but I was more curious to know what was inside than anything else.

"My mother left me a box for the day I mated. It had nothing worthwhile, but..."

"Walk me through this. You grew up here, spent your childhood here."

"Yes."

"And you don't know what's behind this door?" He pointed at it with a thumb, turning to give me an incredulous look.

"No idea," I said, shrugging. "My parents clearly had secrets. I mean, look at what my mother and Devika did to me." I looked at the door again. "What if that's what this door is hiding? What if that's why it's showing up for me?"

"Kaliya..."

"Help me open the door," I demanded, needing to know.

Raphael sighed heavily and reached out to the door, readying himself to shove it open if he had to. I grabbed the handle at the same time. Magic rushed around us, kicking up dust, and sure enough, the handle turned. Raphael cursed as I pushed the door open and entered the room.

Walking into the room, I realized fate was playing with me. That the circumstances of the night had purposefully led me to this place in the world at this point in time.

I *knew* this room, recognized it deep in my

subconscious. This had been where my mother and Devika had done the spell to uncover my previous life. The place where I was irrevocably changed, altered, and ruined, my life taken from me and replaced with the memories of another. The patch job they had done to fix it had been good enough to let me live what seemed like a normal life, but it had only been a patch.

"What is this?"

"Where my mother did magic," I whispered. "This is where they gave me his memories and discovered who I was reincarnated from. This is where Devika sealed them away again."

"Oh, Kaliya..."

"My mother's writings are probably..." Looking at the tables and desks, I started hunting, and I was right. All around me were my mother's scribblings—her work on the spell, why she was doing it, and her most private thoughts. Some were academic journals, while others were personal. Opening it and reading a single page, I could get the gist of a journal. I sorted them until someone grabbed my wrists.

"Kaliya, do you really want to go down this rabbit hole?" he asked me softly, leaning over my shoulder as he held me still.

"I think I have to," I said, staring at my shaking hands. "She left it for me to find when I was mated. Gods, what did she know that I didn't?" I closed my eyes, pain threatening to make me crumple.

"Kaliya, you once told me that knowing she loved you was *enough*. I want you to be certain you're willing to open this can of worms again. Knowing the answers behind the spell and how she did it might not give you any closure. I need you to understand that. You said her letter was enough."

I heard his desperation in every word, and with that desperation was his love for me.

He doesn't want me to hurt about this anymore. How do I deserve this man?

His force to make me stop was a blessing. It let me think and get past the overriding curiosity. Curiosity was the death of me. I wasn't a cat, but I was curious. Always so desperate for answers and normally willing to pay the price for them.

Normally.

Like learning Garuda was reincarnated and was behind it all. That answer had come in its own time, brought by hunting, and it had extracted a terrible payment. A price I hadn't asked to pay, a price I never wanted to pay, even if I could learn the secrets of the universe.

Touching the top of a journal, even as Raphael tried to gently hold me in place, I thought about a little orphan, so like me but so different. Roshni back home, probably giving Eshika hell because her warm rock and safety net wasn't around. If I left these here, someone could one day use this magic on her and ruin her life or the terror twins, two beautiful boys who just needed to take a nap most of the time. Innocent, small lives, just like mine had been once until my mother stole it from me.

That risk wasn't one I was willing to accept. I would never let anyone steal their futures and their choice from them. I would never let anyone put the burden of the past on them or give them enemies they did nothing to deserve.

I had a choice and decided I didn't need the answers, not to these questions—not today, not tomorrow. I would never need these answers. I was angry with myself for considering for a moment to read these, angry this room existed, angry these journals existed. Angry at *her* all over again. Even with them right in front of me, I stepped back from it and closed a door I hadn't realized was still open.

"We'll burn it," I decided, looking over the journals, feeling the wave of anger simmering in my heart. "We'll get rid of all of it once I... no," I corrected quickly. "We'll just burn them. If it's related to the magic she did, we destroy it." Fire was good. Fire seemed like a great idea.

"Are you sure?"

I nodded.

"Yes. It's blasphemy and too dangerous to put in an archive and hope no one discovers it." I took a shaky breath, trying not to be overcome by not only my emotions of loss and pain but the fury as well. "I can't imagine a world where someone does this to Roshni, the twins, or any future children. Even if we think it's useful in a century, think we can use it the right way... it's too dangerous. Too *wrong*. Look at me. Look at what it did to my life, how it changed me. What it led to for my family. No. We have to get rid of it, so we're never be tempted to look for it again. I don't need answers about the magic, not *this* magic. It can all be destroyed."

Slowly, he let me go and backed away.

"I want to keep her personal journals, though." I

turned my back on the tables to look at him. "If we can. Maybe. I don't know."

"We'll sort through them, and the books of magic will be kindling for a fire."

"Thank you."

"After we get some sleep." He grabbed my elbow and dragged me out of the room. "It's not even dawn. We're not dealing with it right now. We have two ongoing problems as it is. We don't need to dive into a third. Not right now. Let's make some headway on the other two first."

"Three if you really break it down. The cambions, the rakshasa, and Garuda," I said, agreeing with him. Closing the door, I did my best to walk away from it. "This will be our fourth problem. I wasn't expecting a new thing to deal with by coming here. I'm sorry. I was curious, but it could have waited."

"You wouldn't have been able to rest if that door stayed locked, and we both know it. It would have kept you up the entire time we stayed here." Chuckling, he dragged me into the courtyard to show me the makeshift camp he'd created out of the old furniture and our stuff. "Does this meet the quality requirements of the *Nagaraja*?" he asked, smiling.

"Very funny... but yes." I smiled back, but my smile felt hollow. "Roughing it doesn't hurt my feelings, you know."

"Oh, I know." Ignoring the dust, he sat down on the floor and stretched his legs out. "Just poking fun, love. You're a little tense, not that I can blame you. It's been a long night."

Sitting across the little makeshift fire he'd made, I thought about what I had just decided. He could poke fun if he wanted to. I didn't mind. Everyone in the compound knew I was a little weird about the pretense of my position among those at home and didn't want to be waited on hand and foot, not there. I wasn't afraid to use the position to remind everyone who was in charge when it was necessary, but I didn't want them to put me on a pedestal.

Thinking about the compound for a moment couldn't keep my mind off the room and what was in it. Raphael took my silence as his chance to open his survival bag and light the fire. Giving me a long look I barely registered, he pulled out two granola bars and put one beside me.

I was going to burn my mother's life's work. Everything she was, everything she had been, was in that room. Her secrets laid bare.

I was going to destroy it for the good of my people. I had to. I didn't even want to read her notes about the magic, none of it. Part of me wondered if I even wanted her personal journals. If they offered anyone even the slightest clue to her project, I wanted them gone.

That's not the only reason, though.

I was still angry with her. My loving mother, who had wanted me to thrive, broke something important, and she was dead, so she couldn't fix it. My father and brothers were dead because of what she had done to me.

I wanted it all to burn. I wanted to let it all go.

The secrets.

The magic.

The past.

Her.

Rubbing my face, I took the granola bar Raphael had put in my reach and ate it in silence, knowing he was watching my every move. Once I finished it, I shoved the wrapper away, deciding I wouldn't litter in my childhood home.

"Sorry for being so quiet. Just thinking about everything. A lot has happened tonight."

"Yeah. I assume you won't be getting any sleep tonight."

"No, probably not," I confirmed, rubbing my eyes. "You can, though. One of us needs to be well-rested. While you sleep, I'm going to... try to think through this. Find our next step, something to start on that isn't,"—I waved a hand toward the hall that held my mother's darkest secrets—"Isn't *that*. The rakshasa attacked tonight, and they could have exposed all of us. I have to think about how we're going to handle that. We need to. They've given us no option but to finish the war they started."

"I'm never coming back to this country," he said, shaking his head. "Ever."

"I won't make you. It hasn't exactly been welcoming."

"Why am I not surprised?" He didn't seem happy about it.

"I know in the heat of the moment, I said I agreed with you earlier, but..." I looked around. "I promised I would fight so my nagas could return. This is our homeland. I have to get this back for them, which means I'll have to come here for my job as queen, even if I don't live here." I pulled my knees up and put my chin on them.

"Even if they decide to stay in America for a century or more, some, if not all of them, will eventually yearn to come back, and I won't stop them, not once I'm certain we can do it safely. I won't make them live behind walls, not here or at home. I'm not doing this to return them to the life they knew but to give them a better one. One where they can live in a village, and their children can have friends. Where they can go to the store if they need milk and eggs. Where they can call each other and meet for dinner."

I wiped my eyes, thinking of things I shared with him, Cassius and Sorcha, and our cambions. The simple things, the easy things of a life outside of hiding. It was so easy to forget how wonderful those things could be, but I would never forget. Having lived both lives, I knew just how important those moments could be.

"I can't promise to never come back. Even if it's hundreds of years from now, I'll be back to visit and check on my people."

His expression told me how he felt about that.

15

CHAPTER FIFTEEN

"I can see you hate it, and I'm sorry, but that's the truth of the matter," I said, not backing down from his clear anger. He backed down first, looking away.

"As much as I hate it, I can't argue with you." Raphael sighed, his anger dissipating. "It's hard to carry the needs of so many people around and try to do your best at every turn, even when you have no idea which direction you should go."

"Yeah." It was something we both knew too well, but Raphael was clearly thinking about something that hadn't happened recently. "Raph?"

"It was Mateo's plan," he mumbled. "At first, but I helped flesh it out when he came to me with it. Sleep with the scientist, use her to get out, free everyone else." His voice grew louder and clearer with every word. "Sammy agreed, though she was vocally disgusted by the part where I slept with the scientist. Everyone... everyone agreed to it." He rubbed his temples as he talked about a time he'd never opened up to me. I knew he'd gotten his memories back from his time in the lab, remembering the moment it happened with ease and clarity, forever marking a change in our relationship I couldn't put a finger on.

He never spoke about them in detail. None of the cambions did, and I understood why, never trying to pry too much. Those memories had to be traumatizing.

"We didn't have any other option. I can remember the weight of their hope... I had five years in those labs, but some had decades. Some had never seen freedom. Some knew their parents had probably passed on, and they would never see them again. Loved ones gone, girlfriends, boyfriends, fiancés—there was nothing out there for most of them anymore except their hope to see the light again." He gave me a sad look.

"I told you I was going to stand by your side through this. You helped my people, so it's only right that I help yours, but... there's something else. I wouldn't let you shoulder that sort of burden on your own. I couldn't even remember it, not when I met you, but the weight... it never went away."

"You were driven to see them free. I remember. Even when you didn't remember them, you needed to figure out what Mygi was doing, why they were chasing you, and you finally had the means to do so, thanks to me. You could stop running and start searching for the answers you knew were important beyond the obvious ones."

He nodded, and I let him stew for a moment, wondering if he wanted to continue. He looked across the fire at me, and I saw the tension in his face grow.

"I felt guilty when I finally remembered. I spent years

running when I had needed to be fighting. All because of what? Some shitty spells that forced me to forget. Not my fault, but they suffered for longer than they needed because I wasn't thorough enough with the plan. Mateo and I had all the means to discover the issue with the memory spell and find a solution, but we missed it, and the other cambions suffered." He finally gave me another sad smile.

"So, I worry about you as your mate, as your lover, as the man who wants to follow you to the ends of the earth, and who will spend eternity with you, but as a man with so many lives in my care, I understand your decisions. I understand why you're doing this, why you'll come back one day. I'll get over my issues with the country by the time we have to worry about it and come back with you. I hate it, hate what this place continues to do to you, but I understand it." With a yawn, he stood.

"I'm going to make a bed somehow and get some sleep. With people coming after us and willing to kill, we should have watches."

"Yeah. I'll leave you to it." I got up as well, walking straight for him. "Sleep well."

"I'll try," he said with a sad chuckle as he looked around.

I reached up and pulled his face toward mine.

"I love you," I whispered.

"I love you." He leaned closer, not fighting me.

Giving him a lingering kiss, I left the courtyard, then the house, needing to explore farther and patrol for anyone who had potentially followed us.

Being in this place gave me no peace. Raphael's words

did, his understanding and his openness to share his experiences as a ruler. I never forgot how we had been in painfully similar situations, but sometimes, I forgot he'd ruled the other cambions for years before I knew him. That he'd been in charge during his time in the lab, on his own, and with everyone against him and his kind. He'd not only ruled, he'd orchestrated a plan of escape and potential rescue, even though it had gone wrong. I met him during a time of confusion for him, a crucial piece of him missing.

He'd made similar choices I had to make, and knowing he understood them...

Meant the world to me.

I strolled grounds I barely knew anymore, sadly leaving my thoughts of my mate behind as I confronted the problems at hand.

"Maybe being exposed is a good thing," I mumbled, stopping at the southern wall, so far from the house, I couldn't see it. "Maybe I don't need to find Rama. What if she hears about someone who looks like her and her father running around with a snake woman? She would be interested in a mating like her own, wouldn't she?" I shook my head at the wall, my invisible conversational partner. "No. Exposure is going to be terrible, and I can only hope there's nothing clear going public. I should call my people and warn them about what's going to happen and why. The cambions, too." Tilting my head to the side, I kept walking beside the wall.

"But a message to Rama, something loud that's bound to reach her? It could work. Her family, even." I focused on them, trying to think of information just about them.

"Sohan might be protective and secretive, but he wasn't a fool. He stayed clear of the nagas, but he wouldn't abandon his own people... would he?" Part of me considered he might just do that. He was so secretive, he might not have heard of the existence of the cambions, even now. So, I moved on to her mother, needing to voice my thoughts to no one.

"Lalika was sweet, but she followed his lead about everything... except Vrindavan. He hadn't wanted her there, but she had gone to help her daughter and son-in-law. She wouldn't abandon them." Chuckling sadly, I stopped again, running a hand through my hair at the distant and fuzzy memories of conversations I hadn't been there for. "I'm neither of those."

Finding the cambion family of my memories seemed impossible. Tears filled my eyes at the futility. I didn't know why I was trying to do this. There had to be other ways, and now, I had other problems.

"I should deal with the rakshasa first," I said, shaking my head. "Just lie in wait for Garuda to show his face again, then track him back to wherever he's hiding and whatever he's doing. Why the hell am I chasing ghosts?" Snorting, I leaned on the wall, looking toward the main house, knowing exactly why this idea had stuck out to me so much.

He wanted me to.

Not Raphael—Adhar. My crutch had wanted me to do this, and it was a possible way forward. Those two men had put this stupid idea in my head, and I couldn't shake it. Knocking it out while also dealing with Garuda seemed perfect. Rama would definitely know how to get to Ramanaka, and Raphael would get to meet some of his own kind who had lived as cambions for thousands of years.

Maybe that's why I shouldn't have been so stupid. This would never work. It's too perfect to be possible.

Now, I was in India, and my course was set, with some detours I had to deal with.

Yeah, that's what we'll do. Deal with the detours. The rakshasa are clearly still a problem, and I need to handle that problem if I want to travel safely. I can't really do anything if they follow me around the whole fucking country, with a bone to pick and not one worry about secrecy.

And my mother's secrets... I can't believe she didn't destroy them and can't believe my father didn't force her to do it or do it behind her back. It's insane they kept that shit here behind a fucking magically locked door.

Not only did she leave it... she left it for me to fix. Damn her!

I slammed a fist against the stone wall and hissed as pain ran through my hand and arm, all the way to my shoulder.

"Fucking gods damn it," I snarled as I continued walking.

I was angry, so fucking angry. As I walked, it grew as I kept going back to that. She ruined my life. She destroyed the family. She brought the enemy's attention straight to us, and got herself, my father, and my brothers killed. For what? For knowledge that wouldn't help her gain anything or help our people. There was no damn reason I could think of that made any sense.

If only time travel was possible. I'd fucking love to go back and give her a damn piece of my mind. Tell her she can't do this to me. To any of us.

I did two laps around the entire estate, and by the time the sun was up, I was walking back inside. The time had done nothing to improve my mood. I was still seeing red as I thought about her and that damn room. Raphael was already up, and I could feel him moving around the courtyard. As I walked into the main area, he turned in my direction with a smile that quickly fell.

"What's wrong?" he asked immediately.

"Just frustrated about things I can't fix or change," I answered, shaking my head in defeat and dismissal of the topic.

"Maybe you should take a few deep breaths. You're lighting up the room in red." Clearly, he was trying to be diplomatic by not telling me to calm down or get over it, only to take some deep breaths.

I looked at myself and saw the red cambion magic swirling around me, giving me an interesting glow. He was right. I was making the room red.

I sagged against a wall, frustrated but now with myself.

"Damn. I could have been a beacon of light for anyone passing by," I said, groaning as I put my head in my hands. The light faded as the magic subsided. "Seeing that room, thinking about it... it just pisses me off, Raphael. I'm sorry."

"Then let's go deal with it, so it doesn't piss you off anymore." He came to my side and held out a granola bar. Taking it, I smiled, but it fell flat, as it had before.

"Having to deal with it is what's pissing me off. Well,

part of it. She just left it here, locked away. She didn't even think she did something so fucked up that maybe she should… get rid of it."

"Maybe she couldn't let go because she had dedicated her life to it," he countered, but not in an argumentative tone. I would have been fine with an argument if he wanted one. Instead, there was sadness from him that made me pity her. "She had done all this work, already damaged one of her children. She probably hoped she could turn it around. There's this thing called the sunk cost fallacy."

"I know what it is," I mumbled, closing my eyes. "Lived my life by it sometimes. I would tell myself, I've already come this far, already crossed this line. What's going to change if I take another step? Who's going to be surprised when I cross the next line?" I snorted, hating how I used to do that. I got people hurt, so many people. Sure, I had done good and had good reasons, which I'd had to hold them close to my heart for years since no one believed me. No one had believed in me for a century, and when they finally did, it was too late.

His words made me see her a bit differently. I didn't want to, but maybe she had held on, hoping she could fix things.

Maybe didn't cut it in my world anymore, though. Not with her.

"What do you want to do, Kaliya? This is your mission. I'm muscle, advice when you need it, and support no matter what, but I can't read your mind, no matter how much I want to." He waited, and I sighed.

"Let's go deal with this. I think we should take care of

these side problems first. We'll contact home while we do this. After this, we need to go back out there and figure out what the hell is going on with the rakshasa. We'll use this as a home base while we deal with them."

"Are you sure? It's a hell of a distraction from your mission to get to Ramanaka and Garuda. I know you didn't want to be distracted. We can avoid them. I mean, it's more dangerous to avoid them and let them strike later, but it's an option. We'll just be more careful, use our fake names and papers when needed, stay out of populated areas."

"They're a problem and are okay with getting in the way. They're okay with the risk. We should shut it down for the good of all three of us and the future. I had really hoped we were done dealing with them, but..." I shrugged. "They're not done with us, and leaving them for later is asking for more trouble. You're not wrong about that."

"I don't like seeing you thrown off your game," he said as he walked toward the fucking door. Since I was in the house, it was there, clear as day. I followed him, not sure what to tell him.

"I haven't been on my game since Pavan got the jump on me," I explained. "I shouldn't have trusted him in snake form. Should have known he would betray—"

"Please, fucking woman, do not start blaming yourself for that," he growled, his exasperation clear. "Not a single fucking person, even those close to him, thought anything was off or wrong. Believe me, I interrogated every one of them while you were fighting for your fucking life. Pavan was standoffish with you, but he wasn't with everyone else. They all thought he just needed more time to adjust and come to his own terms with you. No one thought he was plotting your damn assassination. He admitted he wasn't until he was set off when Aamir made peace with you. How the fuck were you supposed to know? Can you see the future?"

I stood in stunned silence as Raphael grabbed the doorknob and threw it open, hard enough to slam it into the wall.

"No," I finally said. "I can't see the future."

"Then this discussion is over. No one blames you. Don't blame yourself." He looked into the room and snarled. "Let's deal with the legacy your mother left us."

16

CHAPTER SIXTEEN

We pulled out journal after journal, tome after tome, artifact after artifact. Everything was piled into the courtyard, where we could deal with it without inhaling a century's worth of dust.

I started sorting while Raphael called home. Cassius answered the house phone, Sorcha close by. Before any real conversation started, Cassius asked him to wait a moment, and the line was silent. Raphael turned on our webcam, and I saw Sorcha rolling her eyes when she saw me.

"Most dusty books to fight over?" she asked, trying to lighten the mood and make us smile. "And where are you? An ancient temple? Do you want Cassius to send anyone? We can do that with the snap of our fingers."

"No," I answered. "My mother's journals. We're at my childhood home."

She was silent, her sympathy evident. I shrugged one shoulder at her, understanding her sudden silence, before turning back to what I was dealing with—sorting and trying to decide if I should just get rid of all of it.

"We've hit a bump, but as I said to Cassius, I don't want to repeat this three times. Getting everyone together for an emergency meeting and check-in so we can focus on solutions is what we need right now." Raphael was diplomatic and pragmatic with our friend.

"Of course," Sorcha agreed gracefully, then I heard a very unladylike groan. "I wish I could do something. After everything, I can't even imagine what sort of trouble you've already run into."

"The rakshasa are continuing to be a thorn in our ass. I would love your help, but you know how these things go," I said, sighing heavily as I tossed a journal into the burn pile. It had been my mother's research into reincarnation and how other cultures tried to discover their past lives. "This is a problem that involves one specific, tiny piece of the world, where fae have no natural reach. If you get involved, you could give your people an enemy they don't deserve. The rakshasa could see the actions of a Sidhe noble as a reason to attack Sidhe or fae, and the weakest of your people might as well be human in some respects. They grow old and die. They aren't physically powerful, and the rakshasa are supernaturals they probably don't know exist, and if they did, it would only be by name or myth."

"I know it's the responsible choice for all of us," Sorcha said softly. "And I would tell you the same if Cassius and I faced something from the fae or had to fight for our people. Your people are vulnerable, so vulnerable, and I would never dream of asking for your help if it could risk their safety and future."

I nodded, believing in my choice to leave friends at home and glad she continued to agree. It was hard to leave strong allies behind, but this was my battle, and I wasn't going to risk anyone else. I wouldn't open a can of worms on people who didn't ask for it. My people? They knew the fight. It was theirs as much as it was mine. The cambions? They were key to this, even if they didn't ask for it. They also had complete faith there was nothing this world could throw at them they couldn't defeat.

"But it doesn't stop the hurt of not being there for you once again," she continued.

"No, it doesn't," I agreed, closing my eyes. "But these are the decisions of the powerful, where we have to put others before ourselves, think of the needs for many instead of the wants for one. At least, the decisions we have to make if we want to do some good in the world and leave something better behind." I smiled over my shoulder, knowing it probably appeared sad. "This is what we all get for being damn good at what we do and being recognized for it."

"It is." Sorcha smiled back before looking away, a jerky motion to look at something out of sight. "Right on time." She stood up and stepped back from the camera. "Cassius, maybe you can use that other camera? And the television?"

"Of course," he agreed off-screen. "One moment, Kaliya, Raphael."

"Take your time," Raphael said, leaning back to kiss my cheek, then press his lips to my ear. "How did you become one of the most mature people I've ever met?" he teased.

"I always was. You just refused to recognize my greatness," I retorted, then chuckled. "No, I've just learned to be smarter, to take it all more seriously, not that I wasn't serious before. I just had... a different way of thinking about my priorities and how to approach getting what I want might be the best way to describe it."

"It looks good on you," he murmured, kissing me again. I turned around fully to look at the laptop and lean on my mate. I could still reach my pile of books, tomes, journals, and notebooks to sort. The artifacts were for later.

On-screen, Mahavir and Vikrant stood on one side of Cassius and Sorcha, and Mateo stood on the other. I looked at Mateo a little differently now, knowing he had helped Raphael with the plan to escape, and the initial idea had been his. From training with him, I knew he was methodical and highly intelligent. There was a reason he stood there as Raphael's right-hand man.

Without beating around the bush, Raphael and I explained our arrival in India and the events since.

"Getting to Vrindavan was easy," he said after we got past the small events at the airport. "But it's not really for me to say." He gave me a sideways look.

I could hear his questions without him needing to voice them.

Should I tell them about Krishna? Would it only scare them? They didn't need to know about what had happened between me, the god, and the kadamba tree.

Telling Raphael is the reality of mating, but...

"It was uneventful," I said, shrugging. "Personal. We came back to New Delhi and checked into a hotel, then worked on our plans for finding the other cambions, considering our options. We went to bed early, thanks to the traveling. We were attacked by the rakshasa in the middle of the night. That's how we ended up here, my home. It was the closest safe location I could think of. Probably safe, at least." I looked around, seeing the rubble that was my childhood home. "We'll see if it's still fairly unknown in the coming days. If we're attacked again, we'll let you know."

Raphael broke down the attack, from the beginning when he woke up to see me taking care of the assassin to the end. Neither of us had to press the seriousness of the issue. A heavily monitored human establishment in a country where we had little to no backup? It was all severities of bad news.

"Fucking *asura*," Vikrant hissed. I cleared my throat, and Vikrant sent an apologetic look at Mateo. Asura, in some translations, was akin to a demon. Enough of the world used it that way, it was worth considering when using it in a room with cambions. Asura certainly was always used to mean an evil or malevolent being. I wouldn't have anyone call my cambions that. "Forgive me. I just don't understand their reasoning behind yet another attack and certainly one so..."

"Forgiven. We're worried this will interfere with my hunt for Garuda, so we're going to handle it while we're here. We'll deal with some stuff here and the rakshasa, then turn our focus back to the hunt for Garuda."

“What are you dealing with at home?” Cassius asked perceptively.

“I would also like to know,” Mahavir added, nodding in Cassius’ direction.

“Just my mother’s mess,” I answered without details. “Nothing I will let impact the future of our people. Things to burn and ashes to throw into the wind.”

The intelligent minds I was trying to sidestep realized I was keeping so much from them. Thoughtful, confused, wary, all of them except one. Cassius had a small smile, the only one with a clear understanding in his eyes. He’d known me the longest and understood the decision. I had something important, and I was letting it go, which would have been impossible only a year ago.

“Let me know if there’s anything you want me to get for you,” Cassius finally said, breaking the silence. “But if it all must go, then it all must go.”

“There might be some. I’ll send you the coordinates when it’s time,” I promised.

“What is it?” Mahavir asked. “What mess did your mother leave?”

“One we’ll never make again for as long as I’m the queen,” I answered, standing up and moving. The move showed them the piles of journals and tomes. “This is the research and notes my mother made before she unlocked the memories of my previous life. This is the recording of how she and a witch researched and did the spell, then studied how it changed me. Somewhere, there’s probably a journal about how they locked the memories away again. Dangerous knowledge we’ll never see again, not in my lifetime, not in my rule.”

"We could become powerful again. Like you," Vikrant whispered. Mahavir's strong nod told me he agreed.

"Exactly. Why destroy it? We could find better ways to use it."

"These books? These spells? They didn't make me powerful. They ruined my life. They got my mother, father, brothers, aunt, and cousin killed. They got Vikrant's sister killed. They nearly destroyed this community." I looked at the books, then back at the screen.

"You wanted me as queen. This is what you get. We will find other ways. We will persevere without this. Every piece of knowledge demands a price, and I will not make the nagas pay the price of this knowledge ever again. Nor will I let others attempt to reckon with these forces. My mother left this to *me*. This is *my* legacy. And I will it see it burned."

If I had to be the wall between my people and the forces that would destroy them, I would. I would fight Garuda every day in endless war. I would defend against the siege of the rakshasa.

I wouldn't allow my mother's secrets to hurt them again, no matter how tempting the hidden knowledge seemed to be.

"Then what made you powerful?" Mahavir asked; his question was valid.

I didn't have an answer that would help my argument. I didn't know how the path of my life would have changed without my mother's experiment, her mistake. Would I still have mated a cambion, or was my future connected to the past, thanks to her? Would I have still fought Garuda in the end? Would I have discovered a different way to shift?

Those questions weighed on me as I tried to answer him.

"Hard work," Cassius answered for me. "Years of training and dedication made her more powerful than you."

"Exactly," Raphael agreed. "She was always more powerful than the other nagas, even before she mated me, and you can't choose your mate. Not even her mother could have done that."

"Well, mating a cambion had a hand in it," I said, grinning at my mate.

"Maybe," Raphael said, shrugging one shoulder, a twinkle in his eye. "But the fact is, your skill and your intelligence are your power, and you didn't get those from magic."

"All right, back on topic. We'll handle this stuff and the rakshasa. This was supposed to be a fast check in and—"

I heard a cry from off the screen and stopped mid-sentence. I knew that cry. Knew it too well.

17

CHAPTER SEVENTEEN

"Sorry. Eshika has been taking walks with Roshni, trying to get her to settle, and I didn't think to tell her not to come this way," Mahavir said, leaving my view.

"They can come in. I would love to see her," Raphael said softly, and it felt like claws wrapped around my heart, sinking in the vital organ. If I wasn't careful, those proverbial claws would tear the entire thing out.

A moment later, Mahavir was leading in Eshika, a bundle in her arms, little fists fighting the air, then we heard a wail.

"Roshni," I said gently, leaning down to see her better. The laptop screen was suddenly too small. I wanted her on a big screen, every detail clear. "It's going to be okay."

The baby stopped wailing as I spoke, and Eshika gave me the most wonderful smile as she moved Roshni to see me on the screen.

"I thought we talked about this," I said to the baby, trying not to tear up but completely unconcerned about looking like a fool to the room of adults who knew

Roshni was an infant. “Behave for Eshika while I’m gone. When I’m back, we can do whatever you want.”

Roshni’s expression was comical. Her little mouth was in an O, her eyes wide as she stared at my face on the screen before her, then she broke out into giggles, and her arms flailed.

I remembered the too few times I had seen her mother smile and laugh.

“Thank you,” Eshika said as she bounced Roshni in her arms. “She’s been hard to get down for naps or to bed, but she’s eating and staying in human form. We’re looking at the positives. Maybe seeing you and Raphael will help her settle tonight. Do you think we could do this again?”

“Mahavir will let you know when we call. We can’t promise a schedule, but you can step into any conversation. We won’t mind.” I blinked and pulled back, looking at the things I had to do. Right now, so many things in my life made this world too dangerous for her. I had to get back to her and couldn’t waste time. “We should probably get back to work. We have a lot to do, and if we get it done, we can get back sooner.”

“Of course,” Sorcha murmured. “Be safe.”

“Will do.” I reached out and hit the key to end the connection.

“We could have talked for a moment longer,” Raphael said.

I couldn’t decipher his mood. I was already walking away, needing fresh air before I could work again, and I didn’t have an argument. He could have talked longer, but I wouldn’t have been able to focus.

"I need to breathe," I snapped, going toward the closest door to the outside, my lungs feeling paralyzed.

Catching up to me, his hand hit the door before I could open it, keeping it shut as I yanked on the handle.

"Clearly, we need to talk about something." Gently, ever so gently, his other hand touched my arm. "You face the enemy as though you're indestructible. You see a sheer cliff and believe you can climb it. You look at the impossible and wonder how it could be done." His lips touched my ear. "But you just ran away from a *baby*."

No, that's not what happened.

"If that's how you want to see it." I turned around, knowing he had me effectively trapped if I didn't cheat and shift into another form. One massive arm blocked me to the left, holding the door closed. His free hand found a new rhythm to touch me, fingers making a trail of goosebumps on my arm, up and down slowly, an ever-present reminder he wasn't a threat to me. His demand to talk was because he loved me, and I would be an idiot if I didn't know that.

"That's how everyone on the call probably sees it," he said carefully, his tone shifting from concerned and demanding to more cautious as I just revealed a tiny portion of how much he and everyone on the call had misunderstood me.

"I'm sure." Nodding, I looked around him at the laptop still on the floor. "Actually... no. There are three people in the world who know me better than that. Two of them were on that call. The last one is standing right in front of me." I met his eyes. "You know me better than that. I'm hurting, Raphael. I'm not scared *of* Roshni. I am scared *for* her. Every step I take is for her, for all of them." I lifted my hands and stretched out my arms. "I have never felt more vulnerable, yet I have to do the impossible. So, when I am reminded of everyone relying on me, I feel a bit overwhelmed, okay? Because it's a lot, okay?"

"I understand—"

I was sure he did, but I wasn't done.

"I feel guilty I'm the reason she's an orphan. For the first time in my life, the answer was right in my fucking face, and I was *blind*. Knowing I failed her like that just makes me want to work *harder*. The problem is I can't work when I'm bleeding out from a wound, and I can't put a bandage on. There is *nothing* you can say, nothing Sammy, Mahavir, Cassius, or Sorcha could say, that would change my opinion of what happened, but I can stop it from happening again, and I will." I put a hand on my chest. "I didn't run from her, but right now, in this house..."

I walked out of his reach, waving around at the ruin around us. A once happy home left to rot as its inhabitants were crushed by the weight of the world. The story of too many homes, too many families.

"I didn't need a reminder that there's another orphan who needs me. An orphan who needs me not to make the mistakes my mother and even Adhar made with me. It was a little too much for me. So, I just want to take a breather, then get back to work."

I felt lighter when I was done, my chest not so tight, my shoulders relaxed.

He stepped away from the door. We maintained eye

contact until he turned and went to our things in the middle of the courtyard.

Instead of escaping, I followed him and went to one knee at his side. We got back to work together, working through the day, then by firelight. When we were finally done, our campfire was trying its best to consume everything we had thrown into its flames.

"Sorry I blew up," I told my mate after the long day. We had spoken about the small things we found. I didn't read through every page of the journals. I didn't want to. We looked for references to what she had been doing, and if we found even one, it was tossed into the fire. When Cassius picked up what remained, I would give him clear instructions to do the same. I could trust him with it.

However, through the day, I hadn't said the most important thing and had to take the chance to do it now.

"Nothing to be sorry for. I'm glad you did," he said, stretching his legs out. "You'd bottle it up for months if I let you. Emotions take time for you, especially the hard ones, and normally, I'm okay with giving you time to process them before prying. Not everyone can wake up and be comfortable with what they feel every day. I'm lucky that way. You're not. That's just who we are."

I sat beside him, stretching my legs out and purposefully throwing one of mine over his.

"Then why did you this morning? Why pry?"

"It's going to sound ridiculous."

I could see his smile in the firelight, the dopey smile I knew all too well.

"Raph, nothing you can say would sound ridiculous."

"I already love her. I know it's been only a couple of weeks taking care of her, but I really love that girl," he said, turning to me. Even with his face half-shadowed, I could see his dopey smile grow wider for a moment. "You have a voice, and she doesn't. I love fighting with you and… sometimes against you as we try to keep understanding each other. I love that we can talk. We promised each other a fresh slate, and we did it. I know tomorrow, you will still be my mate, and I will always have you standing beside me, no matter what happens to us, no matter what the world throws our way, no matter what we throw at each other. And you know that about me… I hope."

"I know. You've proven it. You were there for me, even when I didn't want you to be. I was the one who walked away. That you have that faith in me…"

"Again, we gave each other that new start."

"We did," I said, smiling. "And I won't walk away again."

"Well, if you tried, I am more than powerful enough to drag you back kicking and screaming." His grin fell away. "But who does she have? She can't tell people how she feels. She can't tell us what she needs. The people who knew and understood her are gone. Saranya would have known exactly what every cry meant and exactly how Roshni wanted to be held. We don't have any of that.

"We're shallow replacements, but we're all she has. I don't know what she'll remember as she gets older, but I don't want it to be us *leaving*. Her parents, through no fault of anyone, are gone. I don't want her to think we're gone, too." Raphael turned back to the fire. "I just want her to believe we will always be there for her. You jumped off the call, and all I could think was how she might remember that. So, I decided to be... her advocate. Decided to pry because in this situation, who was going to look out for her except me?"

"You wanted to be her protector," I whispered, feeling those claws sink a little farther into my heart. "She'll love you for it. One day, she'll be able to tell you that." I put my head on his shoulder.

"It's one reason I was angry at the hotel," he admitted. "We left her behind with Eshika, with nothing to go on when we got here. We could have stayed, had more time with her."

"I..."

"I'm okay. It was temporary anger, and I'm over it. We'll get through this and go back. Maybe this was also your way of finding the time and space you need to process the things you feel." Raphael wrapped an arm around me.

"Maybe." All I knew was that it was time. There were things in this country I had to do. I made promises to myself and my people and had to see them through. I wouldn't leave this life until I finished my business.

Garuda was my business.

We watched the fire together.

"We should get some sleep tonight," he said quietly.

"We should." I had no more energy now that I'd sat down and leaned on him. He was warm, and he was everything. Even as I grappled with feelings I couldn't always handle, he was steady and was there for me.

Leaning on him, I knew I could relax, and my body did just that.

"But someone has to keep watch," I mumbled after too long.

"I'll do it," he promised. "I nap through the hottest part of the day, remember? I'm still feeling pretty awake for a patrol."

I could only nod.

He moved one of the bags behind me, and I used it as a pillow, letting my eyes close.

He loves her. Of course, he does. I already knew that.

And it's totally fine.

I...

18

CHAPTER EIGHTEEN

When my eyes opened, the sun was already up. Still early enough to be right after dawn, but it shocked me enough to make me sit up.

"Raphael?" I called out.

I slept through the whole night. Where's my mate? He should have come to get me. We should have switched. I should have been up hours ago.

I got up, feeling the bond we shared, and used it to point me. Walking out of the house into the wooded grounds that were the estate, I found him at the north wall, letting out a long breath as I approached him.

"Why didn't you wake me?" I demanded.

"You were exhausted, physically and emotionally." He had dark rings under his eyes, but he seemed alert otherwise. "I had planned to be finished with this patrol and get back before you woke up, but..." He shrugged.

"Well, go get some sleep!" I ordered, pointing at the house. "You could have switched with me."

He chuckled as he headed in the direction I ordered,

not arguing. Knowing he had been up all night for me, I smiled at the back of his head.

"I love you," I called.

"I know," he called in return over his shoulder.

Shaking my head once he was gone, I looked around. We'd finished with what we found here, and it was time to move again. We needed to load back into the car and head into Delhi once again, this time looking for trouble. I took a moment to consider what that trouble would be before walking back to the house. Even though I was only moments behind Raphael, he was already asleep.

I changed into fresh clothes, then packed us up as much as I could as quietly as I could. We had to get back to the city to deal with the rakshasa. If they had been in the city to attack me, some were still there looking for me. I wanted to find them and beat out the answers I needed to stop this unnecessary fighting between our kinds.

I also took the quiet time as a chance to email Cassius. I explained that Raphael and I had done the preliminary work and that I would send the information he needed once we were clear of the house. I didn't want him to be in the area while I still was. I wasn't looking to get the fae tangled up with this, just as I had told Sorcha. He replied faster than I expected, only telling me he was making sure his people were ready whenever I was and good luck.

While using the laptop, I also emailed Paden. It was a long shot, but I asked him to reach out to anyone who might have a friend of a friend of a friend who understood the political situation in India and where I could get to the Market from here. I knew there was a door but had never used it. He messaged me back quickly as well, telling me he would call everyone he knew for the second request, and he was pretty sure he could find it easily. He made no promises about the first. As I had known for a long time, it was hard for those outside the subcontinent to get news about what happened inside it. I told him I expected nothing, but his help was appreciated. It felt good to know he was at my back again, even if it was at a distance.

It was nearly noon when Raphael awoke. I had already loaded the car and hid the remaining pieces of my mother's things for Cassius to get later. My mate and the remnants of the fire were all that was left in the courtyard. Using my phone, with its two bars of service, I tried to figure out where supernaturals might hang out in the city.

"Have a quick breakfast. Stretch. I already have us ready to move out except for that last bag." I was leaning on a nearby pillar, smiling as my mate rubbed his eyes. "If you want to change, do it now."

"Are you sure you want to leave completely? We could use this as a safe house while dealing with the rakshasa. I still like that idea," he said, with a yawn breaking up one of the sentences.

"Cassius will need to come here or send his people, which means we can't risk it getting out. If the rakshasa follow us later, it won't be safe for his team. We got lucky they didn't have more people to follow us at the hotel, and I had already cleared our ride of bugs."

"Give me... thirty minutes," he decided as he stood up. "I'll be awake enough to leave soon."

"I'll be waiting," I said with a grin, feeling better today. He gave me a look. "Patiently, I promise. More than likely, Delhi will be an all-night adventure."

The good night's sleep was the source of my good mood, and I knew I had my mate to thank. It also felt as if I was finally going to do something today. It wasn't what I had come to India for, but it was a problem to be solved. I would solve it tonight, and the supernaturals of Delhi wouldn't know what hit them.

They shouldn't have taken me up on my dare. They should have realized I wasn't in the fucking mood for their bullshit.

While he got dressed, I doubled checked everything.

This would be the last time I saw this place, my childhood home. When I gave him directions, I would ask Cassius to leave nothing behind. I knew I would never come back, and the risk of leaving that room, even emptied, posed too much of a threat.

I shook my head as I walked the halls, knowing it was just an excuse to see it all gone.

The place was steeped in grief. I could practically feel it oozing from the walls that still stood as if they remembered what they had seen that day. A family torn to pieces. Lives ruined, then wiped from existence. A place once full of smiles was now rotting under the weight of the trauma it had been forced to carry for so long.

Just like me.

I caught the strangeness, comparing myself to a house.

First a tree, now a house. At least the tree was alive, but I really should stop finding inanimate objects relatable. Raphael will wonder if I'm losing my mind.

I have to raze this place.

'No, not destroy it. That's the wrong way to think about it.

I wanted to give this space *peace*, the way I searched for it every day. A fresh start like I fought for now. If I took away this place so full of memories, the wilds could reclaim the area. In two hundred years, maybe I could come back, but it would be a new beginning for it.

I wanted a future that wasn't haunted by the past. It was the same reason I went to Vrindavan and apologized to the kadamba tree.

I touched my door as I passed it but didn't stop.

Maybe this is what healing is.

I wasn't healed. It was never a goal I had worked to achieve. The idea of healing was for people who didn't have to fight every day, who didn't live in my world, with its dangers around every corner.

As I left the dark, decrepit halls, I didn't feel as though I was injured by a wound I couldn't see anymore or feel as if my feelings should have left me limping. A small ache that would probably never go away, but nothing fatal. Not from this place, not from what happened here.

I didn't see my mate as I stared into space, soaking in this last moment, but I could feel him coming back into the courtyard. He had been walking as well, though I figured it wasn't for the same reason. Getting the blood flowing was a good way to wake up, and I knew there was no modern bathroom in the house.

"I'm ready," he told me as he gave me a drive-by kiss.

"Me, too." I went to grab the last bag, the one that had been his pillow, but he grabbed it first. We walked together out of the courtyard, then I unlocked the gate and let him drive out. He was switching seats as I made sure the locks reengaged once I closed the gate.

"Kaliya?" he called out softly.

I looked over my shoulder to see him standing by the car door, waiting for me to head over before he got back in.

"Sorry. Just…" I looked back at the estate, the once-impossibly tall gate between us. "Just trying to say goodbye."

"We're not coming back on this trip, but one day—"

"We're never coming back. It won't be here. My family loved me, my father, my brothers. My mother made mistakes and did something without understanding the consequences, but she loved me. You were right to remind me of that. It's enough, and I don't need this place to know that. I don't need it to remember the good days. I don't need it to remember the bad ones."

"It's your family's home," he said softly, and I heard his yearning for something I couldn't give him.

"A family that's been gone for over a hundred years, Raphael. It's a piece of the past. My future is with you, in a different country, with different people. A new family, one who knows who I am now. It's not here, where a girl I don't recognize once played with wooden toys and tried to sword fight in a sorry excuse for training. There's no future here."

"I just don't want you to look back and regret losing it."

Walking to the car, a response built as I got in and put my seatbelt on. I methodically checked everything to make sure my mate hadn't moved the seat to a position I didn't like. He had, so I had to fix everything.

He got in and waited in silence.

"A year ago, I would have opened every one of those journals and read every page. I would have believed I couldn't be happy or at peace without every answer those pages provided." I started the bumpy drive back to the road. "When we met, I would have considered taking back my childhood home as a victory, entrenching myself in the pain of being there alone. I would have believed I was winning by surrounding myself in painful memories." I gave him a smile. "Because I didn't know a life without endless and unbearable pain was even possible. I do now. So no, I won't regret losing it."

"Okay." I wasn't sure he understood yet, but he didn't have another argument.

I drove back to the road and turned toward Delhi. Thirty minutes into the drive, my phone buzzed, and I let Raphael check it.

"Paden says he knows where the Market door is. He's provided an address and the way to use it to get into the Market. When did you decide we needed to go to the Market? Aren't we still banned?"

"Yes, but we're not going to the Market. We're going to use the location as a trap to talk to some locals."

"Ah. I have a feeling no one is going to like that." Raphael didn't sound all that worried.

"Then they shouldn't have pissed me off." I tightened my hand on the steering wheel.

19

CHAPTER NINETEEN

It was nearly seven when I parked. Raphael got out first. The moment we had entered the city, we went on high alert. He was the more durable, so getting out and being seen first was better for us both. Even better, I was fairly certain most people didn't know what he looked like yet, while I stood out in a bad way.

My hair going white way too young had made sure I would never blend into a crowd. I was certain there wasn't a supernatural on the subcontinent who didn't know about the white-haired naga who ran away to America and worked for the Tribunal. I had made a splash over the century for a reason. If I couldn't blend in, I would be scary enough for people to leave me be—most people. My job as an Executioner often had very little to do with *most* people. I kept the enemies of my people off my back for the most part but had gained others.

Raphael was still largely unknown in most circles. A young supernatural ruler of a newly established species, people might have heard of him because it was big news, but he wasn't so established that everyone would know his face. As my mate, my partner, people would look out for him, but it was still easier to deal with than my white hair that could be spotted from a mile away.

It made him the right choice to get out first to scope the area before I followed.

He tapped the hood, and I got out and looked around. For the first time since I came to the country, I went to the back and put on my weapons, but nothing obvious—a dagger in each of my boots and one on my back, hidden by my shirt, which was loose enough not to give anything away. I wouldn't be caught by something sharp again. Raphael only took a handgun, unceremoniously shoving it in the waistband of his pants at his lower back.

"Really?" I was putting on a headscarf as I looked at him, trying to cover my hair as best I could. I felt a little bad for doing it when I didn't meet the requirements of wearing one for any of the religions practiced by humans in the country, but I needed to do something about my blasted hair. The ghoonghat was a head-and-face covering worn by some Hindi and Sikh married women. I was mated, not married, a distinction I thought was important. I also didn't want to cover my entire face. I wasn't a Muslim, so wearing the headscarf as a hijab felt *wrong*. I only had so many options, and safety was paramount.

"You know I'm really only effective in close quarters. If I have a chance to get some range, I need to take it," he said, shrugging. "Just like Sammy and Mateo, who have options for the same problem. I won't be a demon here," he reminded me in a low whisper. "I'm not in the mood to be a science experiment again or to accidentally start a nuclear war as the humans try to kill me."

"Of course. It's just that... Normally, we're not held back by those things. I just wasn't thinking for a moment." I stopped fussing with the headscarf, deciding I didn't care what it looked like. Pulling it a little over my forehead, it created shade for my eyes if I needed it.

"No, we're not," he agreed. "Are you done playing around with that, or..."

"I'm done," I mumbled.

Heading toward the door to the Market, we took a roundabout route, trying to stay out of sight and make people think we weren't headed there. I wished I knew what the network of information was like in this city the way I knew Phoenix. Every time someone from any organization saw me moving around the city, I knew they reported it to their boss. If a vampire from the Phoenix nest saw me, word was sent to Imani, the Mistress of the nest. If a werewolf saw me, it was sent to Alpha Wagner. A witch would tell Monica if they were part of her coven.

It wouldn't take long for news from one of them to spread to all of them. I had the legal right to kill people for the government that ruled all of them. I knew they tried to keep an eye on me and were willing to share that information with each other. Often, it would be an exchange of information. Imani would know where I was and would exchange that information with Wagner if he knew whatever I might be working on.

Knowledge is power, but who in this city is willing to talk to who? I knew Imani would never call Monica, who didn't like witches all that much. Wagner might if he wanted something from her, information or spells. What sort of power balance exists here?

The door came into view, a simple door in a small alley. Humans passed it without even thinking, which made me wonder if they could see if or if it was only visible to supernaturals, much like the way the door in my childhood home was spelled to appear when I was in the house. In the middle of a popular bazaar, the streets around us were packed with people on foot, bicycles, and more. Vehicles were stuck in the congestion. Paper, brass idols, and more were being sold all around me. It was loud, the perfect cover for a magical door to a realm created by powerful fae who wanted to barter in illegal goods.

"A Market in a market," I said to myself, shaking my head. "Cute."

"Yeah? Is that where we are?" Raphael looked around. It was pretty clear we were in the middle of a thriving marketplace. I raised an eyebrow at him, and he chuckled.

"Want to know something interesting?" I didn't know if he would consider my knowledge interesting, but we could see the door to the Market, which meant we were now in the waiting game. I didn't want to stand in silence, so fun facts it would be.

"Sure," he answered, crossing his arms.

"I've been trying to retrain my brain. The name of the city is actually Delhi, not New Delhi. New Delhi and Delhi are often used interchangeably, but since we were coming for a more... public visit, I wanted to think about things properly."

"Why is that important?" he asked. "Would anyone care?"

"I have no idea if they would care or not, but it's important because, um, we're actually in Old Delhi right now."

"I see..."

"Right? When I could just zip you through the city, calling it New Delhi didn't seem like a big deal, but we're in the city for a lot of stuff and staying in the country for who knows what, so I figured I needed to establish that mental distinction."

"It is... a somewhat fascinating thing to learn while we kill time waiting for any... people of interest to come by," he admitted. "Do you know the history of the naming?"

"Not well enough," I admitted. "Born in the country, only a quick drive away from the city, yet I'm as much of an uneducated tourist as you."

"Well, not as much. You at least know basics."

I fiddled with the headscarf, not used to wearing something like it.

"Question."

"Answer?"

"Would you consider a mated couple and a married couple the same thing?" It was loud enough, I thought we could get away with the conversation with no one hearing us unless they were paying way too much attention.

He coughed, pounding his chest as he doubled over. I let him get over the shock as I watched for potential supernaturals trying to get to the Market.

When he was standing up straight again, he didn't immediately answer.

"Well?" I didn't want to be pushy, though it took me longer than it should have to realize I had asked him if he thought we should be considered married.

"I, uh, don't know?" he said, rubbing his temples. "Where did that come from?"

"There are things in cultures done by unmarried or married women. I don't know where mated women fall in that."

"I would lean toward marriage, but..."

"The concept feels different, right?" I always thought it had. My parents had been mates, *and* they had been husband and wife. I was raised to think marriage was a ceremony, but mating had none, especially the mating I had with Raphael. There was no ceremony to be found in that basement.

"Yeah, I guess. I might just have an idea of marriage that needs to change. It's always big churches, isn't it? Or a courthouse? Mating feels too... easy, even though I know it's not."

"And the commit thing. Like marriage makes a big deal about the commitment."

"Divorces are a thing," he reminded me.

"Where mating doesn't make a big deal of it, even if it's an unbreakable mate bond like we have. Some supernaturals call their spouse their mate, but there's no magic. They could walk away if they wanted to. The word isn't really misused, but there are different meanings depending on who you are talking to. Marriage, though, means pretty much the same thing everywhere.

Commitment, promising to be with someone forever. It's not forever. It doesn't have to be."

"It's a promise that means something to two people," Raphael agreed softly.

"Mating doesn't require a promise. For those of us with mate bonds like us, it just requires the criteria of the magic to be fulfilled, even without our choice in the matter. It doesn't feel like marriage."

"No, it doesn't, but I don't think it's worse or less than."

"I would never call our relationship less than Cassius and Sorcha's," I promised. "Just different."

"Well, no one can be Cassius and Sorcha. They're so perfect, sometimes I wonder if they weren't actually made for each other, sculpted out of clay or something."

"No one can be Kaliya and Raphael, either."

"I hope not. There doesn't need to be two of us."

Thanks to his look of horror that he'd said that, I couldn't stop a snort of laughter. Trying to be serious again, I didn't look at him. Soon or later, a supernatural would come by or leave the door, and I needed to be ready for that. Licking my lips, I tested the air for any sort, but it was all too much human. It would be easy for humans to cover the tracks of the supernaturals in this kind of area.

"I hope we haven't scared anyone off," I said softly, growing more serious by the moment and resisting the urge to find another topic to kill time. Stakeouts could be boring.

"The sun is still going down. I'm sure someone will

make the mistake of walking too close. If they smell for another supernatural, they'll only smell you."

"A naga isn't exactly normal," I pointed out. "And you stink to the moon cursed."

"But they know it's only you. No other nagas have appeared publicly in what, a few centuries? And just because I stink doesn't mean they'll recognize me as a threat."

"Longer, but you're right. Adhar is the only other exception because he had to go in front of the Tribunal when needed, but those meetings were handled with care," I said with a sigh.

Time ticked by slowly. At nine, wondering if my plan was already ruined, I needed to think of a new play if this didn't work out.

It was closing in on ten when the door to the Market opened, and three supernaturals came out. I didn't bother trying to identify them, just moved to block their path. They were laughing with each other and walked straight up to me. Raphael growled softly as the one in the middle bumped into me, and I didn't move.

"Get out of the way," the one in the middle snarled, looking down his nose at me, then his eyes went wide, and his nostrils flared.

Werewolves. They rely so much on their nose, but this place is so crowded, a lot of human scent probably rubbed off on me.

"My name is Kaliya Sahni," I said with a smile, then pulled back the headscarf, hopefully driving home the point. "You might have heard it before. I'd be surprised if you haven't, but it's polite to give one's name when meeting someone new."

"My mate seems to think everyone has heard her name before. Not that she's wrong to consider it's possible. Her reputation has the habit of preceding her," Raphael said, shifting to stand beside me, shoulder to shoulder. I watched the werewolf's face morph into one of disgust. "I don't appreciate people bumping into her or even touching her. Maybe you should watch where you're going next time."

"What are you going to do about it?" the werewolf finally demanded with all the arrogance of a guy who didn't know who he was talking to when it came to my mate. He definitely recognized me, but he was focused on Raphael and his stink. "Other than offend my nose. Take a fucking bath."

"Make you apologize," Raphael said calmly.

I touched my mate's arm. "Let's play nice," I said to my mate before focusing on the werewolves again. "I just have a few questions."

"We're not answering them," the same werewolf snarled. Since he was doing all the talking, I pinned him as the most dominant in the group. He would decide for the others and was probably the one who knew the most, though lower-ranking werewolves had surprised me before.

"You should. If you do, everyone goes home unharmed. I would like that. I don't want to make this a fight." The thing about werewolves was they needed to tell the truth, and that was the truth. They weren't rakshasa, so I had no reason to bloody them up and make enemies. I just wanted to get a bit of information.

"Oh, really?"

"Yeah. Your nose is telling you I'm telling the truth. Here's another truth for you if that one's not good enough. If you don't answer my questions or if you try to pick a fight,"—I stepped closer—"I only need *one* of you, and *no one* will be going home by the time I'm done."

"Everyone in the city knows you're here. Do you really think you could get away with killing three members of the Delhi Pack?"

"I do, and I will." I nodded. "See, I know your Alpha's bosses. I reminded a werewolf at the airport about this. Looks like your Alpha didn't bother to tell you everything." I smiled wider, knowing my fangs were down and visible. "Those two Alphas might not agree with my choices, but in *this* country, they won't punish me either. Werewolves are the species that doesn't belong. There's a general rule that a supernatural outside of their homeland should respect the natives, and you are no longer a native. Werewolves will never be the most powerful faction in this country."

"Neither will the nagas," he growled.

"Yeah, probably not, but at least I have a chance." I shrugged a shoulder. "If I asked around, I would probably discover humans that become werewolves get the cold shoulder from the native supernaturals. I bet if I told all the other native supernaturals that the werewolves were getting uppity, thinking they were the ones in charge here, I could easily make an army."

He took a step back. It was a completely empty threat,

but not a lie. I had no intention of doing anything of the sort, and I hadn't said I did. It was hypothetical, and the werewolf didn't know that I wouldn't try something of the sort.

"Yeah, I figured as much," I said, crossing my arms. "I've been at this game for a long time, wolf. You're better off answering my questions."

He looked at the two following his lead, then back at me.

"Let them leave, and we'll talk. I can't and won't give you pack secrets, but I'll answer what I can if you spare them."

"Deal."

If I need to know pack secrets, I know how to get them. Besides, if they call for help or backup, I would love to speak to someone more important. If I don't hurt this werewolf, they'll have little reason to hurt me.

And I have Raphael if they pick a fight. They don't have a Raphael.

He nodded to the others, and they turned around, leaving the alley on the other side.

"What do you want to know?" he asked, stepping deeper into the alley, away from the prying eyes of the humans still wandering the bazaar this late.

Finally.

20

CHAPTER TWENTY

"Who is considered in charge of Delhi right now?"

"The pack," he answered, then winced.

"Don't worry, I won't give you a hard time unless you try something stupid," I promised. "Do the rakshasa keep a presence in the city?"

Raphael walked slowly, aimlessly in the alley, looking at things littering the ground, trying not to pay attention.

"On and off. Most of the native supernaturals try to stay out of the bigger cities. *Not* because we pushed them out." His emphasis told me he was trying to make sure I didn't make good on the army threat due to misunderstanding. There was genuine fear in his eyes. "The nagas are probably the most private of the supernaturals, which you probably know, but the others are still pretty secretive. Most don't like that the werewolves are *out* and don't want to risk their own secrecy."

"Of course. That's pretty typical around the world. Witches? Vampires? Fae? Any of those in the city?"

"Vampires and witches, yes. Fae only come to Delhi if they have Market-related business that requires they use our door." He hadn't noticed Raphael had pinned him between us, but he did now. His eyes went wider with the fear of what that could mean for him. He didn't know what Raphael was but realized Raphael was confident enough to be a supernatural, not a stinky human.

"Who is more powerful? Vampires or witches?"

"Witches, definitely witches. They're everywhere. They give the pack a run for our money when it comes to who's actually in charge, but we have more people, and they have issues with keeping everyone on the same page. The vampire nest in the city is small, no more than fifteen or twenty, and as long as they don't kill anyone, we don't care about them."

"As long as they don't kill anyone you'll care about or find," I corrected. "That's the concession made when vampires live in a city. Don't worry. I'm positive they're not mass murderers or anything."

"Kaliya can be a bit..." Raphael trailed off.

"Can I ask a question?" The werewolf kept his eyes on me, but I saw the subtle shift of his body, so his back wasn't entirely to Raphael.

"Sure."

"What is he?"

"A cambion, human-demon hybrid." I remained casual. "Very powerful... very hard to kill. Quite new on the scene and he,"—I pointed to my mate—"is the ruler of the cambions, Raphael Alvarez, Warlord of the

Cambions, mate to the Queen of the Nagas. Anything else?"

"I—"

A phone rang, but it wasn't my ringtone or Raphael's. The werewolf paled, reaching for his. The screen was bright as he lifted it for us to see.

"Who?" I asked.

"My Alpha."

"Answer and put it on speaker. If you don't, I'll take it from you and talk to him myself."

He swiped and answered, luckily before it went to voicemail or the Alpha disconnected. This was a good thing. I would have asked the werewolf to put me in touch with his Alpha to explain I just needed information and no harm was done. I didn't want to piss off more people. Threaten it? Fair game. Make more enemies? Not in the plan.

"Are you safe?" a man asked, sounding a little too young for me to think of him as a powerful Alpha.

"I am, Alpha. They promised to do no harm, and no harm has been done."

"What do they want? And am I on speakerphone?"

"They've been asking about..." He looked at me.

"I wanted to know how the powers that be are stacked up in the city," I explained loudly enough to be picked up. "You're on speakerphone because I told him to put you on speakerphone. I don't plan on killing your wolf. I don't care about your pack. I'm looking for the rakshasa. They picked a fight, and I'm trying to finish it, then get back to more pressing matters."

"You could have come to my office," he snarled, an

annoyed Alpha werewolf who didn't have control over everything that happened.

See it once, see it a thousand times.

"I don't know where that is or how to reach it and didn't feel like asking Callahan or Corissa for a favor for that information. I didn't plan on needing to deal with you." I wasn't too stressed by his annoyance with me. "I don't even know your name."

"Alpha Rahul Varadkar."

"I would say well met, but..." I was in some sort of mood tonight, leaving that on a disrespectful note.

"Are you always like this?"

"Call Adalwin Wagner, the Alpha in Phoenix, Arizona, and find out. He speaks your werewolf language, dominance, and all that. I can give you his number, even."

There was a long silence. I knew enough about werewolves to know Wagner was a name that impressed most, and I wasn't using Wagner for anything he would disagree with. In fact, I had a feeling Wagner would have made the call himself if he knew I was heading into this city and could run into the Alpha here. He would say exactly what I was trying to tell this Alpha. He would say I didn't have the fucking time or patience for werewolf posturing, and not even he could give me a hard time for it.

"Let my wolf go, and I'll answer any questions you may have at my home," Alpha Rahul finally said, his voice a bit more taut, but some of the bluster was gone.

Ah, Wagner, your reputation precedes you. Thank the gods.

"No. I think you can answer the rest of my questions

now. The phone is fine. I'm keeping your wolf with me until we're done."

"I know what happened in April when the rakshasa broke a treaty with you and attacked, everything about the attack down to who died and where it was located."

That part made me take note. That was dangerous intel to know and flaunt.

"I know the rakshasa attacked you on your first night in the city and where they stay while they're in the city. I also know what your mate is and what he can do. If you want information, it should only be said in person. My wolf doesn't need to be part of it. I don't want trouble with you, him, or either of your kind. I only want my wolves safe from the trouble brewing around you."

"Tell me where to go," I said, looking at Raphael. He nodded, confirming he felt confident to take whatever the pack could throw at him if we were betrayed. I had no doubt about that, but his agreement with my choice was always a positive.

"Lakhan, lead them to me. I'll have my second meet you and relieve you," the Alpha said. He hung up, and I was left with the werewolf.

"You figured your friends would call your Alpha," I said, not terribly surprised. He gave me a look, and I raised my eyebrows, trying to figure out what the look was supposed to mean.

"You, the ruler of another supernatural species, show up in the city without warning anyone or telling anyone what you're doing here. Of course, he called our Alpha." He looked at my mate. "Is she daft?"

"No, she expects everyone else to be and is surprised when people aren't," Raphael answered, smiling.

I couldn't help laughing. Tonight was going better than planned. I could stress about meeting this Alpha Rahul Varadkar but didn't worry too much as we walked out of the alley.

Confidence was hard to find in recent days, but dealing with werewolves? It was a necessity, paramount to the success of the meeting. At the very least, I had to project it even if I didn't feel completely confident. Confidence made other predators wary and second-guess their own power. Intimidation, relaxed confidence, teasing behavior—the goal was to make the other person see themselves as the weaker and that they were the only ones who didn't know it.

Some used those techniques to make others feel powerless and helpless, so they would accept whatever abuse came their way. I used them to avoid conflict with those I didn't want to hurt. I didn't know if that was the right way to approach things, but it was what I knew.

"Maybe I'm a bit of a bully," I mumbled to myself as we walked.

"You can be," Raphael confirmed.

Lakhan made a wolfish noise of surprise, clearly not expecting the brutal honesty my mate sometimes had.

"Yeah, I was thinking about how I would rather scare people to avoid having to hurt them," I said lightly. "I would rather be a bit of a bully than actually hurt them. No need for unnecessary bloodshed."

"Honorable bullying... only you could think of it."

Raphael was teasing me, but I chuckled because he

was probably right. Or at least there was no one else who would call it that.

The silence from Lakhan made me think about what I had just said. Even admitting what I was doing, I was acting as if it was easy for me to hurt him, and I was being nice. I couldn't turn it off.

The simple fact was, I wasn't scared of this werewolf, his friends, or even his pack. I was playing nice, although not as nice as I could have been, because I saw no reason to hurt them. I didn't care to make them my friends but was nice enough to keep things from escalating. I wouldn't act scared when I wasn't.

The walk was longer than expected. We weaved down roads and turned through allies. I figured Lakhan was using his normal route, full of shortcuts to avoid potential crowds and the busiest streets. We moved out of the crowded city center into a calmer residential area of the city.

Ah, we're in a rich people's neighborhood. I see. One of those Alphas*... got to have the big house and all of that.*

Lakhan saw the other werewolf before I could, his pace picking up.

Raphael and I kept our pace steady, letting Lakhan get to the other werewolf without us chasing after him. The other werewolf had cool blue eyes, which glowed in the dark as we drew closer. They couldn't be his natural color, not with the way the moonlight reflected off them.

"My name is Kannan, second to Rahul, Alpha of the Delhi Pack," he explained as I stopped only a few feet from him.

"Kaliya Sahni," I said, nodding once. I pointed a thumb at my mate. "Raphael Alvarez."

"Yes, I know. Queen of the nagas and Warlord of the Cambions, respectively. Lakhan, you're dismissed. Go home."

"Thank you, Kannan. Have a good evening." The werewolf jogged in the direction we had just come from.

"I hope he doesn't have to go too far," I said, watching Lakhan disappear. "We could have brought our car and given him a ride here at the least. It's been a hell of a walk, an hour and a half."

"He is not your concern," Kannan warned. "And forgive me, but you seem more than capable of light physical exercise." He lifted his right hand, gesturing to the drive he stood before. "If you would follow me, I will take you to Alpha Rahul."

I knew the game. Sending Raphael and me on a circuitous route here gave them time to prepare. Whether that was for a meeting or a fight was yet to be decided. I was trusting it would be a meeting but was more than aware it could go the other way. Alpha Rahul knew a lot, more than I thought he would.

It also pushed us a little. I wasn't at my best coming back to India, which meant the walk was harder than it would have been a few months ago. I wasn't breathing heavily, but my legs were tired, and we were both sweating. We wouldn't be looking our best for this meeting, that was certain. Or smell our best, but with a cambion in a room of werewolves, they would have been offended by his scent no matter what.

"I must say, the pack wasn't expecting trouble from

the two of you," Kannan said, making conversation as we walked down the long drive toward a mansion.

The grounds were lush, bushes and trees wild in placement, but they weren't. Someone maintained the look of wildness, but there was crucial energy and chaos missing. The home itself was a blend of classic architecture from the area and modern, sharp design concepts.

"We didn't mean for trouble," I said, almost apologetically. "We just wanted some basic information."

"You threatened them," he reminded me.

"It kept them from doing something stupid," I countered.

Kannan gave me a curious look over his shoulder as we turned onto the walkway toward the front door instead of heading in through the garage.

"Is that really what you expect any of us to believe?"

"You can smell a lie," I said with a laugh. "So, you can't use that argument."

He opened the front door in complete silence. I let Raphael enter before me, staying close to his back. We went a few feet inside and waited as Kannan locked the front door once more. He walked past us, down the opulent entryway—everything trimmed with gold details, ornate wood carvings on the side table, a lamp I was offended by, and more. The building dripped wealth.

I saw them as I walked. Werewolves came out of side rooms. Two walked down the main staircase, holding weapons and on alert. I met their stare for a second, then dismissed them, keeping my oozing confidence and lack of fear in the face of the pack. Raphael and I were led into what I could only assume was the central living room for this place. The centerpiece of the room were four black leather couches, positioned in a loose square, with a low coffee table in the middle. The sofas had white and gold pillows, and the table was black, contrasting nicely with the white marble floors and white walls. Even the art lacked vibrant or diverse colors.

There was no missing the werewolves sitting and waiting on Raphael and me. We slowly drew closer, Kannan breaking away from us and heading around to the others. I was grateful to see one couch was empty for my mate and me, but I had no intention of sitting down with strangers. Alpha Rahul wanted to speak, but we could do that in an office, and none of these others would be invited.

Certainly not with the woman crawling on and kissing Kannan as he sat down on his Alpha's right. Alphas were pretty obvious in most packs, and Rahul was the most obvious I had ever seen.

"Welcome, Kaliya Sahni, Queen of the nagas."

The voice was wrong. This wasn't the werewolf who had spoken on the phone.

"Where's Rahul?" I asked, and the room felt as if it froze. Silence and stillness marked the scene in front of me as they all appeared to be shocked. The only thing that broke the silence were the soft footsteps behind me.

21

CHAPTER TWENTY-ONE

"How did you know?" someone asked behind me.

"He sounds... lighter than you." I turned around to see a mirror copy of the man on the couch. Identical twins. It was a game, then. "Jovial. He's trying to cover it up, and he's doing it fairly well, but you had *none* of it in your voice earlier. It's not a feeling, though. It's how you talk. You're a bit more serious, and it changes the way you deliver a line."

"My brother enjoys being the life of the party," Rahul explained, a smile forming. "Normally, people who have never met us can't tell the difference when we try."

"And you wanted to see me from afar to take me off guard while I ran in circles with your twin," I said, nodding. "I can respect that. Smart move. Don't do it again."

"Why not?"

"Others might take offense to someone trying to fool their ruler into speaking with someone beneath their equal rank. You know better."

"Are we equal?"

"No. I rule my species. *You* answer to people." I tried to not have a shit-eating grin as his jaw tightened. He was stupid to imply I was his lesser. I knew how he got the impression I might be, so I addressed that as well. "You might rule this city, but I don't really care if you do since I'm not interested in it."

"What are you interested in?" he asked.

"Your information."

"I want more than that," he said, stepping closer, eyeing me. Raphael shifted his weight on his feet, and Rahul's eyes went from dark brown to light wolf gold, which wasn't as pretty or as true as werecat gold. His nostrils flared, and luckily, the disgust across his face was just a flash. When he looked back at me, I was still relaxed, trying to make no obvious body language for him to feel threatened.

"How much more?" I asked now that his attention was on me.

"You came to this city unannounced, not making appointments with the local powers, including myself. Now, I'm assuming you are after the rakshasa who attacked you, but that still doesn't answer the question of why you're here."

"You remember the rakshasa broke a treaty with my people. I could be here to correct their mistake."

"I don't think so," he said curiously. "We'll talk in private if that's what you wish, but you must know I'll tell my inner circle what they need to know at the end of the meeting."

"Of course. I just won't take part in... this." I waved a hand at the werewolves hanging out on the couches.

"Not much of a party person?"

"My parties and yours probably have *very* different outcomes." When I smiled, he lost his smile.

It took several quiet moments of consideration on both sides before he waved for us to follow him. We went up the main staircase, ignoring the guards on duty. Raphael made every werewolf fight to keep their faces schooled.

Another werewolf jumped forward to open the door to a large office. I couldn't taste human in the mansion, werewolves of both sexes, but not a single human. It was smart. It kept anyone from being fatally hurt if a supernatural lost their temper, which was a real risk.

Though werewolves like finding reasons to kill each other. I honestly think they account for more of their own kind dying than anything else.

The office was empty compared to what I had seen so far. Everything in the house had been packed with detail, but this room was clean. It wasn't too large to feel vast, but its size and sparseness made a stark contrast. The shelves were simple and white, with only a few items on each. There was only a minimal amount of clutter on the center desk. The white marble was still in use, and the furniture was black.

I had a feeling it could be a tranquil place to think.

"So why are you in India?" he asked, sitting on his side of the desk.

"Can I sit?" Raphael asked, grabbing a chair across from the Alpha. By touching it, Raphael was ruining the very reason he asked. He knew scents rubbed off on things and was making sure the werewolves didn't forget about him for a *long* time.

"Go right ahead," Rahul answered, crossing his legs and leaning back in his chair.

Raphael moved a chair and angled it so I could sit and see both of them and easily turn to the door if someone opened it. Then he angled his chair the same way, mirroring mine to give him the same advantage. Once we were both seated, I knew Rahul was probably tired of waiting for me to answer.

What will happen if I tell him the truth? Will he be surprised? Will he play nice until we leave, then make a quick phone call? Will I become the hunted before I even leave these grounds?

There's no one at risk right now but Raphael and me. No one can touch my people at home. They would find themselves in a fight against super-predators. Even the weakest cambion had a healing factor that put everyone here to shame. I don't see the United States werewolf packs indulging in the effort, not at Rahul's behest.

Fuck it.

"I'm here to kill Garuda," I answered.

His eyes went wide, dinner-plate wide, losing the gold and returning to the dark oak brown they had been when I first saw him.

"He..."

"Is alive," I said with annoyance, not directed at the Alpha. "Reincarnated, actually. With his memories and his power. He's the reason nagas are slowly becoming extinct. He's working from the shadows, knowing he can't use the same methods he had in his first life. He's the one who convinced the rakshasa to go back on the treaty I had just established with them. Convinced them they would be heroes, have glory, or whatever people need to hear when they try to kill innocent women and children. He finally revealed himself, wanting to be in the final battle. The rakshasa lost. Therefore, he did and had to retreat." I plucked something off my shirt. It looked like a petal of some sort. It had probably been in the wind. I tucked it in my pocket, knowing I was commanding all the attention.

"I am here to kill Garuda," I said once more. "I am the reincarnation of my namesake and have been named *Nagaraja* for a reason. Things are... how can I say it? This is out of your league. We're a different weight class, one you are *not* ready for. I mean that with all due respect. I don't want to see another species get tangled into this situation, and I don't want to see anyone in this pack killed."

By the look on Rahul's face, he hadn't been prepared for my answer and was struggling. This wasn't something a normal werewolf Alpha had to deal with.

"This war has nothing to do with werewolves," I continued. "So, if you can give me your information since I have given you my truth, we won't bother you again. I'll even tell Callahan and Corissa that you helped me gain justice for my people, a Tribunal species, just like yours. Something the rakshasa and Garuda have never tried to plead for."

"Your loyalties, Alpha, are already decided for you,"

Raphael finished, and damn, the tone of my mate's voice sent wonderful shivers down my spine.

Rahul got up and paced.

"How did we all miss this? How did..." He stopped and stared at me, his eyes still that wide dinner plate thing children often did. "I hear things, as you know. People have spoken about how you were *different* from your kind. When you were declared *Nagaraja*, Callahan called me and told me we had to *pause* our plans for expansion. Your new title created turmoil, and he wasn't certain he wanted to risk werewolves, that we could hold for a century or two."

"Which stops you from growing your pack, from setting up outside homes of operation, and increases the likelihood that one of your own will challenge you for your position. They'll have nowhere else to go and no ability to establish their own pack with your blessing," I said, nodding. "Yeah, I can see how that would cause some concern for you." I lifted my hands. "But we're not talking about you... or Callahan. I really don't like the guy. He's a warmonger and a colonist, and you knew better than to align with that sort of thing."

Rahul winced but made no argument.

"We're here because we're just trying to make sure this situation ends before it gets bloodier," Raphael continued. "And I can make it very bloody."

"We weren't expecting the rakshasa to assassinate us on our first night."

"Why did you threaten my werewolves?"

"I'll tell you what I told Kannan *and* what I didn't tell him. I threatened them because I knew I could kill them.

Things go smoothly when people cooperate. Making sure they understood there was no winning for them meant we could all go home tonight. I didn't target them because they were werewolves. In several hours of waiting, they were the only supernaturals who went into or left the Market. They were unlucky. Lakhan deserves a fat bonus, by the way. He bargained well and got the other two out of trouble to call you."

"I know," he answered softly. "You play a dangerous game."

"I don't know any different. Before I was *Nagaraja*, I was a Tribunal Executioner trained by Hisao, son of Hasan, after he rescued me from human captivity. Before that, I was a girl running for her life as Mehar, King of the rakshasa, murdered her family. All the games I play are dangerous." I folded my hands in my lap. "Tell me what you know."

"Two weeks ago, shortly after the announcement of your appointment, I was visited by a rakshasa, which was nothing new."

"Explain that for me," I said, frowning. I needed to know the politics, and Rahul had opened the door into his connections.

"I had known Mehar, known his mate and his sons. Hearing what happened between you and them was... shocking. I heard tales of your vicious murder of the King and his family, but as you and Mr. Alvarez reminded me, I am a werewolf, loyal to the Tribunal, therefore loyal to the Rule of Law they impose. I asked around my community and werewolf Alphas, and Wagner gave me the truth. You told me to call him, and I did long before tonight. It started in Phoenix, did it not? All this with the rakshasa?"

"Yeah." I wasn't surprised Wagner would know the details of the events, not after so many months. Him, Imani, and probably Monica. Any one else of note or interest in the city. I was never trying to keep it a secret. "Sort of. The recent turmoil."

"You were justified in killing all of them. I learned that from the incident at the Market, which was quite the news headline among supernaturals. Two rulers, one also a Tribunal Executioner, being banned from the Market? That was some news." Rahul came back to the desk and sat down again, finally. "I cut off contact with the rakshasa after that. I can't be seen as a friend to a species that willfully goes against the laws I have to uphold for my werewolves. It would send mixed signals. I only knew the names of the new king and his mate, heard of your treaty, then heard the aftermath of the betrayal. Everyone knew nagas relocated to America en masse, hobbling and running for their lives. Adhar, the oldest of your kind, dead. Nakul, the most dangerous of your kind, dead. And you were named *Nagaraja*, the first in centuries."

"Nakul was the most experienced warrior, but he wasn't the most dangerous naga when he died," I corrected. "I was at the time and still am."

"You speak so confidently." Smiling, something relaxed in the Alpha, and there was clear flirtation in his eyes. "I must say, I like it."

"I'm taken," I reminded him as Raphael growled in his direction.

"I know." Rahul looked at Raphael. "I haven't asked your place in all this."

"She helped free my people from captivity. The cambions consider the nagas our closest and most loyal allies. Our friends. No one else thought to help us. No one else wanted to. If I die, my people will continue to support and follow her, helping her people live safely. I don't play too much of a role, not in this situation. She's the beauty and the brains. I'm the monster who will turn your mansion into your gravestone if you cross the line." Raphael leaned back in his seat. "And if you attempt to flirt with my mate again, I might do it without her permission. My patience is thinner than hers when it comes to others hitting on us. This beautiful woman is mine." Raphael punctuated the ending with a snarl.

The way Rahul paled said he knew all about Raphael, thanks to the events at the Market. My WMD of a mate could make an impression.

"Moving on. You stopped having dealings with the rakshasa. What happened two weeks ago?" I wanted to get to the really important parts of this conversation, and Raphael's sudden possessiveness was weird. I wanted to talk to him about it but couldn't do that here.

"Maurvi came here," Rahul explained.

22

CHAPTER TWENTY-TWO

That wasn't the rakshasa name I expected to hear. My jaw dropped open, but Raphael had to pry further.

"Mahatma's mate?" He sounded just as surprised. "Why?"

"She explained much of what occurred... *without* telling me the Garuda connection. I assume she was scared to say the eagle's name. She was scared of shadows that day," Rahul told my mate, sighing. "She told me how her mate had come upon new information and broken the treaty they had made, then attacked your kind while you were having some sort of community gathering. I was already getting news from the Tribunal, so it was nothing new. She told me the location and about the casualties beyond Adhar and Nakul. You lost a mated pair, too. That must have been a deep blow."

My hands curled into fists.

"Yes," I answered.

"My condolences."

"I'll pass your condolences to their surviving infant daughter," I said, my voice hollow but also a warning. This wasn't a topic I wanted to discuss. Rahul caught the message loud and clear.

"Maurvi left that day, desperate for help. I know within seventy-two hours, four attempts were made on her life. You see, the failure of their attack against your people has left the rakshasa splintered. Maurvi had been vocal that she didn't want the war, not after peace had been decided. Honor and reputation are important. Non-Tribunal species have to work harder if they want to be accepted by Tribunal supernaturals. We outnumber them and control the world. The rakshasa can't be trusted anymore. We all know that, and therefore, offer them no help."

Wheels were turning, pieces coming together, ideas and plans forming.

"And now? That was two weeks ago."

"Maurvi is in control of the largest and most powerful of the rakshasa factions," he said, shrugging. "She realized she was on her own, and when some tried to turn against her for not supporting her mate and husband, she became the tigress she needed to be. It's not stable yet. The ones who attacked you were the same faction who tried to kill her for her perceived betrayal."

"You know about the hotel attack? Are the rakshasa, nagas, and cambions outed? I know nothing has hit national news, but what about the local whispers?"

"No. You both disappeared, which was smart. Maurvi went in and cleaned it up. I caught her while she was there because everyone knows I'm supernatural. The humans called me to see what had happened. I did my part as a Tribunal species and threw the humans off the situation while she destroyed evidence of anything they could use. She was protecting her species, but she also hadn't sanctioned the assassination attempt and as the closest thing to a royal rakshasa left, she is pretending to have that authority. Cleaning it up for you and your mate was the least she could do, or so she told me."

"Gods," I groaned, leaning over to rub my temples. "That's lucky for us."

"Yeah," Raphael said, his relief evident.

"Maybe so much of this could have been avoided if you had reached out when you arrived."

"I'm not here for this," I reminded him, dropping my hands. "You're getting priorities mixed up here. The rakshasa and their mistakes aren't my problem. I defeated them on the open field of battle when they laid siege. They should get the message—they won't win against me. They will *never* win against me. If they're too stupid to figure that out, they'll keep dying. If she wants to limp out of this with a handful of her people, she'll get control of them. She clearly knows that. I'm done here. You've told me everything I need to know."

Standing, I considered this resolved without needing to get involved further. Knowing we weren't outed to the public was enough payment for me to leave Maurvi alone. If she wanted to clean up the messes of her people, she was more than welcome to follow me around to keep the others off my back. It was time for me to get on task.

"Wait..." Rahul stood at the same time as Raphael. The Alpha did so with urgency, while Raphael seemed more confused by my decision. "Are you sure? If this unrest is allowed to continue..."

"I'm not here to solve everyone's problems," I hissed. "Certainly not the rakshasa's and not yours, if you have any."

"No... I was just..." Rahul looked away from me.

"You know something else?" I asked, crossing my arms.

"It's the timing of the situation," he admitted. "And something I heard Maurvi whispering to her second in command."

"What?" When he didn't immediately answer, I walked closer to the desk, put my hands on it, and leaned over. "What did she say?" I demanded again.

"If I tell you, I want a promise of something in return. I have given you a lot of information tonight because of my loyalty to the Tribunal, and in good faith, you won't attack my werewolves, but for this, I want something in return."

I could have said no, but he was right. Fair was fair. He'd told me a lot and had gone to the hotel and helped Maurvi when he found her there cleaning up the mess. He hadn't needed to do that. It put his position with the humans at risk. That was the danger werewolves had to face because humanity knew about them. The humans could turn on them if they made the wrong move.

"What do you want?" I asked, taking my hands off his desk but not stepping back as our eyes locked.

"If the nagas return to India, I want them to be my pack's public ally. I would appreciate being your public ally long before that, a show of acceptance that werewolves are here. We've had... on and off relationships with the other native species. I was born in this country, but they look at me as if I'm a foreigner. I was born in this city and know it better than most supernaturals, better than you, I bet, but because I became a werewolf, I have been... ostracized and talked down to. I know you did it to my wolves."

I felt guilty, seeing the desperation, hearing the pain. I had threatened it, knowing it was probably the case. This was his city, his home. Always had been and always would be, but now, he was an outsider.

Oh yeah, I understood.

"If you agree to be my ally, to accept werewolves in the country without issue, the others might warm up to us," Rahul continued as if I needed to know more when I didn't. "We can do good things for the supernaturals of this country. We would never allow the western werewolves to destroy the culture we grew up with. We could help preserve it, protecting it from other Tribunal species. This is our land, too. Mine just as much as yours. This is my culture just as much as yours. I would never allow the other werewolves to poison this, the way..." He walked around the desk, his eyes still on mine. "I asked to become a werewolf, but that didn't mean I gave up who I am. I will not betray our land or pillage it. I believe I can help it." He touched his chest. "Because of who I am.

"Look at what you have done for the nagas. Phoenix, Arizona, on a separate continent, a naga showed the world what her kind could be and do, which made people respect your people, even though they would never meet a naga in their lifetime. You, the last nagini, did that. You made a werewolf Alpha warn me you weren't someone to toy with, even on a good day. He warned me that I didn't want to see you angry because that was the moment people started dying.

"He also told me you always had the best interests of the city and the region you covered in mind. That you put your body between criminals and innocent lives, defended those who most would never defend, and while he didn't always like you, he respected you and would never raise a hand against you. You made a bond with those who weren't from our home, and everyone in your city has been stronger for it. I know none of you are the natives of those lands, but that is... more complicated in America."

Wagner, you son of a bitch. I'm not sure whether I want to kill you or give you a fucking hug. I'll buy you a drink.

"You did that because you were given the chance," Rahul said as we stood without the desk separating us. Nothing between us. We were both people of this land, and yearning shined in his eyes. "I could do that for my pack here if they would only give me a chance. I could make us all stronger and give them a voice to my superiors, to the Tribunal, but I need one native species to give me a chance."

"I respect those who inhabited those lands long before I did," I said softly. "I don't toy with them or attempt to impose my will on them. I don't go out of my way to rule over it. I have my piece of the desert, and I stay in it, for the most part."

"As I respect those who have come before me and inhabited these lands for thousands of years. I make no attempt to rule the rakshasa or the other natives. I have never tried to rule the nagas… would never try. I have my city, which I am trying to make into a community."

His earnest desperation made me think of children, the ones who took a different path from their parents but still did their best. They just wanted someone to see the work they were doing, trying to make their parents proud, to add to the family, not take away from it. Everyone saw it play out in their life or the lives of their friends.

Oddly, he made me think about Cassius. So desperate to do good by his family, good for his people, good with his power, yet he chose another path. For that, he was ostracized and had to learn nothing would ever be good enough. I couldn't fix Cassius's problems. I wasn't a fae. No matter how much I appreciated my friend, it wasn't the appreciation that would heal his heart and subdue his pain. Only the other royals, the other Sidhe, and the myriad of creatures we called fae could do that.

But I was here in India and could offer Rahul a chance.

"I look forward to working with you in the future, Alpha Rahul Varadkar. I'm sure you and I can have a healthy working relationship when the nagas come back to their homeland. Maybe, in a matter of good faith, others will see your good intentions if you help the nagas establish homes here. I will show you and your pack my commitment to this by publicly speaking about how the werewolves have been a constant help while others in the country have left my people to struggle alone. You are helping us to thrive once more." I held out a hand. "And that will only be step one."

Rahul's smile was more like his twin's, making his face look five years younger. The joy and pride that lit up his eyes were so *human*. Acceptance and a chance were all he wanted, and I could definitely give him those things.

"I look forward to discussing this further when the time is convenient for you. You have much to deal with." He shook my hand but didn't release it. He patted it for a moment, then held it in his, almost as though it was delicate. "I imagine battling Garuda—if you can find him—will be difficult. I hope you can help your people and see them into an era of peace." He let me go and stepped back. "Now, I promised you information in return."

"Right, back to work," I said, laughing. Raphael touched my back, and I gave him a smile. He nodded.

"Well, not before I say something," Raphael said. "Kaliya gave my people a chance to thrive, and we are still building what that will mean for us. Even though it's a work in progress, we wouldn't have had it without her. The spirit of your argument is one I can understand all too well. Thank you. Anything my mate promises, I will do my best to uphold as well." He sat back down. "Now, we can go back to work."

If I could crawl into his lap and unbutton his pants, I would have. Ruling looked so fucking good on my mate, and he was learning to talk like a proper ruler.

It was a turn-on.

"Maurvi told her right-hand man she was frustrated. They must have had a leak. He tried to talk her down, saying anyone in the city could have found you, but she truly believed she was the reason you were found."

Rahul's information made me forget the fantasy as if a cold bucket of water had been dumped on my head. I felt pieces slide into place, and plans continued to shift and form.

I can fix the rakshasa problem.

"I don't know why she would have believed that. Anyone could have found you there. You didn't do anything in secret when you came into the city."

"She sent a messenger," I said softly, looking not at Rahul but Raph. "The witch who wouldn't give me the name of the one who hired him."

"She should have told us—"

"Why would she? If I knew she was trying to contact me for a meeting, I would have believed it was to finish what her husband started," I reminded him. "She couldn't reveal her entire hand in a message through a third party. She would have tried to reach me, knowing I didn't know the current political climate. It was a wild gamble that didn't work for me but didn't hurt her. I didn't go hunting for her without her having a chance to say something. In the end, it went as about as well as it could have."

Raphael groaned, and Rahul was stuttering.

"She tried to reach you with a witch on your first day in the country?" Rahul shook his head. "That's either genius or madness, definitely bold either way. She's lucky you didn't send the witch's head back, considering the circumstances. With your reputation, I'm more shocked that you didn't."

"Fucking politics," Raphael muttered, and just like that, he was tired of this whole thing.

"I wasn't here to find any new fights, only to finish one that's been brewing for five thousand years," I huffed. "I didn't think I was coming here to establish peace between the species, but I can fix this."

"Kaliya?" Raphael wasn't on the same page anymore, but I knew he would understand once I had the chance to tell him. I didn't want to reveal my entire hand to Rahul, not yet. He would like it, but it wasn't his decision. It wasn't even mine or Raphael's.

"We'll get into it later," I promised my mate before looking at the confused Alpha. "Can you get ahold of her? Tell her I'll take that meeting, and as long as no one attempts to harm me, I won't harm her or the rakshasa. Tell her my mate will be in attendance, and we want to resolve this without more violence, if possible."

"I can certainly put a few werewolves out with the message. There are a number of places she could hide in the city, and I wouldn't want to send you on a chase to all of them. The rakshasa won't attack my werewolves, no matter what faction they are."

"How do you know?" Raphael asked.

"If they want access to this city, they'll keep their claws to themselves." His eyes went back to the wolf gold. "We committed no violence on those who came before us. We expect no violence done to us."

"I assume you've proven this point before," I said softly.

With an angry snarl, cut off with a look of guilt, he nodded.

"There are no riksha in Delhi, and I won't allow them in until a discussion is had with their current king," he explained. "An unfortunate incident, shortly after the Indian independence."

I winced.

"Um..." Raphael's confusion was clear.

"Bear shifters of the subcontinent," I said for my very confused mate. "There are few of note in the legends, but they're out there. Never met one myself. No need to get into it today. Forging a united community among the supernaturals of this land will be an ongoing effort for the decades and centuries to come."

"Of course. That's why I can safely send out your message to the different rakshasa safehouses and meeting areas without expecting trouble. As long as Maurvi's enemies don't grow so bold as to attack you before that, everything should be fine." Rahul grabbed a pen and jotted down a note on the closest pad of paper he had. "Can I offer you refuge until we can establish the time and place of the meeting? I will have a werewolf retrieve your vehicle and offer you a guest suite."

"That's very kind of you, but I don't see how it benefits you," I said, wondering why the Alpha was feeling generous.

"I have a vested interest in the political stability of the subcontinent. While Callahan and Corissa would appreciate political instability for the future of the werewolves, they've also paused my ability to expand even an inch, which is... stifling for those of us here now." He put his pen down and leaned back. "Perhaps the expansion of the werewolves can be a positive to a politically stable India, something I can show you, the rakshasa, others. If we go into other cities, we could create thriving supernatural communities of all species and try to make the cities safe grounds for all, which would lead to more doors opening in the Market. But first, we must put an end to a war that shouldn't have started."

"Politics," Raphael muttered again.

"I can't say this is the perfect plan, but it's hopeful for our world," I admitted to the Alpha. "I know Callahan and Corissa and can't promise they will approve. They might think you have divided loyalties, and you should be prepared for that possibility. It could be a deadly way to approach the situation. However, if you mean to do good for India, for the entire subcontinent, I won't let the werewolves from Europe stop you."

"But expect her to stop you herself if she thinks you're getting uppity," Raphael warned.

"I'm certain she will," Rahul said, nodding his head respectfully at my mate. "With your help, I bet, and that's okay. Now, let me have rooms prepared for you. It would be my honor to host you both for however long this may take. You will be free to come and go, meals will be provided at scheduled times—"

"A bed and a shower," I said, chuckling. "Let's get those first."

23

CHAPTER TWENTY-THREE

Rahul was more than willing to give us the rest of the night to ourselves while he passed my official message to a handful of his strongest werewolves and sent them into the city. The room was nice, the bathroom massive, and it was private. I cleared it for bugs, then Raphael and I got into the shower, which had more than enough room for both of us.

That was easily one of the best showers of my life.

"You know, he's using his personal messengers," I told Raphael as I dried my hair while seated in a cushioned chair at the bathroom counter. It was a nice built-in vanity section, not that I had anything much to do at it. I hadn't packed for meeting the rulers of other supernatural species, so I had no makeup or jewelry.

My mate came up beside me, a towel around his waist, which was at my eye level in the mirror. Thickly muscled and covered in scars, my mate's abdomen was on full display. The V women drooled over was right there where I could see it. If I turned my head to the left, I'd be able to sink my fangs into his hip.

My fangs ached at the idea. It had been a while since I let myself indulge in those thoughts. Not that we weren't having regular sex, but when I was up and moving around, I didn't have time to daydream about ripping his pants off.

I don't even need to work that hard. It's just a towel...

His smile was arrogant as he leaned down, putting his hands on the back of the chair I was using to sit in front of the mirror. He tilted my head back by my chin. The view of his chest was magnificent, and his eyes, those warm chocolate eyes, were absolutely sinful.

"We just had sex in the shower," he reminded me.

"It was very good sex," I reminded him.

"We didn't use protection."

"It's fine." I felt okay with it, a surprising change. We were pretty strict about condom use, but I didn't really care. "It was still great sex."

"It was, but I need fifteen minutes."

I licked my fangs. Having bitten the rakshasa in the hotel, I didn't have excess venom.

"We might have an important meeting coming up. You shouldn't waste the venom," he continued. "No matter how much I would love for you to do just that. Besides, we're in a place of practical strangers, and that stuff... is a hell of a distraction."

He was right. Logically, I knew he was, but I remembered how he spoke to Rahul, to the werewolves. It was a side of him I didn't get to see often enough, and it made me want to go another round... seven more rounds.

"You are very attractive when you put on your warlord face. Can't blame a girl for wanting to get in your pants."

"Being that man feels easier every day, just another piece of me. You're right, though. I don't use it often. I don't need to all the time with the cambions, and I don't like to with friends."

"I wish I'd appreciated it sooner," I admitted, lowering my head to look at us in the mirror. Together, our body language was at ease with the position we were in. "There's no going back in time, but I plan on appreciating it every day for the rest of eternity. It's sexy to see you play hardball with such easy confidence." I reached back and pulled off his towel, making him laugh. "I plan on appreciating all of you."

"You are becoming a sex fiend," he said as I threw his towel into the next room.

"You like it," I murmured as he came closer again. He turned my chair away from the counter and mirror, letting me see him in all his naked glory. Every scar was a story he had written on that hard body, but they didn't detract from his beauty, and most days, I didn't even think about them. Raphael wouldn't be who he was without the story they told.

Tonight, they only made him more beautiful.

Leaning in, he used his foot to push my feet apart and open my legs.

"I love it," he whispered before kissing me, then picked me up to carry me out of the bathroom. "I don't see it often enough." He dropped me on the bed. "Business first. You were saying something about the werewolves. What was it?"

I'd been played. Laughing at my defeat, I sat up.

"He sent out his personal messengers," I repeated. "Strong and fast, they're considered the official voice of the Alpha when they pass his word. He's using them to cover who the message might be from. No one will attack his werewolves, but people are even more likely to listen if it's from such a trusted source."

"That's kind of him. I was zoning out through all that."

"I noticed." By the time we had left Rahul's office, my mate wanted to be done with the whole thing. He had run out of patience and stopped having an opinion on anything. Everyone had their limit for politics, and tonight had gone past his. Rahul had noticed and understood as Raphael wandered around, looking at stuff while we finished with the small details.

"Sorry," he said, finding his towel to finish drying off. "Now we're just waiting to see how fast they can get word to Maurvi, right?"

"Yup. And our car is probably already here. When the sun is up, maybe we can see the Taj Mahal."

"Really?"

"Yeah. It's over three hours away, but we could do it in a day..." I trailed off, remembering where the Taj Mahal was. "I should have taken the chance to take you on our first day here. It's just south of Vrindavan."

Raphael was silent for a minute, then laughed.

"Let's save it for another trip," he said, coming to sit next to me. "We still haven't made any progress on our reason for being in this country." His reminder sank my mood, although I knew it wasn't his intention. He was giving me a pass for not seeing more of the normal sights of the country, something I knew he wanted.

Already in the country for days, we were no closer to Rama or Garuda. We were tangled up in different problems, forced to be rulers, and fixing problems neither of us had wanted to deal with.

"I know," I whispered, looking down at my hands.

"Hey..." He touched my cheek and turned my head, leaning in to put his forehead against mine. "We'll figure it out. I'm sorry I gave you such a hard time at the hotel. I have a lot on my mind but shouldn't have lashed out at you for following your gut instinct about coming here because I... I wanted more time at home. I followed you here without complaint and should have said something earlier if I thought this was the wrong time." He kissed me, but not with the same fiery passion as earlier. It was a reminder—a reminder he didn't just lust for me, he loved me.

"Do you think we came too early?" I asked, looking for honesty. "I felt the need to come and—"

"No."

"Why?"

"I think there's no right time for this sort of thing," he said, letting me go. "Even if we... researched for months, something would have happened here. There would have been drama. Or maybe Garuda would have prepared for you to return. Right now, he's probably trying to stop you from hunting him down."

"All that crossed my mind, too, but I figured in the end, waiting and trying to gather intel on the other side of the planet wouldn't be helpful. And..." I tapped my chest. "It's here. This is telling me to be here and do this now, not to wait. My people deserve *action*."

"They do, and if we resolve these other problems while we're here, they might get to come home sooner if that's what they want. I would miss them on the compound, but this is their home."

"Yes." I felt that in my heart. "Maybe summer homes or something. We could... work out a schedule. Buy a private plane for the freedom to travel between the two."

"We'll worry about it when it's time to worry about it." Kissing me again, this one was the one I had been hoping for since I got out of the shower. I moved to straddle him as he pulled me onto his lap.

He touched every inch of me, softly growling when he reached the scar on my side from the fight at the hotel. He had growled about it in the shower, too.

"Don't like it?" I asked, nipping his bottom lip. "I find your scars sexy. I don't get the same courtesy?"

"I don't like that I was unable to stop it," he said roughly, glaring at the scar. "That you got hurt, and I couldn't stop it. *Again*. I know who you are and what you can do. Understand and accept it, but that doesn't make me okay with the consequences. I'm not okay with the toll it takes on your body, on *you*. That's impossible."

I didn't have an argument for that. I had lost my temper when I had known his blood had been spilled, and he could heal a hell of a lot better than I could.

"You're still beautiful," he continued. "Don't worry about that." He kissed me. "Want me to prove it?"

"I wouldn't object." I wrapped my arms around his neck.

Moving us to the center of the bed, he carried me with ease before letting my head hit the pillows. He touched the scar, his fingers tracing it as though he was imaging how it happened. I let him do whatever he wanted because he needed to come to terms with it. I could get it removed. Monica and her coven offered the service, and I paid handsomely. I had done it to several scars over the years, not wanting to look like an abused pin cushion.

A few new scars I hadn't had removed yet. Two small circular scars on my calf and a few from the fight with the rakshasa. I hadn't gotten around to having them removed while we were in Arizona because it hadn't been worth the time or money.

Raphael kissed the new scar then moved on. His warm hands massaged my thighs as he focused on something entirely different.

Pleasure raced through me, banishing the thoughts of how I got every scar. Moaning, I ran my hands through his hair. He could do magical things with his mouth, and I knew I was a lucky woman to have him doing them to me. It was almost criminal that he was only mine, tied to me for eternity. Every swipe of his tongue drove me higher. I could feel it building, and I wanted it so much. Wanted him to take me over the edge.

He stopped before I climaxed.

Feeling robbed, I sat up as he lifted his head.

"Raphael!" I was strung out.

His arrogant smile was breathtaking, but I wanted to strangle him.

"You—"

Kissing me, he pushed me back onto the bed and drove himself into me in one fluid movement I hadn't seen coming. It was more than enough. My orgasm shook me to the bone and left me helpless.

He let me recover before he started slowly thrusting. Everything was sensitive, but I knew that was what he'd wanted. Like a crescendo, he moved faster and faster, taking me back up once again.

When I shattered underneath him again, he came with me. For a few moments, it was just us, together and alone, with nothing else to bother us. He moved to my side after those precious moments and wrapped his arms around me.

At this moment of what should have been bliss, anxiety ran through me. I wasn't sure how my mind had ended up on the memory, but I thought about how Gabi had fiddled with our bags before we left Phoenix. It was the first time I'd thought of it since I had caught her scent on them. I thought about how she didn't really say goodbye to me, and I hadn't been able to catch her to say goodbye to her.

Wide awake, I stayed in bed as Raphael snored softly. I heard a soft knock at our door and got up, putting on a robe before I opened it. Two werewolves were carrying our bags, and I let them put them down just inside the door.

Once the werewolves were gone, I looked through the bags and found what had to be from Gabi, a small envelope in a side pocket of my weapon bag. Raphael never would have looked there, and her swirling, beautiful cursive only said my name. I opened it, wondering what Gabi needed to say to me that kept her from talking to me personally.

It confirmed something I had subconsciously known.

Folding the note, I put it back in its envelope and hid it away in the pocket again.

Numbness took over as I stared at the bag. I grabbed the note again and read it a second time. I kept waiting for a wave of pain or grief, but numbness was all I had.

"I should have asked," I mumbled. "Asked how bad the damage really was instead of trying to ignore it, got a full report." I put the note away again, then ran a hand through my hair.

Looking at my sleeping mate, I felt a soft, aching pain, but it was better than the numbness.

"It's not entirely permanent," I whispered to myself, repeating what Gabi had said. "The scar tissue could eventually subside." I closed my eyes. "Gabi, sweetheart, you made the right choice telling me. Thank you. I'm sorry you carried it, trying to find a way to say it."

I knew what had happened. Gabi had assessed me that first day and tried to tell me how serious it was, but I'd shut her down. I had been grateful to be alive and on my own two feet, even with a long list of other problems to deal with.

Her note had explained why it grew harder and harder for her to watch me ignore what I went through. She had watched us take care of Roshni and how happy it made us. She felt an ethical need to tell me everything, but as a friend, she'd been scared—scared to hurt me. So, she had left a note and prayed we came home, so she could apologize for her cowardice.

I didn't find her actions cowardly, though. It was a hard thing. Now I needed to grapple with the same problem she had overcome. Raphael deserved to know, but I didn't know how I was going to tell him. Just the idea brought home how hard of a conversation it would be.

Wrestling with it, I laid back down and stared at the ceiling until morning.

24

CHAPTER TWENTY-FOUR

I was quiet through the morning, keeping to myself as Raphael called home and explained the sudden change in our situation. Most of the conversation didn't need me. I wanted to make sure we were ready to meet with Maurvi when we received word, and Raphael knew everything going on.

Anything to help me forget the personal thing I had learned the night before.

"What's Kaliya thinking?" Cassius asked curiously but not condescendingly. "Has she elaborated since she said she could fix things?"

I perked up. Raphael didn't know my plan, and with Cassius on the call, it was the perfect time to say something.

"No," I said, jumping up from the bed and walking over to Raphael at a small desk. "I'm going to talk to Maurvi about the rakshasa becoming a Tribunal species."

Raphael spit out his water, luckily not hitting the

laptop, while Cassius went wide-eyed for a second, but only for a second.

"How do you intend to convince her?"

"By telling her what she gets out of it. Right now, she's reckoning with everything Mahatma did by betraying another species and breaking Tribunal Law. No one in power will ally with her. She has no backup to gain control over the misbehaving members of her species. If she joins the Tribunal, others can step in and take out those who continue to break the law. All she needs is a majority vote in favor and to go before the Tribunal. If I can give that to her, we're both bound by the Law to behave, and she's able to enforce it with help. It will require her to make concessions, but if she wants to clean up what her mate broke, that's the price she'll have to pay."

"The best option, if not one she'll entirely enjoy. It's a bold plan, Kaliya, and you'll need me to get in contact with the Tribunal."

"Isn't that the deal we all made?" I asked. "And yes, once I have an answer from her, I will need you to be the guy who handles it while I get back on track. This has completely screwed up our trip, and I'm not leaving to come back later." I drummed my fingers on the desk next to Raphael's arm. "This only works if my suspicions are correct. It could all be a ruse to get me killed, and we know what will happen if that's the case. We'll find out."

Cassius and I discussed what the immediate future would look like if my decision was the right one, and it worked. Adding species to the Tribunal could be tricky. I'd done it with Raphael, but I had options with him I didn't have with rakshasa. There were meetings that would need to happen. None of it would be fast, not this time, but it was possible. If I could get the process started and introduce Maurvi to the right people, I could get back to what I needed to do.

Or that was the hope.

Eventually, I ended the call and went back to my weapons as Raphael left to get us lunch. Alone, I worked, making sure each blade was sharp. When Raphael came back, he didn't come back alone.

"Look who I saw in the hall," he said as he carried in our two plates. I put my sword down to see Rahul and Kannan. Standing, I met them at the table.

"I take it there's news?" I said as I sat down.

"She's willing to meet this evening. I understand the timeline doesn't provide much time to prepare, but she's worried she might not stay in the city much longer. There are other areas of the country she needs to wrangle the rakshasa."

I nodded as Raphael slid my food in front of me, then thanked my mate with a smile. Rahul and Kannan sat down across from me as Raphael ate.

"Time and place?"

"Here." Rahul pushed a neatly folded sheet of paper across the table. "I hope... peace is struck once again, and this time, it is truthful."

"I do, too," I mumbled. Taking the paper, I read the address. "Six isn't too late, and I've been preparing all day. I hope she doesn't expect anything fancy."

"I don't believe that will be a concern or something she'll take offense to," Rahul said carefully.

I studied him before folding the paper and tucking it away in my back pocket.

"When we announce the next peace treaty, I'll stress how the werewolves of Delhi have been gracious and helpful throughout the process."

"Meaning everything relies on another peace treaty," he said, nodding as he caught my stipulation. There would be no credit if this went wrong. I was doing this based on his information, and he would take the fall with me if this turned bloody. The news would be how the Delhi werewolf pack tried to send me to my death, and I would make sure Callahan and Corissa knew how much I didn't appreciate it.

"That's fine," he continued. "I will drive with you to the meeting, or you may follow my vehicle with your own. I won't attempt to join or intrude. I have promised Maurvi my werewolves will be the main security for the event. She will leave everyone but her second-in-command behind. You will have Raphael; she will have him. Kannan and I will be there for the entire meeting, and if there is a need for a mediator, we will both take the role. There will be two for each of your parties at the table, so it seems fair there are two for us if we're needed. Does this sound agreeable?"

"Yeah, we can work with it." I looked at my lunch again. "How far is the drive?"

"In traffic? It could take an hour," Kannan answered.

"We'll meet you in the garage at four-thirty and be on the road by five. I don't want to be late."

"Of course." Rahul stood, and Kannan mirrored him.

"You're well behaved for an Alpha werewolf," I

commented lightly. "Few would play messenger and mediator."

"Since I became a werewolf, I have watched those who have stayed in power and noted those who have lost it. Would you like to know where they were all challenged the most?"

"Sure."

"When to be involved and when to stay out of it. I feel my time is well spent helping improve this situation. As you said, it might backfire. Callahan and Corissa may disagree with my decisions. Good leadership is safe. *Great* leadership requires taking risks, taking action when others may believe none should be taken. Visions of a better future require someone to act, not play safe."

"So you're acting, a decision I know all too well."

He smiled and nodded before walking out of the room, Kannan following dutifully.

"I like him," I said to my mate, who stopped eating with a snarl. "Not that much," I mumbled as I leaned away from him. "*Raphael.*"

"He flirted with you," he muttered, going back to his food.

"Is that really it?"

"Yes," he growled, putting his fork down. "He's *fine.* I've just never had someone flirt with you while I was sitting right next to you. Felt too... ballsy, overconfident, and a little smug. You can't deny he was undressing you with his eyes last night. That I have a major problem with. It's not anything you're doing. I trust you. It's his—"

"Ignore it." I stood and patted his shoulder before going back to the bed to start the delicate process of deciding what weapons could stay in the car during the meeting. "I know no one has really crossed that line before with you around, but I'll tell someone when they really overstep. I don't find it *that* attractive when my mate verbally pees on me to mark his territory when it's unnecessary. I like it when my mate is confident and doesn't see other men as a threat... because they *aren't*."

Raphael's groan let me know it would never happen again.

"Thank you," I called out over my shoulder before picking up one of my chakrams. I would bring all of them. They had been helpful in the last fight.

Getting ready, I skipped lunch. I didn't want to believe I was walking into a fight but had to act as if I was. Always prepared. Always ready.

I'm tired of always being ready.

That feeling, the deep exhaustion I couldn't shake, was why I had forgotten to leave my sword out at the hotel. It was the silent reason I had been in denial about Garuda's spying. I was tired. I had been so willing to believe it was just a normal bird. It was what everyone else believed. I hadn't trusted the fear because I was fucking tired and had wanted to trust the defenses we had in place. I had wanted to trust our ability to move in secret so we could meet without trouble.

There was nothing anyone could say to make me shake the guilt, not a single thing. I had known better. I had been taught the lesson time and time again—be careful about trusting too much. For a long time, it had been second nature—trust nothing.

I'm so tired of living like that.

Arms wrapped around my waist, and I leaned back into the one person who let me take refuge, true refuge. I didn't need to say anything. He just understood, which was why he was holding me.

We didn't stay there long. When we were both ready to leave, I checked the time and nodded to him. We grabbed our bags, not planning on returning here for a second night. I didn't know where we would go, but it wouldn't be here.

We were finished loading them when Rahul and Kannan appeared. A second later, two dozen werewolves came into the garage.

"Good security detail," I said with an appreciative nod.

We loaded into jeeps, SUVs, and trucks. Rahul and Kannan were the only two taking something that didn't look like it belonged in a military convoy—a shiny red sports car.

It was unsurprising.

As we got on the road, Raphael was quiet in the passenger's seat, only groaning when we hit the expected traffic. I kept our car right behind Rahul's while the others struggled to stay with the pack, fighting people trying to cut them off and get between us. I kept my front end on Rahul's bumper, and it worked.

We made it to our destination, a farm outside the city, which seemed simple enough.

Parking next to Rahul and Kannan, I got out, not waiting for anyone to tell me it was safe. It was time to turn on the political show again.

"She'll meet you both inside," Rahul said when he got

out of his car. "My werewolves will patrol around the building. Kannan and I will organize them."

"You know, this would be a great chance for you to kill us," I pointed out, staring at the front door of the farmhouse that held a problem I needed to solve.

"In this area?" Rahul laughed. "No, your mate would find this a great place to show us the demon he is without fear of being caught."

"I was making sure you knew that." I looked at my mate. "You ready?"

"Let's get this done."

25

CHAPTER TWENTY-FIVE

Letting him go in first, I followed close behind him. It was quiet inside, but not silent. Soft music played, old music, with enough distortion to tell me it was a record. I followed the sound, Raphael close enough behind me to brush against my back when he breathed. Close enough for him to grab me and give me cover if someone took a shot.

"It's been decades since I've bothered with records," I said when I found Maurvi and a male rakshasa in the dining room. A record player sat at the end of the table, out of the way.

Maurvi moved the needle, and the music stopped.

"It was relaxing," she said softly as she stood. "It's... Thank you for meeting with me, *Nagaraja*." She bowed her head.

"It's what?" I asked curiously but not demanding.

"It's the song Mahatma and I danced to for a decade," she whispered. "It was a good decade."

There was nothing nice to say, nothing sympathizing

or sweet. I would not offer condolences, pity, or empathy for the woman who had lost her mate.

Mine had killed him, for good reason.

"Where should we get started?" the other asked, standing as well, looking at Maurvi for direction. He was trying to fill the comfortable silence, and I felt some sympathy for him and the challenge he faced.

"With the truth," she said, reaching out to touch his arm across the table before looking back at me. "I told him not to. Begged him not to."

"He did it, anyway." My words were cold.

"He did. When he wouldn't change his course, I broke our mate bond and left. Even if he had won..." She shook her head.

"Please. If he had won, you would have gone to him on your knees, begging to be taken back," Raphael snarled.

"Believe what you will," she snapped. "He didn't win, and I made my choice not to fight with him. I made the choice not to let my people fight with him. He lost a third of his army, thanks to me. So believe what you will, but I know my truth."

"Your people, meaning your faction of the rakshasa," I said, hoping to clarify that.

"We're not the most numerous, but due to recent events, we are the strongest. Not all rakshasa are warriors. Some live normal lives, doing magic tricks to brighten the days of children and to make a little money. Some live alone, others in family units." She looked at the table. "Why don't we have a seat and... start from the beginning. Alpha Varadkar told me what information he gave you, but maybe hearing it from me will... help make this a productive meeting."

I nodded. Her second in command moved around the table, allowing me to sit across from her. Raphael sat close to my side, facing him.

"What do you want?" I asked, cutting straight to it.

"Peacc... and to preserve what little honor my kind have left," she answered. "When I heard you were coming to India, I was close by. I also knew that others would come. Others who would want revenge for the events that have unfolded over the last year. I'm sure that isn't surprising. You've been able to defeat two rakshasa kings, Kaliya Sahni. You faced an army and walked out of it, not only alive, but with a title we haven't heard in centuries."

"My people decided on the title," I explained.

"I believe it's well earned," she said.

I watched her swallow her pride. I had been watching her swallow it since the moment I walked into the room. She had a lot of pride.

"You've been a remarkable example of your species."

"That's not for me to say. A ruler should always wonder if they've done enough and strive to do more for their people. It's a job that's never done, impossible to ever truly succeed, and so easy to fail." I put my hands together on the table. "Flattery won't get you anywhere with me, Maurvi."

"What will?" She lowered her head. "What will get all of us out of this room alive and to a place where I don't have to constantly worry about the retribution my mate has so kindly earned for me? I have little to offer. That's why I wanted this meeting. If there is nothing, take my life now, for I don't wish to work for something better for my people, only to have it destroyed right before I can succeed."

"Gods, he left you guilty," Raphael whispered. Maurvi seemed surprised my mate said anything, but after a second, the pain came.

"My mate betrayed everything," she snarled. "The rakshasa... we are spit on. Always called evil. And yes, we've been on the wrong side of history more times than I can number. We are considered man eaters and evil sorcerers, and we have been both, but he had a chance!" She roared the last word, slamming her hand on the table. "I didn't like you when I saw you,"—she pointed at me—"but you reminded us we could be honorable. Better. That it's been achieved before and could be again." Her hand dropped. "And I thought... this is good, no need to fight the battles of Mehar, with his hunts getting us into trouble when our people didn't ask for it. We were just beginning our rule, and war was ugly. Sure, it would bring bloody glory, but it would hurt the rakshasa in the end. Starting a rule with bloodshed when we were the ones in the wrong?" She growled. "Better to avoid it. I would have accepted executing you. I won't lie about that."

"I would have fought for the same outcome, then walked away when it proved to be more costly than planned. Everything has a cost."

"Yes. We spoke to you, and it was decided that neither of us wanted to pay the price of war. My husband spread this decision and was able to enforce it, thanks to the power he not only received from his throne but also his mating to me, binding him to my… family. We will call it my family. I am related, if distantly, to all of them."

"Very distantly," her second in command said softly, and I heard the stress he put on it as if he was trying to make a point.

I nodded. I was technically related to *every* naga. We all came from the same thousand sons of Kadru. I took the chance I was presented. It was time to reinforce I wasn't here to kill anyone.

"I'm sorry. I didn't catch your name," I said, eyeing him. "And I'm sorry for not allowing proper introductions. This my mate, Raphael Alvarez, Warlord of the Cambions."

"Tanish."

"Well met, Tanish." Leaning back, I put my hands in my lap and studied him for a minute while he remained stoic, unflinching under my stare.

"I'm tired, Maurvi." My words surprised her. "I am exhausted. I have fought every day since I was a child. I have been hunted, beaten, and broken. I've watched families destroyed when they had hurt no one. Our generations were dismantled, and most children reach adulthood as orphans. For over a century, I fought *alone* for my people. I will keep fighting until I can't lift a sword. But I'm tired."

"That seems like a dangerous thing to admit," she said, but even if the words should have been threatening, she was staring at the table. Her head down as if she thought this was my monologue before I killed her, explaining my reasoning.

"Possibly." Leaning forward, I waited for her head to

come up and her tiger eyes to meet mine. I felt my power surging, and my eyes were probably a snake's. "There's only one option for you because I'm too tired to think of another solution that doesn't require killing all of you. If you do this one thing for me, I will consider this resolved and your honor restored."

"Tell me," she whispered desperately. So desperate.

"Enter the rakshasa under Tribunal rule and agree you and your people will follow the letter of the Law. Doing so will give you the resources you need to contain those who are speaking against letting this go. Letting the manipulations go because we've both been a victim of them." I reached into my back pocket for the note with Cassius's information, along with a short explanation of who was on the Tribunal and what species they were. I held it up for her, studying her surprised expression. There was a rebellious streak in there, but I didn't hold that against her. The rakshasa had never even considered bowing to the Tribunal, but now I was telling them they had to.

Or they would die.

"This is the information to contact Prince Cassius of the fae, a Tribunal Investigator I've worked with for years. His aunt and uncle are the King and Queen of the fae and Tribunal members. His father and mother were the founding fae members. If you call him right now and agree to begin the process to join the Tribunal, I will leave and never bother you again with this soured time in our history. I will treat any rakshasa who act against me as bad actors, but I won't judge your entire species because of them."

"You'd rob us of our independence."

"That's the price you pay when you rob my people of everything and want your *honor* back." I put the note on the table. Tanish growled as Maurvi stood and stepped away.

"If you leave, I will *never* offer this chance again," I warned.

"I'm trying to understand," she said, looking at me again.

"It's simple. If the rakshasa join the Tribunal, you, and whatever leaders follow you, will be expected to maintain the Law among your people. Mehar got away with what he did because he purposely left the Tribunal blind. He wanted great hunts and got them in our corner of the world. I am not the advocate of the Tribunal, don't believe I am. The members, those on their fake thrones, got there through bloodshed, murder, war, or tragedy. They are all self-serving and dangerous." I tapped the note. "When your people attacked mine, I called this man. Alvina, Queen of the fae, volunteered her jet to get the nagas out of India because my people and I had proven our loyalty. They won't be the best of friends but will be better than trying to do this alone."

"In exchange for control," she whispered.

"We all pay prices."

"Maurvi?"

Tanish and I were in the same position. I couldn't spare the glance, but I figured Raphael was feeling the same way as well.

There was no telling what direction Maurvi would go.

"But this doesn't resolve *us*," she finally said, walking back to the table. "Me and you."

"This is the offer. It puts you in a place where I can trust someone will keep an eye on the rakshasa. It allows us to be on the same page. It will allow you to rebuild your honor by being a contributing member of a larger whole. They will work with you for the betterment of the rakshasa, and you will work with them for the greater supernatural world."

She nodded, reaching out to take the note.

"I will call. I didn't mean I would reject it because it wasn't..." She handed it to Tanish. "Keep that safe."

"Maurvi, what are you..." Tanish trailed off, a gasp taking the place of whatever else he wanted to say. "You can't mean to..."

She gestured for me to stand, so I did, then walked to the end of the table, so there wasn't a barrier between us.

"Tanish, stay in your seat," she ordered, and I heard the woman Tanish was falling in love with. Or maybe he had always been in love with her, even while she was with Mahatma. Powerful, strong. "This is mine to do."

Yeah, she'll be able to wrangle the rakshasa.

"You offer me a chance at redemption, and I will take it because it's the only thing you will accept right now. But I don't feel it pays the debt my people have incurred. I know nothing will pay that debt, but I would like to offer one more thing."

She held out a hand, and I put mine in it.

"Once, a rakshasa was born to a hero. He mated a naga," she said softly. "His hero of a father could summon him."

"I'm not your father," I mumbled before swallowing a lot of surprise at her story. It was the same one I had referenced when I met her. "This was an ability granted between two people who shared blood."

"My grandmother, many generations back, was a nagini," she reminded me. I had been the one to realize it since she was named for that nagini. Maurvi was one name for the nagini princess who had mated the rakshasa, Ghatotkacha. "And you are all traced back to one mother, Kadru."

"Why are you doing this?" I asked.

"I know who you're going to fight, and this is not just a matter of honor between the naga and the rakshasa. This is a matter of honor between you and me, and this is me getting my revenge on that bird for destroying *everything*." She wouldn't let go of my hand. "I, Maurvi, shall answer the summon of you, Kaliya Sahni, *Nagaraja*. If you have need of me, all you must do is speak my name as if you are calling me from across the fields."

My arm blazed, and even Maurvi seemed surprised as three black lines formed on my right forearm.

Tiger stripes.

She let me go once they were solid and leaned to the side. I stared at the tiger stripes in fascination. They weren't much. Most would look at them and think I had a small tattoo.

"That is something only my bloodline in the rakshasa can do. This is the first time it has been offered to someone other than another rakshasa since Ghatotkacha. The stripes aren't a count or limit to how many times you can summon me. This gift is yours until you permanently release me or either of us dies. Let it be evidence of my commitment to a better future, to what my previous mate failed to do. Just between you and me."

"I do," I whispered, touching the stripes with my left hand.

"I will make that phone call now," she said, sitting down.

I showed Raphael the new addition to my arm, and he was mystified. Sitting while he studied them, I watched Tanish get her a phone, then she punched in the number.

"One thing. You said you broke the mate bond. I didn't think about it at the time, but..."

"I mated Mahatma. Breaking it is... a divorce," she answered. "Severing the bond we had agreed to create."

"It's painful, and it's permanent," Tanish added. "Mahatma never would have been able to mate another, not even Maurvi."

"And I cannot mate another. He made all the mistakes, and I am the one who must live with it," she said softly. "We can only mate multiple times if our mate dies and that breaks the bond."

"Oh, I'm sorry." That sounded rough.

"Don't be."

"I'm sorry," Raphael said, breaking his long silence. "I didn't understand the nature of your sacrifice."

"Why would you?" Maurvi asked. "I certainly wouldn't tell you to garner sympathy. It's better that you know now that we've settled these affairs." She put it on speakerphone, hit call, and I heard the ring.

"Prince Cassius speaking." Hearing my friend on the other end of the call was a relief.

"I am Maurvi of the rakshasa. I currently sit at a table with the *Nagaraja*, and she said you would be the correct person to call."

"We'll start tonight," Cassius said. "Kaliya, I have it from here. The Tribunal has been made aware of the situation and is already preparing." Hearing that, I stood up, Raphael following my lead. "Maurvi, this could take a week or two. Is your life in danger? We can provide safety."

I nodded to Maurvi, and she nodded in return. She pointed at her arm, and I looked at mine, seeing the stripes again before I walked out.

"Always, but I would like to remain in India as much as possible."

I didn't hear the rest.

As Raphael and I left the farmhouse, I took a deep breath of the fresh air.

"Holy shit," I exhaled.

"Agreed."

26

CHAPTER TWENTY-SIX

I didn't move, just taking a moment to think of what I had just put in motion. In retrospect, I thought of another thing.

"You were pretty quiet in there," I said to my mate.

"Yeah..." He frowned and shook his head. "I didn't have much to say, honestly. This was between you and her."

"Are you sure?"

He nodded, but something seemed to bug him.

I looked around, wondering where all the werewolves were. A sense of foreboding suddenly filled me.

"Rahul?" I called out.

"Oh, sorry. Here!" he called from out in the field. He wasn't alone. Other werewolves stood up where I could see them. They had all been lower than the tall grass, which explained the empty field.

"What's going on?" I started walking toward him, Raphael going with me.

"I don't know if you'll believe me," Rahul said as I got

closer. Licking my lips, my feet froze. "Or maybe you will."

"No fucking way," I hissed.

Raphael rumbled when he stopped beside me.

"He was sneaky and breached the outer line of defense," Rahul said, shaking his head. "Trying to stay out of sight. I wish we could say we caught him. He saw us trying to creep up on him and bolted. With only one person, we tried not to make it a... distracting incident."

I stepped closer, absorbing the scent as Raphael growled, a continuous low vibration from his chest. I didn't know why he was reacting that way. I was purely shocked.

"Just one? A male?" I asked.

"Just the one," Rahul confirmed. "We've swept everything around the house. No one else has been close."

"Raphael..." I turned back to my mate, seeing black lines radiating from his eyes, traveling over his cheeks. It had been a long time since Raphael hadn't had a smooth transition from one form to another. A long time since his temper started it in this slow creeping way.

"Raphael, it could be someone we've been..." I looked at Rahul and sighed. "We've been hoping to find some cambions in the country. It's a bit much to explain. Raphael and I haven't found anyone outside of the community he's in charge of."

"Ah..." Rahul nodded. "Something of a side mission while you're in the country?"

Nodding, I looked at my mate, wondering where his aggression was coming from.

"Raphael, I can't read your mind."

"*Enemy*," he snarled, finishing the transition. His skin went grey as he grew several inches taller, and horns erupted from his head. The veins covered his skin, creating the unique marble of the cambions. The werewolves growled in both wolf and human form.

"How do you know?"

"He answers to another warlord," Raphael snarled, coming closer. Not looking down at the cambion's footprints, he looked out, past all of us, his gaze pinned on something. "That makes him my enemy."

"Woah..."

"He was spying on us," he continued.

"Why? How does he even know we're here?" I asked, trying to understand what was going through my mate's head.

"Everyone knows this meeting is happening," Rahul said quickly. "Or was since I'm assuming it's concluded. Just like everyone knows you ended up in my mansion last night. You're the most-watched person in the country right now, Kaliya. A witch probably saw you at the Market door last night and hid among the humans. They would have had spies on us ever since. They would have listened in on our messages with the rakshasa."

"I don't need an explanation why witches, vampires, or any else knew where I was. Only cambions," I replied. "As far as we know, any cambions outside of the community in Arizona have been off the grid and out of touch with supernatural society for *five thousand years*. How did this one know to track me *now* when I'm looking for them? No one knew their species existed until recently. Why reveal themselves to spy on us here?"

It was so much more complicated than Rahul could even dream. Even worse, this could have been Sohan or a cambion I didn't know. I wasn't sure which worried me more. The last thing I wanted was Sohan following me.

He's been possibly killing for longer than the oldest known living supernatural, and that's fucking Hasan on the Tribunal.

"We're following him," Raphael growled.

"Yeah, we are," I agreed. "Drive or hike?"

"If you go on foot, you'll lose him," Rahul said, shaking his head. "And I don't see how you're going to track him in a car."

"Hike," Raphael said. "I don't care for how long or how far. He won't be able to lose me."

I wasn't sure I liked this. It seemed as though Raphael was planning to murder this cambion the moment we found him, and all he did was try to get close. For what reason, I didn't know, but Raphael's sudden flip was counterproductive. There was a lot coming out of my mate's mouth I needed to process, but I had little chance. Turning on his heel, he headed for our vehicle. I shrugged at Rahul.

"The meeting is over. Maurvi has agreed to join the Tribunal, and the rakshasa will become a Tribunal species. She's on the phone with Prince Cassius. You might want to call Callahan or Corissa and give some good words for Maurvi. It may expedite the process."

"That was your idea to fix things?"

"Yup. It was the best I could do. Our business is done. It was nice working with you, Rahul. I hope our efforts will help bring lasting peace to India. If you need me, you can call, though I might not be available to answer. If I'm not..." I searched for another note I had written, this one for the Alpha. Finding it, I held it out. "Those are numbers to my nagas, Vikrant and Mahavir, my seconds in command. They'll do what they can. Raphael told them about the deal we made." I looked toward my mate, then took my car keys out. "If we're hiking, we won't need the car anymore. Would you be kind enough to house it so it's not in anyone's way?"

"Of course." He slowly took the keys.

I walked away, chasing after my mate, leaving Rahul to the rest of this mess. I was done with it, and luck was finally on my side. A cambion tried to get close to us and was caught. He escaped, but we had a scent, verification they were out there. I just hoped *they* included Rama.

"Why do you think he spied on us?" I asked Raphael softly.

He shrugged. "Doesn't matter," he answered gruffly.

"Actually, it does matter," I said, putting my hand on the bag he was grabbing. He snatched it out and put me off balance. "Raphael... look at me."

He froze, and blood-red eyes set in black met mine.

"You are out of control," I said clearly, without anger. "Something has bothered you in a way I've never seen before. You need to hit the fucking brakes. Now."

Veins in his neck bulged as he closed his eyes and snarled, but his cambion form slowly receded.

"Better?" he asked softly.

"No. I still don't know what the fuck is going on with

you," I said softly. "And I need to. How do you know there's another warlord?"

"I can... feel it. In the spot where he stood, I could..." He snarled as he looked over his shoulder. "I get the same feeling with all the cambions. I know who they are, what they are. Warrior, mage, civilian, I can feel their rank to mine. They can feel my position over theirs, but his has another aura tied in, and I knew what it meant. Mine is tied in with all the cambions on the compound. That's how they recognize each other and work together. It helps them... stay cohesive. He answers to another cambion like me."

"Another warlord? Why does that make this cambion the enemy?"

"I..." He trailed off. "I don't know. That was just the... feeling I got."

"Don't Alpha werewolf on me," I pleaded. "Please. This doesn't need to be a fight, no matter what your feelings are telling you."

"I didn't think it would be like that. I've never met another cambion that wasn't *mine*. I'm sorry. It won't catch me off guard again."

He was calming down, a positive I clung to.

"It was bound to happen, eventually," I said, sighing heavily. "What if one of our cambions had children and one was a warlord? You can't be the only one forever."

His jaw tightened as he stared at our bags.

"Raphael, you can't be the only one," I repeated.

"I know," he said, the words so forced and disingenuous, I was unsure how to approach this anymore. The man I mated, respected, and loved *wasn't* a domineering conqueror, but that was what he was trying to cover up. The entire situation felt wrong.

"Let's just get moving," I said softly, grabbing my bags.

He grabbed his bag, took one of mine from me, and we closed up the vehicle. We ignored the werewolves as we walked back through the field, only stopping at the spot where they had been, where the feeling of the cambion was the strongest. The werewolves kept their distance, the closest over twenty feet away.

"How do you intend to track him?" I asked.

"Every place he uses magic leaves a bit of his aura soaking the area. We're going to play connect the dots," he answered. "I use it to track cambions around the compound when I'm wandering. I've never done it on this scale, though."

"What type of magic? This?" I lifted a hand, red swirling around it for effect. "Or something else?"

I really wish you had told me these things a long time ago.

"Anything. When we transition between forms or even just begin to. You always say I smell human until I don't. Those moments leave the residue, that piece of aura."

"All right then. If we hit a moment when we can't find the next one, we'll rely on my tracking skills." I headed for the next field and the tree line beyond it.

"That's what I was thinking." Raphael walked at my side, his words still full of tension as though it was hard for him to speak.

No, it's not hard for him. He's trying to speak in the right way for me. He's holding his own leash. That's what it is.

As we entered the trees, Raphael turned, angling our path as he pointed at a bush.

"He did something here, probably trying to outrun the werewolves," he explained.

"What type of cambion are we dealing with?"

"Mage..." He didn't sound certain and soon elaborated. "Or something like it, I've never seen before. I don't know enough cambions to know if there's a natural... variation, I guess. He could be a mage or something similar but distinct."

As we walked, I stewed.

Night fell as Raphael pointed out places where the cambion had done magic. I looked at the footprints left on the ground—male shoes, larger feet, adolescent or adult. Light steps would make the cambion harder to track, but the ground was soft and wet enough, he couldn't walk, certainly couldn't run without making tracks.

The entire time, I stewed about the revelation that my mate could track his own kind by using the places where they did magic. That *all* the cambions could do it.

Even after a year, none of them had mentioned it to me. This was a hell of a thing, and not a single cambion ever bothered to educate me... not even my mate.

27

CHAPTER TWENTY-SEVEN

We walked all night and well into the next day, ending up in what I believed was the Southern Ridge Forest, a section, at the very least. From a simple web search, the Southern Ridge Forest was 6,200 hectares or just under twenty-four square miles, and the farm where we had met Maurvi was within half a day's walk. However, my phone's location tracking ability was shut off for good reason, so I could only guess.

We didn't make camp. I was walking because Raphael was still walking. He wouldn't stop, so I couldn't. I didn't want to lose this cambion, either, but my legs hurt, and my stomach was growling, but I just pressed on... and stewed about *how* we were tracking the cambion.

Well, we're probably far enough away from the werewolves by now...

"How long have you known you could do this with other cambions? Feeling or seeing where they do magic and being able to identify them?"

"Since the labs, excluding the time I didn't have my

memories. I really noticed it while we were staying with Cassius, catching cambions in each other's rooms and around the compound, but it fades. We could lose the trail because eventually, it'll fade."

Well, that explains why he won't stop.

"You didn't think I would want to know this sort of information?"

"Kaliya..."

"No, don't say my name like that," I huffed. "This is going to sound really petty, but I tell you everything about my people. Do you know how this looks? You've been hiding behind the idea all of you are ignorant and not telling me anything."

"I know," he snapped back. "I know what it looks like."

I didn't get mad because he snapped, just waited for more.

"I..." Raphael kept stomping through the forest. "I wanted to be certain. That's the only way I can describe it. You have a certainty about your kind that I *don't*. That's why I want to find other cambions. So I can feel as though I know my people, to give correct information to you and others, and not feel like I'm floundering or making it up as I go with every little thing. What if I'm wrong about a small detail that becomes important later? That could be life-threatening. So, I don't tell you what I'm not certain about. I continue to explore and test it until I'm certain and ready."

"And you're not entirely certain about this." I understand it even if I disagreed. This was about telling me—his mate. Others, I totally understood.

"Not at all. I don't know what determines how fast it fades because it's not consistent. I don't know if it's what a cambion does or how powerful the cambion is naturally. I don't know if it can be covered up." He growled, but it was frustrated, not angry. "I wasn't going to ask you to rely on this, but I was so... I felt him and knew I could try this. I might have convinced you to do something stupid. We'll see."

Taking a deep breath, I nodded, then tried to let go of the petty anger. It wasn't productive, and I felt bad for even giving in to it. He offered his explanation, and I was fine just listening and accepting it.

"Okay, we'll forget about it. No harm, no foul."

"Really?" His disbelief in my ability to move on made it impossible to do just that.

"I'm hurt," I said, throwing up my hands. "I guess I believed you would tell me what you knew, even if it wasn't perfect. Especially since I spend my every waking moment with cambions. I mean, seriously?"

"I understand. Look, it really was just this one thing." Raphael rubbed his face. "I agree. I should have told you more about this passive stuff earlier. I'm just..."

"Insecure," I said without thinking and instantly regretted it. There were better word choices that weren't so loaded.

"That's a way to put it," he growled.

"I'm insecure, too," I said softly, gently. "Insecure in my position, insecure in my power. So insecure, I broke down when I found Adhar because I wasn't ready to lose him as my *crutch*. If your knowledge about the cambions is all you have to be insecure about, there's nothing to be ashamed about."

"I'm expected to know for them. I'm expected to have the answers, even when they know I don't because they know what I know. It doesn't stop them from having the quiet expectation their leader will figure it out," he explained. "I *need* the answers for *them*."

"Then don't answer them until you're certain, but please don't hide from me. I'm the one person who will help you find those answers, to study them and figure out the truth. We could search for months... years, but I'm willing to hunt them down with you. You *know* that."

"You've been hunting for your own, and my problems are much smaller than yours." "They are, Kaliya. No one is trying to exterminate the cambions anymore. No one is trying to burn our homes or kill our children. I didn't want to distract you from what mattered more."

He probably didn't mean for it to, but those words cut my self-esteem to pieces.

"I never want my problems to be more important than yours," I said, shaking my head. "Don't bury something because I'm dealing with something else. Don't do that to me."

"Realizing we could hunt down Rama felt like killing two birds with one stone. I could help you find the answers you need... and get some of my own."

"What if *they* don't know?" I asked, crossing my arms. "What do you do, Raphael, if they've come to terms with a lack of knowledge and accepted themselves for who they are? What if they can't tell you anything you don't already know?"

His eyes went wide as he struggled to form an answer to my question. I could guess why it was so hard for him. He had built up this image in his mind of ancient cambions who had figured out everything about their kind. They had to because *he* needed that level of detail in his own life. *He* needed to understand.

I had made the same assumption so many times in my life, only to have it backfire.

"Trust me to help you the way I trust you."

He nodded.

"Want to keep walking?" I asked.

He nodded again, so I forced my legs to move again down the trail. As midday turned into evening, the sky darkening into golds and purples, he finally spoke again.

"We're always going to have these conversations, aren't we?"

"From what I understand about lifelong relationships, probably."

"It's a good thing," he said, grabbing my hand. "I like having them."

"Do you?"

"I know you would never make me feel like I was second. After everything you did, everything I remind people you did for me, I know you wouldn't. Then I look at the nagas. I saw Adhar's body, and my problems felt small, even when I knew they were still important. Added to those feelings, I'd become used to this thing I didn't know everything about yet. Your problems are so big, and this little thing, passive and potentially useless, didn't seem like something to bring up right now."

"And when you first realized you had it, how it was working, we weren't even speaking."

"Yeah, that probably contributed to it in the beginning."

"No harm, no foul," I said again, and this time, I meant it.

We continued until sundown. I was struggling. If an hour and a half across Delhi had been hard, this was nightmarish. The only reason I kept going was thinking about my training, the endurance challenges Hisao had come up with. Staggering, I leaned into a tree. He turned around, finally realizing I was a good fifteen feet behind him. I was certain he knew, thanks to our bond, and had just filed it under close enough not to worry.

"I can't. I need to get off my feet, Raphael. It's nearly sundown. Let's make camp and hope the trail doesn't disappear tonight."

He came back to me and nodded.

"Okay."

Sinking to the ground, groaning loudly as I stretched my legs out, I fully intended on kicking off my boots as Raphael pulled out a picnic blanket and laid it out.

"We didn't bring a tent, but I packed this. Forgot about it while at the house, but here, it will keep us out of the dirt."

"Thanks." I was so out of energy, I didn't move. "I'll get over there, eventually."

He stared at me for a minute, then closed his eyes with a pained expression.

"I'm sorry for pushing you this hard. You're still dealing with..."

I winced, remembering Gabi's note.

"Yeah, that." I had worked out every day for two weeks and had been on a special diet. I had picked up some of my weight, but it had been hard. The schedule had been strict, and it did everything it could, but I just wasn't the same after what Pavan's venom did to me. It would have taken me six months to a year to get back to that point, but I *knew* Garuda would not let me have six months to a year.

"Um..." I had just chastised him for not telling me something. "Raphael, I need to tell you something."

"Do we want a fire going? It could be risky, but I can get one started."

"No, we'll be fine in the moonlight. It's not cold, and a fire would draw more attention."

I watched him sit down on the blanket, knowing I should have been anxious, but I was too tired to draw the emotional energy I needed to feel anything.

"Considering I gave you a hard time for not telling me something, I need to tell you some news. I've only known for..." Frowning, I tried to think how much time. "This would be the second night. Gabi put a note in my weapon bag. I had forgotten about it for a few days but finally read it while we were at Rahul's."

"Gabi?"

"Yeah, Gabi," I said, not looking at him anymore. I stared at the trees, unable to focus on anything as I thought of the best way to explain. He was in the corner of my vision, so I couldn't look away completely. "She looked over my injuries when we returned from India. Remember?" When he nodded, I kept going. "I brushed her off and didn't really give her the chance to tell me everything. I mean, she could have told me right there, but that would have been... inappropriate for a lot of reasons. She expected me to ask for more information later, but I never did. I was thinking about how to rebuild my strength as quickly as I could, put on more weight, how to hunt a mythical birdman. I didn't care about my injuries because they would be long term, and I couldn't fix them, so I never asked for details."

"I'm not surprised," Raphael said, leaning forward.

"She avoided me the last few days, then slipped a note in my bag." I pulled my bag to me and opened the pouch where it was still hidden. "More about the damage I took, things she had to carry in secret, unsure how to broach the conversation. She watched us take care of Roshni, and there isn't a person on the compound who doesn't see how you feel about that little girl." I opened the envelope and pulled out the note, rereading it quickly and catching the highlights. "Gabi knew this might come up eventually and wanted me to be informed, but it scared her to tell me. She didn't want to hurt me. Poor girl. She's a sweetheart."

"Kaliya?"

"It might change in the future, but it would take decades, if not centuries. The important thing is I'm infertile now," I whispered. "There's too much scar tissue. It could continue to repair itself, maybe not. This is just the way things are now. Gabi doesn't know. She can't fix something that isn't... *technically* broken. Scars are a natural part of life."

Scared for reasons I couldn't fathom, I folded it up

again and slid it back into the envelope. Hands shaking, the paper tried to crumple as I shoved it away.

"I would be... okay with never having a child," I admitted. "I could go either way, with or without." I finally dared to look at him again. "But I know you."

He sat quietly for what felt like an eternity, and I couldn't bring myself to continue talking. His mind was an unknown, which made me think of older memories and a dark fear I had always denied.

I was scared he might define my worth, the worth of our relationship, by this destroyed possibility. In the back of my mind, comments from men I now ruled and men I buried played on repeat in my mind.

Raphael loved me while I'd kept open the option for children in the future. That option was now closed. Even with all the talk about potentially healing, more than likely, it was permanently closed. Would that change our relationship just as permanently?

"It's going to be fine," he said softly.

I couldn't help an insane laugh, the emotion too overwhelming. It was all so simple to my mate at that moment, and I couldn't believe it. There were a lot of things I couldn't believe, even my own feelings.

"Yeah?"

"Yeah." He seemed pretty set on it, and I couldn't think of a damn thing to say.

He got up, closing the distance between us in only two steps, and hauled me off the forest floor. Taking me back to the blanket, he held me between his legs from behind, his arms around my waist.

"Kaliya, the only person who didn't understand how

badly you were injured was you," he whispered. "I had suspicions we were just avoiding all the possible long-term consequences. I didn't think about this specific one, but it... doesn't surprise me, either. Our relationship isn't defined by your ability to have biological children." He held me tighter.

"I know other nagas made you feel this way, but your worth isn't defined by your ability to continue the species. You know that logically and have fought it for your entire life. So, we already didn't know if we could even have children, and now we have a definitive answer. Oh, well." He leaned down and kissed the side of my neck.

"Oh, well?"

"Oh, well," he repeated, so sure. "But,"—he brushed my hair aside—"there's this little girl without parents we've been helping. I know I've been silent about it. Kaliya, the last thing I want to do is force you to take on a responsibility you're not one-hundred percent sure of. You already have a lot of them, and forcing someone to raise a child they don't want to raise is a recipe for disaster." He kissed me again.

"I know you're still considering it, and I want you to know if you say yes, I will love that little girl as if she's my flesh and blood. If it isn't the time, one day we could adopt. I will love any child we bring into this family as my own and never regret not having biological children. I just want a family with you, no conditions, no expectations, none of it. I want to be a father, and Roshni has helped me learn, helped me feel, I can be a father to any child who needs one. Okay?"

"Thank you," I whispered, my shoulders shaking. "I

don't even know why I want to cry. I didn't care if I had children. I just..." Closing my eyes, I tried to control my breathing. "You said it. I fought it for a long time, but after a century of hearing about how my job was to bring in a new generation,"—I rubbed my eyes—"it's so irrational."

"It's a big thing," he reminded me. "Didn't you promise not to have children until you felt the world was safe enough?"

"I did."

"Maybe you were holding on to that as a hope," he said gently, pulling me back and over, laying me next to him, my legs on his thigh. "Maybe here,"—he tapped my chest—"you wanted to live in a world where you could have children, and they could play safely."

I couldn't keep my eyes open, not just from exhaustion but because of the pain. It had been a bright future to fight for, a good thing to throw in the face of people who told me to get busy, but I realized Raphael was right. Somewhere along the way, I had actually *wanted* that future.

"You can still have that future," he whispered, and I felt his lips on my forehead.

28

CHAPTER TWENTY-EIGHT

I woke up well before dawn, feeling raw but better. My legs were sore, but they would work again. My back was sore from the forest floor, but it also wasn't so terrible some stretching wouldn't fix it.

One thing was certain, through the aches and pains.

"I fucking hate this trip," I said, shaking my head as I untangled from my mate, who was out cold. I had a feeling he'd stayed up later than I had, watching out for things while he held me. He would want to get moving at dawn, so I scoped out our surroundings, making sure I could still find the trail we needed to follow and remember the direction it was going in.

It took me some time to go back to my original thought.

"I really fucking hate this trip," I repeated.

There was only one real answer, at least only one I could find.

I was tired of being emotional.

"I was just fine for a century," I said, keeping my voice

down as I talked to myself in the quiet morning. "Not digging deeper into all... this." I waved a hand at myself. "Now, I feel like a case study a therapist would absolutely delight in speaking to." I crossed my arms, glaring at the forest around me. "Why does everything have to rip my fucking heart out and stomp on it now?"

The more I thought about it, though, the less I hated the trip because of those conversations. I liked who I was today more than who I was a year ago. I liked her more than the woman who had slept with Cassius, more than the woman who had left Hisao's estate, training completed. If the painful, vulnerable conversations that made me feel weak actually were the reason I liked myself more, I would continue to have them.

There were a lot of reasons to hate being in India for the second time in less than a year. The emotional turmoil didn't even make the top five.

"Good morning," Raphael said quietly behind me.

"Did I wake you?" I turned around to see him propped up on one arm. "Didn't mean to. Just woke up."

"You don't sleep to dawn most days. Why would you now?" He stood and walked over to me with stiffness that told me he was having a hard time recovering from our sleeping arrangements, just like me. "I'll pretend I didn't hear you talk to yourself."

"Oh, more went on in my head than what I said out loud." That he had heard some of it was only slightly embarrassing. It was nothing I wouldn't have said to him.

"Oh, I saw," he said, brushing a hand over my cheek. "But I will say... I can't wait for us to have a moment when it's not a tough or painful conversation, for a day that feels... normal."

"Me, too." I touched his hand before looking at our things. "Time to get back to it."

"Yeah..." His sigh was one I felt to my core.

He folded the blanket as I checked my weapons. I saw the date on my phone as I checked the time.

"Can you believe we've only been in India for a week?" I asked as we picked up our bags. "Today is the seventh day since we arrived. Feels so much longer."

"In that time, we've burned your mother's things, convinced a supernatural species ruler to join the Tribunal, and found a cambion... the trail of one at least." Raphael groaned as we started walking. "Yeah, it feels longer."

"Do you still see that... aura thing?" I asked as we followed the tracks that had been leading up to the night before.

"Yeah, but it's fainter. We might have lost time, but if he stops, we'll eventually catch up to him. He had a head start and probably kept running until the werewolves were off his heels."

"That he was faster than a werewolf in wolf form is... surprising. Any of the cambions back home that fast?"

"Haven't tested it officially because I don't like working with Wagner, but I've never been, at least not with the werewolves outside the lab. It makes me wonder if he might be something unique I've never felt, or maybe he's just trained. Or he's talented, naturally fast, which is a bigger boost for cambions. Who knows?"

"Yeah. Just makes me wonder how fast we're talking about when it comes to this cambion."

"We'll find out."

I kept my eye on the trail. Tracking someone through vegetation was a combination of things—broken branches, bits of clothing or hair, tracks. Slowly, the trail we followed turned, veering a new direction.

"At twenty-four square miles, this forest isn't that big," I mumbled. "Average walking speed is four miles or so an hour. We should have already popped out on another side, so why are we still chasing this guy through it?"

"Well, this isn't the first time he's turned. He's barely gone in a straight line." I could hear the shrug in his voice.

"Yeah."

Raphael was right. This cambion was weaving around, doubling if not tripling the travel time with his zig-zag through the deepest and roughest terrain of the forest, and I was getting annoyed. The only thing I was happy about was the sound of running water, and the trail was leading us in that direction.

"At least he's kept us away from populated areas. This isn't an empty forest; it usually has hikers. He's avoided every piece of civilization through it. Probably thanks to the route he's using."

"Do you think he's trying to throw off any... werewolves following him?"

"I don't know," I said, shrugging. "He could use this route to stay out of sight."

The sound of running water grew louder as a small stream entered a pool.

I froze as I saw the man standing in the waist-deep water, eyes going wide before I grabbed Raphael and shoved him down, slamming a hand over his mouth and feeling his body practically vibrating. Once I was down, hopefully out of sight myself, I gave my mate a surprised expression as I let my bags slide off my shoulders.

"Is that...?" I lifted my hand.

"Yes," Raphael said, a growl trying to escape.

"Let me lead?" *Please, let me lead. Do not—*

That got a resounding no as Raphael stood and walked closer, making no attempt to hide. I caught the shift in his scent as I scrambled after him, hoping to keep this from becoming a fight.

"Hey!" Raphael called out.

"Who are you?" the other cambion yelled in Hindi, and I cursed.

"Raphael, let me talk to him!" I pleaded, grabbing the back of my mate's shirt. He was already transitioning into his cambion form. I looked around my mate.

"My name is Kaliya Sahni, a naga. I've been hoping to find one of your kind, and we found your trail outside of the forest in the field." I spoke Hindi, knowing he'd understand. It left Raphael out, but I needed this cambion to listen.

The cambion's jaw dropped open, his eyes went red and black, and the veins grew from them, a scene I knew all too well.

"Please don't run," I pleaded. "We're not here to fight you."

He looked at Raphael, my massive mate. With a snarl,

he transitioned, grey skin and everything, but didn't come for us.

I cursed as he left the other side of the pond, grabbing his things, then ran after him, knowing my long-legged mate was right behind me.

"Please!" I yelled.

The cambion snarled again, a red ball forming in his hand. He threw it, then four others. I dodged all of them, but I heard a roar behind me and looked for a moment to see my mate had been blasted. I was now halfway between the two.

Raphael was already getting back to his feet as I looked back at the cambion, several of the red orbs of power floating around him. Behind him, two orbs were spinning so quickly, they were making a red ring of energy.

All I have to do is disable him for a minute so Raphael can get here. He'll be strong enough to keep this guy in place so we can talk.

I had to sidestep more of those blasted orbs. Destroying trees and blasting the earth, I knew they would kill me if they hit.

With only ten feet left between me and the cambion, the spinning stopped, and I gasped at what I saw. It wasn't the forest we were in. It was a wild jungle, different, greener. He was glaring as he jumped through, and it closed.

"Damn it!" I screamed as I ran and jumped for it, shifting into my snake form at the last moment. I went straight through, shifting back to my human form, then turned around to see Raphael's look of horror as the portal disappeared.

Oh, fuck.

I was stunned as I tried to comprehend what had just happened. I had no idea where I was, and I had just left my mate with no idea how to follow me or how I would get back there.

Turning back to where the cambion had to be, I saw him looking at me with as much surprise as I felt. Then he ran, and I cursed. He was fucking fast.

I gave chase. Since I was already here, alone in a jungle I didn't know, there was no point in losing him now. Following him through the jungle, I was amazed at how easily he could traverse the thick undergrowth, hopping over downed trees and leaving me struggling. Then I saw the house between the trees, the cambion's destination.

Stunned, I skidded to a stop.

Did I find their home?

He made it to the door and flung it open but looked upset when he didn't find what he wanted. I slowly walked toward the house but wasn't really focused on him. I was taking it all in.

Then I heard the clear, sweet sound of metal cutting the air. With no time to react, my feet stopped when the blade stopped horizontally at my throat. The male cambion smiled as though his hero had just arrived and came back toward me, creating orbs that slowly circled him.

Trying not to breathe, thanks to the sword at my neck, I could see her out of the corner of my eye. Blood-red eyes set in black were burning with fury—powerful, righteous, determined.

Exactly the same.

It was as though not a day in the last five thousand years had changed her. It could have been yesterday, but I was frozen, unsure how to process the fact that Rama held the blade against my throat.

“Who are you?” she asked in Hindi.

29

CHAPTER TWENTY-NINE

Metal touched the vulnerable skin of my throat as I tried to think, to find anything to say.

"I will only ask once," she snarled.

"I'm…"

Gods, do I tell her my name is fucking Kaliya? I didn't think this far ahead. I don't want her to kill me, but I will practically be asking her to if I say that.

"Not so ready to talk now," the man growled at me, coming closer now. "Stupid to jump through a portal like that."

"Did she speak to you?" Rama asked the other cambion.

"Yeah. She even had another one of our kind with her. Luckily, I pushed him back from the portal. She was too agile to hit, and the trick she pulled to fit before it closed was something I had never seen."

"What did she do?"

"Turned into a snake! On my honor, she turned into a snake. That makes her a—"

"Naga," Rama snarled, pushing the blade harder against my neck. "Why did you chase him through the portal?"

"Allies of mine caught his scent during an important meeting I was in while they patrolled. He ran. I wasn't coming after him because I wanted to hurt him. I've been hoping to find... more of your kind for a long time. To talk."

Rama snarled, and the male cambion stepped back.

"What were you doing?" she demanded of him.

"I... heard something while going into the city, rumors and stuff. I avoid the wolves like you tell me to. I just..."

"What rumors?" she snapped.

"People whispering about *him*," he admitted as if it was a grave crime to even mention whoever *he* was. "After a bit of looking around, I found out what was going on and realized there must be an imposter, so I went to get verification. I was right. *She* is an imposter." He nodded in my direction.

I was too confused.

"Boy, explain better," Rama ordered.

"She calls herself Kaliya, and people whisper she's the Demon Serpent."

Finally, Rama stepped in front of me, the sword staying in a deadly position, its point pushing ever so gently against the hollow of my throat.

"Who are you?" Rama asked, her voice thunderous.

She was beautiful and terrifying.

"My mother named me Kaliya Sahni. Sahni is my family name, not that many nagas bother to use them on a daily basis. I was named after the naga of the first generation, Kaliya, the Demon Serpent." I took a moment to let that sink in. "I am the reigning *Nagaraja*. I'm close allies with the cambions in North America. Cambions is what we call your kind. The one with me was my mate, Raphael Alvarez."

Rama's eyes grew larger with every word, especially at the end when I explained my mate, but she wasn't surprised for long. A snarl built, and the rumble from her would have made many supernaturals step back.

Or run.

"Liar."

Focusing, I pulled on the cambion power I had, letting red magics form around me.

Her hand and the blade shook.

"Could I do this without one of your kind as my mate?" I asked.

"Rama! Kahan!"

I recognized the voice yelling and had memories of the man who came into view, storming down a trail toward us.

"Here, Father!" Kahan called in return. "I—"

"Messed up, I see," Sohan said, clearly angry when he saw me. "How did someone follow you home? What if it had only been your mother here?" Sohan turned his glare on Kahan, then looked at Rama. "Are you going to kill her and be done with it?"

"She's a *naga*," Rama said, her nostrils flaring with anger and possible frustration.

Sohan lost his anger and looked at me differently now, coming up to his daughter's side as he crossed his arms.

"Do you think they remember the agreement?" he asked.

Rama side-eyed him then growled, "It doesn't matter if they do. I promised him I would never... Kahan, make another portal and dump her somewhere else. She was bold enough to follow you into the unknown, she can find her own way home."

She can't kill me... can she?

Reaching up, I put my fingers on the dull side of the blade, then took a step back and slowly pushed it down and to the side.

"I see," I whispered, watching Rama put her sword away. "So, you can't kill me?"

"None of my family can actually hurt a naga unless you try to hurt us," she answered.

I raised an eyebrow at Kahan, who paled. Rama's gaze followed mine, and I saw an older sibling's frustration, then her sheer need to defend him when she looked back in my direction and stepped between us.

"Do you plan to take offense to his actions? He believed he was defending himself. You're uninjured," she said.

"No. I'll forget all about how he blasted my mate with those fancy magic balls and tried to incinerate me with them... if you and your family will talk to me, answer some questions," I said, keeping my eyes on hers.

"Why do you want to speak to us?" Sohan asked, studying me as though I was the most interesting thing he had seen in the last century.

"I want to ask some questions." I wasn't going to

elaborate. If I said too much, too quickly, I would look like a crackpot.

She grumbled, shaking her head before she looked at her father.

"She's mated to one of our kind," Rama explained. "She's proven that already. She's apparently been looking for more of us."

Sohan perked up, the intense light in his eyes growing as he stepped closer to me.

"Are you?"

"I am," I confirmed. I turned and felt the longing to have Raphael here with me for this. We were so far apart, but I figured he was to the south. Maybe. "I made it through... Kahan's portal, but he didn't."

When I turned back to them, Sohan was a step closer, nearly making me jump out of my skin. He was taller than he had any right to be. I didn't remember him being so tall. Then again, I had a distinct memory of Rama only reaching the middle of my chest, and she was only a few inches shorter than me.

Ah. My memories are from his *perspective.* He *was taller than me.*

"I feel you have a story to tell," he said, still looking at me.

"You wouldn't believe it." I swallowed my fear and anxiety. I was confronting everything I didn't want to confront, missing the one man who I needed to back me up.

"I am very old. I've seen it all. Try me."

"Why don't we... get introductions out of the way?

And possibly get my mate here. He would love to find others—"

"Rama, her mate is like you," Kahan said quickly. "I don't want to bring him here."

I clenched my teeth.

Damn it.

"Then we won't," Rama said simply. "Father, take her inside. She's not a threat. I would rather send her away, but I see you want to speak to her. If you want, you can. I'm going to see Mother, though."

Sohan was still looking at me, his head tilted to the side.

"My name is Sohan," he said, then grabbed my arm and pulled me along to follow him. "To think, after all these years, a naga has come to our home, a rare nagini even." He waved with his free hand as Rama walked away. "Have fun with your mother, Rama." Then he turned to his son, and his mood shifted as he pointed. "You will do a patrol."

"I just got home!"

"And you've forgotten the supplies you were supposed to bring back and clearly didn't stay hidden well enough," Sohan snapped. "Go."

Kahan snarled and walked away.

For some reason, I didn't want to be alone with Sohan. He took me inside the home and closed the door behind us, then turned on a light, telling me they had electricity, and pointed to the table.

"Sit down, Kaliya Sahni, and tell me why you're here," he ordered.

"You know my name." I grabbed a chair and put my

ass in the seat.

"Normally, my son isn't allowed to go anywhere with other supernaturals. Over my long years, I learned which ones were safe to hide around and which ones weren't. It let me hear things." He sat across from me. "I heard of a nagini born, one Kaliya Sahni. I've listened for a century now... small things, whispers of what you achieved, the reputation you built. I'm not completely up to date, but there's only one adult nagini in the world. I'm not a fool." He leaned closer. "Tell me why you're here."

"What was the last thing you heard about me, so I know where to start?"

"That you helped free demon-human hybrids from captivity. You and others call them cambions."

"You're a cambion," I pointed out warily.

"I know."

I stuffed my surprise down. I could ask him questions another time... if he didn't throw me out. I was an intruder, potentially threatening his family and home. It would be a very Sohan thing to do if I understood him even half as well as I thought I did.

"I'm mated to a cambion," I said, trying to figure out what I was supposed to say next.

"You are. That I knew. Heard it in the same conversation." He studied me, then smiled. "You don't understand what I'm asking, do you?"

I had no idea.

He must have seen the confusion on my face, but instead of telling me outright, he lunged across the table. I bit back a scream as he grabbed my throat and squeezed with power, which I knew would only be matched by three people in my lifetime.

Sammy, Mateo, and Raphael.

"How did you know about *us*?" he demanded as I grabbed his wrist, trying to pull him off as I uselessly pulled my head back. I was locked in, and if he wanted to snap my neck right there, he could have. "I never let anyone reveal my family. You found your demons in the western world. What made you look for us *here*?"

I tried to answer, and his grip loosened just enough.

"I... h-have... m-m-memories," I fought to say. "His..."

Sohan released me, but he was still right in front of me, crowding my space as I tried to catch my breath.

"Whose?"

"I was named for Kaliya," I said, breathing hard as I rubbed my throat. "They named me after him because my mother discovered a way to learn I was reincarnated from him, and she accidentally gave me all of his memories."

Sohan fell back into his seat.

"Gods..." He *believed* me. One less battle to fight.

While I had the chance, I told him my story

"When I was a child, my mother and a witch delved into old magics, researching everything they could find about reincarnation and magic. My mother thought it might be useful to the nagas. They devised a spell, each of them doing a part of it, and it worked on me. She revealed my past life, not just to them, but... to me. I gained his memories, and I changed. She had her witch friend block the memories of his life from me. There was a key to unlock them, though.

"I didn't know, had no memory of any of this for over a century, but when I mated, to my cambion, Raphael, I started getting visions and flashbacks. I was blacking out," I continued to explain, taking his silence as a chance to say as much as I could as quickly as I could. The more they knew, the less likely they were to kill me or toss me out. I hoped.

"I had to deal with the block before everything clicked. I grew up thinking I was normal but learned I wasn't. I know about your family because he knew you. I asked you to introduce yourself, but I already knew your name. I know Rama and your mate, Lalika. I didn't know or don't remember Kahan. When we were chasing after a cambion, trying him down, part of me wanted to think it was you, but it wasn't right. I know what type of cambion you are, and Raphael said Kahan was something different."

"Why?"

"Why what? Why did I try to find you? Why..." I shook my head, trying to figure out what he was asking. "Truthfully? I never thought I would find you, but apparently, Kahan heard my name and decided to check it out." I was at a loss.

"Why the need to find us?"

I sighed.

"Your information ends before something terrible happened. I brought my mate to India to meet my people. The rakshasa attacked us after being given our location by... by an old enemy. I was hoping someone in your family would have a specific bit of information I need." I swallowed my fear and asked, "Why do you believe me?"

"Because I'm too old," he whispered. "And I know the gods of these lands do things that are beyond our comprehension. I know nagas reincarnate after they die, new children of a new generation. Have known this since..."

"Five thousand years ago?"

"Time is fuzzy that far back, but yes. I learned after..." He looked at the door and growled softly. "We cannot help you... with anything. You cannot stay."

"What?"

"I won't have you hurt her again," he said, standing up. I jumped away from him before he could grab me.

"I've never hurt her," I snapped. "*He* might have, but *I* haven't."

"But by existing, you will. Leave. Leave before she comes here with Lalika. I'll tell her you asked your questions, and I pointed you to the nearest town."

"No."

"What could you possibly want from us?" he demanded, stalking closer. "What could be so important that you would hurt her? I will kill you, Kaliya Sahni, before I let you reopen these wounds for her."

"I am in India to find someone who knows the way to Ramanaka, so I can kill Garuda. I need to stop his reign of terror." Straightening my spine, I lifted my chin and glared at him. "I know, from memory, one person who used to *live* there."

30

CHAPTER THIRTY

Sohan glared in return, his eyes full of fire.

"Maybe I shouldn't kill you and let Garuda do it," he said softly. "Maybe if he finally does the thing he's always dreamed about, you won't come back and haunt this family in a third life."

"I will haunt you in *every* life if that's what I need to do to save my people," I hissed. "Do you know how many nagas are left? I can count them on both hands, and three of them are *infants*. I will do whatever is necessary to help them. My people are dying, and I am the *Nagaraja* now. I understand this will hurt your family and open emotional wounds that have been trying to heal for five thousand years. I even fought with my mate against this very plan because he wanted to find you before I was given that title. However, I am out of options and would rather pick emotional pain over the decimation of my people."

"I thought Garuda was killed centuries ago," he finally said, crossing his arms.

"I'm not the only one reincarnated and given the memories of my previous life. I don't know how he did it or who did it to him, but he's been at this for a long time. This time, he's been smart about it. He hides in the shadows and works through others instead of trying to meet us in open conflict. He revealed himself last month when… when he killed our last second-generation naga and tried to use the rakshasa to wipe us out."

"Adhar."

I shouldn't have been surprised he knew Adhar's name. He had known mine and known the nagini near his home had to be me. Maybe I was surprised because Adhar's name had been important enough to cross this man's lips. I figured Adhar would have been honored to receive recognition from this ancient. I was honored for him.

But I had to keep fighting.

"Yes, Adhar." I stared down Sohan. "Three thousand years old, he had given everything to his people for so long, including his life at the end. I found him holding the body of a human woman he considered the daughter of his heart. Her mate was dead in the room, the only trained warrior there. Her *orphan* is now in my care, a little girl who had to go into her snake form as an infant to *survive.* A little girl who was in the room when her parents were *butchered*! You're telling me I should value the feelings of a *five-thousand-year-old woman* over that baby's future?" I hissed, revealing fangs, my fury reaching its peak as I made sure Sohan knew I'd go down fighting. "No."

"What do you know about the pain she's suffered?

About the pain you'll inflict on her?" His voice wavered, his argument losing some of its power.

"Enough to know she can survive it," I said, keeping my head held high.

"She might not want to help."

"If she's unwilling to help when she knows the stakes, then she's not the woman I remember and wouldn't be someone I would want in my life now." I hissed. "If she doesn't want to help, I'll find other ways to get the information I need."

His argument to defend Rama's feelings fell on deaf ears now. Now that I had seen her, seen the changes in her from those days in Ramanaka and Vrindavan, I knew she was strong. She was a warrior. She could use a blade and could have cut my head off the moment she saw me.

The silence stretched out until he broke first.

"Infants..." He shook his head, eyes closing. "Killing infants..."

"Skinning us to make bags. Putting our eyes in jars." Everything I said made him more uncomfortable. "You've seen it through the years, haven't you? Did you find nothing good about my people to make you want to stop it? Nothing at all?"

"I have seen those things... and I liked your people," he admitted. "I honored him as a son, Lalika *loved* him, but I told myself... with him gone, with all the ones we knew gone, what could we do? How did we help people who didn't know us?"

"Well, I'm here to finally ask for that help."

He looked at the front door, sighing.

"Yes, you are, but you shouldn't get your hopes up,

Kaliya Sahni. There's something you must understand before I *attempt* to help you. You see, the nagas have been a forbidden topic in this place since he died and Rama returned. I knew of the troubles the nagas faced, but no one else here did. What you say to them will be a shock, and…" He trailed off, then shook his head. "Come, let's speak to Kahan first," he said, then left the building. "There's so much he doesn't know, can't understand, about this situation. It's only right to put him on the same page as the rest of our family."

I followed cautiously, not foolish enough to think this couldn't be a ploy. Kahan could make a portal. As we walked through the jungle, I kept my distance from Sohan for that very reason. We found Kahan sitting on a log, staring at the jungle.

"I thought I ordered you to patrol," Sohan said, walking around to stand in front of his son.

"I'm trying to figure out what I did that was so wrong. If you heard about someone named after him, you would have investigated. They call her…" He turned and realized I was there. "They call you the Demon Serpent."

"Because she *is* the Demon Serpent," Sohan said, looking over me. "Not that she's much compared to the original."

Ouch.

"But…" Kahan stood, confused by his father's declaration. "How?"

"Nagas reincarnate. Normally, their lives are fresh starts. Kaliya Sahni, however, has been burdened by her past life, tasked with, I'm assuming, his unfinished business."

"In a sense." That was one way to put it.

"But—"

"The Demon Serpent was a naga mated to one of our kind, Kahan. She is. She has the powers of it. She proved that to your sister, who knows exactly what is entailed and what to look for."

"Kahan, why don't you say his name?" I asked, curious. I had noticed, continued to notice his avoidance of saying *my* name.

"His sister refuses to speak about Kaliya," Sohan answered instead. "Lalika and I can almost do as we please. Even though Rama is more powerful than me, I am still her father. We knew him. He was our son for a time, a member of this family. However, my boy here was only born five hundred years ago, and Rama, with her imposing will and her endless pain from the loss of her mate, made it clear when he was young, she wouldn't tolerate him asking questions. She also made it clear she wouldn't tolerate Lalika and me to ever truly explain it to him."

Yikes.

"You don't seem surprised by her, Father," Kahan pointed out. "Why aren't you surprised? I mean..." He flung a hand in my direction.

He doesn't act a day over... twenty-one, tops. He's a confused young man, and I can't blame him. He's probably been babied all these years.

"I've heard rumors about Kaliya Sahni for a century. I knew she existed, though her recent titles are new. There's a reason I usually handled trips to areas with large supernatural populations. I am old and knew what sort of information to listen for, what would be pertinent to the family, and what wouldn't be." He rested a hand on his son's shoulder. "You did nothing wrong wanting to see who this new Kaliya was, this new Demon Serpent. Maybe if your sister was more willing to talk, you wouldn't have felt so curious, and..." Sohan squeezed his shoulder and patted his son's cheek, then he looked at me with soulful eyes. "Fate probably would have given *this* naga a different way to find us."

I didn't know what to say. For this entire trip, it felt as if something strange was twisting my path. Vrindavan, a trip I took on a wild feeling I couldn't shake, ended with a meeting with Krishna. My childhood home, where I found the secrets of my mother's dangerous journey into magic. Then handling the rakshasa and Kahan's mistake getting caught because he was curious about me.

I never liked fate or destiny, didn't like the idea of my path being chosen for me, robbing me of free will. It was the same issue I had with naga mating because we didn't get to choose our mates.

Sohan watched me, possibly waiting for me to say something, so I said something.

"I don't like the concept of fate."

"I believe some things happen because they are meant to," Sohan countered. "But it's not an invisible being doing it. A chain reaction of choices, all freely made, lead to an inevitable ending. The ending is what I call fate. Don't like it if you don't want to, but hearing even the... stripped-down version of your tale, I can tell you, this meeting was inevitable." Sohan looked back at his son. “She is the reincarnation of Rama’s mate, Kahan, and you brought her here.”

“I didn’t mean to!” Kahan was so desperate to please. I felt so bad, almost pitying this man. He was five hundred years old, but he could have been nineteen. “I knew the wolves had seen me, but I lost them and didn’t think she and her mate would hunt me down. I was washing up before heading home when they caught me off guard. I had to build a portal while buying time. I tried, Father.”

“I’m not angry,” Sohan said gently. “I’m not angry, my boy.”

“*She* is,” he whispered.

“She is always angry,” Sohan murmured, then kissed his son’s forehead.

He was such a tender man, which I hadn’t expected. No amount of hunting through my memories told me Sohan would be so tender with a son as he was protective with his wife and daughter. “She will be angrier with me by the end of this day than she will be with you.”

“Why?”

“Your father is allowing me to ask her to do something difficult,” I answered, taking the responsibility. Sohan wouldn’t hurt Rama. I was and took full responsibility.

I also had to weigh the feelings of everyone who relied on me, and Rama’s feelings were overshadowed by a greater need.

“I’ll do it as... gently as possible,” I promised.

“I wish I knew what that meant,” Kahan said, fire entering his eyes. I figured it had something to do with the need to defend family.

"It might be best for you to wait for Rama to know as well." Sohan turned his son and kept an arm wrapped around him, directing the young man toward the house. "Go home. Boil some water, clean up a little. Get off your feet."

"Are you sure—"

"There's..." Sohan released his son, looking as though something was giving him pain. He snarled as Kahan grabbed his father's shoulders.

"Father, you can't."

"Desk... journal," he growled. "Read... it." Sohan exhaled, and the pain seemed to leave. Rubbing his chest with one hand, he shoved his son toward the house. "*Go.*"

"What did you just do?" I asked, taking Kahan's place next to the warrior.

"Almost disobeyed an order and exploited a loophole. Sometimes, a loophole is easy to jump through, but sometimes, it's... painful," Sohan answered, still rubbing his chest, not looking at me. "We're not allowed to give him the full story. Rama doesn't want him to know. She believes she's protecting him, and she is... in charge. However, I'm not telling him. I am giving him access to it. There's never been a reason for me to test her before, not really, and it was harder than I expected."

"She's a warlord," I said, the dynamics of this place falling more into place. I had known, but knowing and *understanding* were different. I was beginning to get a grasp of the latter. "In North America, we understand cambions have a strict caste system. Will she know you did that?"

"That's a great way to put it, apt, considering the

situation." Sohan seemed to find dark humor in it, a feeling I knew all too well. "No, she won't know."

"Cambions, like Rama and my mate, Raphael, are what we call warlords. They're in charge of other cambions, able to control every detail. You're a warrior, the second caste. Next, it's mages, or similar, like Kahan. Then a caste we call civilians, who have general cambion abilities but don't have unique ones like warriors and mages. They aren't nearly as powerful as warlords."

"You know much of what I've never been able to discover," he said, yearning in his words.

My fears for Raphael's hopes and dreams started to grow. Even if I could convince them to let him come here, he might be disappointed by what he found.

"You know what you are," I reminded Sohan. "Actually, I was hoping to convince you and your family to bring my mate here. He was left on the other side of Kahan's portal and is probably losing his mind."

"I would be if my mate jumped through a portal to an unknown land," Sohan murmured, a shrewd and understanding nod following. "But if we don't have Rama's permission, he cannot."

"He's wanted to meet all of you so badly."

"Why?"

"He's in his thirties, ruling a group three times the size of your family. He promised them a better life when they were freed, but when they have questions about themselves and what they are, he has no answers. They thought they would never know love or happiness. They thought their kind was infertile. I told Raphael they weren't, and I'm glad it holds true. You've had two children. They don't know how mating works because I'm the only one they've met. You have Lalika, a human."

"Not as human as she once was." Sohan chuckled, but gods, it was sad. "None of them have found human mates?"

"They don't really know how it works or what to look for. They're blind, and Raphael had hoped he could talk to you and learn more."

"So he could give them what they need." Sohan sighed. "Maybe, just maybe, with that argument, I can convince my daughter to allow Kahan to bring him here. You have to promise Kahan's safety, though."

"Raphael won't hurt anyone I tell him not to," I promised. I sure as fuck hoped I didn't just lie to this man.

"It can't be before you speak to Rama." He waved a hand at me. "Who you are, why you're here. Your mate, if he is the same as Rama, will he be okay without you for a few hours?"

"Where is she?"

"She and her mother went to the pools. We'll have to wait for them to return."

"I could—"

"You will not be going there alone, and I am not allowed there when the ladies want private time. Rama left you in my care, so you will stay here with me." Looking up, he nodded. "Dinner will be soon."

I was left with one choice, so I walked with him to the house.

31

CHAPTER THIRTY-ONE

Sohan went to his son the moment we walked in. He paid me no mind as he went through the main room then through an opening. I followed slowly, not wanting to intrude. I had focused little on the house when Sohan brought me inside earlier to talk. Now I studied it. There was a bench by the front door, and I saw leather boots made by hand waiting there.

Should I take off my shoes? He didn't, and maybe I'll have to leave. I don't want to lose my shoes. I don't have replacements.

Deciding against it, I kept looking around. The front door opened to a large room that looked like a living room and a dining room shoved together with no visible barriers. One side had a fireplace and in front of it, chairs, with a low, small table in the middle. The other side was the dining table.

The space was sparse. This was lean living. There were no pictures on the walls. There was very little to show that proved I was in the new millennium. Except for the electricity, the house could have been built centuries ago.

Or thousands of years if they had considered this sort of architecture that long ago.

Passing the wooden table where Sohan nearly killed me, I went to the arch, seeing a library of sorts, a few built-in bookshelves, the same shade of wood as everything else in the house. I touched the beams that made the arch, feeling how the wood had been sanded smooth but was relatively untreated.

How often do they have to rebuild because they don't have the proper materials? This wood probably rots so quickly.

I stood there, letting Sohan check in with Kahan, and watched them. Kahan was sitting on a stool with a leather-bound book in his hands, the paper old and fragile. Sohan was nodding, then flipped the pages, pointing out a specific passage.

"This is a good place to start," the father said softly.

It was then I realized they weren't even dressed for the proper era. Kahan was the closest, probably able to pass if someone saw him on the street, but Sohan was dated by at least a few centuries, with his linen pants and leather boots.

He noticed me studying him and straightened up.

"Is there something you want to say?"

"I was just taking this in," I answered. "How do you stay hidden? Not here, but when you see people go into villages or anything like that? You don't... dress like people do now."

"I have other clothing. This was what I was comfortable wearing today," he answered, looking down at his wardrobe. "I know how to match the humans, and when I go out, I pay attention to the attire they prefer. I often pick the most prevalent, then get a new outfit and wear it for my next trip. I'm never more than a decade behind the trends of humanity."

"What do you do about money?"

"We steal," Kahan answered. "Father and I are good at it. He taught me how."

Sohan gave his son an uncomfortable look that went unnoticed by the younger man. He grabbed me as he walked out of the room, forcing me to follow him into a back hallway. There were doors around me, but he took me to a door at the end of the hall.

Like a father about to chastise me, he put me in a spot and glared.

"Don't judge what we must do to survive," he warned.

"I wasn't planning to." I saw his shame and knew its source. "There's no shame in surviving. I wasn't considering it."

"Then why did I see you look like you pitied us?" he asked, his dark stare intense.

Did I have that expression?

"I wasn't... pitying you. However, I saw the way *you* looked when Kahan said that. You didn't like him telling me, and I get it. You were once a warrior, able to receive work for those skills. You once participated just enough with the outside world to maintain your family with a small pile of gold when trading was necessary."

"The world doesn't need warriors anymore."

"The human world? No, they don't, at least not in that

way. It's illegal unless you join one of their armies, for the most part."

"Exactly."

"You could have worked with other supernaturals. You did once before. You were friends with the nagas or those you knew. Why didn't you try that route?"

"I was friends with some of them." This time, I saw very real regret. This close and isolated family probably weren't all that used to covering how they felt, masking so others couldn't read them. "But I can no longer have those relationships."

"What are you hiding from me? What do I need to know, Sohan?"

"We're not allowed to come out to the supernaturals," he said softly. "You already knew of us, but we're not to tell anyone new. It's an order I haven't been able to break."

"Sohan?"

"When he died, she lashed out," he explained, turning away. "No more friends outside this little bubble. No more potential allies. No more interaction with other beings who weren't completely human. I got close a handful of times... so close."

I walked around him to see his face as he spoke, and his eyes were closed.

"With a young male naga who was with a mercenary group for a short time. We were both new recruits to the group, both hiding what we were. I knew he wasn't human—I had heard him singing to snakes at the river's edge—but he didn't know I wasn't. He didn't love being a warrior. It was something he was learning out of necessity. He was skilled but not particularly talented, and that skill was born from his hard work and dedication. He loved other things. I wanted to so badly to tell him I had once known his father."

"I'm sorry."

"His name was Adhar," Sohan whispered.

I remembered a scene that had unfolded in the courtyard. Adhar walked in, a sword in hand, and with a single practiced swing, he beheaded Pavan, then walked away. He took no glory in it, had no love for it, but knew how to do it.

His story of Adhar's youth wasn't surprising in some ways and quite surprising in others. I wasn't surprised they had crossed paths. The world was good at bringing people together and then pulling them apart. So good at it. I was surprised to learn this small piece of Adhar's life from the most unexpected of places.

"He wasn't the only naga over the years who I came so close to knowing once again, but I could never break myself from my daughter's angry declaration in those early days after he died."

"Sohan, what did she do?" This could change everything about how the later conversation went.

His eyes opened, pain in them.

"She hated them, so she returned here and... lashed out. She banned us from purposefully making contact. She banned us from trying... anything. Kaliya, we're still here, living in this place, in this isolation, because she has refused to interact with the world ever again. I *love* my daughter, but I have known for thousands of years, I am trapped by her."

"Hated who?"

"Them.... his brothers... all of you." Sohan relaxed, leaning against the house as he met my gaze once again. "You, even though you weren't born yet. Other supernaturals, even humans. She hates everyone, my daughter. She trusts no one unless it's absolutely necessary. We're forbidden from interacting with the rest of the world. Kahan got away with what he did because he was out for supplies." He lifted his hands. "Which my son did not bring home."

"Why Delhi? You live pretty far away."

"I figured Kahan would have a more difficult time hiding in a smaller village when I started training him. The city? It's easy for one person to disappear, to not stand out. It's only become easier as time passes. It makes thieving easier. So many people to hide among. He had gone with me several times. He's also the only one who can reach the city. We've developed his strength to make portals, which has allowed us to go farther away from home to make sure people don't recognize us. His range has only increased with age. The farther he tries to go, the longer he needs to recover, but it's been a boon."

"Oh, so he can hit cities all over the country, and no one will notice him. At least, they wouldn't put together his appearances as easily."

"Exactly. This time, I didn't feel like doing the supply run, so I let him go with a list of what we could use. He picked Delhi. He knows it better than other cities, so he picks it more often. He broke some rules. He's not supposed to spy on other supernaturals, and clearly, he's been practicing without my permission."

"He's curious. You, Lalika, and Rama were once part of the outside world. He's been locked up here."

"I think that's why he started making portals," Sohan admitted. "Because you're right. He has been locked here his entire life and has always been so desperate to see more of the world. Rama thinks she's protecting him, protecting all of us." Sohan shook his head. "You're easier to talk to in this life."

"Sure." I nodded. "Or maybe you just haven't been able to speak honestly for a few thousand years."

"No, I haven't," he confirmed.

"When I think about you from the past, that man would have been okay with this. You were isolated back then. Five thousand years of isolation changed you."

"It was my choice. Lalika needed to be kept safe, and Rama was so young. I'm a grown man without choice now." Sohan didn't continue that, and he didn't need to. I understood. "You remind me of him."

"My predecessor?"

"No. In a way, you remind me of Adhar. He was easy to talk to, wiser than he let on for someone so young."

"He would laugh to hear you say that. I think he would try to have you committed to a mental institution." I was considering it.

"I know what those are."

"Good."

Sohan laughed, although I wasn't sure why.

"Were you two really so different?"

"Yeah. We didn't get along for over a hundred years," I explained. "He took me in as the ruler of the nagas when my parents were murdered. My mother had been the female ruler, and I was the last nagini. I was the only option as her replacement. I ran away and didn't talk to him again until I was in my thirties. We disagreed about everything for so long and only started to understand each other right before the end." I blinked, realizing my eyes were wet, but no tears rolled. All of that had come so easily. Sohan was easy to talk to.

"I'm sorry."

"Me, too," I said as I wiped my eyes.

Sohan looked to his left, and I dropped my hand.

"What is it?"

"They're coming back. Unless they ask you, stay out of the kitchen. They enjoy cooking together. Lalika might enjoy the help, but Rama will not."

We didn't head in. Sohan moved around me, blocking me from view.

"I heard we've had a visitor," Lalika called out. Her voice was still warm and musical.

"Father?" Rama was more careful.

"We still do," he replied, stepping aside to reveal me.

Rama snarled as Lalika gasped. Sohan stepped in front of his daughter as his mate approached me. I took in her rich, dark mahogany hair and brown eyes. She had a gold nose ring, a very simple one.

"My name is Lalika," she greeted sweetly. "Welcome to our home."

"It's a pleasure to be here," I said, bowing my head low in respect to this kind woman, still as welcoming today as she had been five thousand years ago. "My name is Kaliya Sahni."

"Is it?" Lalika was surprised as she turned to her

husband and daughter. "Rama, you didn't tell me. She only told me a naga had followed Kahan home."

"I thought she would be gone by now. Father, why is she still here?"

"Well, she said she wanted to speak to us," Sohan reminded her.

"I—"

"And it's *my* house," Sohan growled, cutting off Rama. "You have one down the trail that you are more than welcome to reside in while I entertain."

It has to be hard, the caste between parental roles. At least he's not afraid to hold some sort of boundary with her.

"Mother, do you want to have dinner with me this evening?" Rama asked, looking beyond her father.

"I..." Lalika looked at me again, but I didn't have an answer for her. She looked at her mate, then back to their daughter. "I would like to be a hospitable host for our guest," she told Rama. "I'm sorry."

Rama looked hurt, but the anger that came next wasn't directed at her father or mother.

Oh, no. Those blood-red eyes in black were pointed at me.

I tried not to be scared.

It was a difficult task.

32

CHAPTER THIRTY-TWO

"My heart, Kaliya is the current *Nagaraja*, a nagini. Can you believe it?" Sohan smiled and went to his mate's side. The way he dismissed his daughter's brewing rage was bold and practiced. "She's also mated to one of our kind."

"Oh, are you also the nagini who saved the cambions across the world?"

"How does she know that word?" Rama demanded. "And that story? Where did that come from? What is she talking about?"

"I hear things when I'm out and about, and I tell your mother, just as I tell you when it seems important enough to report," Sohan answered. "This is that nagini, Kaliya Sahni, named after him. She's had a very interesting life. I think we should let her stay a few days a—"

"Stop," Rama snarled.

His mouth opened, and he shook as he tried to close it, his own cambion nature rising to the surface.

"Rama!" Lalika was stunned, trying to move her mate, to help him.

"He knows the nagas can't be trusted," she growled at her mother. "I am doing this to protect us. Our family."

"Rama—"

"Quiet," Rama quietly ordered, and I watched as Lalika's eyes filled with tears as she couldn't speak. Rama seemed pained for a moment, but she quickly got over it as she turned to me. "I don't know what you've said to my father, but you are *not* welcome here."

"I told him the truth." I met her stare, unwilling to back down. "I think you need to hear it before you pass judgment." This was not the woman he had been in love with. This was not the woman I had feared hurting.

I kind of wanted to hurt her now.

"I don't care what your truth is. You should start running." Her skin was turning grey, and she grew taller as the black veins spread. She became taller than me, but not by so much, it was intimidating. Her horns grew, twisting like a ram's, and she started walking toward me.

I put a hand on the hilt of my talwar, the other reaching for a chakram.

"I don't run from cowards," I hissed.

She roared, scaring birds from the trees. I heard their calls of fear and realized Rama wasn't just smothering.

She was a dictator.

A tyrant.

I can't let this go on.

"My name is Kaliya Sahni," I started, taking steps back as she advanced on me. She was so confident in her power, she didn't feel the need to lunge.

Or she doesn't want to eviscerate me in front of her mother.

"I am here to find the way to Ramanaka to defeat the great eagle, Garuda," I continued.

"Not my problem," she snapped. "I don't know how you found us or why you think we know where fucking Ramanaka is, but you will leave, or I will make you leave."

"I know your family's role in the legend of Kaliya five thousand years ago," I said, keeping distance between us.

"Legend?" Rama's glare promised she would open a door to hell itself and throw me in if I didn't start saying the right thing. "You mean the time you let my husband die?" With no animals to terrorize, only silence remained at the end, a silence I knew I had to continue to fill.

"I wasn't there. I wasn't born yet. My parents weren't born yet. My grandparents weren't born yet. So no, not the time *I* let your husband die." I dared to glare back at her. "Don't you dare put that on my shoulders. That blame isn't mine to carry."

"It will always be your fault," she growled.

Kahan ran outside at that moment. I saw him burst through the backdoor over Rama's shoulder, his eyes filling with horror at his mother's inability to speak and his father's frozen body. I felt the heartbreak as Lalika tried to push him back inside, but Kahan was stronger. In the ways sons do, he pushed her in and closed the door before going to their father.

All the while, I kept backing away, keeping ten feet between Rama and me. I was doing my best to lead her away from the house, knowing exactly what sort of destruction she could unleash.

"Why?" I finally asked. "Why am I to blame for what others did five thousand years ago?"

"You vilified him," she snarled. "When all he wanted was to protect his family. His brothers rejected him and let Krishna murder him!"

"Is that what you think happened?" I asked, shaking my head. "Do you want to know what he *did*? He went to someone else's home and killed *countless* living things."

"I don't care about trees!" Rama roared.

"It doesn't matter!" I screamed back. "It was selfish! It was cruel! It might not have been purposeful, but he did it and didn't stop when someone brought it to his attention. He put his own fear over what was good for everyone else. The willful ignorance of his faults doesn't look good on you, Rama. He loved a better woman."

"You have no idea—"

"I know everything about you," I hissed. "I have *all* of his memories. I'm his reincarnation."

That made her stop. In her moment of processing, I continued.

"I wanted to let you know in a better way, but I will not bow to the whims of a *tyrant*. I know all about your mating with him. It's how I knew about your family. I knew your name before I got here. I didn't know what I would find when I looked for you, but it wasn't this. It wasn't a woman who has completely lost everything he used to love about her."

I knew when I had made this plan that every word I said would have an impact. That it would be so easy to get it wrong.

I got it wrong.

"Liar," she snarled and lunged for me.

I pulled my sword as I jumped back, and before I landed, my lower body shifted. My clothing became armor, old and historic, hailing from a distant past. My lower body morphed into a snake's, black scales reflecting the glow of late evening.

With a hiss, I dodged her attack, grateful she wasn't as fast as Sammy, my best sparring partner. I cut upwards, grazing her arm before making more distance from her. She looked at the injury with fascination, black blood dripping down her arm until it healed, leaving a black scar over grey skin.

With a snarl, she focused on me once again.

"Rama, no!" Kahan yelled.

Oh gods, no.

He appeared between us, his hands up.

"Please, we should listen to her—"

Rama grabbed his brother's throat, forcing him to his knees.

"Stay out of the way," she snarled before tossing him toward the house.

I saw him go through the wall and Lalika's silent, horrified scream as their son disappeared inside.

When I looked back at Rama, I truly believed she didn't know what she had just done.

"He's your brother," I said, unable to comprehend just how mad with grief a person had to be to go this far, to be willing to do this.

"He's a man who knows better," Rama growled. "This is between us."

I flipped my sword in my hand once, spinning it before bringing it up between us.

"I don't want to kill you," I said, a promise to myself more than anything.

"Then it's a good thing you can't," Rama sneered. "I promised him I would never raise a hand against one of his people, but I'm certain he would make an exception for a cheap mimic, a far cry from who he had been and the power he had."

Oh, that's bad news for me.

She transitioned again, and I had to distance myself from the growing demon. She wasn't as large as Raphael, but that meant little. There had been a time I couldn't defeat a demon barely taller than a horse. Rama was the size of a small elephant. She wasn't the same size as Raphael, but I didn't practice fighting cambions in their demon form. I never expected to, not without Raphael with me.

She attacked with a vicious, single-minded focus. Black claws tried to snag my snake form. Blood drool flew from her mouth. Her demon form was faster than Raphael's, at least from memory. It was impossible to get around her or behind her. I could only fight defensively as she came for me. I threw my first chakram, watching it embed in her eye, but it only slowed her for a moment.

She reached up and put a claw through the hole in the center and yanked it out. With a snarl, she let it fall to the ground as I watched her eye heal.

Yeah, she heals just like the rest of them. Just what I needed.

I wasn't surprised, but the verification was nice to

have and let me put another hundred feet between us, my body coiling anxiously.

I sheathed my sword, grabbing two more chakram. I figured she would rip me in half if I gave her a chance. Knowing I had to be careful, I attempted one more bid for peace.

"Rama, I don't want to kill you! Don't make me. All you have to do is listen to what I have to say. If that's not good enough, I will leave and never come back."

She roared, running for me. My hands shook as I let her.

I had to do something. The idea was insane. If Raphael could witness this, he would chastise me until I was hollow and broken. It was stupid and risky. It was everything I was known for. I didn't like to lose fights. I had been tested, every battle harder than the last. This was no different, but this time, I couldn't go directly to the easy way out. I didn't want to kill her, which meant I needed to do something insane.

I have to try everything.

My hands were shaking as she closed the distance. Every time her feet hit the ground, it shook. Taking a deep breath, letting muscle memory take over, I spun the chakram on my fingers, time slowing as I took aim. Her body was lumbering, her head lifting and falling with every gallop.

It's muscle memory, right, Nakul? You said I could do the things he could, that this was just another type of memory. I've been practicing, you know. You got to teach me more for those few weeks. I kept practicing.

Let's hope it's paid off.

Once she was too close for me to escape, I threw my chakram, each hitting true.

This time, I got *both* eyes, and the chakram went deep.

As she roared in pain, I surged up and grabbed her fur as she thrashed. I shifted back into my human form so she had less to grab as I climbed. As she was busy trying to regain her vision, I unsheathed my sword again, stabbing downward in the middle of her bony back. I knew if I wanted to kill her, I would go for her head, but I was desperate not to do that. Instead, my sword went through two vertebrae, and Rama's roar of agony nearly burst my eardrums. I had to leap from her as her body crumbled, her back legs useless.

"Do you want to continue?" I screamed, facing the demon as she turned on me, her legs heavy and useless for her back end.

In only seconds, she put weight on them.

Horror filled me. I knew they could heal, was around them often enough to know. I had chopped off Sammy's hand because I knew it could be fixed.

But a severed spine?

There were times in my life when things felt hopeless but never been like this. I was faced with the impossible. There was no disabling a cambion, not long enough to matter.

She roared again.

This time, someone roared back.

A feeling of *closeness* flooded me as something felt as if it had been put back into place.

I was still staring at her when a bigger demon barreled into her. The tumbling battle, black blood, and fur flying, sent the two giants rolling into the thick jungle around the house.

Stunned, I didn't react or attempt to defend myself as someone grabbed me, pulling me farther away from the brawl.

"Come!" Kahan demanded, and I took the chance to look at him. He had a bloody hole in his shirt but looked fine otherwise. "I made a portal to get your mate, made sure he could see the fight, and he jumped through."

"Are you okay?" I asked him, pulling open the hole to see a scar.

"A piece of lumber ran through me," Kahan answered. "Took me a minute to get up. You're good, though, holding her off like you did."

A roar took both of us away from the conversation.

"She's lost her mind," I whispered.

"She's never had it," Kahan replied sadly. "I didn't know what else to do. He's going to kill her, isn't he?"

"I..." I could see them. Two giants attempting to destroy each other, Raphael with more experience in this form, and more weight behind him, and he was winning.

Part of me, the horrified, nearly killed part, wanted to let him finish it. I truly did, but it wasn't the right call. I ran toward them as Raphael sank his fangs into the back of Rama's neck, shaking viciously before slamming her through trees that toppled like dominos.

"Are you mad?" Kahan yelled after me.

"Protect your parents!" I roared back, my eyes only on my destination.

Raphael tossed Rama like a rag doll. I saw her chest heaving as my mate prowled toward her, slamming a heavy foot on her chest. He raked her open, exposing bones as her healing tried to recover.

"Raphael, no!" I screamed. "It's Rama! Raphael, that's Rama!"

He snarled, barely glancing at me.

My legs burned as I ran underneath him. I climbed on her, laying my body out over hers. Black drool or blood, I couldn't tell, dripped down on me, covering everything, my hair, face, body. I wiped it from my eyes as I tried to maintain my composure. Panting, I held on to her, staring down my mate.

"It's Rama, and she's hurting. She's been hiding here for a long time. We need her, Raph. We can fix this. Please. We can't kill her."

His reply was a snarl that made sure I knew he hated every word coming out of my mouth.

"Please," I pleaded.

I was tired. Tired of fighting. Tired of struggling to survive every day against the odds. Tired of making enemies. Tired of finding enemies, I had done nothing to except exist. Tired of being forced to throw my life on the line for the things I believed in. Tired of being laughed at for my convictions. Tired of the centuries of grief piling up on my shoulders because no one else could carry it.

The thing I was most tired of?

I was tired of *death*.

I wouldn't see it today. Not today.

Raphael took one step back, growling, but when I wouldn't move, it wasn't as if he had much choice. There were things my mate would never do. Purposefully hurting me was one of them.

He didn't shift back to his human form, not yet. He went to Rama's head and snarled. Her reply was a whimper. When he looked at me, he nodded his big head, then stepped back again, distancing himself from us.

I slid off Rama and distanced myself as well. Her body crumpled and transitioned through her forms, all the way back to her human one. Covered in blood, her injuries still apparent, she stared blankly at the sky. I couldn't take my eyes off her, wondering what might be going through her mind at that moment. I jumped when someone touched me, turning to see Raphael back in his human form as well.

Without a word, I threw my arms around him.

33

CHAPTER THIRTY-THREE

He let me go after a moment, forcing us both to face the situation we were in.

"Let her heal for a moment," he murmured, then turned away, walking toward the house. Holding my hand, he pulled me with him. He stopped in front of Kahan, giving the youngest of the family a nod.

Kahan went to one knee, bowing his head.

"This is Kahan," I explained. "Sohan and Lalika's youngest. He's five hundred years old."

"Good to meet you, Kahan," Raphael greeted before looking at Sohan and Lalika with a smile. "I have heard about you both. Sohan and Lalika, it's a pleasure to meet you." He extended a hand, but Lalika opened her mouth and sighed, and Sohan still couldn't move.

"Rama has them under orders—"

"Not anymore, she doesn't. I release you," Raphael said, his temper flipping back on like a switch.

"Is my daughter alive?" Lalika asked, looking beyond us in horror.

Shocked to hear her speaking in English, I didn't reply. It was heavily accented, but it was English.

"Yes," Raphael growled, turning to glare at me. "She is."

"We need her."

"She was going to eat you," he snapped, forgetting all about the people we were with. "Damn it, Kaliya, you jumped through a fucking portal and left me behind. You're lucky he thought to get me!" He pointed at Kahan. "You're powerful, but you never could have beaten her!"

"I wasn't trying to beat her!" I snapped, responding to his anger with my need to defend my choices. "I wanted to talk to her. She's the one who lost her fucking mind! This was never supposed to be a fight! We were supposed to talk, then Kahan was going to be asked to bring you to us. It wasn't supposed to go like this."

"Excuse me, but I need to know what's going on," Sohan said, slowly coming toward us. He'd also switched to English, and I was mystified. "How did you override my daughter's order?"

"She's not in charge anymore," Raphael snarled.

I wasn't sure if he was mad at me, Rama, or the entire situation. Probably a combination of all of those.

"*I am*. You, Kahan, and Lalika are mine now. She has nothing and will never, in my lifetime, have anything again."

"What?" Lalika gasped. "We're her family."

"*Mine*," Raphael growled.

"Raphael, no one understands you right now," I said, putting a hand on his chest, which was heaving as if he could barely contain himself. "Explain. Burn off some of this. It's over. We need to talk and need to do it with clear heads."

He growled, his neck bulging as he shifted into his cambion form. Sohan went to the midnight form of the warriors, stepping back, then grabbed Lalika and pulled her behind him. Kahan was the only one who showed no fear, looking at Raphael with a stunned, nearly adoring expression.

"I have conquered this community. It belongs to me now. You all belong to me now. If it wasn't for Kaliya, I would have killed Rama. I still *want* to. She threatened something that is mine and has lost everything. She's a ruler with nothing to rule. You will never answer to her again. You will answer to me."

"Raphael, you can't just... take them like they're property."

"He's right, though," Kahan said softly. "I can feel it. It's been the same with Rama for a long time. I didn't realize that was what made me feel this." He stood and stepped closer before turning to his father. "Do you feel it?"

"Yes," Sohan answered. Slowly, he transitioned back to his human form. "I always knew we were locked in some sort of system. Demons I have fought over the centuries had some sort of structure when there were more than one or two of them. We, as... cambions, have this as well. Kaliya explained to me they use terms to denote different types of our kind. Talks for another day."

"Yes," Raphael agreed.

"Thank you," Kahan said.

The words shocked Raphael enough to send him

back to his human form, everything demonic receding until I could see his chocolate eyes for the first time since he arrived.

"What?"

"Rama was ruling them like a tyrant," I told him, swallowing as I sent a guilty look to Sohan. "I'm sorry, Sohan. It's unkind to say, but—"

"It is true. She was. We..."

"She's our daughter, and..." Lalika was also at a loss, the guilt visibly eating her alive. "We couldn't help her. Couldn't convince her to let go of the pain. She wouldn't... let us." Lalika cried, nearly falling. Sohan grabbed his mate and held her, giving her the strength to stand.

"For five thousand years, we've been prisoners in our own family, unable to speak truthfully, unable to speak at all when Rama was in a foul mood. She forced us to continue to be a perfect little family." Sohan shook his head. "This is for the best."

"I did it to *protect* all of you," Rama growled softly. "And I will *always* protect you."

How she ended up right behind me, I would never understand. The way she had come up so quietly was nightmare-inducing, and I had a feeling I would spend the rest of my life wondering if she would be right there.

I reacted before anyone else could think.

Naga reflexes made me faster than anyone there. In the blink of an eye, my sword was out and pressed against her neck, ready to do the very thing I had just saved her from if she forced my hand.

My speed scared her and stopped her outstretched

hand from grabbing me, leaving it frozen in the air. It took another second for me to realize she was going to grab the back of my shirt, probably to yank me back and kill me.

"It's over," I said, adding the punch of finality to it. "Touch me and lose the hand."

She dropped it as my blade cut into the skin on her neck. The tables had been turned.

"You have lost everything," I explained as tears filled her eyes. "You lost your mate because of his actions. You've lost your family because of yours. Whether you lose your life is up to you."

"I just wanted to protect them," she repeated. "From them. From all of them. The outside world is—"

"Beautiful. Dangerous. Scary. Loving." I leaned in, letting my blade slide, extending the cut. "*Worth it.*"

"You will never understand—"

"What I understand is that he loved you," I whispered. "Loved you the moment he saw you. Loved you when he sank his fangs into your thigh and made the mate bond."

Her eyes went wide.

"He loved your power, your kind heart, the way you cherished them." I pointed at her parents with my free hand. "He knew if he died, you would be strong enough to survive without him worrying," I hissed.

"I *also* understand he didn't blame his brothers. That he loved his nephews and the new, precious nieces he called princesses."

Rama's lips quivered.

"I understand *everything*. From your most intimate

moments to the days you were forced to spend apart and how he ached for you. I understand the pain. Damn you, Rama, I *know*!" Then I gave her the horrifying truth I had to live with. "*I still feel it*."

It broke her.

She fell to her knees and sobbed.

I let my sword arm hang limply, the hilt sliding from my fingers. Touching my cheeks, I felt the tears on my own cheeks and wiped them off, then turned away from her to look at her family.

"It's over," I repeated.

Lalika was the first one to walk toward us. She hadn't known. Sohan and I hadn't had the chance to say anything before Rama attacked. She had probably heard me screaming the truth to Rama, but there had been a lot happening at that moment.

She extended a hand for Rama first, then closed it, looking away from her daughter to me. Reaching out tentatively, she touched my cheeks.

"Are you really..."

"I'm not *him*. Just his reincarnation, cursed with his memories."

"What did I say to him when he thought he lost the most precious thing in his life?" she asked me. "And what was that precious thing?"

I swallowed as the memory came rushing to the forefront of my mind. I hadn't remembered they had this moment. Perhaps I had trauma blocked it. Perhaps I hadn't known what to think of. It was hard remembering things when you didn't even know what to remember.

"He lost his mother. He wanted to introduce Rama to Kadru," I started, seeing it unfold in my mind. Closing my eyes, I lived in the memory. "He was excited and nervous but so happy. He took Rama to meet her with your blessing. With Sohan's blessing, for neither of you had ever let Rama go so far from home. She was still young enough to worry over." I felt the pain of my past life.

"Kadru rejected Rama, and in turn, rejected her son. She knew Rama wasn't fully human and disliked her immediately. He never understood why his mother felt the way she did, but it cut him so deeply, he left with Rama and never darkened his mother's doorstep again." I opened my eyes. There was something I was missing about that memory, something he hadn't wanted to remember, but it wasn't worth looking into yet. "He took Rama back to you, heartbroken. You told him you could never replace her, but you would love him like a son, no matter what. Later, you, Rama, and Kaliya moved back to Ramanaka, but he never acknowledged that his mother was just on the other side of the island, and she never attempted to reach out."

Lalika cried as I answered. She pulled me in and held me, her tight hug as though she was holding onto a lifeline. I let her, and some piece of me enjoyed it.

It had been years since someone hugged me with the maternal love she was pouring into the hug. Sure, it was directed at a dead man, not me, but I was okay accepting it.

After a long time, she pulled back, touching my cheek again.

“Thank you,” she whispered. “For finding us again. For coming here.”

“I’m not him,” I repeated.

“No, you’re not, but I would like to know you.” She grabbed my hand and pulled me away from her crying daughter.

I wondered if anyone else felt oddly guilty. Looking back to see Rama still on the ground, no one going to her, I felt as if I had just stolen her mother. Raphael stood the closest to Rama, his face shockingly blank. He didn’t seem fazed by the breakdown happening at his feet. Sohan and Kahan were together, watching Lalika and me. Sohan was even smiling a little.

“What about Rama?” I asked finally, stopping my feet until I got this answer.

“Rama…” Lalika looked back, and I saw the deep, unhealing sadness in her. “Rama has held on to something painful for a long time, refusing to let us help her. She must purge herself of the pain now. As much as I hate to say it, my daughter is an adult woman who has forced her own family into the dark because she refused to see there was still light in the world. I will always love her, but right now, I am going to have a moment without her… truly free to make my own choices again for the first time in five thousand years.”

Lalika kept walking, and I didn’t resist her pulling.

“Sohan, Kahan, come,” Lalika called without turning around again.

“Raphael, will you…” I didn’t even know what was going on here.

"I'll keep an eye on her and won't kill her," Raphael promised.

"We're just going inside. Join us when you're ready."

I hadn't been paying attention to our direction. Sure enough, Lalika sighed at the hole in the house, then pulled me through the backdoor. Sohan and Kahan followed us. Once inside, Sohan threw an arm over my shoulder and guided me to sit at the table once again.

This time I got to sit with the family.

"I wish we could reminisce, but I'm here for an important reason I can't put off," I started, not wanting them to absorb me into the family as their lost son-in-law.

"Yes." Sohan sat across from me while Lalika stayed at my side, holding my hand in both of hers.

"What is it?" she asked us, curious and worried, then realized. "Ramanaka. Garuda."

"Yeah." I gently pulled my hand from hers. I was tired of explaining this but started once again. "That. We recently discovered Garuda has also reincarnated, with his old power and memories of his previous life. He's been systematically hunting down my people and killing us. He's funded people from the shadows, used cover stories, attacked from all sides… until recently. Thinking he could get the death blow on my people, He revealed himself. He failed and retreated while his rakshasa allies finished dying in his stead. As the *Nagaraja*, it's my duty to my people to free them from this. It's been a long road to get here, but here I am to ask Rama for a way back to Ramanaka."

"It's more than that," Raphael said behind me. I

turned to see that he held Rama by the back of her shirt. "Krishna told the original Kaliya to go back. He didn't."

Rama hissed, and Raphael practically tossed her into the center of the living room area. She looked healed, her eyes wild, but there was nothing she could do to beat Raphael.

Stop testing him, Rama. It's suicidal at this point.

"Rama started talking the moment you went inside. I decided she needed to hear this, to hear what her mate left others to face," he explained.

"He made mistakes," I said, shaking my head. "He didn't hold ill intent, but his choices hurt so many people, and he still had to face the consequences of those." I touched my chest. "I went to the kadamba tree and apologized for them. It was the first thing I did when I started this hunt. I met Krishna that day. Only a week ago—"

"And you didn't take revenge?" Rama demanded, glaring at me, the fire back.

"Revenge for what?" I scoffed. "Protecting his childhood home and the people who relied on the river? Vrindavan was one of the most important places in his life. Stop forgetting that Krishna told your mate if he went back to Ramanaka, Garuda wouldn't act against him or you. He promised, and if anyone could promise it, it was Krishna. Kaliya spat in his face and threatened the lives of innocent people."

"They could have moved," she mumbled.

"Selfish," I snapped. "That's what you are. You'll do anything to justify your hate, and you know what? I don't have fucking time for it anymore." I turned back to her family, particularly Lalika.

"As I explained to Sohan earlier, I had to come here, no matter how much it might pain everyone involved because there are too few nagas left. We're dying. Orphans are being left behind when their parents are butchered. If the enemy had the chance, they'd kill our babies too." I watched the newfound horror take over Lalika's face.

"There are less than ten nagas left on the planet. If I didn't act, if I don't succeed, then... we might be able to steal a few centuries, but the ultimate end will be the extinction of my people."

"How did I not know?" Lalika turned to Sohan. "The nagas are dying?"

"I didn't want to tell you that part," Sohan admitted. "But yes. I've known for some time."

"We might have been able to help them," Lalika said, a tear rolling down her cheek. "They were our only friends in this world."

I turned to look at Rama again. This time, instead of indignant rage or the selfish need to blame others for her mate's failings, I saw *guilt*. She pulled her legs up and wrapped her arms around them.

"These things are tied together," Raphael said from his place by the wall near Rama.

Sohan looked at me. Choices. Over thousands of years, people made choices. Kaliya, Krishna, Rama, him, me, my mother, Garuda. We all made choices, and eventually, they led to an inevitable moment in time.

His concept of fate.

"I will return to Ramanaka and find the peace

Krishna once freely offered to Kaliya. It forces me to face Garuda, who can only be using Ramanaka to hide, as he has for so long. This allows me to save my people. I will kill him and make sure my people can heal and recover. If he returns one day, we'll know to be ready." I chuckled. "He told me it would be harder for me than my predecessor because the circumstances were different." I looked around the room. "He was right."

"Rama, will you tell them how to get to Ramanaka?" Sohan asked.

"Tomorrow," she whispered. "I will tell them tomorrow."

"Good enough." It really was. I had forced this woman to look at herself, forced her to see who she truly had become over the centuries and the pain she had caused her family. I was fine with giving her one night before I made her take an ancient journey to a land she hadn't been to since before her mate died.

Rama got up and walked out of the house.

"Let's settle in for a visit," Lalika said, standing. She gently touched my shoulder. "I was speaking from the heart when I said I wish to know you. I hope we can spend some of this evening talking."

I could only nod.

34

CHAPTER THIRTY-FOUR

"Where is she going?" Raphael demanded a second later.

"Probably her home, a short walk down the west trail," Sohan answered. "Unless you want her to stay under lock and key. You will need to go get her. Kahan and I aren't powerful enough to do that for you."

I never knew my mate to be in a rancid mood, but he was. He growled softly but didn't move. I had only suspicions about what he was feeling, thanks to the day's events. His mate was beside him, then across the country in moments. He had been left alone in a park in the middle of Delhi. When someone finally gave him a chance to catch up to me, he had to save my life, then I didn't let him kill her.

Added to that was his reaction when we started following Kahan. There was something deeper at play here, a quirk of the cambions. None of the others had ever threatened him, even when they attempted to. Sammy could rage all day in his face, even try to attack him, and he never broke a sweat. He might get a little mad, but he was never on guard with her. It was the same with Mateo, who was the deadlier of the two warriors back home, in my opinion.

The idea of another warlord had my mate seeing red.

Rama had him bloodthirsty.

Knowing that and understanding the source, I didn't talk him down from his bad mood or judge him. He could take his time to process his emotions. These were just as new to him as they were to me.

"It's fine," I said, shaking my head at Sohan. He gave me a look, promising there would be a conversation later. It was a look I hadn't gotten since I was probably eleven when my father had given me the same look. Adhar had tried a few times as well. Sohan's left an impression. I wouldn't avoid a conversation with him the way I could anyone else.

"Kahan, you can help me in the kitchen today," Lalika decided, ignoring everyone's small dramas. She led him out of the room.

"Where's the kitchen?" I asked Sohan, frowning.

"It's mostly outside, around the side of the house, thanks to how we have to cook."

"I bet. I was impressed to see you had electricity when I got here. I bet an oven would have been more difficult, though."

"Yes, a modern oven would have been impossible. We use a hand-built, wood-burning stone oven. I like electricity, though, and wish I could do more with it." He looked up at the lights installed in his ceiling. They were basic, not even behind drywall. Now that I had time, I could see how they were wired. "I run everything off a generator. Kahan was supposed to bring back gas. We still have enough for a week if we're careful, but..." He sighed. "Well, I'll deal with it later."

"You won't need to."

Sohan and I turned toward my mate at his simple declaration.

"You'll be living with Kaliya and me in our community once we've finished things with Garuda. In Arizona." Something unintelligible rumbled from my mate. "For a time. Until things settle down and we get you adjusted to the world. I'm guessing there's a lot you're not prepared for, thanks to staying here under her thumb. Once we're all comfortable that you're ready to live a different life, you'll be free to move out on your own with Lalika. I would appreciate if you stayed close by when that time comes, but that's a different discussion."

I waited for the fallout. Sohan didn't know my mate and probably didn't have the best impression yet, but to my surprise, Sohan sagged in his seat as relief washed over his face.

"We'll have choices," Sohan whispered. "Thank you. I look forward to seeing..." He looked around. "Something new, somewhere new. I have wanted to leave this jungle for a long time."

"We live in a desert, so it will be a change of scenery," I promised. "You know English, which is a positive, considering the area is mostly English speaking. When we first tried talking to Kahan, he pretended he didn't understand us."

"Yes." Sohan chuckled. "Pretending there's a language

barrier is an easy way to stop people from bothering us and allows us to play fools. Gives an excuse to act differently and use it to our advantage if we're caught stealing, for example. But we learned, and I would come home to teach Lalika as a safety precaution. We've learned many languages over the years in case people stumble over our home, and we need to protect it. Many times, it's convincing a few human hunters, campers, or hikers to turn around. We don't want to kill anyone. If people go missing in this jungle, others come to investigate."

"That must have been centuries of constant study."

"Yes, but once you learn a few root languages, others are easier. It takes me somewhere between ten to fifteen years now to be fluent in a language. Another twenty teaching Lalika, though her need is less pressing than my own..." He trailed off.

"Because she was never allowed to leave?" Raphael asked with a growl. I could feel his slow stalking toward the table. He sat beside me and leaned on the table. "Is that right?"

"Yes," Sohan whispered. "It must look foolish, two adults held hostage by a daughter we love. If we could have found a balance, we would have." Sohan gave me an apologetic look. "I know I tried to convince you to leave. I didn't want to hurt her and cause her to take more extreme measures like forcing us to become hunter-gatherers with no outside contact. What we had was already so limited, and I didn't want to lose it for my mate or son. I didn't want to lose it for myself."

Disgust for Rama curled in my belly. Even knowing

Lalika was outside with Kahan, working on a meal, made me a little sick. Food didn't sound appetizing.

I knew all about overprotective measures and didn't always agree with them. Variations, different levels of freedom, circumstances of the situation—I had seen it all and had to look at those small details before passing judgment.

Raphael made the cambions check in and check out when they left the compound. There were security protocols, and if they weren't followed, the cambion lost their travel privileges for a week at a minimum and up to a month.

I grew up with harsher conditions, and as a child, I had no say. As an adult, Adhar had never tried to chain me and drag me back. He never took my choice from me. We made other security measures.

I felt sick about Rama's actions in a way not even the nagas had made me feel about the estates and compounds. Her measures were downright abusive, completely uncalled for, and out of proportion to anything she had experienced. There was nothing to justify her decisions.

"Don't hold on to the anger," Sohan warned, drawing attention to the fact that I was letting everyone see my own feelings. "It's how we ended up in this position, Kaliya."

"I'm going to talk to her tonight," I decided. No need to drag this out. I knew she was in a house down the west trail. Seemed like easy directions.

"Please don't," Raphael muttered.

"I need to." With a sigh, I gave Sohan a sad look. "Think she'll try to kill me?"

"You ask that as if you think I know my daughter anymore," Sohan said, shaking his head. "I can only assume the worst. I misjudged her today, thinking I could slyly get her to let you sit down with her, that after so long, she might just give it a chance. She tried to kill you. She's also promised to tell you the way to Ramanaka tomorrow. Perhaps she doesn't want to see you until tomorrow. I wouldn't test it."

"Then I'll talk to her at dawn. I'll head over there before everyone is awake. That's still tomorrow, isn't it?"

"Your ability to tell time is correct," Sohan confirmed, shaking his head at me. "On to more positive topics... Arizona? What is it like?"

"A desert," Raphael and I said at the same time. I chuckled when Raphael gave me a look.

"I told him why you wanted to meet him." I patted Raphael's hand.

"Yes, yes. We know different things, you and me. I wouldn't say I know more since it's hard to know anything when you have no one to test the knowledge with. Maybe I can tell you some very interesting things. Maybe you have interesting things to tell me. Ask your questions and I shall answer, then ask my own." Sohan looked excited.

"Do you know what *makes* us?" Raphael asked tentatively. "I was born human, but I'm a cambion now and never found the thing that did it. Of all the records we searched, that was one thing they never put on paper."

"Ah, yes. That is a bit of a history lesson. Once, the barrier between our world and the world of demons was... thinner, more like the fae I hear about. Apparently, there are many doors between the fae worlds and ours. They come and go more readily. Mind you, those were times when the gods regularly walked the earth instead of making short appearances. That has certainly changed as the centuries slipped by."

Sohan stood and walked to the fire, threw in a few logs, then some dry bush, those twigs and leaves people used for simple fire starting. He got it going in less than a minute. With the glow of the fire, he turned off the lights.

"I have to save fuel."

"I think you want to be dramatic, with the lighting to match," I accused teasingly. Sohan looked around, then took his seat again.

"While we can take monstrous forms, the grey skin is our natural one. It's very similar to their natural form as well. They can all take the forms of the beasts, though. And there are the ones who are just beasts."

"I think I remember something about that." I just couldn't recall any of the details.

"The lab believed the realm demons come from is like the fae one. An entire world with its own ecosystem, possibly culture or society. Maybe even its own laws of physics," Raphael filled in for me. "And we might just call them all demons, the same way we do with the fae."

"It's probably true. If we have culture and society, why wouldn't intelligent beings from another realm have them? Plus, to have children with humans, well..."

Raphael's face was pale, but he nodded.

"Some of them had children, and most of those children were forgotten about, abandoned to die or survive on their own. Some lived perfectly normal human lives. They were *all* forgotten by their fathers, but not all of them were abandoned by their mothers. Some had mothers who told them all about their fathers. The monsters who rode great beasts pillaged their villages and raped them. Some had mothers who handed their sons swords and sketches of the beasts." Sohan's eyes turned red and black. "And sent their sons killing without a care for the young man's life.

"I rode out, barely a man with a sword in my hand, given to me by my mother. I trained and hunted for years. Then I found one while working with a mercenary group while we were protecting a village. I didn't kill it. I landed blows, though, enough to make it bleed. I was covered in it." Sohan looked at his hands. "It left me for dead, off to continue its rampage. I changed."

"Demon..." Raphael leaned back, his face another shade paler. "Demon blood?"

"I was stronger, faster, more powerful... and felt the terrible urge to kill. It consumed me," he said softly. "And then it faded. I don't know which of us slaughtered the mercenary company... or the village." Sohan closed his eyes. "But I was the one still alive. The demon, just one of the beasts that can slip out of their world sometimes, was dead."

"You just... kept going?" I asked.

"I went home," he said, smiling. "My mother killed herself when she saw I had become too much like my father. It was... oh, I couldn't tell you how long ago. I don't remember her name. I barely remember what she looked like." Sohan looked at Raphael, reached out slowly, and patted Raphael's hands. "You wouldn't be a direct son the way I am. It's been thousands of years since I've seen a true demon who could sire one of us."

"We always thought it was... distant relationships, several generations back," I said, nodding. "You might be the only direct son of a demon in the world."

"I'm the only one I know," he said, pulling his hand back when Raphael didn't react. "Though, outside of my family, I was never certain others of our kind existed at all. I am so very excited to meet more. I was when I heard about the ones living in America... yours. It's odd to be the only one for so long. It was decades, if not centuries, before I met Lalika. It was love. I felt this pull to her, needing her. Needing to see her, be in her life, hear her laugh. I'm really not sure what happened. You'll have to ask her. Somehow, she ended up ingesting my blood, making our connection permanent. Even with the mating, I was still the only one. She was a human changed by me, but not like me. Then we had Rama."

"How are cambion children?" Raphael asked.

"From our relationship, my children have grown naturally into their abilities."

"Start a cambion family, have cambion children?" I looked at Raphael, who exhaled. "You were worried we would need demon blood for every child, weren't you?"

"It's a nightmare to go through that," Raphael said, nodding. "I'm glad the others will only have a cambion child if they have the chance to find a mate. An immortal mate, too..."

"Yeah, that's nice to know." I leaned over and kissed his cheek. "I'll let you both talk. I'm going to ask Kahan for another portal to get our things."

Raphael shook his head, grabbing my hand before I could get away from the table.

"I threw it all through the portal before coming through," he explained. "You'll probably find it lying around outside."

Leaving them there to get the bags, I headed out the backdoor, and my eyes were drawn to the damage to the jungle around their home.

It'll grow back, but... I'm sorry it happened.

I saw our bags and grabbed them quickly. As I walked back inside, Sohan was already in the hall with Raphael, one of the doors open.

"You can stay in this room." He held the door open enough for me to get through. "I know it's not fancy—"

"It's perfect," I said, looking over the sparse, undecorated room. There wasn't an actual bed, either, only bedrolls that could be picked and moved easily. "It has a roof and a door. You're giving us space in your home. That means a lot to me." I put the bags down, Raphael trying to help. Looking at Sohan in the doorway, I tried to shoo my mate away. "We're not taking someone else's room?"

"No, not at all." Sohan looked around it before shrugging. "We sometimes use this for storage when we have extra supplies. Camping gear as well. I'm not sure why it's empty right now."

"Choices leading to an inevitable end," I said,

nodding. "Why do you need supplies? You're going to go home with us."

Sohan's laughter filled the room with joy.

"Put your things down, get what you need to change, and I'll show you where you can wash up for dinner," he said, giving me a warm smile before closing the door on us.

"Inside joke?" Raphael asked me.

I shook my head. "Sohan's concept of fate. I like it."

35

CHAPTER THIRTY-FIVE

Raphael and I were shown to a stream the family used to clean off and wash other things. It didn't leave us, by modern definition, clean, but it made us feel better. When we were in fresh clothes, Sohan took our dirty clothing, promising they would be washed and ready by the next afternoon.

"We're efficient," he said when I questioned that. "They'll be hung up in here to dry in a warm room with an active fire, not in the humid jungle." He nodded to the table. "Now sit down. Lalika and Kahan will bring in dinner any moment."

As a guest in this house, I didn't argue but was amazed Raphael was letting Sohan order him around. Once Sohan was out of the room, I leaned in and elbowed my mate.

"How are you feeling? Sohan is ordering us around, which isn't something you enjoy from the cambions at home."

"Good." Raphael wrapped an arm around the back of

my chair as he looked at me. "Sohan... is fine. He's interesting, not what I expected. I thought he wouldn't accept outsiders, but knowing what he's experienced over the last several thousand years, it would make sense he's ready for a change. We brought change."

"Yeah. I really like him."

"You two certainly have that... click. That's a good thing. It could have gone the other way like it did with Rama." Raphael growled her name. "I like Sohan. I need more time with Lalika and Kahan, but I don't see any reason I wouldn't like them. They're mine now, no matter what. I won't leave them to *this*."

"They did their best," I whispered, hearing the judgment in his voice, not of the people, but of how they lived.

"They did. *She* didn't," Raphael countered. "I won't let her on the compound in Arizona. It'll take a long time before I'm ready to make nice with her, Kaliya. I hope you understand that."

"I do," I promised. "But don't ban her family from seeing her. Sohan is a good man, and she's his daughter. If they want to rebuild some sort of relationship in the future, let them."

"I won't stop them from being a family, but I'll never allow her to have control over them again," he said, shaking his head. "Never. I promised better for all the cambions. That includes this family."

"You know, I started this conversation to ask if you were okay with Sohan ordering you around."

"I'm in his house," Raphael said, softening for a moment, a small smile forming. "I respect him. He's older and has clearly experienced a lot. He can teach me... so much. Not *everything*, but he won't be another Mateo or Sammy. Not to me. I won't lower him to the level of much younger cambions. He's earned some privileges even though we just met."

I heard a door, and the conversation died before I could tell Raphael I agreed with him.

Lalika and Kahan came in with several dishes.

"We need to make a second trip—"

"I got it, Mother." Kahan kissed her cheek and pushed her to a chair. "You just sit down. I can do the rest."

"Oh, you sweet boy," Lalika said, smiling as she let him push in her seat. "Fine."

Kahan brought the rest of the food inside in two trips. As he was putting out plates, Sohan came back and sat down, and we realized they only had four chairs for the dining table. With Raphael's and my help, we moved all the food and sat in front of the fire, using the floor cushions and low table there.

"This is even better," Lalika declared. "I hope you enjoy the meal—"

The front door opened slowly, but Rama's appearance wasn't tentative. I watched her over my shoulder as she realized we were eating on the floor, not at the table as she was probably used to.

Talk about bad timing...

"Can we help you?" Raphael asked before anyone could think of something to say. Seeing his expression, he wasn't happy at all to see her.

"I came for dinner... if I am allowed to eat."

For several tense moments, we all waited for

Raphael's answer. It was a defining moment. He had to show her family how much he would control this relationship.

His face went blank.

"Are you comfortable?" he asked, directing the question to the table, not Rama or me.

"She can join us if she promises to listen and not start any more fights," Lalika said.

Rama nodded.

"You can sit down," Raphael said.

It was so awkward, watching her move closer, trying to decide where she wanted to sit. Raphael claimed the side that left our backs to the front door. Sohan and Lalika were staring at the fire. Kahan was across from me, in the middle of his side, looking uncomfortable at the idea she might sit next to him.

It left Rama to sit with her back to the fire, her parents in front of her, Kahan to her left... and Raphael to her right. Alone on her own side, she was next to the one person in the room who would kill her without a second thought. The one person who *could* kill her.

Once she was settled on a cushion, Kahan slid to her, Lalika started making a plate. She held it out to me, leaving me surprised when I took it. Lalika made every plate at the table, handing them out, then starting the next.

As if he saw my interest and confusion, Sohan leaned closer.

"Lalika enjoys playing host, handling the plates to make sure everyone gets a fair portion. It's helped during our lean times to have one person manage the portions, so no one is going hungry."

I could only nod, wondering how much extra food they had to use to feed Raphael and me.

By the time Lalika was finished, there were no leftovers in the dishes. She sat down with her plate, just as full as everyone else's. That was the best part I saw in this situation. She wasn't going without to feed us.

"Now, you may eat... and *talk*. Kahan, aside from the obvious, how was the trip to Delhi?" She smiled as Kahan's eyes went wide.

Is he surprised by the question? I bet Rama controlled the conversation topics during meals, and everyone had to walk on eggshells.

"Oh, it was good," Kahan answered tentatively. "Um... Father, I traveled back while the food was in the oven. The supplies are behind the house."

"Wonderful. They'll make us comfortable until Kaliya and Raphael come back." Sohan's eyes twinkled, reminding me of the sly way he had gotten me away from Rama. He had talked around it, talked through it, and gotten her to wander off, so he could investigate me.

"Come back?" Kahan looked at us, his mother, then his father again. "Really?"

"Well, it's dinner, so we should get the big news out of the way. And..." Sohan looked at Raphael. "Could this be a family decision?"

Oh, we're just getting straight into this. Okay then. I figured we would enjoy our food for a moment before we set off the nuclear warhead that came to dinner.

"I would be willing to hear arguments against it, if

any," Raphael said, shrugging one shoulder. "Although they may not change the decision."

"Pragmatic and honest," Sohan said, chuckling. "Not bad traits in a man."

I could feel Raphael puff up. He might not say it yet, but I had a sneaking suspicion he saw Sohan the same way I did—a potential father figure, something neither of us had for a long time.

"Lalika, Kahan..." Sohan took his wife's hand, bringing it up to his lips to kiss softly before continuing. "Raphael, leader of the cambions in America, has told me he wants us to live in America with more of our people."

"Ordered. Let's be completely honest. I plan on seeing that through," Raphael corrected. "And it won't just be our people."

I glanced at Rama while Raphael looked at me. I could see them both, but the dawning realization on Rama's face made me worry about what Raphael clearly expected me to say.

"We have a compound in the desert. It was started for the cambions we freed, but it's also the refuge of the remaining nagas in the world. When Garuda attacked, I took them there. And yes, we would love to have your family live with us there."

The silence at the table was a long one. I decided I was going to eat. That made Raphael start eating too, giving the cambions time to absorb. Sohan was the only one not purely shocked or surprised. He was smiling, but I also knew he was watching his daughter carefully.

"You're going to come here... disrupt my home... and

take my family away?" Rama asked, defeated. Lost. Hollow.

I put my wooden fork down and met her gaze. There was only the small bit of fire, but most of it was pain, shell-shocked pain.

"What did I do to you?"

"You lack a certain sense of responsibility," I said, wondering if she truly thought I was a grand evil mastermind, there to ruin her life. "You locked your family into this life. Did you ever think to ask them if they wanted something else? Kahan is five hundred years old. Have you realized he's a man who can make his own decisions? Your parents are older than you, and you kept them here, unable to talk openly about the things they enjoy or even dream of having a different life. If you didn't try to kill me, Raphael might have asked you to join us, but you tried to kill me, so you're not welcome. When your family wants to visit you, they'll have that option."

Rama looked at her parents, and all I saw was a terrified *girl*. Not a woman five thousand years old, but a girl who never knew a single day without a support system. Not someone who could live alone and face the future by herself. That was the biggest difference between her and me. She was utterly dependent, abusive, to fulfill her need. I could be toxically independent, hurting others so they couldn't hurt me.

I was growing past my own troubles from a traumatic life, but Rama was only beginning to take very small steps and they were against her will. I tried to pay attention to the rest of the table, but I wanted to keep my eyes on Rama as she processed this.

"In the end, they don't really have a choice. I won't let them live like this anymore," Raphael said, taking the attention off me. He took another bite of his food, looking at Lalika. "Are you okay, ma'am? I really would like to know how you feel. Maybe we can make the transition smoother. We've helped people adjust to the modern world before. You don't have to worry about—"

"I would love to meet the other cambions. I would love to see a new country and meet new people," she said, making me turn to see her smiling as she grabbed a small cloth and wiped her eyes. "Oh, I would really love it." She held up a hand and cried harder. "I don't know why... why I'm like this." She reached out and tapped her son's shoulder. "Kahan, do you want to go?"

Kahan looked at his sister, who didn't react. The ground had been taken out from under her feet, and she appeared to be in shock. Kahan looked at his parents, then at Raphael and me, then nodded.

"Yes."

"When we're done, we'll help you move home with us," Raphael said. "Let's finish dinner. It's delicious, Lalika. I know many people who would want to know how you did this."

"Thank you!" Lalika's smile was accented by another wave of tears.

The rest of dinner was excited discussion about the idea of moving. I knew it wouldn't all be perfect. Lalika would need the most help, but I understood her excitement. She'd heard stories of the modern world as it kept evolving but never got to see it. Based on their home, I assumed they had no cameras or internet. Kahan and

Sohan at least had peeked and learned quickly to avoid cameras.

Once dinner was over, Kahan and Sohan cleaned up. Rama never moved. Once the men were back, we sat around the fire, and I wasn't sure where the conversation would turn next.

"Perhaps, love, we can tell Raphael about you," Sohan suggested. "While he tells us about Arizona and our people there. When we get there, we'll have some understanding of who we'll share a community with."

"Oh, you mean about me being human? I can do that." Lalika pulled her husband to sit next to her. I had seen it all evening. Lalika was sheltered, but she embraced being the caretaker, able to shower her husband in love without reserve.

"I would love to tell you about the other cambions," Raphael said, leaning forward and resting his arms on the small table. "Actually, I'll start, because... well, we don't have any human mates. Only Kaliya and me for now."

"Oh, and I'll be able to answer everyone's questions then when they start finding their own mates," Lalika said, her eyes practically glowing with excitement. This woman would throw dinner parties, holiday parties, get-togethers, playdates for children not her own, and whatever other function she could think of.

As Raphael started talking about the cambions, our friends and community back home, Rama finally lost her patience and stood without a word. I let her get all the way out the door before I got to my feet.

"If she hurts you—"

I put my hand over his mouth.

"I'll be fine," I said softly, kissing the top of his head.

I couldn't be the only one of us who saw what was happening. Rama's parents were pretending she wasn't even there. Kahan feared her but was slowly realizing Raphael wouldn't let anything happen. Rama was watching her entire world come crumbling down and how her family was *happy* about it.

I would be, too, if I was forced to live like this.

But I wanted to make sure she would help us tomorrow. Had to make sure.

She came to dinner. Maybe that was a sign we could try talking through some of this.

Raphael nodded, so I took my hand off his mouth and walked out, following Rama.

She was twenty steps from the door, her head down, back turned to me. I could see her shoulders shaking as I drew closer, but I kept my distance. At ten feet, I felt safe enough to say something.

"Rama, can we talk?"

"About?" I could hear the tears.

"Any of it," I said, taking another step closer. "I didn't know how any of this would go when I came looking for you. Make no mistake about it, I came looking for *you*. Raphael has wanted to meet more of his kind, but I needed you."

"If I give you the way to Ramanaka, will he let me keep my family?" she asked, turning enough for me to see her profile in the moonlight.

"No."

"Then there's nothing to say," she said, walking away.

36

CHAPTER THIRTY-SIX

"Wait a minute!" I snapped, and it got her to freeze. I stormed around her, making her look me in the eye. "Do you really see yourself as the ultimate victim here? Answer me honestly, Rama. I'm trying so hard to understand your logic. You held your family fucking hostage—"

"Why do you care?" she growled. "You don't know them. You don't know me. Even with my mate's memories, you don't know us. You certainly don't know Kahan. Why would you come here and destroy our life when you don't know us?"

"My mate said it best... they deserve better," I answered. "If you loved them, you would have given them *better*." I pointed at the house. "Instead, they're happy to get out of this. Do you have any concept of the outside world? The time that's—"

"Are you going to turn me into a villain, too?" she asked softly.

"I don't need to turn you into anything. You're doing a

pretty good job of being one," I hissed. "At this point, you're not even trying to say you're protecting them. You're trying to buy them back like they are things that go on your shelf. Do you care about their feelings at all?"

Rama crumpled before my eyes. Before she could cover her face, I saw tears roll down her cheeks as she fell to her knees, and gut-wrenching sobs came.

Letting her cry, I took a knee. Seeing Rama cry brought up memories, and there was a shred of sympathy, a shred of memory I couldn't repress.

"Rama, I'm sorry he's gone." They were the most honest words I could give her that weren't some form of condemnation.

"I didn't *know*." She straightened, and her head fell back. Staring at the skylight, her chest heaved as another wave of tears came. "I didn't *know* they were unhappy. I didn't mean to *hurt* them. I just want them safe, and..." She closed her eyes. "I just can't lose this. I can't go back out there. There's no place for me out there. I lost it when I lost him." Covering her face again, she bent over her legs again, and the tears were never-ending. "I can't be *alone*. I've *never* been alone."

"It's been five thousand years. It's time to let them go," I said as gently as I could. "You understand that, right?" She nodded, and I breathed a sigh of relief.

"I didn't mean to hurt them," she said in a whine. "I *didn't*." Sitting up again, she shook her head in denial. "I..."

I don't know what she saw, but something changed. Her head tilted to the side as her bottom lip quivered.

"What's wrong?"

"You have his eyes," she whispered. She reached out, prompting me to move away. The flash of hurt was clear, but I couldn't let her touch me. There was no way I trusted her enough for that.

"Oh." I closed them and rubbed, hoping to get rid of the snake eyes. I hadn't realized my eyes weren't their natural color anymore.

"I always liked that they were nearly like mine," she explained. "You and him... same coloring, the eyes, and black scales... I'm sorry I called you a liar." She hiccupped. "I can't say I like that you exist, but that doesn't mean you're lying. You remember..."

"Everything," I said softly, nodding, then made a regretful click of my teeth because it wasn't entirely true. "Sort of. Big moments are easy to recall. Small things, like what he ate for breakfast? It's the same kind of things we deal with, and our people have none of his writings left. I know better now, but for a long time, we really only had the story of what happened to him and pieces passed down in families. I'm certain I would remember more if I could remember what to think about. Your mother did that. I had no idea they had that conversation. I didn't know he and Lalika had such deep personal moments together. She reminded me." I dropped my hand and sighed.

She looked like hell, but that was what people looked like when they had a mental breakdown and walked out the other side of it.

"What do your people say?" she asked, looking away.

"That he made a mistake and paid for it. Mistakes happen. We know the human legend isn't completely accurate. Krishna is their hero, and he *is* a hero. Sometimes, bad guys are just people making mistakes, and history is written by the victor."

"Why do you want to kill Garuda after all these years? Why pick a fight not even my mate wanted? None of the nagas wanted it."

"We actually killed Garuda once before." Her eyes went wide, but she didn't interrupt, so I continued the story. "In Vrindavan. We passed down his bones. The current Garuda is like me—a reincarnation with the memories from his previous life. Just because many of the beings from your time are gone doesn't mean we all stopped living. So much time passed." I sighed.

"I'm going to kill Garuda before he finishes us off. Less than ten nagas remain in the world, Rama, and three of them are infants. Our last naga over one thousand years old was murdered last month. I'm the *Nagaraja* because we have no other options. I'm trying to finish this." I chuckled darkly. "The number of times I've had to repeat that information… it hurts every time, but I do what I can."

"How old are you?"

"One hundred and nineteen… and I might not live to see one twenty."

"You're so young,"—Rama shook her head—"to be here, talking about any of this. I was five hundred when he died."

"I am an adult, and—"

"I did this all wrong, didn't I?" She stood, and I quickly followed, not wanting to be in a vulnerable position while she was moving around. "I did this all wrong."

She walked away, and I wasn't sure if she wanted me to follow. It took her a moment to realize I hadn't.

"Come, let me show you."

I didn't know whether I trusted her, didn't know if I ever could. My feet moved, though, thanks to the regret she wasn't trying to hide.

Following her down a thin trail worn into the jungle floor, we came upon a smaller house, and she led me inside. I was fidgety as she closed us in. Everything could be seen from the main room, including the one door to another room. She went into that room and brought out an ornate chest, which looked like the entire wealth of the family, put it in front of me.

"Look," she ordered as she unlocked it.

Opening it, I saw papers and took the top one to read. I put it back and grabbed a leather-bound book, but not how we bound books now. It took little time to confirm what I believed this was.

It was *everything.*

I was right. Rama had stolen all of it. Every single piece of his writing, his private journals...

"What..."

"I thought I was protecting his legacy," she explained. "But hearing you... he was never evil to you, was he?"

"No..." I answered, looking over the chest at her. "Rama, this is—"

"Yours," she said, nodding quickly. "You are—"

"No." Shaking my head, I stood. I closed the chest to

make sure this was just her and me, no allure to keep looking at his writing. "No, you don't need to give this to me, but a loan would be appreciated. We can make copies. The world is bigger than it used to be, and I know people who can preserve them better, so you can have them five thousand years from now. All I would like are copies."

"If this will make me closer to... the woman he fell in love with, *please* take it," she pleaded. "Because I know how much I've *fallen*. I know. I knew when I told my mother to be quiet and when I hurt my *brother*, neither the first time." She cried again. "I'm not worthy of him anymore. I'm not. He would have never hurt his brothers. He honored his mother until she hurt him, and even then, he never acted against her. *Please* take them."

"I can't, in good conscience, leave you with nothing when there's another option." I wouldn't do it. "You can keep these. He would have wanted you to keep these." In my heart, I knew that was true. I didn't need his writings. I could use them going forward, but I didn't need them.

"I guess arguing with you would be pointless, wouldn't it?" she asked, chuckling sadly. It was the mad chuckle of someone about to collapse again, about to lose control of their grief and let out more pain. "I guess arguing with me seemed pointless to my family all this time. Now, I know how they feel."

"You didn't let them argue, Rama," I reminded her, trying to say it gently.

"No, I didn't," She sat on a lonely stool, the tears coming silently as she stared at me.

"But you can't do that to me," I said as I walked around the chest. "How did we end up here? How did you end up with these? Will you tell me? In exchange for keeping them? I just want to know the timeline. I need that understanding."

"I don't know where it went wrong," she admitted. "I came back after he died... and they, my parents, said I could take all the time I needed. I know they didn't mean forever. I knew it then, but the years... kept turning. It didn't happen all at once. First, my father would bring me news of what was happening in the world, news of new births among the nagas, a new *Nagaraja*... Then my father told me he heard Kaliya's name on the lips of a human. I was so *angry* to find out the legacy my mate was left with... so angry. I... banned them from ever speaking to the nagas about me again. I already hated the gods and humans, but that made me hate the nagas." She leaned against the wall, staring at her hands as she curled them into fists. "This was their brother, their uncle, one of the most powerful of them... and they let him be a villain. My mate was *not* evil." Her words went up an octave as she fought tears.

"So you went to find all this?"

"No, I forced my father to," she countered. "Oh, he was so angry when I first told him what I wanted. My father, mercenary and warrior, but *never* a thief. He had never been a dirty thief, as he said. Said it wasn't fair of me to steal important memories from other families. The more he argued, the more I realized I could just..."

"Take his will away," I whispered. Now, I knew just how uncomfortable Sohan had to have felt when Kahan revealed their thieving. It was so much deeper than the honor of a warrior. It was also tied up in the power of

Rama and the abuse she'd inflicted on everyone while trying to protect herself.

They all need therapy.

"That's right. That's what I did. My father had no choice in getting this back for me. I keep them here because he… he always refused to look at them when I lived in the main house. Refused to read them with me. I built this place with my bare hands and have rebuilt it several times since. I felt as if no one in the family understood me anymore, so I built this place and brought them here." She looked around, then shook her head. "I would stay here for days on end without eating or sleeping, rereading every letter, every journal."

"You lost time, even your perception of it, didn't you?"

"I did. My family tried to argue with some of my decisions. My mother asked if she could leave with my father to see a local village, and I banned her from ever leaving this place. I told myself it was to protect her. The reality was, Kahan wasn't born yet, and I would have been alone."

I feel as if I'm watching the tail end of a horror movie. That eventually, this obsession and need for control would have gotten so bad, she would have killed them to puppet their dead bodies. Gods, this is all fucked up.

"Over the years, I just made more rules whenever they upset this bubble I needed."

"You didn't need it… you wanted it. There's a difference," I said, this time saying it strongly. "There was no *need* to abuse your family. You wanted it to their detriment, and you had the power to make it happen."

"Fine, I wanted this. I wanted to never go back out there. If I did, it would be to kill all of them... all of you."

Rama still had that fire in her. I knew I had to tread carefully, but my fuel tank was emptying.

"Part of me also... wondered what it would be like if I left, made a new identity, and never came back. Part of that sounded appealing, to... never be Rama, mate to Kaliya again. I could never take that step, so I stayed here."

"Taking any step would have implied you were moving on. You didn't want to move on." I moved closer. "I won't say I don't understand or sympathize, even if I really don't like the actions you've taken. It took me over a century to move on from my parents' murder. In fact, I'm still dealing with it, but it's not what drives my every decision anymore. It was hard coming to this point in my life.

"For over a century, I jumped into battles and got dear friends hurt or killed, all in the drive that I could avenge them. I refused to let it go. I hurt many people when there were probably better ways to do what I was doing. I can't imagine what it feels like to lose a mate. I try my best not to consider a world without Raphael in it."

"Horrendous... it's horrendous," she whispered, her long black hair falling over her face as she let her head drop. "It continued like this for... I don't know. Kahan was born, and I was... jealous. I couldn't let him know I was broken. I had to be the powerful sibling, or this new baby would take away my parents' love and affection. I treated him so unfairly."

"He's scared of you," I pointed out.

"For good reason," she said, shaking her head. The tears came back with a vengeance—a tide, unstoppable, ebbing and flowing. "I never wanted to hurt them… I didn't. I just needed to protect *me,* too."

I gave her time to recover, watching her wipe her eyes when she was cried out once again.

"And now you're here."

"I am."

"I'll take you to Ramanaka tomorrow, but I'm going with you." She swallowed and cleared her throat. "Don't tell me I can't. I can't be here when my family leaves. I won't be here when they do it. I'll stay in Ramanaka for a little while until you decide what to do with those. Then I'll come back."

"Are you sure? I don't know if you're in the best place to be making big decisions."

"You can't go to Ramanaka without me, so don't argue with my decision," she said. "And you'll need me. I know the island, and its inhabitants probably have changed little since I left, at least where they live. There are some areas that will be safe for you and some that won't. You might remember some of that, but I know. You'll need me." She gave me a once over. "You won't succeed, you know. I'll begrudgingly admit you're valiant for this quest you're on, and you're right about things I wish you weren't, but you won't kill Garuda."

"I've beaten impossible odds before." I didn't know if I would walk away this time, but if I died, I was going to take Garuda down with me. "I'll have my mate fighting alongside me, and we'll do what we have to."

"Well, with his help…" Rama growled, the low chest

rumble I knew from Raphael. "You might have a chance. However, you're just... so weak compared to my mate. He knew how to do things that would have changed your world."

"I'm sure, but I have one thing he doesn't."

"What's that?"

"Belief that I can win." I stepped back. "Have a good night, Rama. I'll see you tomorrow." I walked out before she could respond. Walking back to the main house, I found the cambions still talking. Raphael looked relaxed as Sohan said something. He looked at me, smiling.

"Did you get what you wanted?"

"Well, things happened and were said. I don't know what I wanted or expected, but I'm still alive, so we'll call it a win." I shrugged and took two steps toward the room where Sohan was allowing us to stay. "She's coming with us tomorrow. Her reasoning is reasonable, so... she's coming with us."

Then I went into the backroom, shutting the door quietly. Leaning on the wall, finally letting myself feel the exhaustion, I slid down and closed my eyes.

One step at a time. I just need to keep going one step at a time. That's all I can do.

But I am so tired.

37

CHAPTER THIRTY-SEVEN

Raphael gently woke me up. He was already dressed and moving, his face hanging in the air over me. I was still on my back, but okay otherwise. My feet were cold, but I couldn't remember taking my boots off.

"Breakfast will be on the table soon," he said softly, pushing hair from my face. "Are you feeling all right? You were asleep sitting up when I came in last night. It looked like you just closed your eyes and shut off. I tried to make you comfortable. Lalika helped when I needed an extra pair of hands."

"Just tired," I answered, pushing myself up. He backed away, pointing to a neatly folded pile of clothing. I could only nod, then waved him out of the room. "Go sit down. I'll be there soon."

I changed into the clean clothes, found a place to handle my morning business, then headed to the stream to wash up for breakfast. I was tired but wouldn't be a rude guest. Sohan made it clear washing up was expected before meals, so I would go out of my way to do that. When I got to the water, I tried not to look in Kahan's direction, listening to him hum to himself. I had no idea if he was wearing anything under the water level and wasn't in the mood for naked men.

"Good morning," he called.

"Put on clothes before talking to me." I splashed water on my face upstream, needing the jolt to wake up more. "Breakfast will be ready soon."

"Oh, um..."

I heard splashing around but continued my small morning ritual, using water to help tame my hair and clean up the braids. I was redoing one of my braids as Kahan loudly walked up behind me.

"Why do you braid your hair? I didn't think you would be someone who... liked doing her hair. You're a warrior, a fighter."

I tried not to turn and hiss. The assumption rubbed me the wrong way.

"You know, it's okay for a warrior to be feminine. If I said it's because I like the way they look, I would expect you to accept that. As it is, that's not why I do it. It helps me keep hair out of my face."

"There are easier ways to do that," he countered.

Why are we discussing my hair?

"My mother taught me to braid my hair, to not put it in a ponytail," I added, shaking my head as I stood. Turning around as I finished the braid, I looked him over. There was something so boyish about him. Now, it was unsurprising. The entire family, their ability to grow for centuries, had been stunted.

"You've been hidden from the world for five hundred years. You deserve a warning." I smiled, fangs down. "The women of the world are going to eat you alive if you make comments like that all the time. Be careful who you make judgments about or ask personal questions without thinking."

"It was just a question," he said, stepping back. "And no one can be as scary as my sister. I'll be fine."

"Sammy is going to destroy you," I mumbled, walking past him. "It's going to be hilarious, but you'll grow from it."

"Oh, come on." Kahan snorted. "Really? Raphael was talking about her last night, but she's not *Rama*."

"No, she's not Rama... she's worse." I chuckled as I stopped next to Kahan. "Look... I'm just trying to look out for you."

"Tell me one thing that might make me scared of her," Kahan said, shrugging a shoulder. "She's what? Over four hundred years younger than me?"

"Rama didn't get a single hit on me. Sammy nearly killed me once." That made Kahan stumble as I kept walking toward the house. "Anything else?"

"Why do you have white hair?"

"It went prematurely white starting when I was a teenager."

"How long have you known about our kind? Been with Raphael?"

"Just over one year... to both."

"What did you say to Rama last night?"

That made me stop and study him.

"You were warming me up to answer anything,

weren't you?" I saw his renewed interest. It was a smart play, so I gave him an answer. "Hopefully, I got her to see herself in a mirror. Everything she did to you, to your parents, was born out of something that wasn't evil but injured or broken. That doesn't absolve her, but maybe, just maybe, she'll be able to move forward and do better to others. She'll heal a little."

"Does she… deserve it?"

"That's not for us to decide," I said softly. "One day, I'll tell you the story about my Uncle Nakul. Great evil was done to him, and he committed great evil against others. I found myself the person who had to stop him, and I watched him begin to heal, but I could never decide how I wanted or should feel about him. Love, hate, pain, regret… There was no resolution between my uncle and me. There may never be for you with Rama. You learn to accept it and move on."

"Okay."

When the house was in view, Raphael walked out with Sohan. Raphael's eyes fell on me while Sohan was looking around. Raphael tapped Sohan's arm and pointed at us.

"Ah, good! Breakfast is ready." Sohan held the door for Kahan, then had a stare-off with Raphael. My mate went inside, leaving me blocked by Sohan as the door closed.

"Say something," I demanded, wanting to eat and meet the day sooner rather than later.

"Rama is already seated for breakfast and ready to leave. I don't know what you said to her last night, but thank you." He opened the door for me. I opened my mouth, but he lifted his free hand, silencing me. "No need to say anything. Just accept the gratitude."

I went in and sat down next to my mate. We ate in silence, and I realized the plans were already set. After whatever happened on Ramanaka, we would find our way back here to let Kahan make a portal to Delhi for us. It seemed so easy.

Just do this thing and go home.

Too bad it wouldn't be like running a simple errand.

Breakfast was cleaned up, and Rama stood, looking at everyone.

"I'll be staying on Ramanaka for a little while. I won't be coming back with them, might never come back. I don't know yet. I love you, and I'm sorry. Goodbye." She walked out, leaving her family in stunned silence.

"Just like that." Sohan stared at the front door, his words shaky as he broke the silence. "I hope she finally finds healing."

"That's up to her," Lalika said, wiping her eyes. "I wish we could help, but it's up to her now."

"Yes, it is," I agreed, standing. "Stay inside until we're gone. I don't know what Rama has in mind, but I would rather..."

"We'll stay inside," Sohan promised. "Go. Good luck."

"Yeah, good luck," Kahan joined in.

Lalika got up and kissed my cheek, then Raphael's. Wiping her eyes again, she disappeared into a back room.

Raphael grabbed my weapon bag, the only bag we were taking to Ramanaka. He'd let Sohan clean the blades, sharpen the chakram, and reorganize everything. I didn't mind. It was an honor to have a warrior with his level of experience show my weapons such loving care.

I gave one more thankful nod to the old cambion and walked out, Raphael behind me. Rama was in the same place she had been the night before.

"Are you ready?" she asked over her shoulder.

"Yeah. How are we doing this?" I stopped beside her, Raphael on my other side. Rama was the one who knew the way. I was expecting something, but not what she held up—a pebble. Naturally smoothed by water, the pebble was a neutral grey with flecks of blue and purple. I had no idea what it meant and tried to understand, but there was a memory just out of reach.

"Let me tell you something of what you'll find in Ramanaka," she said, fingers curling around the smooth stone. "This was given to my Kaliya the day she rejected me, and he promised he would never see her again. Her rejection of me broke the relationship between them. I felt so guilty, but that's not the story. As he grabbed me to leave, Kadru followed him, asking him not to disappear. Asking him to come home someday if he felt the need to leave now. He yelled at her, and she grabbed his wrist—"

The memory flooded my mind, and I wasn't able to stop myself from repeating the line. It was the thing I couldn't bring myself to remember earlier.

"And said, I am your mother. I will only ever be a stone's throw from you," I whispered. "It wasn't what he wanted. He wanted her to apologize for saying you weren't good enough for him, but she wouldn't give him that. She gave him the pebble." I crossed my arms. "So... you throw it, then what?"

"Well, a portal probably," Rama said, shrugging. "I've never actually tried it. It was his. His mother intended it for him, not me. There's more you should know. Ramanaka is saturated in magic. It was back then, and I highly doubt it's changed. There may be things, people even, you need to be careful with. Or we might not see any of them. It's just something to remember."

"It's a land lost to time, so I assumed it would be potentially dangerous."

"Yes, it is. It's good we're on the same page. One last thing." She pushed her hand out, the pebble still in her palm. "I'm not going to throw it. You are."

"But—"

"You're her child," Rama reminded me.

"It's... sort of mad," I countered. "Actually, it's insane. I've never heard of a spell like that."

Rama rolled her eyes.

"Sure, but that's the time you are stepping into. Look, you are a shadow of what my mate was. I thought about what you said, the last part. My mate, my Kaliya, did things you wouldn't dream of because he believed he could. It's how he poisoned the damn river. Not everything worked or worked the way he intended, but he could do things others couldn't. You believe you can defeat Garuda, something he never thought was possible, not without magic and prophecy on his side. You can be sure to believe this stone, imbued with Kadru's power, will work."

I took it, but my mind wasn't on the stone.

"Is that how I healed?" I asked myself.

"From Pavan's venom?" Raphael sighed heavily. "Maybe."

"So you've done it?" Rama's curious and surprised question made me look at her. "You've been able to do something impossible before?"

"I survived the bite of another naga, which should have killed me. We weren't able to give me his blood to neutralize it fast enough. Can all cambion mates do stuff like that? Impossible things?"

"No. My mother can't. This is only you and him..." Rama made a face. "Though you are the same person, so maybe it's just *you*. A specific combination of you and us. Your soul or maybe being a naga. Humans aren't powerful in their base nature. Cambion magic gives them immortality, a little more strength, a little more healing. I bet it would be the same for every human. What it does to a naga... well, there's only been two of you, and there's only one human mate, but that's how I always looked at it. It explained the differences between my mother and my mate."

"I see..."

I rolled the stone around in my hand, focused on it, and felt something interesting.

It *did* have power. It was a magical object, meant to do something. Rocks weren't alive, which meant someone had to put this magic on it or in it.

Just believe, huh? Well...

I threw it. Not hard, because I didn't need it soaring into the jungle where we couldn't find it. Hearing it land in the vegetation, for a second, I felt the disappointment of being right. That it had been insane.

Then a boom echoed out, shaking trees, scaring animals, and even making all of us take several steps back.

"I thought I knew magic," I whispered as I stared in wonder at what was happening. Trees grew and bent, becoming an arched doorway, and beyond that door was a new land. "But…" I started walking, knowing I would find myself on Ramanaka when I went through. Before I went inside, Raphael took my hand. Rama jogged ahead of us, stepping through first.

"Let him come through. It might close when you pass through."

I pushed Raphael in, then stepped through. The trees remained, but the portal was gone. Turning around, I didn't see the home of Sohan, Lalika, and Kahan. I saw an unfamiliar forest or jungle. I didn't know. I didn't care. It was wild and full of magic. The magic permeated the air in such a way, I understood why it had been lost for so long.

Ramanaka was a realm of its own.

And I was finally here.

38

CHAPTER THIRTY-EIGHT

"When... when did it become its own realm?" I asked, not to anyone in particular.

"It used to be... closer," Rama said, sounding bored. "Like if you went to the right spot in the ocean, you would slip through the barrier and arrive. No one who has ever come here has left in the same way. Many never left. I don't think the realm is fully explored. For all I know, it might just be this island and endless ocean."

It was a realm of magic. It was entirely possible it was only the island, and something made it impossible to leave. There were stranger things in the fae realms, not that I had personal experience with them. I made it a point never to go to other realms, certainly not the fae realms.

I could only look around, taking it all in. It didn't take long to see the house, sitting between the trees in a clearing. Behind it, a waterfall came down the cliff, with a lazy river to the side of it. It was a beautiful place, as though someone had taken the greatest architecture of every temple, then crafted a cabin instead of a palace.

It was so beautiful, I couldn't speak. It touched places in my heart that made everything blurry.

"That's Kadru's home," Rama explained, seeing what I was looking at.

"Let's go say hi," Raphael said, stepping forward.

"No. Only she should go. Kadru won't be happy with us. If you want her to give you a safe place on this island... well, you need to get her to warm up to you first. We would make a bad first impression."

"Okay." Taking a deep breath, I started walking. "Both of you stay safe. Please."

My heart was racing. I was nervous.

I was the first naga to come home in thousands of years, if this could still be called the home of the nagas. I didn't know how she would feel seeing me—not one of her sons, but a cheap knock-off, a descendant who wasn't even the right sex.

Finding the walkway that showed me through an arch to enter what I assumed was a yard or garden, magic rushed over me, blowing my hair back. I kept walking but felt pulled to the river. The stone wall didn't separate the garden from the river. I hadn't been able to see all of it previously, but now, I saw her, wearing an ornate sari, standing at the edge of the water, staring at the river. She didn't turn, her black hair floating in the wind as if it was actually in water.

"So, you've come home, have you, Kaliya?" she asked, making my feet freeze as my breathing stopped. How did she know who I was? "After everything, you come here.

After you lost everything... only *then* do you feel you can return to your mother. Well, it's better than dead."

Wrong Kaliya. She thinks I'm him... which means she recognizes who you're reincarnated from.

"I go by Kaliya, but I haven't lost everything yet, Mother of Nagas." I spoke in the language she did, using the ancient Vedic Sanskrit. "I'm sorry to disappoint you, but I'm not your son, only a distant granddaughter." I couldn't let her continue to think I was her long-dead son.

She turned slowly, a frown making her confusion known. It didn't last long. She looked me over like a slab of meat she wanted to buy from the butcher.

And I wasn't worth the cost.

"Ah, one of you," she said, shaking her head. The entire time, her hair looked as if it was floating in water.

Is... is that because she was turned into a river that one time?

Focusing on the mystery of her hair allowed me to ignore the dismissive way she spoke and the deep pain it gave me. I wasn't in the mood for someone to carve into my emotional state.

"One of me... do you mean a nagini or a reincarnation?"

"Either... both. My sons loved their daughters, but... granddaughters aren't as good as grandsons. There was a reason I had so many sons, a reason lost on my children."

"Why not?" I asked, putting my hands in front of me.

"Don't bother me with questions. What are you doing here?"

"Saving the nagas." I decided to do something that

could have been seen as foolish. She had dismissed me; I would dismiss her. I found a tree and leaned on it, studying her as she studied me.

"Oh really?" She found me *so* funny. "Do they need saving by a little girl?"

"There's only,"—I did a mental headcount—"eight of us left, and the ones who remain named me the *Nagaraja,* so I think they'll take whoever they can get."

"Excuse me?" She came closer. "What do you mean there are only *eight*?"

"I mean just that. Your thousand sons are all dead. Their children are all dead. Their descendants are struggling to stay alive as they are hunted to the last member. There are only *eight* left. I didn't know what to expect meeting you, but not this. I will take my leave." Pushing off the tree, I wondered what I was thinking. I didn't know this woman. *He* had barely known her. I was walking away when she spoke again.

"They made a nagini into the *Nagaraja*?"

I froze, unable to keep walking. My feet were glued to the ground. I looked down, trying to yank them.

"Yeah, they did."

"Weren't there more powerful nagas?"

"No, nor warriors as skilled as I am."

I heard soft footsteps as she circled around me, and I finally judged her height. She had to be over six feet tall. I wasn't short or even average at five foot ten inches, but she was *tall.*

"Tell me how my children have ended up in this position," she demanded.

It spilled out of me, a child trying to explain to a

parent. I told a story repeated through the ages of persecution, of pain. I told a story of secrets hidden in the shadows, of dark mistakes and obsession. I gave her the story of the pain the nagas were suffering and what I had already done to fix it. I kept much of my personal life story to myself, not seeing it as relevant to the journey. Knowing how she'd reacted to Rama, I kept Raphael to myself. Knowing she already recognized me as her son's reincarnation, I didn't tell her of all my memories. On that topic, I only told her I knew I was the reincarnation, thanks to magic done on me.

She wanted to know about the nagas, so I told her everything I knew.

"You found Rama." She made a face, then shook her head.

"Are you angry I found her? I understand you don't like her, but I needed a way here."

"No," Kadru said, turning away from me. "Unsurprised."

"And the rest?"

She walked away, shaking her head again. Finding my feet free, I followed her into the house, knowing I was taking privileges that could cost me my life, but I couldn't let that threat stop me, not *now*.

"You can't fight Garuda," she said as she went into a very traditional kitchen, with no modern appliances or anything else. Standing there, I remembered it more clearly from my previous life and realized it hadn't changed at all. This really was a land out of time.

"Why not?" I demanded.

She frowned when she turned in my direction.

"Don't use that tone with me," she snapped. "You can't because you won't win. If the nagas are in such a position where they can't suffer more losses, you shouldn't throw your life away. Have children. Protect the others. Any child you may have could be powerful enough. Or you'll need an army to defeat him. Take your pick, child."

Biting my tongue, I tried not to hiss, thinking carefully about what I wanted and needed to say. Reduced to something small, one task—only the one.

Well, I need to say something. She's waiting on me to say something...

"I can't have children. I've taken a serious injury. I'm not ready for them, anyway. I have a duty to my people, so we'll leave the baby for another time. I am here for one purpose, and it's not to have that discussion with you."

"To give your husband strong sons... is your duty," she said softly, eyes narrowing. "And you can't?"

"I don't care what you feel marriage is and what wifely duties are, but in the world I live in, it's not the most important thing I bring to the table... not by a long shot. And it's a discussion that only involves two people, my mate and me." I crossed my arms.

"I didn't come this far only to meet you and be turned away. I'll walk all over this island until I find where he roosts. I don't need your blessing to do that. He started the war. I'm finishing it."

"It's been a long time since one of my children has disrespected me," Kadru hissed.

"Yeah, but you take every opportunity to disrespect us. Maybe that's why Kaliya tried so hard to forget you." I knew the comment would cut deep. "It's so fucking hard to remember you when I remember everything about Rama. The way he loved her. The way she loved him. There was no judgment between them, but then I get here,"—I shook my head as her eyes went wide—"and the first thing you did was dismiss me."

I wasn't that surprised. She had one-thousand sons for her husband and only two daughters. One of them was left mostly forgotten, and the other... well, there were disputes on who her father actually was.

"*Don't.*"

"Just like you dismissed Rama. No wonder."

"You don't know him. You could never know him."

"I remember him," I snapped. "Gods, I am running around and dealing with people who can't realize the world has moved on. You, Garuda, Rama... none of you realize and accept that it's been thousands of years since those days. Sure, I'm a nagini. I am a woman, not one of your precious sons, but I'm going to do what none of them could. There is nothing you can say that will stop me."

I turned to walk out, too tired to change this woman's mind. Too tired to keep fighting these arguments and these battles. Kadru wasn't a threat to the nagas.

"What couldn't we do?" a man asked as he walked in. He eyed me as if I was dirt someone tracked in. I didn't know what they were feeding people on this island, but he had to have been nearly seven feet tall. Licking my lips, I realized he had asked me a literal question.

He was a naga.

He was one of the *first*, one of Kadru's true sons.

"Don't mind her, Nahusa," Kadru said with a heavy

sigh, another dismissal of me. "A nagini who found Kaliya's little asura girl. She's here to get herself hurt, but we'll talk her out of it and let her go play with the others."

"Play with the others?" I hissed in Kadru's direction, fuming. "You mean the seven others left? After everything I just told you, do you really think this is a game?"

A hand grabbed the back of my shirt, yanking me off my feet and into a wall. I struggled to push away from it, but Nahusa wasn't letting me go or giving me any sort of leverage. My feet weren't even on the ground.

"You will never speak to our mother like that," he hissed. "If she believes you should go home and stay there, you will do so." His voice softened, brotherly, loving... and condescending as hell. "Don't make this difficult. Just be on your way. Don't play games here with things you can't understand. Find your mate, make a home, and let others handle things."

"No," I snarled. Summoning power, red swirled around me as my fury rose.

I had worked too hard for this. I had bled and sweat for too long. A powerless, shouting voice against time, clawing for every inch of ground. I had lived in the dark, suffered through shame, and was silenced whenever someone had the chance to silence me.

I had been broken and brutalized to come to this place at this moment.

Nothing would make me turn back now... not when I was so close.

Pushing off the wall, pain shot through my arms as I roared in rage. Once I was clear, I transitioned, my snake body filling up the room. It gave me the ground back, though. I coiled, forcing him to let me off the wall entirely. Once he lost that, he let me go.

I rose high, letting my fury roll through my body, black scales glittering in the home's firelight.

"I have been declared the *Nagaraja* by the nagas remaining in the mortal realm," I told him with a hiss. "I will not be told what I can and cannot do. Not by you, a naga who has abandoned his people for centuries. Never think you can speak to me like that." I looked across the room at Kadru. "I won't be told what my worth is or what my duty should be." Power rolled through me, and Nahusa went to his knees. "Do you understand?"

Kadru was still, eyeing me with curiosity and surprise, and I couldn't see Nahusa's face. I moved, swooping him up by the front of his tunic to get on his feet again.

"Answer me," I ordered.

"I submit to the *Nagaraja*," he said, bowing his head. When it came up, his eyes were a vibrant green. "We have waited… a long time for one to come."

Kadru laughed.

"She's just like him, isn't she?" Kadru said softly, and I had no idea if she was talking to herself or her son, my distant uncle. "She's Kaliya's reincarnation, finally doing as Krishna asked of her."

"Yes," Nahusa agreed, smiling.

I let him go, rocking back as I reeled in complete confusion.

39

CHAPTER THIRTY-NINE

"Oh, granddaughter…" Kadru walked across the room, reaching out to gently touch my long tail. "We've known about every naga. Even when you lost track of your generations, we have kept them."

"How?" I transitioned back to my human form, her touch making me a little uncomfortable.

"I have the ability to track and find other nagas," Nahusa explained. "When all of my brothers went into the world, I realized we could and would lose track of them if no one did something. While our people have tried to stay somewhat organized, there were periods of different factions rising and falling among my siblings and their children. Records were lost for all time. It was a good thing I took the job I did. I kept my own records, able to find any naga at any time, and brought them here for safekeeping. Mother made a spell, so younger generations who didn't know me would never notice me. I didn't want to disrupt everything by suddenly appearing then disappearing." He turned to Kadru. "And Mother played a part."

"When you die, your soul passes through here." Kadru looked sadly out a window. I walked slowly to see what she was looking at and saw the river. "I record the name of the son I see when that happens. How many lives each of you has lived... I know. Only a handful of my sons never drifted down my river... your soul was one of them." She turned that sad look on me. "Krishna sent you to Patala. Straight there. No need to pass down the river."

"Why do we have two realms in Patala?" I asked, always wondering. It was a mystery that stumped me as a child.

"Don't concern yourself with it," she said, shaking her head.

"Please?" I was so curious and could finally find the answer to this innocent little mystery.

Just let me get one more answer before I abandon these hunts. Just one.

"I can tell you the difference." Kadru sighed like a tired mother. "*Nagaloka*, the lowest realm, holds the majority of certain souls, Sesa and Vasuki reside there for most of the time, for example. Those two boys... so powerful they can't be reincarnated completely. They're gods now and can't abandon their duties to live mortal lives."

"So, they use avatars," I said. "Like Krishna was an avatar of Vishnu."

"Exactly," Kadru agreed. "A piece of them continues to experience life, the world, and reincarnate eternally with their brothers. *Mahatala* is for those who haven't found that great power and purpose yet, and maybe never will. A place where the family can be together, in *peace*, between the cycles. It's a place where all of your lives come together, all the memories. When you're reincarnated, you forget your time there... until you go back, with new life experiences to share."

"Sounds wonderful, doesn't it?" Nahusa said softly.

I had practically called him a coward, but now I understood his *sacrifice*. His brothers had moved on, finding their realm, a place of peace between the cycles of life and death. He never got to experience that.

"It does, but I'm somewhat attached to living right now," I said, touching his arm. He was anything but a coward. He'd denied himself happiness for the sake of duty and that was honorable.

"Of course." Nahusa chuckled. "You have reason to be. Surprising, though. The world has been cruel to you. You picked up his karma, but still, I know it might feel unfair. It's been hard watching you grow up."

It took a moment for me to realize Kadru had already known everything. She had known the nagas were suffering. Known her children were dying out. The whole thing had been a test of my will.

"Karma has no expiration date," I said, knowing that to be true. "So... you think I can beat Garuda?"

"I think... you're the first naga in a long time who has the chance to," Nahusa said. "Though we had hopes for your brothers, they never made it here."

"Why them?"

"We won't tell you who they were reincarnated from, so don't ask," Kadru said simply. "There are some things, like that information, that will change your perception of the men you knew. We will not do that. Nahusa has said too much." Kadru gave her last son a silencing look.

"Forgive me." Nahusa glanced at the front door.

"So, was everything a test until this point?" I asked. "You already knew of our troubles, didn't you?"

"Yes. For so long, we have hoped someone would come, a *Nagaraja* willing to fight this battle. However, I can't just point a young naga to Garuda. I had to see what you were made of. I apologize if that hurt you. I see you. I see who you are, granddaughter. I see when he ended, and you began. I see the accidental way the pieces of you have tangled together, unable to be separated. I knew where to strike, so I did, for I need you to be absolutely sure this is what you want."

"But—"

"You're asking a mother to send one of her children to possibly die," Kadru reminded me. "Once, I was more callous about the lives of my children. I had so many of them... Then I began losing them."

I could only nod. There were stories of her getting nagas into precarious situations.

"Now that we've answered your curious questions, answer one of mine. Who are your guests? I take it the two hovering outside of Mother's yard are yours."

"Yeah..." I looked carefully at Kadru then went to the door, a little worried about calling in Raphael and Rama.

"One is Rama. I recognize her," Nahusa said. "Mother, would you be willing to see her?"

"I will tolerate her," Kadru said softly. "And the other one, whoever he may be. I know this child of mine likes her asura. I saw the magic." Kadru sighed. "I made my sons powerful, and Kaliya found a wife more powerful than him. *Kaliya* has found a *husband* more powerful than her. I said it earlier... unsurprised. Some things repeat in every life, for the soul remembers, even if the mind does not."

"Cambions," I corrected. "They're demon-human hybrids. Rama was once good. My Raphael *is* good, not asura. If you don't like them because they're more powerful, then you wouldn't like many people I keep as friends."

"*Vinata* made Garuda more powerful than all of you. She had a son she could point at mine to hurt them. Forgive me if I have a difficult time with my children spending time with those who could hurt them."

That was an explanation of sorts. The way Kadru said her sister's name, though?

Damn. Nothing has changed between them, has it? Still the sibling rivalry. Still the cunning, sly nonsense.

"I'll invite them in now, then we'll talk about where Garuda is," I said, pulling open the door.

The moment I made eye contact with Raphael, he started walking toward the house like a one-man army. I didn't need to say anything. Rama was left confused as I waved for her to follow. She followed tentatively, but she came. I held the door open for them.

Raphael came in, straightening when he saw Nahusa. His transition to the cambion form was smooth, giving him height against the first-generation naga, who seemed impressed and a little worried, though I wondered if my distant uncle was also amused.

"Well, they made you bigger than they made Rama," he said, crossing his arms.

My mate crossed his arms, not even looking in my direction. Before I had the chance to translate, Rama came inside.

"Funny," Rama snarled as she saw him. I wasn't surprised she understood the language everyone was speaking. "Nahusa."

"Rama, it's... a change to see you." Nahusa nodded in her direction. "I spent many years wandering the world, tracking my people, but never caught wind of you. Mate of my brother, I would have liked to have known you were still alive."

"Nahusa, this is Raphael," I said, wrapping my arm around Raphael's. I had to say everything in two languages. "Raphael, this is my Uncle Nahusa, I guess. The woman over there is his mother, Kadru, mother of all nagas. My most distant ancestor."

"Good to meet you," Raphael said in English, and Nahusa laughed.

"You don't hide as well as Rama," Nahusa said in English, looking over Raphael again. "Not that I think anyone could expect you to. Someone needs to teach you a better language. English is so... crass. Mother, can you?"

"Oh, it's no worry. I don't like that Kaliya has to translate for me, but I'm trying to learn," Raphael said with a sheepish chuckle. "We haven't been together very long, so I've had little time."

Kadru sighed, turning to us again. She had busied

herself with something in the kitchen and lifted a cup made of clay.

"Taken care of," she said. "Kaliya, your mate can drink this, and it will give him an understanding of things said around him... for a time. When you said his name, I inferred he didn't speak any of our languages. He still won't be able to, but he'll at least understand."

"Mother..."

"We already have one of them who can speak. I don't need *two*."

"Mother." Nahusa was more firm than exasperated this time. She looked displeased, but grabbed a few bottles down from a shelf and added drops of them.

"The things I do for you children."

I went to get the cup, eyeing Kadru warily.

"I won't kill him. There are lines even I will draw. If I didn't like Rama as much as he believed, she would be *dead*. She's not." Kadru seemed to be an eternally annoyed woman. She waved a hand over the cup and the liquid glowed for a moment. "*There*. It will let him speak in our native tongue as well, and it will be permanent. He'll have to get used to it. Giving someone a language can lead to some mental confusion that will pass shortly."

I handed the cup to Raphael, who sighed. I explained what Kadru had said, and my mate rolled his eyes so far into the back of his head, I was certain they wouldn't come back. He drank from the glass, though.

"Better?" Raphael asked, frowning. The Vedic rolled off his tongue in a deliciously attractive way, fluent and unaccented. "Thank you, ma'am."

"At least he has a nice-sounding voice," Kadru said.

"Now that we're all together, why don't you stay here for a handful of days? Rest. Prepare."

I knew it was still early in the day. The idea of staying here, talking to Nahusa, getting into the long rivalry of Kadru and Vinata was appealing but not appealing enough. I couldn't keep getting lost in the past and the troubles of others.

It was time I faced the one I came here for.

"No." I shook my head. "We left just after breakfast. There's still a lot of daylight left." I looked out the window, fear rising of the possibility that forced me to say goodbye to my friends and family. I was here, in Ramanaka, dealing with the mother of my people, and somewhere on this island, Garuda waited.

"Kaliya?" Raphael's voice cut through, and the fear subsided. He would be there with me. With him, I had less to fear.

All I had to do was find him.

"Tell me where he is. When this all said and done, come visit me. Come visit the rest of the nagas."

"I don't leave Ramanaka," Kadru explained. "If you never come back, this will be the last time we see each other."

"Then I *will* come back one day. Before then, we'll let Nahusa pass letters between us. Plus, he'll have to show me the way. He clearly goes into the world and comes back on his own." I had no idea why he worked on his records in secret, but I knew about him now, and I was the *Nagaraja*. "Will you do that for me?" I wanted to know if he was comfortable with it.

"I can do that for the *Nagaraja*," he said with a bow.

"When all is said and done, I will go see your kingdom in the sands. I will bring a letter from our mother." He spoke with hope, and I prayed I could do him proud. "I will take yours back. When you are ready to visit, I will bring you, and during that trip, I'll teach you the route I use to travel to and from this place."

"You can't share it," Kadru said. "You hold a title that can't be denied, but this world is not the world of the nagas any longer. The others can't return to visit or live. Don't worry about an old woman. I will see them again one day." She gestured to the window, indicating the river. "When they flow past me on the waters, I will see them, so I am always standing vigil for my children."

"That must be lonely. Waiting for your children to die..."

"No... Nahusa brings me the records. Come, daughter. I will point you to the roost of Garuda. I hope it doesn't lead to you floating down my river." She walked through us, her head high.

I followed her, knowing the men followed behind me. Kadru went to the river's edge, looking up and to her left. When I was at her side, she pointed to a mountain. Ramanaka was mountainous, as well as tropical. There, on that cliff, was a home.

"That is Vinata's home. Near it, will be Garuda's roost. As you approach, you will not be welcome. She will not speak to you. Garuda will think you are a threat and will come for you, a great eagle in the sky," Kadru explained.

"And that's when we'll learn the fate of the nagas." I hoped I sounded brave. Confident. Secure.

That's the place where I'll defeat Garuda and save the nagas...

No...

I was staring at the place where I was certain I would die. Before the day ended, I was going to see Patala. All I could hope was that I dragged Garuda down with me and stopped his reign of terror over my people.

40

CHAPTER FORTY

Before we started our short hike, I sent Nahusa and Raphael inside.

"I have to handle something," I told Raphael before kissing his cheek. "It won't take long."

He grumbled but let Nahusa guide him inside.

"What is it?" Kadru demanded.

"Oh, don't," Rama growled.

"Rama wants to stay on Ramanaka when this is over. She's broken from his death and has never healed. I want a promise that you won't chase her out. I don't care if you two don't like each other. I won't come back to find an endless war on the island between you."

"Nahusa can find a place for her to set up a home and spend her days," Kadru said, eyeing Rama. "And I will stay with my river. So long as she doesn't disturb me, I won't disturb her."

"Rama?"

"Why would I want to spend time with her?" Rama asked. "Let's go kill Garuda and deal with this after."

"Wait, you're coming?" I didn't remember that being decided. I knew we were using her to get to Ramanaka, but I couldn't remember her asking to fight Garuda with us.

"I don't see what other choice I have," Rama whispered. "It's what he and I should have done all those years ago. I can't live here if he's here. I can't go back to the mortal world. I don't belong there anymore."

"If you're sure, I can't and won't stop you. You know how to use a sword." Rama had brought hers, which should have been a sign, but I was so used to seeing people with their weapons on them, and she hadn't left her jungle in years.

"A sword and my demon form. I'm not as big and powerful as your mate, but with the three of us, we might just have a chance."

Yeah, a pretty damn good chance, but we're going to take a loss though. I know it.

"I wish you all the best of luck," Kadru said, stepping back from me. "Kill Garuda and usher in an age of peace for my children. Let's give Vinata the tears she has forced me to cry for thousands of years."

Unable to say anything to that declaration, I decided to leave. Truthfully, Kadru's words left me deeply uncomfortable, but it was a feeling I didn't have time to untangle.

"Raphael! We're done out here!" It was time to get moving, so I could face this.

He was out the door faster than he had gone in it, carrying my weapon bag and unzipping it as he approached.

Silently, I strapped on my weapons. Talwar and katana, one at my hip, the other on my back, throwing daggers in a row across my chest, and my chakram stacked on my other hip. A fully loaded handgun was on my outer right thigh, a dagger in my boot, with a second dagger on my outer left thigh.

When I was done, everyone was staring at me.

"I'm a trained assassin. It was how I survived."

"I know, but I don't believe you are anymore. You've become a different type of warrior." Kadru was, once again, unsurprised. She said she could see *all* of me, and I realized she wasn't wrong. Or Nahusa had told her when he brought back records. I still wanted to ask him more about that.

Maybe in the next life. Or maybe not. It's not the end of the world if I don't know everything.

I said goodbye to the mother of my people by kissing her cheek, surprising her, then hugged Nahusa. I barely knew either of them. I didn't try to sort through what Kaliya knew of them. He didn't want to remember his mother, which made those memories a little more difficult to reach for.

I also didn't care. Those were his life. I had to make my own. If meeting Rama told me anything, his memories weren't the best view to pass judgment on anyone. I had to decide who someone was to *me*.

It doesn't matter anymore.

I was ready to get moving. Ready to see what waited for me at the end of this.

I was tired, but I had to take one hike up a mountain to find who I needed to find. I was tired, but it wasn't about me anymore. This entire trip was never about me.

This was for Roshni. I hoped one day she could meet this uncle and grandmother. They would adore her, and she deserved to be adored.

I started walking, my eyes on the mountain where I needed to go. Raphael and Rama followed me. I looked back once to see Nahusa standing beside Kadru, both seeing us off.

It was an honor to meet you both.

Looking forward, I kept walking, leaving them behind. As fear coiled in my gut, I thought about the people I had to do this for. I had their names like a list on my heart, and as we hiked, I repeated every one of them to myself. This wasn't about me. This wasn't for me.

It was for Devesh, the start of a bright future, a new generation that could see a better world as he entered adulthood.

It was for Eshika, Basanti, and Eleanor. Humans but ours, standing beside us as we faced eternity and our own mortality. Mothers just as much as Kadru. Beautiful, loving women. Strong women, all in their own unique ways.

It was for Dalar, a soft heart and doting father. It was for Vikrant, a quiet warrior, watching and waiting for his time to finally rise, to prove the depth of his character. It was for Mahavir, a man who understood honor, family, and responsibility, even if he sometimes needed a reminder.

My heart stumbled on a name.

This is for you too, Nakul.

Tears filled my eyes, and Raphael reached for me, but I waved him off. I would be fine. By the end of this, one way or another, I would be fine. I would get to rest, and that would make it fine.

Every step was a name.

Every step was a memory.

I thought of my parents and my brothers. I thought of Nakul's wife and mate. My aunt by blood, my mother's sister. Their son and my cousin. I thought of Adhar, Saranya, and even Aamir.

I miss you, Adhar. I hope she's there with you, the daughter of your heart. This is for all of you, too. All of you.

When this was over, I would get to rest my weary soul, and perhaps, I would see them again, names carved on my heart. I climbed, not for my revenge but for their future, not only for the living but for those waiting to be reborn into new lives.

We were on the incline when Rama stumbled.

"Are you okay?" I asked her as she pushed herself up.

"Yeah. I just tripped over a root," she explained. "It's been a long time since I walked the trails of Ramanaka. I forgot how... little wear they had. They've always been treacherous, and I wasn't paying attention. I was thinking about stuff."

"We should all be on guard," Raphael reminded us, but I was just as bad as Rama. Lost in memories, it was hard to focus on the world around us.

"I was thinking of a time when I climbed similar trails with him," she said, tears shining in her eyes as she looked at me, ignoring Raphael's comment. "I was right to come back here. Even with Kadru, seeing

Nahusa was nice. He was always a kind man, a good brother-in-law."

"Maybe, if we ask him nicely, he'll deliver letters for you."

"I..." Rama nodded. "That sounds lovely. I'll wait for my parents or Kahan to reach out first, though. They deserve time without me. If they never want to... well, it's what I deserve. Really. I can live with it, here in this land out of time. No one will count the years against me here. There's no one for me to hurt. Maybe Nahusa and I could have tea, and he could tell me how everyone is doing. Maybe."

"Let's keep moving," I said, swallowing a lump of fear in my throat. I started the hike again because I was okay with what waited for me at the top. My fear was a mortal thing. No one wanted to die.

I wanted to be *free*, and I wanted that for my people, my family of all spades, the ones I loved more than anything.

If my death could give all of us that, I would die a thousand deaths. One for every son of Kadru. I would take it for them. That was a reasonable trade.

Nearly at the top, my heart wasn't racing. It was calm, a steady beat. I saw the home on the cliff, saw a woman standing at the door. She looked so much like Kadru, but her hair didn't float. If Kadru was water...

Vinata was fire, and that fire blazed in her eyes.

"We're here to see Garuda," I called, remembering Kadru said this aunt of mine would not speak to me.

Vinata turned, walked into her home, and slammed the door.

"Well, Kadru wasn't wrong about that," I said, shaking my head and remembering how Kadru had said Vinata's name like a curse. "If those two want to hate each other forever, they can do that." I glared at the house. I was angry with both of them. "I just wish they would stop using their children as weapons against each other."

"They'll never stop," Rama said with a huff.

"But I have a choice not to be a part of it anymore," I said softly. I knew why Kadru had pointed me here. It wasn't just about saving the nagas, though the need was there.

It was about killing Garuda to hurt Vinata, as Vinata had let Garuda kill the nagas to hurt Kadru.

Back and forth, over and over.

"Then why are we here?" Rama asked. "This is the way things are."

"No," I whispered.

"We can't turn around. We have to stop Garuda from killing more of the nagas, love. We've come so far. Think of Roshni."

He was right. He had to be right. I had to do this. It would just repeat the violent cycle, but I had to save my people *now*.

"I am. Don't worry... I'm always thinking of Roshni."

An eagle cried, and I looked up to see him flying. He went over the sun, casting a shadow over us for a moment. Circling, he was waiting for the moment to strike. We'd been told Vinata would see us, and Garuda would come. Again, Kadru was right.

Drawing my sword, I readied myself for the hardest battle I would ever fight. I shifted to my true naga form, black scales catching the sun as my body coiled and lifted me. Raphael and Rama both transitioned from human to cambion to their demon beast.

In the same breath, I accepted the inevitable ending waiting for me and stepped up to face my destiny.

"Garuda! As *Nagaraja*, I challenge you!" I cried out. "Stand for the crimes you've committed against my people. Today is the day of your reckoning!"

41

CHAPTER FORTY-ONE

A gust blew over us as Garuda flapped mighty wings. He seemed small in the sky, but I knew he was the great eagle, and he was massive.

"Then face me, Demon Serpent! Alone as honor demands!" he cried in the air.

My body was lifted by the next gust of wind. As my body was whipped in the air, I grabbed Raphael.

I need my allies! Damn it!

Rama tried to move behind me, and I felt Raphael slide as the strong winds tried to peel me from him. My arms shook as I tried to pull myself closer to him. Every inch was a terrible struggle against gale-force winds I wasn't meant to fight. I tried pulling my body up. The snake-half of this form was both a positive and a negative. It was massive, and its muscles were much more powerful than my human ones, helping me fight against the winds Garuda was sending. On the other side, it was long and was whipped around by the wind.

Raphael turned his body, trying to block the winds,

but it was quickly useless as the gust turned into a vortex, swirling around us. Rama was slowly sliding around us, trying to keep her claws deep in the earth. Raphael was losing his purchase as well, his muscles tensing as he tried to hold steady for me. It started with an inch, then another. Eventually, the winds were so strong, Raphael was nearly sliding as badly as Rama. As the winds grew, she couldn't stay on her feet any longer, and roaring against the inevitable, she was flung away.

One of my hands slipped, and I closed my eyes as I tried to quickly think of a plan. I only had seconds before I was ripped off Raphael.

I have allies even if I lose these two. They'll follow. Garuda will be focused on me... Maybe I can find some way to disable this when that time comes.

Letting go of my mate, I let the wind pull me away from him. Rama roared as she saw me soar by. I was thrown into trees nearly a hundred yards from the cambions.

Fucking hell, Garuda. When did you learn to do that?

I pushed myself off the ground, making sure everything worked as I searched the sky. I didn't see him until the last moment, already in a fast dive.

"Shit!" I tried to jump out of the way, but he hadn't aimed for *me*. He grabbed a section of my snake body and yanked me back into the air.

I surged, bending to grab him as he took me into the air. Every beat of his wings sent gusts that were nigh impossible to move against, but I needed to grab something. If he let go, I was in for a fall I was unlikely to survive, but each of those gusts put me back at zero, limply hanging from his talons. I could see my cambions still fighting the wind, each beat of those blasted wings making them lose purchase and fight to follow us.

He continued to climb into the air. Once we were at a height he enjoyed, he no longer beat his wings, letting the natural updrafts and currents move us.

My mate became a dot on the earth, and I couldn't see Rama. I tried to throw myself up to grab Garuda's legs and missed the first time as my fingers grazed his leg. He shook me hard, realizing I had nearly gotten a hold on him, and his talons sank in deeper. Throwing myself up again, screaming in pain, I grabbed him, fangs ready, but I never had the chance to deliver the bite I hoped would kill him. He rolled, throwing me around again, disorienting me, and I wasn't prepared for the dive, either. I wasn't sure what speeds Garuda could reach, but I knew they had to be faster than any natural bird of prey.

Bracing for impact, I covered my head with my arms, pulling my snake half to coil around me in a tight ball as a defense, and could only pray it was enough.

He let me go, and my impact to the ground was fast and brutal. I bounced several times, feeling bones break in this form. If I transitioned back to human, I would be healthier, but I didn't think I could fight him in that form.

"Smart," Garuda said as I uncoiled.

Every flex of muscle made me want to whimper, and I could feel every break. He was back in his human form, studying me.

"Not going to kill me while you have the chance?" I hissed.

"As I said... if this is to be a challenge, let's do it the

honorable way. Just us. No asura to help you." He drew his sword and circled me in a wide berth.

I tried to move in my naga form, but the pain was too distracting and took my breath away. Shifting back to my purely human form, I was grateful to find that the injuries didn't find new places to form.

"You couldn't do that the last time we met," I pointed out. I tracked him as he circled me, also using the chance to take in where he brought us, gaining an understanding of the terrain. "The winds..."

"I am whole again," Garuda said, spreading his arms. "With the last pieces of my previous life, I regained my full power. Now, there will be nothing that can stop me from killing all of your kind. That's what you face, Kaliya, and what the nagas will face when I have finally dispensed of you." He pointed his sword at me. "When you die, the last thing you will think is how there will be nothing that can stop me from killing off all of your kind."

I can buy time, hold him off. Raphael and Rama... they'll chase. They'll come looking for us. Raphael would never let me fight alone, not for long.

I looked beyond Garuda, swallowing. I just had to make sure he didn't throw me off the cliff waiting only ten steps behind him. From the view I could see, we had to be on the tallest cliff on the island. There were no mountains taller than this one.

I drew my talwar.

Time to fight.

"Have no words?" Garuda chuckled. "Come, let's see how powerful you think you are."

He came at me faster than I thought possible. I had fought him before, and he had been winning that fight until I had help. This was faster.

Scrambling to block his first lunge, I moved, remembering my footwork to keep from losing my balance. Normally, that was second nature, but the speed I had to move would make it so easy to slip. I had to rely on reflexes only Nakul had ever pushed me to as I dodged a slash aimed for my gut. The sheer force of his sword hitting mine was enough to shake my arm.

I tried to find that peaceful zone I'd had with Nakul that day in the courtyard and found it on the third block, letting his downward swing slide off my sword to reduce the impact force on my arm. Before the action was over, I responded with a fast kick to his abdomen, forcing him to take a step back.

Relentless, he came in for another attack. I sidestepped him and didn't block because he was going to miss. Instead, I launched my attack, trying to disable him. Slowing him down was more worthwhile than fatal blows he would be ready for. I cut his thigh open, leaving a line of blood against his leather to spread over the material as Garuda glared at me. I smartly took three steps back, spreading my feet shoulder-width apart, taking a stance Hisao had taught me. One that would give me the proper positioning to move if I needed to. I couldn't properly attack from the angle I had, but I could easily defend. Sword in my right hand, I pointed my left shoulder to Garuda, keeping my body to the side as we stared each other down.

All the while, I watched Garuda's bleeding leg. It

didn't heal. He wasn't invulnerable and didn't heal like the cambions—both positives.

"I have a question," I said, spinning my talwar in my hand as Garuda approached more cautiously. He hadn't expected to be injured, and I was glad to surprise him. "You talk about *honor*. Do you even know the meaning of the word?"

He gave a warrior's cry as he charged.

Lifting my sword to block, wincing as it shook my bones up to my shoulder, I pushed forward but not with my sword, which was locked in place with his. If I faltered, he would cut my arm off. No, I shoved my shoulder into his chest, knocking the air out of him. Only then did I push away his attack and move quickly to the left. As I went, I cut across his chest. It wasn't as deep as I had hoped since he was already moving with me. I threw my weight to my left foot, then darted back to the right as he attempted to keep up with me.

It was the wrong move. He saw the fake-out coming, and his sword made purchase on my side, cutting open my waistline. I kept moving before it was deep enough to cause serious damage, but the sting of the injury followed me as I made distance again.

"I mean, really," I scoffed at him. "You convinced someone to break a peace treaty. You used other agents for centuries to continue your genocide of the nagas. No longer a warrior on the field of battle." I shook my head as we circled. "No, only a coward too afraid to show his face, hiding and sneaking around until you believed you had the victory in hand. And you drag me here, talking about *honor*." I lifted my arm. "Let me show you what honor is. Maurvi!"

Garuda's eyes went wide as I felt her arrival. She walked up, her form becoming more solid with each step. She took stock of what she was being summoned into and drew her sword. She was solid by the time she was behind Garuda, a tiger's smile as she realized I was giving her a chance to get back at Garuda for his willful abuse of her people to feed her late mate's ego.

"You," Garuda said with disgust.

"Me," Maurvi snarled joyously.

"Maurvi, do you practice the illusion magic of your people?" I asked, launching to attack Garuda while he was distracted by her arrival.

"Absolutely!" she answered.

Garuda spun to meet my attack. We clashed at speed, swords hitting and bouncing back with every clash. I had no idea what sort of illusion Maurvi would try, but if it disoriented him, I could take him off-guard fast enough to kill him.

I saw the moment it took hold. Garuda's steps faltered, and I lunged, pushing my sword through him but not hitting his heart as intended. It went into his shoulder, finding that blasted pocket where it ran through him and out the other side. The angle of the attack left me right in front of him, and he was a warrior smart enough to catch that. I tried to pull my sword free quickly enough to get away from him, but his boot connected with my chest and sent me flying, skidding, and rolling over the dirt of the mountain summit.

Before I could get to my feet, Garuda shifted into his

eagle form and launched himself into the air with a gust of wind that had me sliding closer to the cliff's edge. Sinking my fingers into the earth, I tried to hold myself as he rose into the air. As soon as the gusts weren't powerful enough to move me, I got to my feet.

Something sliced my arm. Confused for a moment, I saw the feather buried in the earth, and dozens more started landing around us, hitting the ground like daggers. Another sliced my thigh before it buried into the earth.

"Maurvi, take cover!" I roared, running for the trees. She was already jumping for a large rock. As I found a place to hide from the onslaught, I tried to piece together this ability. Peeking over the log I was hiding behind, I saw him spin and throw his wings out, sending dozens more feathers hurtling to the earth and into my log, making it crumble enough to worry me. I ran for another tree, trying to keep it between me and the eagle, and the cover was helpful.

He can't aim them directly, so he's going for widespread destruction. If he hits us a few times, he can come back down and fight more effectively. He might get lucky and hit someone fatally.

I grabbed my chakram, knowing this was the perfect time. If I took him out of the sky, too injured to fly again, I would have a real chance with Maurvi's help, though I couldn't give up hope Raphael and Rama would find their way to us. It would be a hell of a climb for them, but I believed in my mate and believed in Rama's need to do this for herself.

Revealing myself to Garuda, I threw two chakram as

he bore down on Maurvi. One missed as he went into a spin, but the second hit a wing as he spread them. With a great cry as feathers flew out, one slicing my cheek, he fell to the ground, and I was running before he finished shifting. As I tried to close the distance, Maurvi attacked him, sword in hand, roaring as she tried to cut off his head.

Garuda was too fast for her... much too fast. The sword went through her abdomen, leaving her stunned, and I knew what would come next. He would pull it free and deliver a final, permanent blow.

"Maurvi, I release you!" I screamed. I could only hope someone was on the other end to help her as she faded.

Garuda roared, realizing he couldn't finish the kill.

"You and your tricks grow tiresome, Kaliya!" he roared as I slid to a stop, sword up.

"Tricks?" I shook my head. "I won't let you kill the next ruler of the rakshasa. She's needed alive and elsewhere. How's the arm?"

I could see just how badly injured he was. It hadn't been his sword arm, but his arms and wings were the same body part, it seemed. Without a wing, he was grounded.

"Let's fight down here from here on out," I said, smiling.

42

CHAPTER FORTY-TWO

He launched into an attack.

I knew it would be a war of endurance, so I tried to fight conservatively. With no allies, it was his sword skill against mine, his raw strength against mine, his speed against mine.

I could match him in speed. I was confident in my sword skill, though I knew he had centuries more experience. However, his raw strength far outclassed me. I wasn't bulked up, my muscles were tired and worn, and I was only just recovering from the emaciation from when Pavan had tried to kill me. I had known when I left on this mission and had been reminded of it every time something pushed me physically.

I wouldn't beat him, but I could potentially wait him out. I wouldn't resummon Maurvi and get her killed.

Raphael, I need you.

Sword to sword, we danced. Even with one arm gravely injured, Garuda maintained the pace and skill expected from someone considered one of the greatest warriors alive. If others had been watching, I knew it would have been one of the greatest showings of swordsmanship in the long history of the world. As it was, it was a clash of ancient enemies, neither willing to back down, falter, or fail. Songs would be written; legends would be spoken by firelight; epics would be penned; art would be created.

But we were alone on this mountain summit of the magical island of Ramanaka. It was us, the tropical-like wilderness, and the rocky clearing before the cliff.

We dueled as the sun slowly moved overhead. I tried to aim for his weak arm and take advantage of that disability, but he was clever about keeping it away from my reach. He was using his clear advantage in strength to keep me positioned where he wanted me, needing to defend, but my speed was a match to his own, and he never found an opening to do real damage.

Until my body caught up with me, the damage I had to fight through. I was at my best in form and skill, but my body couldn't maintain it as long as I needed. Even if I healed the minor cuts as they happened, it was still a drain.

My legs started moving sluggishly as I tried to keep up the pace. He pressed harder, forcing me to step backward, unable to see where I was going. He was in control, able to stay on the offensive as my lungs ached. I felt a stone and nearly tripped over it as I tried to move, avoiding another potentially fatal swing of his sword.

"Surrender!" he demanded. "It will be a clean death if you do."

"No," I hissed.

"Fine." He lunged again, and I tried to dodge, but he disarmed me, my talwar flying away as a slice opened on the back of my hand. I reached for my katana, shifting my left foot back, only to discover the worst possible scenario.

I was at the cliff edge. Horror filled me.

He herded me into position. Shit.

When he came for me again, I jumped to the side. I stayed on the cliff, but I hit my injured side. As I scrambled, trying to get on my feet, he was there.

"Pitiful."

He kicked me in the ribs, and I couldn't stop from rolling over the edge. I tried to find purchase, grabbing rocks, fighting to hold on to anything, but he stomped on my fingers, and I screamed as I fell another six inches.

"Sad," he said as I lost another foot and could no longer see over the edge of the cliff.

I saw the rocks jutting off the cliffside and did the insane. I found places to put my feet and took my hands from his reach before he could stomp any more on my fingers. As I tried to grab with my left hand, a sharp, awful pain came from my ring finger. It was broken, changing my grip as I held on to the cliffside. As I struggled to maintain my grip, the damn finger healed wrong, bent out of place.

The ground rumbled, and my fingers nearly slipped. Finding new holds for my hands, I lost another foot of distance from the cliff. I looked up to see Garuda turn away. The rumble grew, and so did my hope. I hadn't held out as long as I had needed to, but I knew only two creatures that could make the ground shake as they ran.

I listened as Raphael's deep roar washed over the mountain. Garuda's eagle cry told me he was going to try for the air.

Good luck, asshole.

I tried to climb up as the battle waged out of my sight.

"KALIYA?" Rama screamed. She came into view, looking over the cliff ten feet to my left, searching for me.

"Over here!" I yelled. I tried to find a way up, to reach the cliff's edge to pull myself, but I couldn't reach. With my hand outstretched, she arrived and grabbed hold. It was firm, her hand steady and strong.

For a second, we made eye contact. This was her chance to kill me if she still wanted to. I had arrived at her home and disrupted everything she had built to protect her heart. If she wanted to, she could throw me off the cliff.

She pulled me up as if I weighed nothing, and I fell to my knees, grateful to have the ground beneath me again.

"You look like hell," Rama pointed out, on one knee beside me. "Any serious injuries?"

"No... just exhaustion, some cuts, a broken finger." A roar got our attention. My head snapped up as I got to my feet, watching in stunned silence as Garuda held a tree over his head. It was a struggle, but his grip was firm. I ran once again.

Raphael was running for him, and Garuda was playing chicken. As Raphael got closer, he lifted a mighty front paw.

"RAPH!"

Garuda, using all his strength, shoved the tree at him,

hitting my mate just beneath his ribs. Raphael's momentum didn't work in his favor, sliding him down the thick trunk. Garuda got out of the way of Raphael's landing.

It was sheer horror for me as I watched my mate struggle without hands to pull the trunk out of him. It was lodged in, stuck, and his body was trying to rapidly heal the damage.

Rama roared, but I held up a hand.

"Help him!" I ordered her, pointing at Raphael. "Only you can. Let me take on Garuda!"

She understood my meaning.

If you help him up, we can all take him on together like we planned. We can win this, no matter how strong he is.

With a nod, she ran for my mate, and I went for Garuda. He was ready for me, his stare one of fury. As I reached him, he stepped aside and forced me to correct.

"Futile," he taunted. "Look at what I can do to your demons."

As I was correcting, trying to face him, he kicked me hard to the chest, sending me back toward the cliff. The impact knocked my sword from my hand, broke ribs, and my hip slammed into a rock. My head bounced on the ground, blurring my vision as I tried to push off the ground. Looking up at Garuda, I saw Rama pull the tree trunk from Raphael. My vision was too blurry to tell how close she was to finishing. I tried to move, but the world spun from the knock to my head.

"You grow *weaker* by the moment. You might injure me, but my power won't fade. Not now that I have become whole. Your demons will falter."

He was right. I handled his blows earlier in the fight. I was fast enough to fight him. He was endless, but I *wasn't*.

I dove for my sword, and he kicked it away as he brought up his own, preparing his swing, aiming to cut off my head.

Rama was there, knocking him away before he had the chance to make that final blow. Yanking me to my feet, she tried to push me to run.

"Go! Raphael is down! He has too much to heal right now. He can barely keep his eyes open. You need to get him on his feet and run!" she roared, shoving me.

I tried to find my sword. I couldn't just run. Garuda would never let me escape. "Let me—"

There was suddenly a sword coming through her chest. I couldn't believe it. The sword was pulled back, and I wasn't fast enough to pull her out of the way in time.

Rama lost her head.

I was paralyzed as her body fell. Garuda was there, shaking his head.

"I don't know why you fight," Garuda said. "You will never be free of me, Kaliya. The nagas will never be free of me. Even if you killed me, somehow, I will be reborn by my mother once again to continue destroying the terrible children of Kadru."

He's right. We'll just repeat this. Another wave of nagas reincarnated to be slaughtered by a new Garuda.

I had an idea.

An impossible one.

The pieces fell into place as I decided on something new—a new fate, a new outcome. There was no destiny in our culture. There was karma, the weight of our actions and thoughts. Every choice we made dictated our future.

I was going to make a new choice, one no one could have made before me.

He came for me, sword cutting through the air as it tried to finish me. I had no weapon, but I didn't need one anymore. Without needing to figure out my own attacks, dodging as my sole objective, I kept him moving away from my downed mate. This time, I purposefully brought him to the cliff.

At the last possible chance, I jumped back, stopping on the edge. I summoned my power, thinking of Kahan and his portals. I thought of Krishna, who had sent my previous incarnation straight to Patala, a different realm entirely.

I was going to take Garuda on a one-way ticket to the next world. I had no idea if it would kill us or not, but this would be over.

I hoped. All I had was hope.

Garuda came in for an attack, and I only leaned to the side, letting the sword reach beyond me and over the edge. Grabbing his wrist, I twisted, disarming him. I could bite him, let my venom do the work, but my plan wasn't about killing him.

I wanted to stop the cycle, the repeated abuses. He killed some of us. We killed him. We struggled, tried to survive, and for what? For him to return. For us to be reborn. For it all to happen again—breaking homes, breaking families, destroying culture and people, turning good men into villains on every side.

Krishna had offered peace once, but it had been rejected because my predecessor hadn't believed it possible.

I believe in peace. I'm willing to do anything for it. I'm so tired of death. I can't breathe anymore, suffocating on it every time I pick up my sword. My arms shake and grow weary.

All I want is peace.

I wrapped my arms around Garuda as my power surged.

"Let's end this, cousin," I whispered as I flung us off the cliff, him trapped in my arms.

As we fell, the portal formed, and we went through it.

43

CHAPTER FORTY-THREE

Something stopped me from landing hard, catching me in the air as I let go of Garuda. He slammed into the ground, but I drifted gently and turned to land on my feet. Inhaling the sweet fragrance of the air before looking around, I found *clarity*. I believed in this decision, and I would see it through to the end.

Standing in *Mahatala*, the fifth realm of Patala—home of the nagas who are in between their mortal lives, with all of the experiences from each life they had gotten to live—I believed I was making the right choice.

If I wanted this to stop, truly stop, I was making the *only* choice.

I could feel my power in ways I never had before. Rama told me what my predecessor could just do, and many times, it worked. All he had was confidence, a belief in himself.

I understood. I didn't know if I could ever reach this height of power again, but for just a moment, I understood and felt as if I could do *anything*.

And I wanted to do the *impossible.*

Garuda was struggling to stand, groaning as he tried to regain consciousness.

Ignoring him, I walked slowly as I took in the realm around me.

It was gorgeous, a stunning underworld. The world was dark but captivating, thanks to distant lights filling endless skies, illuminating the world beyond distant mountains. I walked up a lush hill and gasped.

Beautiful groves grew around large, clear lakes. People walked together, laughing as they spoke, smiles on their faces. One pair came close, not realizing I was there, then the woman noticed me, her eyes going wide. Her visage flickered into a man, then flickered into another. It didn't stop as she got the attention of the other beside her.

That one took my breath away. I didn't recognize him, not at first, but he seemed just as surprised to see me. I caught the flickering of who he was, and tears filled my eyes as I saw he only had two, and the second was Adhar.

More came closer as my arrival caused a bit of a stir. All of them flickered as they looked at me. With heartbreak and joy, I understood what I was seeing. As I saw my mother in one's face and my father in another, I understood.

They're nagas... and when you look at them, you see the lives they've lived.

"Where..." Garuda was finally moving, and I knew I had to finish this. "Where did you bring us?" he demanded.

"Welcome to *Mahatala*," I said, looking over my

shoulder at him. He was climbing the hill to reach me. He had no weapon, and I couldn't summon the need to fear him. Not here. Not at this moment.

He reached the hill beside me and fell to his knees.

"How..."

"We're not dead," I said, looking back over the gorgeous landscape. "Thankfully. I was worried, but we're not dead. We would be like them, flickering, our faces changing." I nodded to my people. "This is where my people go when you end their mortal lives."

"I know," he said, the contempt in his tone almost strong enough to make me falter.

"Why do you kill us?" I asked softly as I looked at the world where I might one day end up permanently. "Answer honestly, Garuda. This is your *only* chance to. Once this is done, you will not be given another chance."

"Because it is my destiny to destroy the nagas."

"Our culture doesn't have a real concept of destiny," I said, looking down at him. "I recently spoke to a man who surprised me. He said it was fate that I would meet him. I disagree with the idea of fate, the same way I disagree with the idea of destiny. I don't like either concept because they both rob us of our free will. No longer can we choose what we want to be in our lives, what will happen to us. He said he believed fate was the inevitable outcome of our choices. Every choice we make, we set up a series of possible futures until one day, there is only one possible outcome." I nodded. "I like that. Do you know what it tells me?"

"I should kill you," he said, pushing himself to stand.

"You can't." Red magic wrapped around his feet,

holding him in place. "Not today, at least. You're going to listen for a moment, cousin."

"We are not—"

"We have always been family," I snapped, getting in his face as my magic grabbed his wrists and pulled them behind his back. "Every time you have raised your sword to cut down a naga, you have killed a member of *our* family. *You* made that choice. *You* picked your destiny. The gods didn't give it to you. In fact, a number of gods have stopped you from killing my people before. *You* chose this."

"If you want to talk about family, let's discuss the crimes your mother has committed against mine!" he roared. "I will stop at nothing to see Kadru feel the pain my mother has!"

"That's a choice, not a predetermined destiny." I pulled him to his knees with the bonds I had holding him. "Garuda, we can choose something else."

"No!"

"Yes," I said, kneeling in front of him.

"You have no idea—"

"I met Krishna at the base of a kadamba tree, one I had done great wrongs to in my previous life." Based on his surprise, he didn't know. Clearly, Garuda didn't hear and see all the events in India. "I met him in the place he had killed me once before. Unannounced and unwelcome, I entered that space, looking for something. I offered forgiveness and hoped to receive one thing... *peace*.

"He could have killed me the moment he saw me, had the right to, but he chose differently. He gave me a chance to prove I wouldn't make the same mistake again, then he let me walk away, to live another day and to make a new choice... to pick a new fate, a new *destiny*. He gave me a chance to *change*. He told me if I wanted peace, I would have to believe in it."

I reached out and touched my cousin's cheek, hurting at how much he hated me. Hurting because I hated him. Hurting because I was asking myself to do the impossible—offer Garuda a chance to change. If I didn't, this cycle would only repeat. More people would die in the conflict, more innocents would be lost as collateral damage.

We would have no peace. Our lives would still be saturated in death, and I was so tired of death. We would still fight battles of the past, refusing to see that we could have futures, and I wanted a future. I yearned for it.

"As Krishna led by example, giving me a choice and a chance." I stood. "I, Kaliya Sahni, the reigning *Nagaraja*, curse you."

Beyond Garuda, in the distant landscape, a mountain moved. I watched in wonder as it *coiled* and the lights beyond the mountains illuminated *scales*. Looking around, I saw all the mountains doing the same.

Then, shadowed so I couldn't tell their colors, the great heads of cobras rose. With their hoods open and gems on their heads, they sat up to see upon *Mahatala*.

It took a moment for me to realize these snakes weren't *in Mahatala*. They were so massive, they were bearing witness from *Nagaloka* to what I had said.

These were the members of my people who had become gods, silent and still as statues, watching and waiting. The nagas around me in *Mahatala* were watching and waiting as well.

I'm the reigning Nagaraja, not in this realm, but they're waiting on me. They would hear my declaration... and accept it.

I looked back at Garuda and knew he saw the gods as well, his eyes wide.

"As *Nagaraja*, I curse you," I repeated. "Your punishment shall be imprisonment to the realm of *Mahatala* while continuing to live your current life. You will do no harm, and no harm will be done to you." I waited for a moment. None of the nagas made to move, in *Nagaloka* or *Mahatala*. They only witnessed. "You will not age or die, as immortal here as you would be in the mortal realm or Ramanaka. You will not have access to any weapons. You will not train. You will not plot." I lifted a hand, and Garuda was forced to stand.

"You will *listen*." Opening my hands wide, I gestured to all of them. "You will hear the stories of my people. You will hear of the lives they have lived and the loves they have found. You will hear the stories of their most joyous moments ... and the heartbreak of their worst. You will listen to it all." I touched his cheek. "And you will tell them your story, and they will listen in turn."

For the first time, the burning hate subsided.

"Why?"

"To give you the ability to make a choice. Your imprisonment *can* and *will* end one day. You will have the choice to decide how."

"Tell me. I will tell you my choice now!"

"You won't be able to make it today," I said, sighing. "Not today, cousin."

"Stop calling me cousin!" he roared.

"Why? You are my cousin." I shook my head. "There are two ways you can leave your imprisonment here. The first is simple. At which time every soul here is reborn, and one-thousand *adult* nagas live in the mortal realm, you will be granted a passage to return. Your wing will be healed by then. You can once again soar in the skies and continue to make the choice to kill my people." I stepped close to him, chest to chest. "And I will be waiting with an army, ready to once again deal with you. You will be dealt with swiftly. Then I will wait for your rebirth, ready to do it again."

"That could take..."

"Thousands of years? Oh yes, I *know*." I smiled. If he wanted to pick hate, he would have to wait a very long time, longer than the mortal world might even exist. "But there's another choice."

"What is it?"

"As I now see you for who you are, I ask that you see the nagas for who they are. I see you as a son who has only wanted to please his mother, to defend her from a sly and cunning sister. To get in the middle of the vicious rivalry they fostered and carried for thousands of years. You chose your destiny to please Vinata, and she has *used* you to hurt Kadru. Just as my mother, Kadru, allowed me to challenge you this day, not just to save her children, but in hopes that I would kill you to hurt Vinata." I put my hand over his heart. "Their fight does not have to be our fight. It has never had to be our fight.

"I am asking you to leave their rivalry behind and find a new path. If you can let go of your hate and resentment, if you can find it in yourself to leave behind the petty treacheries of the past, you will be free. I will welcome you back, not with an army, but with open arms and an open *heart*. I am *tired* of living in the past. I am tired of death only to be reborn and pick up the same fight. Together, we could have a bright future, unburdened by the past. When you are ready for that, you will be *free*. And we will have *peace*. Choosing peace could be our destinies, Garuda. Peace could be our legacies."

"You ask for the impossible," Garuda said, his nostrils flaring as he breathed hard, glaring at me with eyes full of hate.

"I know," I said, stepping back from him. I was asking for the impossible for not only him. I was also asking it of my people, so hurt by him, for they would have to open their hearts to this as well.

And I asked it of myself, but I was willing to do the impossible. I was ready to do the impossible.

"That is my decision as the reigning *Nagaraja*. You have your choices, Garuda. Choose wisely."

I looked upon my people, and the ones in *Mahatala* went to their knees in deep bows. In the distance, mountains moved, coiling and bending until they went still in new places, the heads of great snakes gone from my sight.

Knowing my judgment was accepted, Garuda screamed behind me for me not to do this, and I thought of my mate. I focused on him through our mate bond, so faint it could have not been there at all.

My power rose once more, and a portal opened. I stepped through it and looked back to see Garuda. We maintained eye contact until it closed.

I wouldn't see him for thousands of years and planned to live until the end of his imprisonment, at the very least. I intended to rule for as long as I needed to so I would be here to handle him when it came time.

I had given him choices.

I hoped he picked the second, but I would be ready for the first.

When I turned away from the portal, I saw Raphael stumbling away from the cliff, his eyes on me and tears in them.

"I couldn't feel you," he whispered as he grabbed me. "Kaliya—"

"Shh." I put my fingers over his mouth. "I'm here. It's done. Let's go home." I thought of the future ahead of me and smiled. "And take care of our daughter."

44

CHAPTER FORTY-FOUR

It took four days to get home, and it was a quest in and of itself. The moment I told Raphael we were going home to take care of Roshni, I collapsed. Nahusa and Kadru tried to keep us for several days, wanting to see me recover fully before I traveled. I agreed to one night because home was calling me. I accepted one night because it was what I needed to tell them of the battle. I told them both what I had done in *Mahatala,* then promptly ignored their opinions.

I was the *Nagarāja*. I could do that.

In the middle of that night, I asked Raphael to carry me up the mountain to Vinata's home. I couldn't make the walk. We stopped outside her door, and I only said one thing to the woman I heard crying inside.

I'm sorry to have hurt you. He will return one day.

Kadru let us leave the next day, opening the portal her stone had given us previously. She knew Raphael and I had made the short trip to Vinata but said nothing about it. I decided not to address it, either, asking her to take care of Rama's body instead.

"I will handle her body with respect," Kadru promised. "It's what she is due as my daughter-in-law."

"Thank you. She wanted to stay—"

"No. She wanted to *die*," Kadru corrected, touching my cheek. "You were the only person who didn't realize that, too colored by your memories of her from your life with her. She had to look at you, new and different, with a new heart and someone to care for it. She had to look at how much she had changed. She called this island a land out of time. She was a woman past hers, and your arrival in her life made her see that." Kadru leaned forward and kissed my forehead. "However, she died for you. In the end, she died for you, and possibly, that has put her spirit to rest."

"Where will her soul go?"

Kadru gently pushed me through the portal.

"Don't ask questions that don't concern you, my little naga," she said, a warm and sad smile on her face. "Go. I might not agree with your decision about Garuda, but I will make no efforts to interfere. Know that I carry you and all my children in my heart. I look forward to sharing letters through Nahusa."

Raphael at my side, we watched the portal close.

"She's complicated," Raphael said, sighing.

"Yeah, and our relationship with her will always be... strained. The love is real, but the manipulation is just as real. Both will always play a part with her." I turned around and saw the house I had only left behind the previous morning.

"Sohan!" Raphael called out. The warrior cambion came running out, his mate right behind him, and Kahan came darting around the building. "We're back. It's done."

We met halfway. I was the slowest, limping, broken ribs, a concussion. I had expended so much power to take Garuda and me to a different realm, then to curse him, I was *spent*. I would recover but had a strong feeling it would be slower this time.

Lalika noticed my injuries and hugged me gently.

"It's done?" she asked me softly.

"Garuda won't be a problem for a very long time," I answered, holding her. "And there's more."

Raphael and I stayed one night in their jungle home. We told them the story we had told Kadru but had to expand parts. Lalika was the only one who cried when we told them Rama's fate. One silent tear rolled down the mother's cheek before she nodded.

"Then she will be at peace," Lalika declared. "Now, let's feed you, then get some sleep. Tomorrow is a big day for everyone."

She got up and went outside, Kahan following to help, while Sohan told us stories of Rama's innocent childhood. I busied myself as he spoke, booking flights for the day, blowing too much money on them, but making sure we would get comfortable seats in the best first-class money had to buy. A small treat to myself I didn't feel guilty about. I sent a few texts to friends, telling them Raphael and I were on our way home and bringing some extra people with us. Cassius told me Maurvi was mysteriously injured, but she would be fine, everyone expecting a full recovery.

Good. The rakshasa need her.

After dinner, Raphael and I went to our room and curled up for a good night's sleep.

I dreamed of *Mahatala* and wished I could have stayed to speak to the souls there, but I knew that wasn't the natural order. It was right that I left. One day, I would join them and we would have great conversation about how the lives we'd had unfolded, but that day was a very long time away.

Hopefully, they'll join me first, and I can watch them experience a new one.

I woke up with a smile, having slept in past the sunrise. Everyone was ready to leave by the time I dressed and left the bedroom.

"Is everyone ready to see Delhi and get on a plane?" I asked, crossing my arms as I watched Raphael inspect what they were wearing. Lalika wasn't wearing the most modern clothing, but a sari was always in style. She would get away with it.

"Ready? We're going to fly through the air in a tin can!" Sohan's nostrils flared.

I laughed as Kahan made us a portal to his favorite spot in Delhi, the pond where we had found him. The trip to the airport was a hike, but we made our first flight.

And I said goodbye to India from the window, my heart aching.

"Ten days," I said softly.

"What's that?" Raphael asked.

"We were only here for ten days. Feels like we left a

lifetime ago."

"I know the feeling. Thank goodness it wasn't, though. We would have missed her growing up." He pulled out his wallet and showed me a picture of Roshni. I wasn't sure when he had taken it, but I was the one holding her. He had kept his dream with him the entire time. "Are you sure?"

"Positive," I said through tears. "I've never been more certain of anything." I touched her face in the picture, my heart healing. She looked like Saranya, but it didn't cause me pain. Saranya had been a loving, cunning woman, and I would make sure her daughter knew all about her. She would know everything we could tell her about both her parents, but I no longer looked at her face and felt the weight of the past, the deaths we had suffered.

I saw the brightness of a beautiful future. A future where I would get the chance to listen to giggles and laughter in the open air. To take my child to the park, on a hike, or to school. I wasn't scared of being her mother, nor did I pity her for being my daughter.

I only loved her and was ready to let that be all that mattered.

The second plane we were forced to take touched down in Phoenix without incident. With Roshni on my mind, I got off the plane with renewed excitement. I couldn't wait to see her... to see all of them.

Twelve days. It had taken only twelve days.

"Kaliya!" Sorcha cried out.

I met her in a bone-crushing hug that left me crumpling in pain as she yelped.

"Okay, let's just get you sitting down!" she said,

ushering me to a chair while we waited on our bags. "I'm sorry!"

"It's fine! I didn't mind. I'm drained, not healing as fast."

"Oh, shit. Well, tell me all about it," Sorcha said as she sat next to me.

"When we get home," I promised. "No Cassius?"

"He's waiting with the cars," she explained with a smile.

I saw him again when we had our bags. His hug was much gentler, but he was observant enough to catch my limp.

"Don't ask. All will be explained when we get home," I said, holding up a hand when he tried to ask.

"It's good to have you back," he said with a smile. Then he saw the cambions, really eyeing them. "Seriously, do you just go to India and bring home strays? Is this going to become a pattern?"

I thumped his chest. Cassius didn't joke often, but that was a good one. I hated it.

The journey home continued once we had the seating arrangements handled. I was riding with Sorcha and Kahan, who was eyeing her with interest.

"She's married to the guy driving the other car," I said, not bothering to give him the opportunity to embarrass himself. "And he's a Prince. You don't stand a chance."

"Not one," Sorcha confirmed.

Rolling into the compound, I looked for Eshika and Roshni. I didn't see them immediately, but I saw a certain curly-haired Nephilim. Heading her way when I got out of the car, she tried to duck and hide. Sammy moved out of the way, snorting as she looked me over, and I pointed at Gabi.

"I need that one," I explained to the warrior.

"Go ahead, but I get the next one." She grabbed Gabi gently and pushed her toward me.

I pulled her into a hug.

"Thank you for telling me. I'm sorry. I'm sorry you carried it alone. It's okay. I will be okay. Raphael will be okay. We are okay."

Gabi finally hugged me back, and I heard her sniffle. Warmth spread through me as she healed all the injuries Garuda had left me with. When I let her go, she wiped her eyes.

"I'm sorry I didn't say goodbye."

"Don't be," I said, holding her cheek. The moment I let my hand drop, Sammy scooped me up. I was healed, but Sammy's hug still hurt.

It was never-ending, trying to say hello to everyone and let them welcome us back. The cambions were the most forward, patting Raphael and me on the shoulders, but my nagas stayed back, more subdued.

This trip had meant the most to them. I walked up to them as their heads lowered.

"It's done," I announced, lifting a hand to stop questions as Mahavir's mouth opened. "When we get inside, I will tell you all about it, but first..." I went to Eshika and the bundle she held. "I hope my daughter was well behaved. I'll take her now."

Eshika gasped, and I saw the tears in her eyes.

"Do you mean..."

"Yes." I slowly took Roshni and held her close as her

eyes opened. She smiled and babbled at the sight of me, and I damn near broke into tears. "With all of my heart, yes."

Eshika kissed my cheek, then Roshni's head.

"Saranya wanted you for a reason," Eshika said, pushing my hair behind my ear. I hadn't bothered with my braids in days. There was no reason to. I had no more battles to fight, not for a long while. "And she was right."

I nodded, believing that. Trusting it. Trusting myself to handle this precious gift of life.

Then I led my people inside to the conference room. The cambions followed, Gabi among them as she always was. There was some tension in the group when I saw Mateo and Sohan eyeing each other cautiously. Raphael snapped his fingers and silently pointed each of them to different sides of the room.

"We'll handle all of this later," he said, then walked to my side. I showed him our daughter but didn't give her up. He smiled, kissed us both, then sat down in his favorite chair. I sat next to him and looked over the room.

"I left for India in search of Garuda, and I found him."

"And you killed him," Vikrant said, filling the pause I had left.

"No. This won't be a story of violence, pain, and repeating cycles." I looked at my daughter, rubbing her head as tears overwhelmed me. All of this was for her. "This is a story about letting the past go and healing. A story about second chances. A story about choosing new destinies. Most importantly, a story about *peace*." I smiled at all of them. "Let me tell you a story of *believing* in peace and maybe, just *maybe*, finding a little of it."

EPILOGUE

A DISTANT FUTURE

I stood on the edge of the cliff, looking over the beautiful island of Ramanaka. A soft breeze held the scent of ocean air drifting over the tropical jungle, blanketing the island. On the highest peak, I waited in the world unchanged and untouched by time. It was not my first time on this cliff. There was not a day I didn't think of it and the choices I had made while standing on the edge.

I didn't wait for long as a gust blew my hair around. Soft feathers floated in the wind, one brushing my cheek, a gentle caress over an old scar. A soft thump behind me announced the one I waited for.

Turning slowly, I extended a hand as I saw him.

"Are you ready, cousin?"

He took my offering, his hand warm in mine. The touch was tentative, but it was also gentle.

"Yes," he whispered, his words nervous. "Yes, cousin, I am ready."

"Then let me be the first to say..." I weaved my fingers

with his. "Welcome home. Everyone has been waiting for you."

He smiled, nodding.

Together, we walked away from the cliff.

We would never see it again.

DEAR READER

Goodbye Kaliya Sahni. (Sort of. Keep reading.)

Before you email me demanding why you didn't get a different epilogue with say... teenage Roshni or anything, hear me out. Kaliya Sahni belongs to a **shared world**. It's still continuing (includes series like Jacky Leon and Everly Abbott, with more to come). Kaliya, Raphael, Roshni, and everyone else will show up again as side characters. So, instead of doing a five year or ten year epilogue, I decided to show you A Distant Future. A Distant Future also gives the proper closure to the proper story. Kaliya's journey started with finding out why her people were being murdered and stopping it, even if others considered her goal an impossible task. A Distant Future shows us she did it, she achieved the impossible.

There's a lot of things I want to write near Kaliya, like a romance novella about Sohan and Lalika, going back over five thousand years to when they met and fell in love. There will be shorts about what happens in her life after this moment. She has, however, retired from being the main character for her own series. She's walked her road and now others need to walk theirs.

As for right now, I don't have a book to tell you to go preorder. A new series may or may not launch in November to replace Kaliya in the rotation. My newsletter is the best place to hear things as soon as they happen.

Sign up now!

Also, I have a Patreon, where I write a monthly short story or novella. In June, there will be at least one Kaliya Sahni related short for everyone's enjoyment. Patreon.com/knbanet

And remember,

Reviews are always welcome, whether you loved or hated the book. Please consider taking a few moments to leave one and know I appreciate every second of your time and I'm thankful.

THE TRIBUNAL ARCHIVES

The Kaliya Sahni series is set in the world of The Tribunal. Every series and standalone novel is written so it can be read alone.

For more information about The Tribunal Archives and the different series in it, you can go here:

tribunalarchives.com

ALSO BY K.N. BANET

The Jacky Leon Series

Oath Sworn

Family and Honor

Broken Loyalty

Echoed Defiance

Shades of Hate

Royal Pawn

Rogue Alpha

Bitter Discord

Volume One: Books 1-3

The Everly Abbott Series

Servant of the Blood

Blood of the Wicked

The Kaliya Sahni Series

COMPLETE

Bounty

Snared

Monsters

Reborn

Legends

Destiny

Volume One: Books 1-3

Tribunal Archives Stories

Ancient and Immortal

Hearts at War

Full Moon Magic (Rituals and Runes Anthology)

ACKNOWLEDGMENTS

Every book is hard work from the beginning to the end. Thank you to everyone who helps me get through them. My husband, Nick. My editor, Sandy Ebel. My proofreader, Michelle. My dear friends, Leigh, Becca, and Erika, who all provide love and support. My PA, Andi.

And you. The reader.

Made in the USA
Middletown, DE
03 May 2025

75090511R00276